For Kate Bradley –
thank you for taking a chance on me.

For Liam Brophy

Part 1

The Dawn Chorus

Prologue

The autumn wind rustled through the trees, and it was as if the building was sighing. The Georgian house was still beautiful, with its yellow paintwork, white pillars either side of the double front door, a curved gravel driveway and a long-dry fountain. The September sun made the tall grass of what must have once been a manicured lawn shimmer invitingly.

But the black, wrought-iron gates were rusted closed, an ancient-looking padlock and chain adding an extra layer of security. The house had been empty for over fifteen years and, behind its elegant exterior, the cracks were expanding, the sturdy bricks and plaster giving way to trails of ivy and birds' nests, crumbling to dust after so much neglect.

It still looked proudly over Meadowgreen, the village it had once been the beating heart of, and the Meadowsweet Nature Reserve, its decay shielded behind tall, redbrick walls. But grass, brambles and bushes thrived where there was nobody to tame them. The mansion would soon be lost to nature, only an echo of the home it had once been.

A ruby-red Range Rover drove past the walls and into the village, slowing to a near stop as if the driver were lost, before turning right into a narrow, tree-lined road. Then, towards the south corner of the house, where Meadowgreen's main thoroughfare met a street of cosy terraces, a young woman, her dark-blonde hair in a ponytail, breathed in the clean, countryside air and started walking, a handsome husky trotting alongside her.

Suddenly, the air was full of birdsong: blackbirds chorusing, the high, repetitive call of a chaffinch, the conversational tweet-chat of a flock of starlings. If anyone had been paying attention they might have noticed the flash of the afternoon sun in one of the upstairs windows, or heard the sudden rush of wind that made each blade of grass stand to attention, almost as if Swallowtail House was waking up.

Chapter One

The robin is a small, brown bird with a red breast, that you often see on Christmas cards. It's very friendly, and likes to join in with whatever you're doing in the garden, especially if you're digging up its dinner. It has a beautiful, bubbly song that always stands out, much like its bright chest.

— Note from Abby's notebook

Abby Field was off the reserve.

She didn't know how it had happened, but one minute she was treading the well-worn woodland trail, intent on finding the perfect spot for the ladybird sculpture, the final creature in her nature treasure hunt, and the next she had pushed her way through the branches of the fallen elder and was standing at the side gate of Swallowtail House, looking up at the impressive, empty building. As always, she strained to see inside the grand windows, which remained free of any kind of boards, as if she could discover what Penelope's life had been like all those years ago.

She wasn't sure why she had ended up here now, deviating from her course and slipping away from the nature reserve, but something about this beautiful, deserted building captivated her, and not just because it belonged to her boss, and had been standing empty for over fifteen years. She wondered if any furniture remained, or if the large rooms had been stripped bare of everything except cobwebs. She passed the house's main gates on her way to and from work every day, could imagine the trail of cars that had, at one time, driven through them. But now they were kept secure, the huge padlock not to be messed with.

The house might be abandoned, but Penelope Hardinge was still intent on keeping people out.

She owned the Meadowsweet estate, the greater part of which was now the Meadowsweet Nature Reserve. Only Swallowtail House, abutting the reserve but secluded behind its redbrick wall, was off limits. The stories Abby had been told by long-term residents of Meadowgreen village varied, but it seemed that Penelope and her husband Al had started the reserve soon after their marriage, that Al's death sixteen years ago had been sudden, and that Penelope's flight from Swallowtail House had been equally hasty.

She had left it as if it was plagued, purchasing one of the mock-Tudor houses on the Harrier estate, a five-minute drive out of the village, leaving the grand, Georgian mansion to succumb to the nature she and her late husband loved so much, although she had continued his legacy. She had been running Meadowsweet Reserve with a firm grip ever since, showing no signs of slowing down even though she was now in her sixties.

For the last eighteen months, Abby had been a part of it. She had found a job that she was passionate about, and while she occasionally bore the brunt of Penelope's dissatisfaction, and sometimes felt her confidence shrinking in the older woman's presence, she could understand why Penelope had to be so strict, especially now the reserve was in trouble.

Abby closed her eyes against the September sun and listened to her surroundings. The wind rippled through the woodland, the dancing leaves sounding like the rhythmic churn of waves against sand. A robin was singing its unmistakable, bubbling song, and she wondered if it was the young one who, for the last few weeks, had been landing on the windowsill next to the reserve's reception desk, curiosity winning out over any fear of humans. He was a fluffy bird, his feathers never entirely flat, as if he hadn't quite got the hang of preening, and she and Rosa had named him Bob. But she wasn't sure he would stray this far out of his territory, and the reserve wasn't short of robins delighting the visitors with their upbeat chorus.

Somewhere in the house's overgrown grounds was the melodic trill of a warbler. It could be a blackcap or a garden warbler, their songs so similar that, even now, she found it hard to distinguish between them.

Opening her eyes, Abby turned away from the house and towards the laid-out trails of the nature reserve. She often wondered if Penelope ever returned, if she walked through the rooms of her old home and found it calming, or if her husband's death had forever tainted the place in her memories.

Abby didn't know why she was drawn to it, but ever since she had moved to the village she had found herself frequently staring up at the serene house, as if it held answers to questions she didn't yet know how to ask.

The swallowtail butterfly it was named after wasn't a regular visitor to north Suffolk, making its UK home exclusively in the Norfolk Broads, and this in itself was intriguing. She wondered if, at the time the house had been built, the population of large, yellow butterflies had been much more widespread; like so many other species, its numbers had declined, crowded out by the constant expansion of humans. Stephan, who ran the reserve's café, had told her that since Meadowsweet records had begun, there had only been two swallowtail butterfly sightings, and those were likely to be visitors from the continent. In some ways, it added to the house's mystery.

Threading her slender legs through the fallen elder and the tangle of brambles, she stepped onto a narrow track that led to the woodland trail. When she had first been shown round the reserve she had noticed the house, and as she found out more about its history, had decided that when Penelope and Al had lived there, this must have been their main route to the old visitor centre. She thought that the fallen tree might even have been left there on purpose – discouraging people from heading towards the abandoned building.

Back within the confines of the reserve, Abby turned her focus to her job, to the place she would now have to work so hard to rescue.

Meadowsweet wasn't the only nature reserve that looked after the lagoons and reed beds around Reston Marsh in north Suffolk. But whereas Penelope owned Meadowsweet, Reston Marsh Nature Reserve – already more identifiable because of its name – was run by a national charity. That the two were so closely situated had never been a problem up until now; the habitats were worth protecting, and while the visitor experience was a little less polished at Meadowsweet, it hadn't stopped people coming to enjoy the walks, weather and wildlife on offer. There was enough to go around, as Stephan always said, and Abby liked the slightly less kempt trails she walked along every day, the sense that nature was always on the verge of taking over completely.

But Meadowsweet didn't have a committee to make the decisions, to test ideas collectively. Penelope kept everything close to her chest, and no amount of gentle encouragement or forcefulness could persuade her to share. Nobody had yet worked out how to chip away at her firm, upright exterior.

And now the reserve was in trouble. The last few months had seen falling visitor numbers, the damp summer not helping, and recently there had been another dark cloud hanging over it, something which Abby was convinced was the subject of the staff meeting Penelope had called for later that morning.

She was nearly finished. The ladybird was the final piece in her nature trail, a new activity she had devised for the school visits that would happen throughout the autumn term. She found a particularly gnarly root, easily visible from the wide walkway that cut a swathe through the woodland, and secured the ladybird beneath it, writing down its location in the notebook she always carried with her. The sculptures had been made by a local artist, Phyllis Drum, crafted from twigs and bound with twine. Abby liked the hedgehog best; it must have taken Phyllis hours – days, maybe – to put his spines in place.

When she got back to the visitor centre, she would create the map and the questions that would lead intrepid groups of children across the reserve to each of the crafted creatures.

It was the first week in September and the sun was still strong, sparkling on the surface of the coastal lagoons, but

9

there was a faint chill to the air, a clarity that made Abby shiver with nostalgia for fireworks and bonfires, crunching through drives of shin-high leaves. She loved autumn; the sun bold but not stifling, the ripples of leafy scent and pungent sweetness of apples, the way everything burst forth in a blaze of colour, as if refusing to succumb to winter. She picked up her pace, hurrying along the trail that was one of the reserve's main arteries. Paths led off it down to the water, to the heron and kingfisher hides, to the forest hide, and along the meadow trail.

She greeted a couple in matching navy parkas, a tripod slung over the man's shoulder, the woman's rucksack bulky with extra camera lenses.

'Anything doing down at the heron hide?' the man asked, spotting Abby's reserve jacket, the logo of a sprig of meadowsweet and a peacock butterfly on the breast pocket.

'A little egret, and some bearded tits were in the reeds in front of the hide about half an hour ago.'

'Excellent, we'll head there first. Thank you.'

'No problem,' Abby said, and waved them off.

The visitor centre was a round, high-ceilinged building constructed out of wood and glass, the huge windows cleaned regularly, letting the weather encroach on the indoors. It was only eighteen months old, and was welcoming, modern and eco-friendly. Inside, it was split into four sections that reminded Abby of the Trivial Pursuit wedges. Penelope's office, the storeroom and the kitchen made up one wedge, the reception and enquiry desk made up another, the gift shop was the third and, leading out onto a grassy area with picnic tables that looked out over the lagoons, Stephan's café was the fourth.

When Abby walked in, Rosa was behind the reception desk, looking elegant in a loose-fitting teal top, her black, springy curls pulled away from her face in a large butterfly clip. She handed over day passes to two men dressed in camouflage and shouldering impressive telescopes.

'Busy so far?' Abby asked once they'd taken the map Rosa had offered them and headed out of the door.

'Not very,' Rosa admitted, her shoulders rising in a sigh. 'But it's still early. And lots of people go back to school and work this week so it's understandable that it's quieter than usual.'

'Of course it is,' Abby said, their false enthusiasm spurring each other on. 'Give it a few more days and we'll be heaving.'

'I truly hope so.' The voice came from behind Abby. It was smooth and calm, but with a steel to it that made her heart beat a little faster. 'How is the treasure hunt coming along?'

'I've placed everything along the trails,' Abby said, turning to face Penelope. 'I just need to finish the paperwork that goes with it.'

'Good.' Penelope raised an appraising eyebrow. 'When is our first school coming in?'

'Next week. The first week back was too soon for most of the teachers I spoke to, but they're also keen to come while the weather's still good. I think the possibility of forty children going home to their parents with muddy trousers was too much to bear.'

'And how's Gavin getting on with clearing the area around the heron hide?'

Abby's mouth opened but nothing came out, because she had no idea.

Penelope stood with her arms folded across her slender chest, her long grey hair, streaked with white like a heron's

11

wing feathers, pulled back into a bun, waiting for the answer. She had used her usual tactic, lulling Abby into a false sense of security by asking her questions she could answer with confidence, then sneaking in the killer blow once she'd become complacent.

'He's been working since seven,' Rosa said, rescuing her. 'He told me he was making good progress when I saw him half an hour ago.'

'I wonder, though,' Penelope said, 'whether his version of *good progress* would be the same as mine?'

Neither Abby nor Rosa dared to answer that one, and Penelope pursed her lips and glanced in the direction of the café, from where the smell of cheese scones, as well as a rather ropey *a cappella* version of 'Bat out of Hell', was coming.

'I want you in my office in five minutes.' She spun on her heels and walked away, closing her office door firmly behind her.

Rosa leaned her elbows on the desk. 'Why do we put up with it?'

'Penelope's not *that* bad,' Abby said. 'She has the potential to be friendly – it's just that she's been on her own for so long, she's forgotten how.'

'She's not on her own though, is she? Her life is the reserve, and we're all here. You, me and Stephan, Gavin and Marek, the volunteers, the regular visitors. She probably sees more people on a daily basis than most other sixty-six-year-olds. My parents don't have as large a social circle as she does, and they're eternally happy.'

'Your mum and dad don't understand the meaning of the word miserable.'

Abby had met Rosa's parents several times since she'd

started working at Meadowsweet, and they were the most cheerful people she'd ever encountered, living in a cosy bungalow in the Suffolk town of Stowmarket. Rosa's Jamaican mother was always laughing about something, and her dad had welcomed Abby with open arms, and was easy to talk to. Abby couldn't help feeling a pang of longing and envy that Rosa had such a loving family close by. Not that Abby didn't have Tessa, her sister, but it wasn't the same as doting parents.

'My mum and dad don't take anything for granted,' Rosa said, 'which is the best way to live your life. Penelope has this whole estate, she has the houses – Peacock Cottage and that gorgeous, deteriorating pile that could be *so* wonderful, yet it's lying in tatters. And she still walks around as if she's sucking a rotten plum.'

'Yes,' Abby said, leaning over the reception desk and lowering her voice. 'But the reserve is in trouble, isn't it? We both know what this meeting's about.'

Rosa sighed in exasperation. Her dark eyes were sharp, inquisitive. She had spent several years in London, buying products for a department store, and had moved back to Suffolk when her mum had had a stroke – one which, thankfully, she was almost completely recovered from. A nature reserve gift shop was undoubtedly a backwards step, but Rosa had told Abby she liked being able to put her personal stamp on it, and the products she had sourced since being at Meadowsweet were good quality and highly desirable.

'Maybe it won't be as bad as all that,' she said. 'Maybe we're reading too much into it.'

Abby shrugged, hoping her friend was right but not believing it for a moment.

* * *

13

Ten minutes later, with Deborah, one of the volunteers, covering reception, Abby, Rosa, Stephan and head warden Gavin were seated in Penelope's office, in chairs crammed into the space between the door and her desk while she sat serenely behind it, her grey eyes unflinching.

'I think you know why I've called this meeting,' she said, without preamble.

'*Wild Wonders*,' Stephan replied quickly, and Rosa shot him a look.

'Gold star for you, mate.' Gavin crossed one overalled knee over the other.

'Thank you, Gavin,' Penelope said. 'And Stephan. Yes, you're right. I've had confirmation that *Wild Wonders* has chosen Reston Marsh Nature Reserve as their host venue for the next year.'

There was a collective exhalation, a sense of sad inevitability, but Abby's heart started racing.

'Year?' she blurted, because while she'd been expecting bad news, this was worse. 'They're going to be filming there for a whole *year*?'

'Got to cover all the seasons, haven't they?' Gavin said. 'Shit.'

'I don't need to tell you,' Penelope continued, 'that this is not good news for Meadowsweet. While it's not the most competitive industry, and many of our visitors frequent both reserves, the pull that *Wild Wonders* will have is considerable. It's prime time, and as I understand it, they will broadcast a live television programme twice a week, supported by a wealth of online coverage: webcams, competitions and social media. We need to be as proactive as we can.'

'In what way?' Rosa asked.

'In increasing our numbers, and our reach,' Penelope said.

'Making Meadowsweet at least as attractive a proposition for a day out as Reston Marsh, if not more, and becoming more visible. You all have your own areas of expertise, and you have to get thinking. We need visitors who will return again and again. It's not going to be easy, but as a small reserve with no regular funding, we, in this room, are the only ones who can make a difference.'

Abby ran her fingers over her lips. Up until that point the events she'd organized had been fairly standard: walks through the reserve and activities for schools, stargazing and bat watching, owl and raptor sessions, butterfly trails. They'd been well attended, but they weren't unique, eye-catching, untraditional. Maybe now was the time to start thinking a bit more radically.

'I have some thoughts,' she said. 'I was toying with the idea of—'

'Excellent, Abigail.' Penelope met her gaze easily. 'I'm encouraged that you have plans. After all, your remit is visitors and engagement, so the weight of responsibility is angled more in your direction. But don't tell me now; this is not the time for brainstorming. All of you go away, come back to me with written proposals and we'll take it from there. I need to see an almost instantaneous change.'

She indicated for them all to leave, which they did slowly, scraping their chairs back and filing out of her office, gravitating to the reception desk where Abby took up her post from Deborah and waited for an influx of visitors.

'Not a huge surprise,' Stephan said sadly.

Rosa shook her head. 'I've got some ideas, but it's still going to be a tiny shop in an independent nature reserve, without a national television show raising its profile.'

'That's the spirit,' Gavin said, giving her a playful punch

on the shoulder. 'I'm sure your defeatist attitude is exactly what Penelope's after.'

'We just need to shake things up a bit,' Abby said, 'look at new ways of attracting people who would never ordinarily pick Meadowsweet as a day out. And if we can get the yearly memberships up, then we'll already be on the way to winning the battle.'

Stephan's smile was tentative. 'Exactly, Abby. And I can work on my recipes, expand my scone flavours.'

'See?' Abby said. 'Run a few more lines in the shop, Rosa, and concentrate on the online catalogue. That way we make money without anyone even stepping through the doors. There are lots of small things we can do.'

What Penelope was asking was straightforward. They had to attract more visitors, sell them more scones and sausage rolls, get them to walk away with bulging paper bags full of mugs and spotter books, boxes of fat balls. They all had their tasks, but, as Penelope had reminded her, Abby was doubly responsible because if she couldn't improve the reserve's popularity, then the café could have the best cheese scones in the world, but there would be nobody there to eat them.

She pushed down a bubble of panic. Would a few more walks, a few more members truly be able to make a difference against a television programme? In only eighteen months she had come to see Meadowgreen as her home, Meadowsweet Nature Reserve and its staff as her sanctuary and family. She didn't want anything to threaten the small, idyllic world she had carved out for herself.

The silence was morose, and as Stephan went to check on his trays of flapjacks and Rosa returned to the shop, Abby watched a young man with fair hair and a blue-and-white checked shirt walk through the door.

'Hello,' he said, bypassing the reception desk and going over to the binoculars before she'd had a chance to reply.

'Hi, Jonny,' Rosa called.

'Oh, hey.' Jonny turned uncertainly, as if Rosa was the last person he expected to see in the shop that she ran.

Abby had almost started a pool on when Jonny would actually buy a pair of binoculars, but then decided it was cruel, and that if he ever found out he'd be mortified. It was the regular customers who kept the reserve going, even if most of them only bought a day pass and a slice of carrot cake rather than a £300 pair of Helios Fieldmasters with high-transmission lenses and prism coatings.

'I need to fill up the feeders,' Abby said to Gavin, who was leaning on the desk alongside her, turning a reserve map into a paper aeroplane.

She went to the storeroom and lifted bags of seed, mealworms and fat balls onto a small trolley, then wheeled it outside to the bank of feeders just beyond the main doors. It was often awash with small birds: blue tits, great tits, robins, chaffinches and greenfinches. Occasionally a marsh tit would find its way there, or a cloud of the dusky-pink and brown long-tailed tits, their high-pitched peeps insistent. Small flocks of starlings would swoop down, cause a couple of minutes of devastation and then leave again. Squirrels regularly chanced their luck, and rabbits and pheasants waited for fallen seed on the grass below.

Often, before visitors had even stepped through the automatic door of the visitor centre they had seen more wildlife than they found in their own back gardens, and once they were on the reserve, the possibilities were almost endless.

Abby waited for a male greenfinch to finish his lunch and fly away, then set to work.

Her job title, activity coordinator, didn't encompass all that she did for the reserve, but she didn't mind. There wasn't anywhere she'd rather spend her time, and her role mattered. She belonged at Meadowsweet, and if Penelope wanted her to get more creative, to double the number of visitors, then so be it.

Gavin had followed her out, pulling his reserve-issue baseball cap on, and Abby noticed how muddy his ranger overalls were.

'That was a kick up the backside,' he said, speaking frankly now they were well out of Penelope's earshot.

'Not unexpected, though,' Abby replied. 'There have been rumours about *Wild Wonders* for ages, and taking a fresh look at how we run this place wouldn't be a bad thing, would it?'

'We could talk about it over a drink in the Skylark later, if you and the others are keen?'

'You've got a pub pass, then?'

'Jenna's taking the girls to her mum's for tea, so I'm jumping on the opportunity.'

'I'll see who I can round up,' Abby said.

'Grand. I heard it was someone's birthday at the beginning of the week. We should do a bit of celebrating.'

'How did you—?' Abby started, but Gavin placed a full feeder back on its hook, then grinned and sidled off, whistling.

She got back to her task, exchanging pleasantries with visitors as they strolled down from the car park. That was the thing about working on a nature reserve – nobody turned up grumpy. They were all coming for enjoyment, to stretch their legs and get a dose of fresh air, spot a species they loved or discover something new. There were the odd children who were brought under duress, but there was enough on offer to engage a young, curious mind once they gave it a chance.

On the whole, the reserve was a happy place, and she wished that Penelope would embody that a bit more. She had always been a strict, no-nonsense boss, but even so, Abby had noticed a distinct cooling over the last few months. She could put it down to the threat of *Wild Wonders*, but Abby had a feeling there were other things Penelope was worried about but had so far failed to share with her team.

But then, everybody had things that they wanted to keep to themselves. Abby had made friends here, but the thought of any of them – even Rosa – knowing her deepest insecurities, her past mistakes, made her feel sick. She hadn't even realized she'd told anyone when her birthday was. She liked to keep them quiet, but she had to concede that a few drinks at the pub would be nice, and nothing they didn't already do.

On Monday, the August bank holiday, Abby had turned thirty-one. Her sister Tessa, Tessa's husband Neil, and their two children Willow and Daisy had thrown Abby a birthday picnic in the garden of their modern house in Bury St Edmunds. Abby loved spending time with them. She was helping with the pond they were creating and had started trying to come up with ways to describe the wildlife that Willow, at eight, would be enthusiastic about, writing some of her ideas down in her notebook. Three-year-old Daisy was still a way off being converted, though Abby had her in her sights.

But thirty-one somehow felt even more of a milestone than thirty had. Abby had no children of her own, no husband or boyfriend or even a glimmer of romance on the horizon – not that, after her last relationship, she felt inclined to dive into something new. It had been a long time since she'd shared her bed with anyone besides a large husky with twitchy ears and icy-blue eyes. Raffle wasn't even supposed to go in her bedroom, but it had taken about five minutes from the moment she'd picked him up from the rescue centre for that rule to get broken.

Working on the reserve, and the long morning and evening walks that kept her husky exercised, meant that Abby was fit, her five-foot-four frame slender but not boyishly flat. Her dark-blonde hair was shoulder length, often in a ponytail, and she wore minimal make-up, usually only mascara to frame her hazel eyes. Being glamorous wasn't one of her job's remits, and the village pub didn't have much higher standards.

As she tidied up the visitor centre later that day, Abby decided an evening in the Skylark with her friends was just what she needed. She took her usual route home, knowing the land like the back of her hand.

The approach road that led from Meadowgreen village to the reserve's car park was long and meandering, forcing cars to slow down, twisting around the larger, established trees, and a single building. If Abby followed the road it would take her three times as long to get home, so instead she cut through the trees and came out halfway along it, opposite the building it curved around: Peacock Cottage.

Part of the Meadowsweet estate and therefore owned by Penelope, Peacock Cottage was a quaint thatched house with pristine white walls, a peacock-blue front door and four, front-facing windows – two up and two down – as if it had been drawn by a child. It was isolated, surrounded on three sides by trees, but also encountered regularly by visitors going to or from the reserve, the approach road passing within a hair's breadth of the low front gate. Abby didn't know who tended to the hanging basket – she'd never seen anyone go in or out of the cottage, though it still managed to look immaculate.

She wondered how many people driving past, or walking the less-trodden paths through the surrounding woodland came across the cottage and thought about who lived there. Was it Mrs Tiggywinkle? Red Riding Hood's grandma? Did the witch who lured Hansel and Gretel in hide inside, behind walls that appeared completely normal to adults, the true, confectionary nature of the house only visible to children? Abby had conjured up all kinds of interesting occupants, something that she'd never done when peering at Swallowtail House, perhaps because she knew Penelope had once lived there.

Once she'd left the cottage behind and emerged from the trees, Abby was in the middle of Meadowgreen village. She walked past the post box and the old chapel that had been converted into the library-cum-shop, and was run by her inquisitive next-door neighbour, Octavia Pilch, its graveyard garden looking out of place next to the newspaper bulletin board.

Then – as always – she crossed over the main road and walked along the outside of the tall, redbrick wall that shielded Swallowtail House and its overgrown gardens from the rest of the world. As she got to pass the main gates of the house twice a day, she didn't quite understand her need to visit it that morning, except that it had drawn her to it, as if it wanted to give up all its secrets.

She crossed back over as she came level with her road, unlocked the red front door of No. 1 Warbler Cottages, and was greeted enthusiastically by Raffle. The evening was warm so she discarded her reserve fleece, attached Raffle's lead and set off on one of her husky's favourite walks, neither she nor her dog ever tiring of being outdoors. Pounding through the countryside would help her think about how she could rescue Meadowsweet from the threat of closure, something that, until today, she hadn't even allowed herself to contemplate.

Chapter Two

A goldcrest is a tiny, round bird like a greeny-brown ping-pong ball. It has large eyes, and an orange crest on its head if it's male or yellow if it's female. It has a call like a high-pitched, squeaky toy, and it rarely sits still, like Daisy when she's watching a Disney film.

— Note from Abby's notebook

The Skylark was a typical village pub. Its paintwork was yellow, but duller than the exterior walls of Swallowtail House, as if it was a slightly desperate copycat. But it had a healthy wisteria over the front door – though its blooms had ended for the year – and picnic tables outside. The wooden floorboards and chocolate-coloured leather seating inside gave it an air of opulence, and while it did a good trade in lunches with local walkers, the evenings were another matter, and Abby had never seen the pub more than half full, even on a balmy summer night.

When she walked in there was the soft hum of voices and Ryan, a few years older than Abby and a big, gentle bear of a man, gave her a cheery welcome. 'They're through there,' he said. 'Got you one in, unless Stephan's particularly thirsty.'

'Thanks, Ryan.' She made her way to the large table by the window, where they always liked to convene and were very rarely unable to. The window faced the reserve's approach road, and Abby liked seeing who turned onto and out of it. The visitor centre shut at five, but at this time of year, when the sun took its time going down, people could still park and walk the trails, though signs reminded them they were doing so at their own risk.

Stephan pushed a pint of pale ale in her direction as she sat down, Raffle settling on the floor next to her chair. Along with Gavin, the other full-time warden, Marek had made an appearance, even though it was his day off. This was the largest their gathering ever got; it was rare for them all to be available on the same day.

'Happy birthday, Abby,' Marek said, holding up his glass as everyone else echoed his words. 'What is it, twenty-four, five maybe?'

Abby laughed. 'You charmer. Thank you, everyone.' She took a sip of beer, her eyes automatically going to the table. They were all her friends, it wasn't exactly a surprise party, but she still felt self-conscious. How was it she could lead an activity at the reserve in front of forty strangers, and yet being the centre of attention with people she cared about made her want to hide in a cupboard?

'If I'd known, I would have baked you a cake,' Stephan said.

'You still can,' Rosa replied quickly. 'A few days late won't matter, and cakes can be enjoyed by more than just the birthday girl. That's what makes them so brilliant.'

Stephan laughed, his eyes bright. He was in his mid-fifties and had run the café at the reserve for the last eighteen months, coming on board at the same time as Abby and Rosa, the supposed turning point for Meadowsweet, when the new visitor centre opened and the venture was supposed to be more professional and profitable. Abby had noticed that Stephan never seemed to have an off day, never appeared grumpy or downcast, and she wondered how much of that was forced, how big a role he'd had to play both to his wife, Mary, and the rest of his friends and family while Mary was dying of cancer.

Sometimes she wanted to ask him how he really felt, sure that he couldn't be upbeat all of the time, but she knew any delving would be a two-way thing, and she wasn't prepared to reveal too much about her past – she'd need another decade getting to know them all for that.

'What did you do, Abby?' Gavin asked.

'I met up with my sister and her family at their house in Bury.'

'No wild nights out on the town? Bury's got a good night-life. Relatively speaking.'

'Tessa's got a young family, so she's usually asleep on the sofa by half nine, and besides, this is my night out – what could be better than you lot in here?'

'Abby, Abby, Abby,' Marek said pityingly, his accent softening the words. His family had moved to Suffolk from Warsaw nearly twenty years ago, and he'd worked on the reserve much longer than the rest of them, when it was still Penelope and Al's pet project. He was happy with his position and hadn't begrudged Gavin the role of head warden when he'd started the year before. 'This is the best you can do?'

'It is for me,' Abby said, patting Raffle. 'Besides, I have to

25

get going on a plan to save the reserve in the morning, and I don't want a sore head when I'm doing it.'

'Bloody *Wild Wonders*,' Gavin said. 'What a fucking curse, eh?' His glass was empty, and the swearing – usually quite prevalent anyway – had ramped up a notch, which meant he was already on his way to being drunk, making the most of the pass he'd got from his wife.

'It's good for the area,' Stephan said carefully. 'It might mean more publicity for Meadowsweet as well as Reston Marsh. I don't think Penelope would have appreciated me saying this earlier, but we shouldn't knock it until it's started.'

'They're here already.' Rosa turned to Abby, filling her in on the gossip she had missed by turning up later than the others. 'Stephan passed three trucks emblazoned with the logo on his cycle over this evening.'

Stephan nodded. 'I went home to feed Tilly her Whiskas, and I passed them on my way back here. Great big bloody things, I wouldn't be surprised if they get stuck in the mud at some point. I wonder, did they not do a recce when they decided to come to Reston Marsh and realize that the reserve is, unsurprisingly, in *marshland*? Even car parks and properly built trails won't always cut it for fifty-ton trucks in this kind of environment.'

Marek chuckled. 'You would have thought the name would give them a clue. Wouldn't it be great if they started off with a huge disaster like that? All the expensive filming equipment lost, because one of the trucks tipped over into the mire.'

'I'm not sure even that would be enough to raise a smile from Penelope,' Rosa said. 'She's so austere – more so than usual.'

'She has a lot on her plate.' Stephan echoed Abby's earlier words. '*Wild Wonders* is real. And I'm the only one who thinks it could be a bonus for us, instead of a problem.'

'It's like putting two mobiles on the table,' Marek said. 'One's the latest iPhone, and the other's the Nokia 3330 with the tiny buttons and the snake game. No matter how nostalgic you feel, you'll go for the iPhone, 100 per cent.'

'But why can't people have both?' Abby asked. 'The iPhone for the cool features, the Nokia because it reminds you of simpler times. Why won't people go to Reston Marsh for the thrill of being somewhere they see on the TV, and then come to us because it's more peaceful?'

'I'll give you a reason,' Gavin said. 'Flick Hunter. That's why.' He sat back, a smug grin on his face and tried to drink the now non-existent dregs of his pint.

'I'll get another round in.' Rosa stood and disappeared to the bar, but not before Abby had seen the eye-roll.

'Who's Flick Hunter?' she asked. 'It sounds like a made-up name.'

'*Wild Wonders* TV presenter,' Marek said. 'She is a hottie. Blonde hair, long-limbed, twinkly eyes. A reason to watch all on her own, never mind the wildlife.'

'But she'll only be there when they're broadcasting, surely?' Abby tried not to be annoyed at their obvious objectification of this woman.

'But people will still go to Reston Marsh on the off-chance,' Gavin said. 'Hell, I'm trying to come up with a detour home so I can get a glimpse of her striding through the trees.'

'Oh God.' Abby put her head in her hands. 'I can't believe the success or failure of Meadowsweet is going to come down to a television presenter who probably doesn't know that much about wildlife in the first place.'

'It's not that bad,' Stephan said. 'The lads are exaggerating. Thinking with their lower halves. We'll be fine.'

'Yeah, right.' Gavin gave a humourless laugh, and the table settled into quiet, not remotely jubilant contemplation. Beside her, Raffle whined softly, and Abby scratched his ears, reminding him that he wasn't forgotten.

'I thought we were supposed to be celebrating Abby's birthday, not bemoaning the fate of our workplace,' Rosa said, returning to the table, Ryan behind her with the tray of drinks, his large hands making the glasses look like they belonged to a child's tea set. 'Can we stop talking shop for five minutes, please?'

'Go on then.' Marek folded his tanned arms. 'If you can beat the *Wild Wonders* gossip then I'll get the next round in, and a bag of crisps each. Push the boat out.'

'Fine.' Rosa gave them a wide, confident grin, her dark eyes sparkling, and then delivered her news. 'Someone's moving into Peacock Cottage.'

'Oooooh.' Gavin waved his hands in mock excitement.

'Shut up, Gav,' Rosa said. 'It's good gossip.'

'Why?'

'Because Penelope owns it, obviously, but like the big house up there—' she pointed, and Abby cut in, her interest piqued by her friend's news:

'Swallowtail House.'

'Thanks, Abby, like Swallowtail House, it's been empty ever since I've worked on the reserve. So, why is Penelope moving someone in now? And is it someone she knows, or is she renting it out to boost her income, add another string to the Meadowsweet bow?'

'I don't understand why she doesn't sell Swallowtail House if the reserve's in trouble,' Marek said. 'That would surely go

28

for a pretty packet and help fund the reserve for a while to come.'

'She won't,' Abby said. 'It's a reminder of her life with Al, isn't it? She can't bear to part with it, that's what everyone says.'

'It's a shame she and Al never had children, someone to inherit it or live in it, even if Penelope couldn't bear to.' Rosa sipped her wine.

'All these romantic notions are very well and good,' Gavin said, 'but can you imagine Penelope with kids? Poor fucking kids!'

'Gavin!' Abby squealed. 'You can't say that. She might have been a wonderful mother; we don't know her well enough to pass judgement.'

'She could do with a little bit more humanity,' Rosa said quietly.

'How do you know about Peacock Cottage anyway?' Abby asked. She wanted to have faith in Penelope. Nobody who cared about wildlife as much as she did, who had – along with her late husband – put all her money into turning her private estate into a nature reserve, could be heartless. But the news about Peacock Cottage was safer ground. No longer would little Red Riding Hood's gran live there, but someone real. It *was* good gossip.

'I overheard Penelope on the phone,' Rosa said. 'I was in the storeroom getting some more coaster sets out, and the office door blew open a bit. She was talking to some guy called Leo. Said something about them being able to move in whenever they liked, the sooner the better, and that it was a "quiet little cottage that was hardly ever disturbed". Guys,' Rosa added, 'I heard Penelope laughing.'

There was a moment of stunned silence.

'*Laughing?*' Stephan said the word as if it were a foreign language.

'Christ,' Gavin shook his head. 'Are you sure it was Penelope?'

'Yup,' Rosa said. 'She said something like "He'll be perfect, Leo. We can see if there's hope left for either of us." Maybe she thinks the rent money will go some way to restoring reserve fortunes?'

'She's not telling the truth about Peacock Cottage, though,' Marek said. 'It may look quiet, nestled there in the trees, but visitors go past it all the time. If Penelope's using that as a selling point, it's false advertising.'

'And it's right on the road to the car park,' Abby added. 'With cars slowing to go over the speed humps. You didn't find out who was moving in, though? Or when?'

'Nope,' Rosa said. 'We'll have to wait and see, I guess.'

Gavin grunted. 'I expect Octavia knows, has their shoe size, their health history and the exact minute they're going to pitch up here. She's probably already picked out a selection of library books for them based on their reading preferences. Bloody woman.'

There was genuine, hearty laughter round the table, Gavin's scathing tone being mostly false.

Octavia, Abby's next-door neighbour, kept gossip circulating like blood through Meadowgreen's veins. She had a handle on everything that was happening in the village and, to a certain extent, on the reserve, but her heart was in the right place. The community library would have disappeared a long time ago had it not been for her selfless commitment.

'You're probably right,' Rosa said. 'I'm almost tempted to go and ask her.'

'Imagine if she's unwittingly rented it to one of the *Wild Wonders* crew members?' Marek's eyes widened.

'Or Flick Hunter herself,' Stephan added.

'No way,' Gavin said, breaking off to down his pint in three long gulps. 'No fucking way would it be that fucking interesting. Come on, guys, this is Meadowsweet we're talking about here. England's most sedate fucking visitor attraction. If a squirrel farts it's the highlight of the day.'

Abby laughed at Gavin's crudeness. He, as much as anyone, was dedicated to his job and looking after the wildlife on the reserve, even though he sometimes did a good impression of not caring.

She felt a slight change in atmosphere round the table. Things were already so precarious with the confirmation of the *Wild Wonders* team turning up at Reston Marsh, and a new tenant in Peacock Cottage shouldn't be a massive deal, but she was sure everyone else was having the same thoughts she was.

Any relative or friend of Penelope's would stay with her on the Harrier estate – she had enough room in her house there – so it seemed unlikely that was the answer. Had she brought someone in to try and rescue the reserve, a professional project manager because none of them were up to the task? Or could it be someone who was interested in buying the Meadowsweet estate, Swallowtail House and the reserve included, and wanted to spend some time there first, getting the lie of the land? Penelope wasn't the type to rent her property out to a complete stranger; she was far too private a person for that, unless the financial situation had become so desperate she had no choice.

That last option would, surely, be the worst of them all, and would suggest they were in even more trouble than Abby had first thought.

Chapter Three

The Dawn Chorus is when birds start singing very early in the morning, as the sun rises. It's most notable in the spring and summer – because that's when birds are most active – and can start as early as four o'clock, which is pretty annoying when you've had a late night, but helpful if you've forgotten to set the alarm on your phone.

— Note from Abby's notebook

For the next week, the gossip in the pub was at the back of Abby's mind, hovering like some forgotten item that she meant to add to her shopping list. It would occasionally burst to the surface, sending a twinge of apprehension through her, though she had nothing to be concerned about except the imagined upsetting of the equilibrium of her life at the reserve. *Wild Wonders* and an increased workload she could cope with – in a way it was better that they knew about it now, the certainty much easier to deal with than worried speculation. And she enjoyed throwing herself into her job, poring over the short evaluation questionnaires she had drawn up for the school visits, reading the comments, bristling slightly when they said 'dull', or 'boring', or 'who cares about blackbirds anyway?' and looking for those that would help her to improve the activities and information she was trying to inspire the children with.

One of the comments stood out: 'Instead of a fake treasure hunt with wood creatures, why can't we look for real birds and animals?' It was a good point, Abby conceded, and enough adults took their spotter books around with them, ticking off godwits, teals and chiffchaffs when they came across them. There was no reason school visits couldn't include an element of this – she'd only held back because she didn't want to create disappointment when a whole class failed to find anything she'd listed. If she kept it simple, included a few plants and trees they would be guaranteed to come across as well as the more common birds, then it could be a success.

She was leaning forward on the reception desk, adding to the written plan Penelope had requested while there was a lull in new customers, when Gavin walked out of the office, his hands in his pockets, Penelope following.

'Thanks for that Penelope,' he said. 'I'll get on it tomorrow, once I've finished at the heron hide.' He winked at Rosa and Abby, then turned to face the older woman. 'By the way, is it right that someone's moving into Peacock Cottage? Only I wondered if you wanted me to do any work on the back garden, clear the bindweed?'

Abby gasped and started coughing. Rosa stopped reorganizing the pens on the counter, and Gavin waited for an answer to the prying that, Abby had to admit, was quite well disguised as an offer of help.

Penelope, her claret silk shirt done up to the neck, seemed

unmoved, her face impassive. Abby wondered what was happening behind it, whether she was trying to work out who had spilled the beans.

'That won't be necessary,' she said. 'The garden has been dealt with. Thank you for the offer.' She walked back into her office and closed the door.

Gavin let out a low whistle. 'Bloody hell, she's good. Neither confirm nor deny. Do you think she was a spy in the war?'

'She's sixty-seven this week,' Rosa said, 'not a hundred and seven. And she was never going to indulge us, was she? However good your attempt to break through.'

Gavin rested his elbows on the desk. 'Do you think she's like the Snow Queen? She used to be all soft inside but something's frozen her solid? Surely it's not natural to be that icy about *everything*?'

'Oh no,' Rosa said with false sympathy. 'Did she give you a hard time?'

'She didn't actually. She wanted to know how I was getting on with the reed beds around the heron hide. I told her and she nodded, which is as close to a compliment as I've ever had, and it gave me the confidence to ask about Peacock Cottage. Thought she was going to answer me properly for a second.'

'If someone is moving in we'll know about it soon enough,' Abby said. 'We all go past there every day.'

'Yeah, but when it comes to Meadowsweet, gossip's the main currency. What's the good in knowing *after* the fact? We need to have the info now, then we'll hold all the power.'

'Anyone would think the ranger job isn't stimulating enough for you,' Rosa said, grinning. 'I promise the moment I find out anything else, you'll be the first to know.'

'Scout's honour?' Gavin asked.

'Brownie promise,' Rosa confirmed.

As Gavin sauntered back outside, his workmen's gloves sticking out of the waistband of his waterproof trousers, Rosa gave Abby a wicked smile. 'I do have news, actually,' she said, glancing at the closed office door before slipping out from behind the shop counter and joining Abby. 'When I was driving in this morning, the postman put something through the letterbox of Peacock Cottage, which means that whoever is coming has already told people or had their post redirected.'

'It's happening soon, then.' Abby chewed her bottom lip. She wondered how she'd feel if she was the object of so much interest simply because she'd moved house, then remembered that when she'd moved into Warbler Cottages, Octavia had been on her doorstep within half an hour of the removal van driving away with a bottle of wine and homemade lasagne, and realized it was simply natural curiosity. Still, the position of the cottage, Penelope's ownership of it and the fact that it had remained unlived in for so long, not to mention the rumours around *Wild Wonders* being somehow connected to the new arrival, did make it a bit out of the ordinary. Or maybe Gavin was right, that so little generally happened in the quiet Suffolk village that any news was important currency. She hoped whoever it was didn't mind a bit of attention.

'Definitely soon,' Rosa said, bringing her back to reality. 'Imminent.'

'Rosa,' a voice called from behind the office door. 'How is the Baywater crockery promotion getting along?'

'Oh, fine,' Rosa called back, her eyes wide with horror. 'I've got some great figures to show you, actually.'

'Excellent,' Penelope replied. 'Looking forward to it.'

'How is she able to hear us?' Rosa hissed at Abby, her cheeks blushing pink. 'We know to keep our voices down.'

'How do you know she did? She could have coincidentally timed it to perfection.'

'Or she's got a webcam trained on us,' Rosa said, 'and she sits in her office and listens to our conversations all day. Maybe she *was* a spy.' She scurried back to her counter and pulled out the sales figures she'd promised Penelope.

If she had been a spy, Abby thought, she must be feeling underwhelmed. Adder and nightingale sightings probably didn't compare to cracking international codes and chasing down terrorists. Abby's mind drifted towards what the mail might have been, and who would be on the receiving end of it when they arrived in their new home.

She was distracted by a young couple, a tiny baby strapped onto the father's chest in an expensive-looking carrier, and Abby's imagination was quashed by practicalities, explaining where the facilities were and giving a rundown of the different habitats and the day's sightings, and it wasn't until she was walking home, eager to get back to Raffle and a long stroll in the balmy, early autumn evening, that she was reminded of the conversation with Rosa and Gavin.

As Abby emerged through the trees, the picture she was usually faced with seemed wrong, distorted somehow, and it took her a few moments to realize it was because there was a car parked in the narrow driveway in front of Peacock Cottage. It was a Range Rover, square and squat, the roof fractionally lower at the back than the front, giving the impression it had been slightly squashed. It was ruby-red, impossibly shiny and definitely expensive. Her eyes trailed to the number plate, expecting to see something personalized like *RANG3 1* or *C0UNTRY K1NG*, but it looked like a standard number plate, though it wasn't local.

Resisting the urge to walk up to the windows of the cottage

and peer inside or, even worse, knock on the front door, feigning a sprained ankle or pretending she was lost, she picked up her pace, texting as she went. It would seem that, this time at least, she held all the currency.

The next day, Saturday, it seemed the whole of Suffolk had decided to descend on the reserve.

'Perhaps they've shut Reston Marsh to get it ready,' Stephan said as he handed Abby a cup of tea, a part of their morning routine that she never took for granted. It was early, but there were already people spilling from the car park towards the visitor centre, the Indian summer bringing everyone out into the fresh air. 'You know, give it a makeover before it gets spread all over the television.'

'When is the first programme?' Abby asked, sipping her milky tea.

'Monday,' Stephan called. 'Seven o'clock. You going to tune in? I'm curious.'

'I'm definitely going to watch some of it,' Abby said. 'I don't think Penelope can expect us not to be interested when it's so close to home. Thanks for the tea, Stephan.' She slipped her mug onto the shelf under the desk and put on her brightest smile for the queue of waiting customers. 'Would you like day passes?' she asked two women in brightly coloured outdoor jackets. One of them, she noticed, was holding a white stick, her eyes staring straight ahead. 'It looks like the weather's going to hold.'

'Yes please,' the taller of the two said. 'Is there a concession for disabled people, for my sister?'

'Of course.' Abby pressed a couple of buttons on the till and issued them with their passes.

Her feet barely touched the ground all morning, and she

could see things were the same in the shop and café. Just before lunch, Penelope emerged from her office and took her place behind the reception desk as a young, enthusiastic boy pleaded with Abby to help him identify a bird he'd found.

'I know you're busy,' his mum said, smiling apologetically. 'I wouldn't ask, except we bought Evan a wildlife book for his birthday and he does nothing but pore over it when we're at home. Even the iPad's been abandoned, unless he wants to find out some more information about a particular species.'

'That's wonderful,' Abby said, smiling at Evan. 'You're going to save the planet, you know.'

'I am?' he looked up at her with wide eyes, his whole body jiggling in anticipation. 'I'm nine now.'

'You and people like you – and it's never too young to start.' She glanced at Penelope, who made a shooing motion with her hands. Abby could see amusement, and something like warmth, in her grey eyes. For what seemed like the first time in months, her boss was in a good mood, and Abby wondered if it was just the busyness of the reserve, or something else, that had lifted her spirits.

'It might fly away,' Evan whispered seriously, reaching out to take her hand.

'Come on then.' She let him lead her down the path, past the bird feeders and into the trees, his parents following.

'It's here,' he said solemnly, already aware that excitement had to be tempered around wildlife. Abby followed the line of Evan's finger to where a fat bird sat contentedly on a low branch, its song high and trilling.

Abby grinned and spent a few moments listening. Evan seemed happy to do the same.

'What is it?' he asked eventually.

'It's a mistle thrush,' Abby said. 'They're not as common

as a song thrush, and much more speckled. Look at its tummy.'

'Like bread-and-butter pudding,' Evan said, 'with all the currants.'

Abby stifled a laugh. 'That's a great description. The mistle thrush with plumage like a bread-and-butter pudding.'

'Do you name the birds?' Evan asked.

'No,' Abby said. 'We have so many it would be hard to keep track of them. Except, there's this robin who comes and sings on the windowsill sometimes. We call him Bob.'

'Why?'

Abby shrugged. 'It seemed like a good name. Robin, Bob. And he does bob quite a bit, he's very inquisitive.'

'Inquisi—' Evan tried, stumbling over the word.

'He wants to know what's going on with everything, like you do with the birds.'

'So I'm inqui-si-tive? Is that a good thing?'

'A very good thing,' Abby said. 'The best, in fact. I'll leave you to your walk, but if you spot anything else and you don't know what it is, write down a description and when you come back to the centre for some of Stephan's chocolate cake, which I'm sure you will,' she glanced at Evan's parents and they smiled, 'I can try and help you identify it. And the more you come, the better you'll get. Soon, you'll be helping *me* identify the birds.' She pulled a small notebook out of her jacket pocket – she always kept one on her, in case she needed to make notes or take down a comment from a visitor – and handed it to him, along with a biro.

'Thank you, miss.' Evan held out his hand again, this time for her to shake.

'You're very welcome.' She shook it. 'I'm Abby.'

'Thank you, Abby.' He grabbed his dad's hand, and began

pulling him further down the path, deeper into the woods. 'There's a hide down here, Dad, let's go and see.'

'That was very kind of you,' Evan's mum said. 'I saw how busy you were.'

'Busy is good, and so is inspiring people like Evan. If everyone loves their local wildlife they'll want to protect it, and that's all we can hope for.'

By the time she got back to the centre, the queue had diminished. As she took her place, relieving Penelope, the older woman patted her hand and Abby felt a surge of pleasure that this stern, proud woman was happy with what she was doing.

She went back to welcoming customers, directing them to different areas of the reserve, talking about the highlights – the kingfisher, the pair of marsh harriers soaring close to the heron hide – as if they had been put on specially. It was only when it got to five o'clock, and they began closing down computers and shutters, that she realized Evan and his family hadn't come back with a list for her to look at. She was surprised by how disappointed she felt, how much she'd looked forward to firing his enthusiasm even more.

She said goodbye to Stephan and Rosa, stayed behind for a few minutes to tidy up the reception desk, then called goodnight to Penelope and stepped outside.

The sun was still warm, but it had begun to sink below the trees. Abby could hear at least two blackbirds, and a tree creeper somewhere in the distance, and the reserve felt peaceful now that most of the visitors had gone. Taking her usual shortcut, she registered that one of the downstairs windows of Peacock Cottage was golden with a soft, welcoming light, and not only was the Range Rover parked outside, but there was another car, a silver Mercedes, pulled up onto the side of the road, blocking it in. Abby found herself slowing, wondering who was inside. As she'd almost passed the cottage, she heard the echo of an opening latch in the quiet and, before she'd realized what she was doing, had slipped behind one of the older, sturdier trees and was peering out at the doorway.

A man stepped onto the path, and then turned and called back into the house. 'OK then, don't work too hard. Actually, I shouldn't be saying that, should I? Work your socks off. It's not like you'll have any distractions here.'

There was a response from inside that Abby couldn't hear, to which the man threw his head back and laughed, an open, unselfconscious gesture. He looked to be in his late forties, slender, with close-cropped dark hair, his navy trousers and grey jumper somehow too smart for a Saturday evening. Abby watched as he unlocked the Mercedes, climbed in and started the engine, then spent several moments turning the car round in the narrow space. Abby moved further behind the tree as he passed with the windows down, the sonorous sounds of the radio slipping out into the still evening air.

She stayed where she was, waiting for something else to happen. Were there two new occupants of Peacock Cottage? But the man's words had made it sound as if he wasn't staying: *It's not like you'll have any distractions here.* Was this a friend, lover, brother? Had a woman or a man moved into the idyllic cottage? Briefly she entertained the idea that this was Flick Hunter's older boyfriend, and then pushed the thought aside. The presenter would surely be staying in an upmarket hotel, or somewhere less remote, at least.

After her WhatsApp to Rosa, Stephan and the reserve wardens the evening before, there had been a flurry of interest about her discovery, but she hadn't had a chance to follow up with them today.

I saw someone leaving Peacock Cottage tonight! She sent to the group as she walked. *NOT the owner of the Range Rover – whoever it is has visitors already! The plot thickens!*

As she picked up her pace, she wondered what the new resident of Peacock Cottage was working on, and why their friend was so keen for them to get on with it.

When Abby returned from lunch on Monday afternoon, Gavin was leaning on the reception desk, intent on a piece of paper that Penelope and Rosa were also poring over.

She had sat outside on one of the picnic benches, staring at the memorial wall Penelope had installed as a feature of the new visitor centre. It was metal, with space for bronze, bird-shaped memorial plaques that people could purchase. In the middle was a plaque to Al, which had been the first. If questioned, Abby was sure she would be able to list all the names and dates that were up there now, she had spent so much time eating her lunch alongside it.

Today, the breeze was strong, the freshness autumnal, the sun and wind conspiring to create glistening ripples on the surface of the water, making her squint as she had walked back inside. The reserve was busy, despite *Wild Wonders* premiering that evening, and she was starting to wonder if Penelope had been over-cautious.

Now, though, Gavin looked up at her, raised his dark eyebrows and said, 'Houston, we have a problem.'

'What's the problem?' Abby asked.

'This.' Rosa handed her the piece of paper they had been looking at.

The first thing Abby noticed was that it wasn't actually a piece of paper, but a large Post-it Note with an illustration of a honeybee in the top corner. Rosa sold them in packs in the shop, the drawings alternating between bee, ladybird, toadstool and dormouse.

Abby peered closely at the handwriting filling the note. It was narrow, slanted to the right as if it was teetering, on the verge of toppling, but also neat, elegant, beautiful. The words, however, were not:

Dear Meadowsweet Nature Reserve,

Is it customary for people to tramp through the garden of Peacock Cottage on their way to, or from, your front door? The incessant cars I can just about put up with, but surely the boundaries of the cottage itself are sacrosanct? How am I supposed to concentrate when there is constant chatter outside my windows? Not to mention the blatant invasion of privacy. If you would address this issue then I would be most grateful.

Yours, JW

As Abby read it, her hands clenched into fists. 'What the fuck?' she whispered. '*This* is the new tenant of Peacock Cottage? Moaning because people are daring to walk near the house?' She thought of the man she'd seen laughing as he climbed into his car, and his assertion that whoever was inside would have no distractions. Clearly, they didn't agree with their friend.

'The letter does seem to suggest that they're walking *through* the garden,' Rosa said.

'So why doesn't he or she tell them not to? And how do they expect us to stop them? And what's with the flipping *sacrosanct* business? Penelope . . .' she said, '. . . isn't this sort of your business? It's your lodger.'

Penelope's sigh was almost imperceptible. She was wearing

43

a thin black jumper and a necklace of large red beads that glinted in the sunshine. Abby was struck by how beautiful she still was, how imposing.

'Abigail,' Penelope said, 'he is complaining about the reserve, the impact it has on the cottage – not anything to do with the cottage itself. I've tasked you with increasing footfall, encouraging visitors, and this man is against that. I see it as your responsibility to remove this disturbance before it becomes more serious. Placate him, tell him that the cottage boundaries *are* sacrosanct. Do what you need to do to make this go away.'

Abby stared. 'Seriously?'

'I'd pop on the charming face instead of that one, though,' Gavin said. 'You'll scare him off. Mind you, under the circs, that might not be a bad thing.'

'Do you know who he is?' Rosa asked Penelope.

'Of course I do,' Penelope said. 'I believe he is a very suitable candidate for the cottage, once this wrinkle has been ironed out. Something, Abby, I know you will do with the utmost professionalism.'

Abby gripped the desk. 'Right. Sure. No problem. I've just got to—'

'*Now*, Abby,' Penelope said. 'I'm sure you'd agree that it's best we nip this in the bud immediately.'

'Of course,' Abby replied. Catching Rosa's eye, she turned and walked outside, a blue tit abandoning a feeder as she stomped past.

This was not her job. Mollifying Penelope's personal tenants was not part of the role of activity coordinator, even if the cottage was on reserve land. What was the activity – damage limitation? She took her usual shortcut, gritting her teeth as she saw the squat, overpriced Range Rover in the driveway. It looked smug. Whoever JW was, she was sure he was smug, too.

She walked up the path and knocked on the front door. A late, lazy bee drifted off the purple heather in the hanging basket and droned towards the garden that was the object of so much consternation. She listened, hearing no sounds inside, and so followed the path of the bee, round the side of the cottage and to the back garden.

It wasn't really fenced off from the surrounding land, she had to concede that. There were no wooden posts, no wire mesh, no walls, but then she supposed that if it had once been the groundsman's cottage on the Meadowsweet estate, it wouldn't necessarily have needed them. Still, there was a small patio and a square of well-manicured grass, surrounded by beds that looked like they would be full of flowers in the spring. Beyond that, the grass became unkempt, rough, full of the bindweed Gavin had mentioned, before dissipating as the ash, beech and birch trees took over.

Abby knew people hiked through the woodland, the more experienced walkers not wanting to stick solely to the reserve's trails, but she couldn't imagine anyone would walk purposefully on the lawn behind the cottage or come up to the patio. JW was clearly just agitated that he could hear people outside the house. Where had he come from, a hermitage?

Walking round to the front door again, Abby pulled her trusty notebook out of her pocket – she had replaced the one she'd given Evan on Saturday – and leaned it against the white wall to write.

Dear JW,
  I am sorry to hear of your dissatisfaction with the nature reserve, and its impact on your wellbeing. If you'd

like to discuss it further, you can find me at the visitor centre, or call me and I will happily return to see you. We would like you and our visitors to live in harmony while you are staying at Peacock Cottage. Anything within my power I can do to make that happen, I will.

Kind regards,
Abby Field.

She had almost signed it off with her own initials, and then remembered that Gavin liked to remind her that AF could stand for *As Fuck*. She didn't want Mr High-and-Mighty JW to get the impression she was angry with him – *Kind regards, angry AF* – although as she stood there and read her letter back, noting at least three cars passing in the short space of time she took, she wondered if it was a little on the passive-aggressive side.

Sighing, she ripped the page out of the notebook, folded it and shoved it through the letterbox, then made her way back down the path, peering into the passenger window of the Range Rover as she went. It was all cream leather seats and a dizzyingly busy, glossy dashboard.

She had reached the end of the path and was waiting for a Volvo to pass before she could cross the road, when she heard the door of Peacock Cottage open behind her, and a voice call her name.

'Abby? Abby Field?'

She closed her eyes, summoning up some inner patience, ready to be as charming to the mysterious, already irritating JW as she could manage.

Then she turned, took a step towards him and found that, while at least her anger disappeared in an instant, she couldn't actually speak at all.

Chapter Four

*The mistle thrush is a large brown bird with a spotty
tummy like a bread-and-butter pudding. It got its name
because it likes to eat mistletoe berries from the plant
people kiss beneath at Christmas. Its song is a bit like a
high-pitched recorder – it's pretty, but can be quite repetitive.*

— Note from Abby's notebook

'You are Abby Field, aren't you?' the man asked. 'You left
me this?' He waved the piece of paper she had pushed
through his letterbox, and she felt her neck heat with embarrassment.

'Yes, I – we got your note, at the reserve.' It was a coherent
sentence, which she was thankful for. She wasn't sure who
she'd imagined JW would be – someone more obviously
curmudgeonly, perhaps a contemporary of Penelope or a
similar age to the man she'd seen leaving the cottage a couple
of days before. But he wasn't, and neither was he Red Riding
Hood's grandma, or the witch who ate children.

He was, quite simply, gorgeous.

About her age, she thought, tall and slim built, but with wide shoulders and a suggestion from the definition of his arms under a navy, cotton jumper, that he kept himself fit. His nose was straight, his jaw firm, defined, and beneath the thick wavy mane of chocolate-coloured hair and matching brows, he had blue eyes. They were looking at her sternly, her notepaper scissored between the ends of two fingers, held with disdain, on the verge of being discarded.

'And this is your response?' he asked. His voice was deep; every word enunciated perfectly, no hint of a Suffolk accent. He could easily, she decided, be Penelope's son. He had that same air of entitlement about him, the same chiselled features, a frown that was probably etched in permanently.

She took two steps forward. 'You didn't answer when I knocked, and I didn't want to go away without responding. We don't want you to be unhappy here, far from it, Mr—' she stopped, realizing she had no idea what his name was.

'I'm Jack,' he supplied. He held out his hand, and she took it.

His skin was warm and dry, the shake firm. Closer to him, she could see the faintest hint of stubble, and a dink on the left side of his jaw – a friendly dimple that he probably despised. He smelt expensive. Of citrus and bergamot, like a posh cup of the Earl Grey you only got with champagne afternoon tea in fancy hotels.

'So, you're going to do something about it, are you?' His voice had softened, questioning rather than accusatory when Abby continued to be tongue-tied, and she relaxed a fraction. 'Only I don't know if *living in harmony* is achievable, as nice an idea as it is.'

His expression was neutral, but was his eyebrow raised a

millimetre? Was he making *fun* of her? She took a deep breath. 'Jack,' she said, 'I am terribly sorry you feel so aggrieved by visitors to the nature reserve passing your cottage, both in their vehicles and on foot, and if there is anything you think I can practically do to help reduce the stress it is causing you, without closing the reserve down, then please let me know what that is. I've had a look at the garden, and I think it's very unlikely that walkers are actually crossing your lawn, and the woodland around it is accessible to all. The reserve has been open for decades, and you – well, you've been here a couple of days.'

Jack looked down at her, and Abby felt scrutinized in a way she hadn't been before. She fidgeted, pulling her short ponytail tighter, widening her feet to give the impression of being steadfast and unwavering.

Eventually, he spoke. 'How am I supposed to get any writing done when there's a constant thrum of chatter outside the windows, walking boots pounding the gravel, cars groaning past at four miles an hour, every three minutes? I had thought this property was secluded.'

'It's not exactly Piccadilly Circus, is it?' Abby shot back. 'If you wanted to be completely undisturbed, why didn't you rent out an island in the Hebrides?'

Jack folded his arms. 'None were available at the time of asking.'

'Right, well then. Not much more I can say, is there?'

'So that's it, you're not going to do anything about it?'

Abby inhaled, waiting for her lungs to fill. 'I'm very sorry, but I don't know what I *can* do. I can't stop people walking and driving past, the reserve's in trouble as it is, and my job is to encourage more visitors, not send them away. I can't afford to soundproof your cottage, and while Penelope probably could, I'm not sure it would be a priority, and other than that I'm at a loss. Can't you put on some really loud classical music or something, to drown them out?'

'I can't write to music. It needs to be quiet.'

'Where did you write before this, then?' Abby couldn't help it; she was intrigued.

'I have a flat in London, but—'

'London?' Abby laughed. 'And you're complaining about a sleepy Suffolk nature reserve?'

'I went to libraries, clubs – there were always places to go in London where I could think straight.'

'So, go back there then,' Abby said. She hadn't meant it to sound so harsh. She bit her lip.

Jack rewarded her with a humourless smile. 'Point taken. If you do think of anything, I'd be keen to hear your ideas. I'm tearing my hair out here.' He stepped back, one hand on the open door, and Abby knew it was her cue to leave.

'Sure,' she said, because she was feeling bad about her last comment. 'I'll put my thinking cap on.'

Jack nodded once, and then gently closed the door. Abby turned and walked back to the reserve, the blackbirds' song drowned out by her clamouring thoughts.

'So, come on then, what is this fucker like?' Gavin flicked ash off his cigarette, shoulders hunched against the chill. Rosa wrapped her cream wool duffel coat more tightly around her.

The temperature had dipped that afternoon, the clouds barrelling over like they were late for an important engagement, and by closing time the reserve was chilly and grey. The three of them were standing at the far end of the car park, where the designated smoking area was. Rosa and Abby were ready to go home, while Gavin had said he needed to stay and finish clearing an area of scrubland but couldn't wait any longer to hear about Abby's unsuccessful visit.

'He's . . . he's a bit posh,' she settled on. No way was she going to tell Gavin she found their new neighbour physically attractive, even if his personality left a lot to be desired.

'And? Come on Abby, spit it out.'

'He's tall, untidy dark hair, blue eyes, cross face. He genuinely wanted me to send all the visitors away and seemed very disgruntled when I couldn't. Then I told *him* to go away.'

Rosa gasped. 'You did *what*? I thought you said to Penelope you'd placated him?'

'He wasn't shouting at me by the end, which is a good sign, and that comment was a mistake. He said there were loads of places he could write in peace in London, so I told him to go back there. I didn't mean it, I was frustrated.'

'Hang on a moment,' Rosa grabbed her arm. 'He's a writer? What's his name?'

Abby grinned. Rosa was the biggest bookworm she knew, and probably, along with Octavia, was the reason the community library managed to stay open. 'He won't be well known.'

'How do you know that? How many authors would you recognize if you bumped into them in the street?'

'J.K. Rowling,' Abby said, raising a finger, and then hesitated.

'Exactly!' Rosa clapped her hands. 'So, we know he's called Jack, and he's tall with dark hair. Age?'

'My age, probably, maybe a couple of years older.' Abby pictured him again, surprised how easily she could conjure up Jack's face in her mind, and then felt a prickle of something, as if a shadow was passing through her thoughts. 'Maybe I did . . .? No.'

'Did what?' Rosa asked, excitement threading through her words.

'Perhaps – I mean, *maybe* I'd seen him somewhere before. But I think that's just because you're suggesting he might be famous. It wasn't like – wham – there's Al Pacino or anything. He was . . . he acted like he was owed everything, though. Like it was his right to have all the peace and quiet in the world, because he'd moved into the cottage.'

'Snooty sod,' Gavin said. 'Not inclined to sort out the bindweed now.'

'I will!' Rosa said. 'Not sort out the bindweed, but I'm going to have to go and see if he is a well-known writer. Just imagine if he was?'

'What difference would it make?' Abby asked. 'We can't exactly advertise him as a feature of the reserve, in the same way Flick Hunter's going to draw the crowds to Reston Marsh. He's already made it clear he wants no distractions.'

'It'll be exciting for us, though,' Rosa said. 'A real live celebrity in the vicinity.'

'A real live, pain in the ass celebrity,' Gavin added.

'We don't even know that he is,' Abby said. 'He could write medical textbooks, history magazines, dull business reports – anything. Just because he said he was a writer, doesn't mean he's Stephen King's hot nephew.'

'Oh, so he's hot, is he?' Gavin asked.

Abby cursed inwardly.

'Tomorrow,' Rosa said, clasping her hands together. 'I'll find an excuse to go there tomorrow. See how he's getting on, that kind of thing.'

'Poor guy's not going to know what's hit him, with all this interest and fluttering about.' Gavin waggled his fingers and shook his head.

'Two minutes ago you were calling him a snooty sod,' Abby protested.

'Yeah, well . . . maybe I've changed my mind. Us guys have to stick together.'

The following day began with a short, and somewhat depressing, debrief. *Wild Wonders* had started the previous evening, and Abby – along with all the other staff at Meadowsweet – had tuned in to see what they were up against. The resounding conclusion was that it was professional, interesting, and made nature accessible to people in a way Abby managed to on a much smaller scale.

The female presenter, Flick Hunter, was the perfect anchor. Undeniably beautiful, she treated the camera as if it was a close friend, speaking to her unseen viewers with warmth and passion about the wildlife being uncovered, day-by-day, at nearby Reston Marsh. Grudgingly, they all admitted that, while it might not be ideal in some respects, promoting nature could never be a bad thing.

Later that morning, Jonny was hovering by the binoculars. He looked friendly and cosy in a cornflower-blue jumper, his fair hair neater than usual. The reception desk was momentarily quiet, and so Abby left Maureen, one of the volunteers who was working alongside her, to cover it and went over to say hello.

'How's it going, Jonny? Any closer to making a decision? You could always get Rosa to go over the specifications of a few pairs with you.'

'Oh, err, no thanks. I'm fine. I'll get there in the end. Good of you to offer, though. Where is Rosa, by the way?'

'Funny story,' Abby said. 'She's gone to spy on the guy

who's moved into Peacock Cottage, you know that white house on the approach road to the car park? Thinks he might be some famous author or something.'

Jonny frowned, and Abby wondered why until a hand landed on her shoulder. Looking down, she saw it had talon-like red nails.

'Octavia,' she said, turning. 'What are you doing here?'

'Just dropping these off for Rosa. Where is she, my love?'

Octavia held up a wicker basket full of the crocheted birds that she made for the reserve's gift shop. Abby loved them. She already had four on her bedroom windowsill – a puffin, wren, blue tit and greenfinch – and from a quick glance, could see that she would be buying half of Rosa's new stock before she'd even put it on display.

'They're gorgeous,' Abby said, picking up a robin that was fat, round and utterly desirable.

Octavia gave her a kind smile, slowly took the robin back and popped it in her handbag. 'I'll take this one home with me, and you can come and pick him up later. I'll bring Rosa a new one next week.'

'Octavia, you don't have to give me the robin!'

'What robin?' She winked, her eyelid a shimmering green, which went well with her dyed, carroty curls. Slightly shorter than Abby, with a large bosom always clad in bright clothing, Octavia was a good-natured whirlwind in Meadowgreen. Her vantage point in the chapel library and convenience store was the ideal spot from which to gather and circulate her gossip. Abby loved her, though didn't always feel in the mood for her outgoing, inquisitive nature. She was equally blessed and cursed living next door to her.

'That's so kind of you,' Abby said. 'And Rosa will be back in a moment, she's just nipped over to Peacock Cottage.'

'Oh yes,' Octavia said. 'This new resident. What do you know about him? Is he a personal friend of Penelope's?'

Abby glanced at the office door before replying. 'He's already complained about reserve visitors trampling through his garden. He seems—'

She didn't get to finish her sentence because Rosa burst through the door, emitted a high-pitched squeak, and gestured to Abby to follow her into the centre's airy café.

'Will you be OK here for a bit?' Abby asked Maureen.

'Of course, chuck,' Maureen replied, her glasses chain shaking. 'Take as long as you need.'

Abby arrived at Rosa's table in the café to find that Jonny and Octavia were already there. She felt a spark of sympathy for Jack, who was clearly the object of this impromptu huddle, and thought how ironic that the complaint about his invasion of privacy had, in only a day, sent everyone digging deeper.

'Come on then,' Stephan said, bringing over a tray of hot drinks and doling them out before sitting down. 'Tell us all.'

'OK.' Rosa took a deep breath, and then jiggled excitedly, her curls bouncing. 'Oh my God, guys, the man living in Peacock Cottage is Jack Westcoat!'

Abby frowned, trying to dredge the name from her memory, and found she couldn't. Stephan and Jonny looked as perplexed as she felt.

But Octavia clapped her hands over her mouth, and Abby wondered if she was about to burst into tears. Then, she exploded.

'Jack *Westcoat*?' she screeched. 'As in, acclaimed thriller writer, puncher of fellow author at recent awards ceremony, once-glowing reputation now in tatters, all-round literary bad boy Jack Westcoat?'

'That,' Rosa said, 'is exactly right. And wow, is he smouldering in real life too.'

Abby's frown deepened. She had perhaps seen something in one of the café copies of the *Daily Mail* about some scandal involving two famous authors, but there was nothing concrete to hold onto.

'This is incredible,' Octavia was saying, her eyes flitting between them as the cogs worked. 'Think what he could do to raise the profile of the library.'

'I'm not sure he wants the publicity,' Abby said slowly. 'He seemed quite keen on maintaining his privacy when I met him.'

'And not after what happened,' Rosa said. 'I mean, the story is *crazy*, like something from a soap opera. But he was polite to me, if not exactly delighted, when I turned up on his doorstep to see how he was getting on. Like you, Abby, I'm not sure what he expects us to do. He's probably just venting his frustration.'

'He must have a lot of it if he goes around punching people,' Stephan said, sipping his coffee.

'That was just the once,' Octavia said. 'Before that, he was one of the country's up-and-coming author superstars. Granted, he'd put a murky past behind him – university high jinks that got out of hand, apparently, but he'd become a true golden boy by all accounts, until this latest incident. I'll have to find out what happened now, why the punch got thrown. Goodness me, it's really him?'

'I recognized him from the photographs I'd seen in the paper when it happened.' Rosa hugged her mug to her chest. 'He must be hiding out here, that would make sense, wouldn't it? Writing his new book, staying out of the limelight.'

'I wonder if Penelope knows who she has staying in her

house,' Stephan said. 'It's not exactly got the same kudos as *Wild Wonders*, has it?'

'But he's not going to be involved in the reserve, is he?' Abby pressed. 'There's no reason anyone else should know that he's here.'

'Do I sense some protectiveness there, my love?' Octavia asked.

Abby shrugged. After his initial priggish note and their less than friendly encounter, she suddenly felt sorry for their new neighbour. Everyone had areas of their past they'd rather keep quiet about, and it must be worse if everything you did played out under a media spotlight. Stephan clearly thought there was no excuse for him hitting someone, and maybe it was unforgivable and Jack was a world-class dick, but nothing, Abby knew, was ever as simple as it seemed.

'I just don't know if we should go spreading it about,' she said. 'Especially as he's so adamant he doesn't want to be disturbed.'

'Ah, Abby, you always were the sensible one.' Octavia patted her hand. 'Still, no harm in asking, a few months down the line once he's integrated himself a bit more in village life, if he'd fancy giving a talk at the library. I expect I could rustle up my biggest-ever crowd.'

'Octavia,' Stephan said, 'he punched someone at a very public event, and now he's taken up residence in a secluded cottage on Penelope's estate. He's unlikely to want to advertise his presence by coming to talk to the great and good of Meadowgreen.'

'In a couple of months, I said. I'm not that much of a dragon.'

Abby sipped her tea. She couldn't help but think that

having Jack Westcoat here, with all the interest and scandal he seemed to have brought with him, was going to complicate things.

She had to focus on bringing visitors to the reserve for all the right reasons, and now not only did the new resident of Peacock Cottage seem averse to other human beings, but he might draw unwanted attention all of his own. Did authors get paparazzi appearing on their doorsteps like actors? The man in the Mercedes had clearly been Jack's friend – the words she'd overheard were much friendlier than her encounter with him. But was he really that much of a celebrity? If he was, then she couldn't imagine anyone – the press, regulars, holidaymakers – being interested in the nightingales on the reserve when there was a real-life, disgraced superstar author in their midst. And – Abby thought ruefully as Jonny, who hadn't said a word the whole time, quietly excused himself – an incredibly attractive, disgraced superstar author to boot.

As the weeks passed, the Indian summer they had been enjoying slipped slowly out of sight, like a shy guest leaving a party, and autumnal weather took over with full force. Abby noticed there was a new vibrancy about the reserve, not necessarily because it was busier, but because there was suddenly a whole lot to talk about. *Wild Wonders* had been an instant ratings hit according to Stephan, who was watching every episode. Gavin and Marek were also unashamedly regular viewers, and Abby was finding their conversations on the subject more and more juvenile.

'Did you see what Flick Hunter was wearing last night?'

'Bit low cut, wasn't it?'

'Is anyone complaining, though?' Marek said thoughtfully,

leaning on his rake handle like something out of *Lady Chatterley's Lover*.

Penelope even weighed in on the discussions occasionally, much to everyone's surprise.

'How are our figures?' she asked one Friday afternoon, when Abby was rolling her neck, thinking about the weekend and a visit to see Tessa. 'It seems those television bods may not have sunk us, after all.'

'Didn't I say?' Stephan said, walking over. 'It's not the world's most competitive market, is it, nature? Enough to go around.'

'There may be enough *nature* to go around, but are there enough *visitors*? That's what we need to determine.'

Abby looked through the figures on the computer. 'We're down fractionally on last week, but the weather's been much greyer over the last few days, which would account for this small a drop. It's pretty consistent.' She smiled, hoping her positivity would rub off on her boss.

'Consistency is a start,' Penelope said, 'but what we want is to be aiming higher, scaling that mountain, not strolling through the foothills. How are your walks going?'

'They're quite successful. I've got one next Tuesday that's fully booked.'

'Keep it up. Well done. Good work.' She addressed them each in turn, Rosa's eyes widening at the unexpected encouragement.

'Dear God,' Stephan whispered once Penelope had retreated. 'What's got into her?'

'Maybe she's been on a social skills course,' Rosa said. 'What about Monday, when she was in London? What was that about?'

'Who knows?' Abby shrugged. 'It's not like she's going to

come back with goody bags for us all and share her escapades over a hot chocolate.' The image made them laugh, Penelope's good mood infecting them.

'Seen any more of our literary antihero recently?' Stephan asked as he wheeled the mop back towards the café.

'Nope,' Rosa said. 'Not a peep. He's backed down easily.' She raised an eyebrow at Abby.

She was wearing a denim shirt that would have looked outdated on anyone else, but Rosa, with her beautiful colouring, her bold Jamaican hair and dark eyes, was always stylish. Sometimes Abby wished she had her friend's elegance, but as lots of her time was spent out on the reserve, helping the wardens, running walks and messy activities, jeans or cargo trousers paired with a reserve-brand T-shirt or fleece were ideal for her, if not exactly eye-catching.

'I've not heard from him either,' Abby said, though she'd heard enough from everyone else about their new neighbour.

That was the other talking point adding to the buzz on the reserve. The fact that Octavia had been here when Rosa returned from her trip to establish Jack's identity was the undoing of everything. Abby had noticed more familiar faces at Meadowsweet than she ever had before, people who she said hello to in the Skylark in the evenings, or bumped into at the chapel store, and who wouldn't be able to tell a blackbird from a bullfinch. She just hoped the buzz stayed within Meadowgreen, and no journalists got hold of the news. She'd had to rub *The lesser-spotted Jack Westcoat* off the sightings blackboard on two occasions over the past couple of weeks.

She didn't know how she felt about her encounter with Jack. He had been stubborn, certainly, and unreasonable to begin with, and finding out about his recent fall from grace should have been enough to cement her dislike of him.

But the truth was, her mind had returned to those few minutes on the pathway of Peacock Cottage more often than she would have liked, though she wouldn't admit it to anyone. She had enough to deal with – her booked-out walk for one thing. It was only a few days away now and the weather looked like it would be dry but cold. The thing she hadn't told Penelope was that there were a couple of names on the list of attendees that she recognized.

The local councillor, Helen Savoury, and her husband, had booked places. She didn't know if there were any council grants available, but she thought that if she did a good job, they would at least see how beautiful, and valuable, the reserve was to the local area.

The forecast, inevitably, had lied. Tuesday turned out to be warmer than planned, but with a constant drizzle that penetrated almost all types of clothing within minutes. Bob the robin was perched on the top of the feeder station as Abby set off with her group of visitors, serenading them as they passed.

'Good morning, everyone,' she said, facing the expectant crowd and clapping her hands together to get their attention. 'Welcome to Meadowsweet Nature Reserve on this glorious October day.' There was a smattering of laughter. 'I'm Abby Field, and I'm your lead on today's walk. I'm going to start by taking you through the woods, and then we'll angle left, down towards the coastal lagoons to look at the waterfowl and migratory birds, and then back along the meadow trail which, while without its butterflies at this time of year, has beautiful views across the water and some autumn wildlife all of its own.

'Please ask questions as we go, and if you spot anything

and can point it out without disturbing it, I – and I'm sure some of you – should be able to help identify it. Is everyone covered up well enough? Luckily not many of our bird or animal species are put off by a bit of rain, though some of the birds of prey will wait until it's dry to go hunting. Still, I'm hopeful we'll see a lot today.'

She took a breath, realizing that her introduction was too long, hoping she hadn't lost everyone's attention completely. Mr and Councillor Savoury were hovering at the back of the group but, she was relieved to notice, looked interested. Helen Savoury was a solid, imposing woman who dressed impeccably and had a kindness to her dark eyes. Today she was wearing a light-grey, fitted waterproof jacket, the hood pulled up over her bobbed brown hair.

There were also the two women – sisters, she remembered – who always came together, one with a white stick, the other leading her. Abby had seen them several times over the last few weeks but had never got their names. They always wore bright colours, today waterproof jackets in lemon yellow and coral pink, so different from the camouflage browns and greens that people often donned to visit the reserve.

'Right,' she said. 'Let's get going.'

Two hours later, things were looking up. The rain had abated, though after the first half an hour Abby was sure everyone was too wet to care anyway, and they'd spotted a marsh harrier, a reed warbler, two herons and a cluster of bearded tits, which were always popular with their dusky gold-and-grey colouring, bouncy, toy-like movements and ping-pong song. As they reached the beginning of the meadow trail, however, Abby's plan faltered. It was far too muddy for any of them to pass easily, even with sturdy walking boots on.

A woman in her forties with spiky red hair, who Abby had decided was the world's most enthusiastic visitor, walked ahead of her.

'I don't think we're going to be able to go that way,' Abby called. 'The mud is deeper than it looks.'

'It'll be fine,' the woman said, waving her away.

'I'm not sure all of us are as intrepid as you are,' Abby replied. 'Our warden, Gavin, tried to walk through a similar patch a couple of days ago, and came back to the visitor centre looking like a golem. The best thing to do is probably head straight to the café for coffee and cake.'

There was a low muttering as the group discussed the options.

'What happens in that direction?' Helen Savoury asked, pointing at a smaller, less worn track through the trees. 'That looks like it could go around in a loop to the visitor centre, but in the opposite direction to the meadow trail. It doesn't look too muddy, either.'

'Oh, that way,' Abby said. 'It does, it comes out at the top of the car park, but—'

'Sounds perfect then,' the red-haired woman said. 'We've got thirty minutes left, so why don't we follow that path and see what we can see?'

Abby paused. She didn't want to curtail the walk unnecessarily, and she should listen to what her visitors wanted, but that route would involve going past Peacock Cottage. She would be directly responsible for the behaviour that Jack had complained about, and it seemed like the problem had gone away. The last thing she wanted was to resurrect it. Still, if she stopped the walk now, she wouldn't get perfect feedback from her visitors – Councillor Savoury included – and word would get back to Penelope.

Jack might not even be at home, anyway. It seemed the lesser risk.

'OK then,' she said. 'Let's go.'

At first, the gamble paid off, and within minutes one of the visitors had picked up on the loud rat-tat-tat of a great spotted woodpecker. After creeping through the trees – a movement Abby was practised at, but which always made her feel like she was in a slow-motion film – they found the culprit, high up in a beech tree, his red, white and black plumage startling in the gloom.

With a sense of satisfaction, Abby led the group out of the woods and along a small section of the approach road. Cars were limited to five miles an hour here, and encouraged to slow further by the speed humps, so it wasn't as precarious as it could have been, but still Abby kept the pace up, wanting to get off the road as quickly as possible.

'This is a pretty house,' said a voice from the middle of the group, as Abby tried to hurry them past Peacock Cottage.

'Oooh, lovely,' said another. 'So picturesque. I wonder who lives here?'

To Abby's horror, everyone slowed behind her. She heard her footsteps distancing themselves from the rest of the group and, closing her eyes momentarily in despair, turned around.

'Come on, folks,' she said. 'We really should get—'

'Do you know who lives here, Abby?' It was the woman with red hair.

Abby chewed the inside of her lip. 'It's part of the Meadowsweet estate, rented out, so it's a private residence and I think we should—'

She heard the unmistakable sound of the door opening. She turned her head, the slow-motion scene becoming a horror film as she anticipated the scowl on Jack's face. She wasn't disappointed, either by her premonition, or by seeing him again, and her feelings clashed. The shame of causing him aggravation, anger at her own stupidity as it could have easily been avoided, anticipation of the harsh words she was about to receive, and the joy of being able to top up the memory of his looks, to redefine the image that was so often in her thoughts. She was surprised how much that feeling rode above the others, how pure a jolt of happiness it was, when the outcome of him seeing them could only lead to another complaint.

'Abby,' he said, his voice already resigned. 'Could I have a word?'

Her visitors were looking eagerly between them, this human interaction matching the wildlife for intrigue. She wondered if any of them recognized Jack, whether he had been reluctant to show his face to more than just her, but she noticed he was hovering inside the doorway, the shadowy hallway doing a half-good job of hiding him.

'Give me ten minutes to take my visitors back, and I'll be with you.'

'Good. Great. See you then.' His eyes did a swift sweep of the cluster of people with Abby and then, bowing his head slightly, either to get out of sight or as a goodbye, he closed the door.

'*Who's that?*' the red-haired lady whispered loudly.

Abby made sure they were a few paces from the cottage before responding. 'That's Penelope's tenant. I don't know much about him.'

'But he wants to see you?' She was curious, shameless, thinking that because the exchange had happened in her presence she had as much right to the details as she did to knowing the number of nesting pairs of cuckoos on the reserve. Abby pushed down her irritation.

'He wants to see me because he wants to complain to me,' she admitted.

'Love and hate are two sides of the same coin,' the visitor said, as if that was somehow reassuring.

'I know that,' Abby said under her breath. It made her feel worse.

Chapter Five

Bearded tits are small, attractive orange-and-grey birds with long tails. The males have black markings either side of their beaks like a moustache. They feed and live in reed beds, and communicate with each other in loud, short squeaks, a bit like when Mum is calling for you and you ignore her.

— Note from Abby's notebook

By the time she had got everyone safely back to the café, spoken to Helen Savoury for twenty minutes about the future plans for the reserve and then introduced her to Penelope, Abby was almost half an hour later than she had told Jack she would be.

As she took the shortcut back to Peacock Cottage the rain began to fall again, which seemed entirely appropriate. She was already soaked through to her underwear, despite her supposedly waterproof jacket, and had begun to shiver. She wasn't averse to a bit of rain – she had experienced much worse over the last eighteen months – but she wanted to appear professional and firm in front of Jack, which she couldn't do if she looked like a drowned rat with chattering teeth.

She walked up the path and banged the brass knocker twice.

The door opened seconds later. Jack's eyes widened, then the perma-scowl was back.

'I'm very sorry about today,' she started. 'I had never planned for us to—'

'That's not what I wanted to talk to you about,' Jack said. 'I left another note at reception, but you've clearly not seen it yet.'

'What?' Abby took a deep breath. 'But I thought that—'

'It did seem coincidental, though, you bringing your touring party right past the front door. Almost as if you were making a point. Hang on.' He disappeared inside, leaving Abby on the doorstep, the warmth of the snug cottage inches away, perhaps with a burning fire and a cup of cocoa on the table, a blanket on an impossibly soft, leather sofa . . . She snapped out of her daydream when Jack reappeared, pulling on a navy padded jacket. It was Arc'teryx. Of course it was. Ten times the price of her own reserve-issue coat. He probably went skiing twice a year at an exclusive Swiss resort.

'Look at this.' He walked past her and crouched next to his Range Rover, pointing at a spot above the wheel arch. Abby tried to keep her sigh silent and crouched alongside him. She peered at the glossy, rain-splattered paintwork.

'What am I supposed to be looking at?'

'This.' He jabbed his finger at the car. Abby peered closer, and spotted the faintest, almost non-existent white line.

'What is it?' she asked, her mind whirring, trying to get ahead of the game.

'It's a scratch,' he said. 'Caused by the pheasants that come stalking through here constantly, hooting like roosters.'

Abby closed her eyes, bouncing on the balls of her feet as she started to stiffen up. 'You're complaining about the wildlife now?' she asked quietly. 'Your cottage is in the countryside. Even if it wasn't on a nature reserve, you're going to get pheasants, deer, birds crapping on your precious Chelsea tractor.'

'What?' His voice was sharp. He looked more shocked than angry, as if he wasn't used to people answering back to him.

'I can't do anything about the pheasants,' she said, more gently. 'And this scratch – I can barely see it, you need a magnifying glass. I honestly don't know what you want me to say. I can't close your cottage and garden off from the rest of the world, wrap it up in bubble wrap.'

Jack stood quickly, and Abby wondered how outraged he'd be if she used his shiny car to hoist herself up, envious of the fact that his knees worked better than hers. Then she looked up and found he was holding his hand out to her. She took it, and he pulled her to standing, the momentum closing the gap between them.

The raindrops were beading on his coat like pearls, and his hair was slowly losing its volume, flattening against his forehead.

'I just need to write,' he said. 'How am I supposed to do that with all these distractions?'

Abby shook her head. 'Can't you . . . be inspired by them, instead? It's an idyllic setting, the roses in the garden, the hanging basket, the birds singing, even the pheasants. There's Swallowtail House a short walk in that direction, beautiful and mysterious. And in the spring you'll have bees again, butterflies – can't you use all that in your writing? And surely overhearing conversations is helpful. Isn't people-watching a writer's favourite pastime – after writing, obviously?'

Jack put his hands on his hips. 'My writing doesn't contain many butterflies. It's usually quite dark.'

'Oh yes, of course. But . . . weren't there butterflies – or moths, at least, in *The Silence of the Lambs*?' She could picture the DVD cover now, a girl's face with a moth covering the mouth. It was a death's-head hawkmoth, though she hadn't known that when she'd first watched it.

'What do you mean "of course"?' Jack asked.

Abby frowned, trying to put herself back in the conversation. 'I – uh.' Her teeth chattered violently, and Jack pulled her by her sleeve until they were huddled under the half-shelter of the porch. She could smell the heather in the hanging basket, its scent enhanced by the rain, even though it was close to the end of flowering.

'You said "of course" when I told you my writing was dark. Why did you say that?'

'Because I . . . oh.' It was common knowledge who was living next to the reserve, but news of the interest it had aroused obviously hadn't reached the man himself yet, probably because of his self-imposed seclusion.

'So, you know who I am, then? Who else?'

'I didn't know to begin with,' Abby said. 'I didn't recognize you. But Rosa, who works in the reserve shop, was just . . . we were wondering, when you told me you were a writer, and I . . . she came by, and said that—'

'Who else knows?' Jack prompted.

Abby looked at her sodden walking boots. 'Pretty much everyone who works on the reserve, and in the village too, I would have thought.'

'Fuck.' It wasn't directed at her. Jack was staring over her shoulder, his jaw clenched, the muscles so tight Abby thought they might lock together.

'It's a normal village mentality,' she said, shrugging. 'Gossip spreads like wildfire, every arrival and departure is noticed, and especially into a cottage that's been deserted for years. If you didn't want to be a—'

'A what? A talking point? A figure of fun?' He looked at her now, his eyes blazing. 'So, I should have figured out there'd be all this wildlife, I should have known I'd be assailed by bloody twitchers, or whatever you call them, and that I wouldn't be left alone from the moment I arrived? Well, I'm sorry I'm not psychic. My agent said it was ideal, that it would give me the space I needed. That's all I want – some peace and quiet to write my book.' He ran a hand through his damp hair, pushing it off his forehead and spraying Abby's face in the process.

She would have been annoyed, except she was already too angered by what he'd said.

'Hey. *You* were the one who came to *me*, complaining about the reserve. If you hadn't, none of us would have knocked on this door, probably ever. You would have been left alone to moulder slowly away, moaning to the furniture about who was disturbing your precious writing time.'

'Technically, I left the note for the reserve in general, not you specifically.'

'Don't be so smart! Why not talk to Penelope? She's your landlady. Shouldn't any complaints have gone to her? And anyone with any common sense would have realized a country cottage would come with wildlife. We can't just turn it off, can we? Flick a switch, goodbye butterflies and deer and robins. It's called Peacock Cottage – didn't that give you

71

a *clue*?' Abby stepped out from under the shelter of the porch. The rain was heavier now, streaming into her eyes.

Jack folded his arms. 'So first you're berating me for being too smart, then you're implying I have no common sense? Come back in, you'll get drenched.'

'I'm *already* drenched! I have been since ten o'clock this morning, and if it hadn't been for you and your minuscule scratch on your glossy, squashed-frog car, then I would have been dry ages ago. I couldn't *be* any wetter, and you didn't even invite me inside, just under the crappy little porch, so it's not like you're actually bothered!'

'Squashed-frog car?' Jack was struggling with a smile. It made her even madder.

'I don't have time for this! I have to get back and start working on my next event, which I will make absolutely sure doesn't come anywhere near your precious blue front door.' She whipped round, skidding on the slick paving slabs, and stormed up the path. She gasped when he grabbed her arm, swallowing another mouthful of rainwater in the process.

'Come inside for a moment,' he said. 'Come and dry off.'

'I need to get back to work.' She twisted round, and his eyes held hers. They were icy blue, cold, somehow, and yet so captivating. The dimple made him look like he was smirking.

'I need to go,' she said again. 'I'm sorry we know who you are, but none of my friends would use it to their advantage. They're just intrigued. It's not like they'd call the press or anything.'

He nodded. 'And the wildlife?'

Abby laughed. 'I'm not apologizing for that. It comes with the territory. Why don't you come on one of my walks, see if you can't learn to love it a bit more, realize there are more important things than scratches on your paintwork?'

'Of my squashed-frog car?'

'It looks like it's been trampled on, OK?' She flung her arm in the direction of his Range Rover. 'And it's just a car. You need to sort out your priorities.' She shrugged out of his grasp and skidded down the path, thinking bitterly that she wouldn't have done that if her walking boots had been £250 Arc'teryx models, and began to walk back to the reserve. When she turned, once, immediately wishing she was stronger than that, she saw that Jack was still there, leaning against the doorframe, watching her. She almost gave him a wave, realized she couldn't guarantee the sarcasm would be obvious, and so left it.

Let him stand in the rain and get soaked, she thought. What did she care?

Abby's sister Tessa and her family lived in a new development in Bury St Edmunds. Quite like the Harrier estate five minutes from Meadowgreen, it was a warren of roads and closes, the houses not quite identical. Abby wasn't sure how she didn't get lost every time, and always felt a surge of panic when she turned onto the estate, but somehow her hands turned the wheel and found the right driveway, the pale-pink front door and the cuddly Peppa Pig in the upstairs window.

She hauled her craft materials out of the boot of her aged Citroën Saxo, took Raffle by the lead and, propping her pile of paper, fabric, pens and paints under her chin, managed to press the doorbell with one, straining finger.

'Abby!' Her sister opened the door and took the stack off her, leading the way through to the large kitchen at the back of the house. The garden was small but neat, with beds Tessa worked hard on and an immaculate lawn. There was a wild-life area at the end, which she was slowly developing with her daughters – and Abby's advice – and with the wall of windows and French doors, the kitchen was somehow an extension of the outside, a haven of calm. If she lived here, Abby would spend most of her time in this room.

'What can I get you?' Tessa asked. 'Tea, coffee, wine? Are you staying tonight?' Abby's sister was older by three years, taller, and, since giving up her job as a swimming teacher to be a full-time mum, even leaner than Abby, which she attributed to running around after Willow and Daisy all day. But Abby knew she was conscious of her appearance, much more so than Abby was, and had her dark-blonde hair dyed a strange violet hue that somehow made her look much younger than her thirty-four years.

'Tea for now, thanks,' Abby said. 'Not decided about staying.'

'You're not working tomorrow, though?'

'Nope. This is my challenge for the next two days.' Abby settled herself at the island in the centre of the room and spread out her craft materials. Raffle did his usual slow peruse of the space, and then lay at Abby's feet. She'd taken him for a two-hour walk this morning, knowing that he wouldn't get as much of a run around in the evening. The following weekend was her first big event – Penelope was calling it the autumn flagship event, a term that made Abby feel slightly nauseous – and she had this weekend off to prepare. Which was what she was hoping to rope Willow into, maybe Daisy too, though a three-year-old was perhaps slightly too young to design Halloween bunting.

'Are your events going well?' Tessa brought the teas over along with a plate of pastel-coloured fondant fancies. She had a grey jumper pulled over her hands, the thin fabric threaded through with silver, and her nails were the colour of fresh lavender.

Abby glanced down at her own outfit, a navy jersey dress. She'd rolled the sleeves up, and the fabric had started to tear at the hem where she'd walked Raffle for hours, catching it on endless twigs and bramble bushes. She pushed her hair away from her face, and Tessa reached out and pulled a strand forward again, appraising her silently in the way she often did.

'They're fine,' Abby said. 'It's mainly been walks and school activities so far, trying to widen the reach of the reserve. We've sent emails out to all the schools in Suffolk, as well as some just over the border, and we've got the county and borough councils to link through to our website on their days-out pages. Take-up's been good, and the feedback so far has been positive. Next weekend, though, that's the biggie.'

'Halloween,' Tessa said. 'Willow's been talking about it non-stop. I think some of the other parents are really into it, having parties and all sorts. She'll love that you want her to help with all this.'

'Where are they?' Abby asked.

'Neil's taken them to the park, making the most of it while the weather's still good. They keep asking about your bird book, and when they're going to get to read it.'

'Oh God,' Abby said. 'I should never have mentioned it. It's ridiculous!'

'No, it isn't. It's a lovely idea. Have you done any more?'

'A few notes,' Abby admitted. 'We had a boy at the reserve a few weeks ago who described a mistle thrush as having a bread-and-butter pudding tummy, so I'm going to steal that.'

'It's perfect. See – get young people to help you create it, then they'll definitely be able to identify with it.'

'Hmm.'

'Come on, then.' Tessa picked up a packet of pumpkin-shaped confetti and wiggled it. 'What's the plan with all this?'

'Bunting for the visitor centre, and I'm running a scary drawing competition. I wondered if Willow and Daisy would like to do some examples for me, so I've got something to show the children when they turn up. I think if we keep it light, I won't end up with pictures full of blood and gore.'

Tessa laughed. 'Of course you will – they're children. No risk assessment will ever prepare you for the imaginations of small people.'

'You think I should stick to a nature theme?'

'I think,' Tessa said, picking up a fondant fancy and biting into it, closing her eyes in ecstasy, then waiting until she could speak again, 'you could theme it around kittens and you'd still end up with some unexpected drawings. Go with horror – at least it'll be entertaining.'

'You're not helping to calm my nerves.'

'What do you have to be nervous about? You've got this, Abby.'

Abby toyed with the yellow icing on her cake. She debated telling Tessa that she thought Penelope's financial concerns were bigger than she was letting on, that she was beginning to feel the weight of responsibility on her shoulders, and that she had this irritating, left-field problem she was thinking about more than she should be – because how much of a risk was he, really, with his petty notes and his non-existent car damage?

'There's just a lot to get done,' she settled on. 'But if Willow and Daisy aren't around, how good are you at drawing bats?'

That evening, once Willow, Daisy and Raffle had worn each other out running around the garden, and two of them were upstairs asleep, and the other was snoring gently in front of the fireplace, ears twitching, Abby, Tessa and Neil sat in the snug living room, a bottle of wine open on the table. Abby had relented and decided to stay over, as she often did, the thought of going back to her homely but silent terrace unappealing after spending time in her sister's boisterous household.

'We've been watching that *Wild Wonders* thing on the TV,' Neil said into an easy silence, earning a slap on the arm from his wife.

'Ssshhh, no we haven't. Not *every* episode, anyway.' Tessa looked mortified, and Abby laughed.

'I've watched some of it too – I had to know what we were up against.'

'And what do you think? Does that presenter, what's-her-name, know anything about nature at all?'

'Flick Hunter,' Neil supplied.

'The name on the tip of every Englishman's tongue this autumn,' Abby said. 'I don't know. She seems competent enough, and they've got a good range of experts to provide the detail. It's well put together, and it's a great advertisement for Suffolk nature reserves.'

'You're not losing customers because of it?'

Abby wrinkled her nose. A month ago, she would have said no, absolutely not. But over the last couple of weeks the footfall had dropped off, takings had dipped and Abby hadn't found a reason for it – unless the popularity of the television show was growing, and customers who ordinarily would have taken a punt, picking either Meadowsweet or Reston Marsh for their day out, now automatically chose the latter because they'd heard of it.

'I don't know,' she said. 'Possibly. The thing is, I don't have the answers, and Penelope won't like that. She wants to know why we've lost visitors, and what I'm doing about it. The drop-off is too vague, too gradual, and I need to work on reversing it. But we've got a night-time wildlife walk, mask-making, apple bobbing and now, with our stunning drawing examples, who wouldn't want to come and see us? If I can make this Halloween event successful, then the ripples will perhaps be enough to get us back on track.'

'It seems like she's put a lot of the responsibility on you,' Tessa said. 'You're not the only member of staff.'

Abby shrugged. 'I know, but Rosa's got the shop and Stephan's in charge of the café. My remit is activities, visitor numbers, memberships. It makes sense that I should be the one driving it, but everyone mucks in and comes up with ideas. I'm not on my own.'

'That's good,' Tessa nodded. 'And all this, for Halloween, is bound to be a sure-fire winner, even without leggy blonde television presenters to lure people in.'

'I'm blonde,' Abby said. 'Not so much of the leggy, though.'

'You're gorgeous.' Tessa drained her wine and reached for the bottle. 'How's lovely Ryan in the pub? What did you describe him as – a fuzzy St Bernard?'

'Subtle, sis.' Abby rolled her eyes. 'Ryan's got a girlfriend, and even if he didn't, I'm not attracted to him. He's a friend. They all are.'

'Yes, I know. Gavin's married, Marek's not far off being a granddad and even before this girlfriend development, you couldn't possibly date Ryan because you couldn't get past his beard to kiss him. There are excuses for everyone, but I refuse to believe there isn't someone at that reserve, one of the volunteers maybe, or a guy in the village, who hasn't piqued your interest. You can't stay single forever.'

'Why not, Tessa? Why can't I be happy, just Raffle and me? Why do I need someone else to complete me?'

'I'll open another bottle,' Neil said quietly, slipping from the room.

'Of course, I'm not saying that.' Tessa scooted closer, drawing her knees up in front of her. 'But I also know that ever since you finished with Darren you've stayed away from men and dating as if the mere concept could damage your health. Just because Mum and Dad's relationship was . . .' she searched for the word, '. . . volatile, doesn't mean we're going to turn into them. Look at me and Neil.'

'I know that,' Abby said, already weary at treading over well-worn ground. 'But doesn't it make sense to stay away from relationships that look like they could go that way? With Darren, I let it go on too long, and before that . . .' She rubbed her hands over her face. 'I get it wrong, Tessa. Every time, I go for the guys who *aren't* like Neil, who *aren't* kind and gentle and decent. And then, it's as if what happened with Mum and Dad is playing out all over again, that somehow I subconsciously go looking for it.' Her voice dipped, the pain of those memories still able to hurt her despite the time that had passed. 'It's easier if I just stay on my own.'

'But you got out,' Tessa protested. 'You put up with Darren's crap for far too long, but you left him. You didn't let it get like Mum and Dad, and you are not the same as them, neither of us are. The way Dad behaved was unforgivable, and you

79

have to give Mum credit for fighting back, even if walking away would have been better for everyone.'

'Tessa—'

'I understand your reservations. You haven't made the best decisions with men in the past, but you can't let it hamper your whole life. Not every guy is going to be like Darren, or Dad.'

'Except they're all I've experienced.'

Tessa shook her head. '*No*, Abby. Don't let Dad's failings stop you from having a rewarding, healthy relationship. He's caused both of us – you, especially – enough pain. Don't give him that satisfaction, too.'

'But whenever Darren raised his voice, or I lost my temper with him, I thought—'

Tessa took Abby's hand. 'No relationship is without arguments; what matters is how you deal with them. Dad *never* got it right. Darren was an idiot, and those guys before . . . Abby, it doesn't mean every man is like that, or they're the only ones you'll ever come into contact with. You can't live your life believing that, because you'll lose out on so much. You've had a bad run of things, but you're much more settled now, with your house and your wonderful job. I don't see why a loving relationship can't follow.' Tessa gave her an encouraging smile. 'Besides, you're going to get overheated about stuff unless you're the Dalai Lama. You need to build up a head of steam then clear the air sometimes. It's all part of it, and making up can be the best thing.' Her smile turned into a cheeky grin, but it faded quickly when Abby didn't reciprocate.

'But what if they frustrate you every time they open their mouth?' Abby said. 'And you feel this rage building up inside you, and you want to scream and pummel their chest, and then every time you imagine doing that, you picture them taking hold of your arms and silencing you with this kiss, this amazing, powerful kiss, so that you don't even feel the rain or—' She stopped suddenly, heat going to her cheeks.

Her sister was staring at her with a look of shocked delight, and Neil was standing in the doorway, open-mouthed, holding a bottle of wine.

'Who the hell is *that*?' Tessa asked.

'Nobody,' Abby said hurriedly, stretching her glass out towards Neil, who had recovered and was holding the bottle aloft.

'Bullshit is it nobody,' Tessa whispered. 'That is a very well-formed fantasy, and I need to know right now who the man is.'

'It isn't anyone real,' Abby said. 'It's just . . . Octavia got this book for me, from the library. She clearly believes, as you do, that my sex life is somewhat lacking. Anyway, this ridiculous novel is full of—' she glanced at Neil, who was intent on his iPhone, his nose almost pressed into the screen. She was embarrassing everyone, though in some ways that was better than continuing the depressing conversation about her parents and her own, less-than-happy relationships. 'It's a bit raunchy, that's all. Not what I'm used to.'

'With a dashing, infuriating hero who you argue with in the rain?' Tessa hugged her knees. 'It sounds like the *Pride and Prejudice* film with Keira Knightley and Matthew Macfadyen. That scene in the downpour is perfection. Whoever this author is,' Tessa said, and Abby jolted upright, almost spilling her wine, 'then they've clearly been watching that film. You'll have to give me the details.' She glanced at her husband then winked at Abby, and Abby felt all at once like she'd been let off the hook and dug herself a deeper hole.

81

She wished she'd remembered that film adaptation and pretended it was the reason for her over-excitable imagination. Now she would have to invent an author and a book title that sounded convincing – but then Tessa would look online and not be able to find it, or else she'd have to search through Octavia's stock and see if she could pick out a book to match, which sounded like a hopeless task, and one which would no doubt result in the rumour being spread around the village that Abby Field was looking for erotic literature.

The irony was that the person who would probably be best at conjuring up novel titles was the one who was responsible for Abby's ludicrous outburst. If only he hadn't stood there in the rain, in his expensive jacket with his scowling, sea-blue eyes and perfect jawline, and then pulled her beneath the porch with him, she would never have let her imagination run away with her in front of her sister in the first place.

But as long as she kept it to herself and had no more slip-ups like that, then the unhelpful feelings were bound to go away and Jack Westcoat would simply be her irritating adversary, until he realized the delights of the reserve were too much for him and skulked back to London to write his dark books. She was confident that he would be a short-lived problem, and she would soon be able to tick him off her to-do list for good.

Chapter Six

Contrary to some beliefs, pheasants are not known for damaging cars – unless they fly into them, which sadly happens quite often. They are beautifully coloured game birds, with shiny orange and green feathers, and they have a mechanical walk, as if the floor is cold and they want to make as little contact with it as possible. Their loud call is, perhaps, a bit like a hooting rooster.

— Note from Abby's notebook

Abby had to admit that Destiny, the face painter she'd hired for the Halloween event, was top-notch. A little boy was running around with his features covered in an intricate web, a sinister spider crouching, poised, at his hairline. The pumpkin faces were terrifying or friendly, depending on the age of the child, and now she was creating a kestrel's elegant face on a small girl who was sitting impeccably still.

The drawing table was full, the café had been taken over by mask-makers when the sequins and feathers started blowing away in the wind gusting through the picnic area, and there was an air of happy chaos throughout the visitor centre. Abby wondered how the real wildlife was coping, but a quick glance showed her that the coal tits and chaffinches decorating the feeders weren't remotely bothered by the noise and hubbub.

She waved at Rosa as she hurried back to the picnic area, the wind not disrupting a competitive game of apple bobbing, currently being overseen by Gavin. She gave him a grin as he handed a goody bag to a successful bobber, and went to stand next to him.

'Going well, Gavin?'

'Never better, Abby. Bloody cold out here, though.' He rubbed his hands together. 'I was planning on dunking your head in the bucket in celebration of all your hard work, but I don't think even I can be that cruel.'

'Thanks!' Abby laughed. 'I think. It is November in a couple of days, we can't expect balmy weather.'

'Yeah, don't I know it. The girls have already written out their bloody Christmas lists. I've told them to talk to Santa, because I'm not interested.'

'Gavin! You can't—'

'They said they wanted them from Santa anyway, so we're on the same page.'

'Except Santa's not real, so you will actually have to go and get the toys.'

Gavin shrugged. 'There's loads of time yet. *Loads.*'

Abby held her hands up in submission. 'Fair enough. And thanks for the no-dunking thing. I'm leading the night-time walk later, so I could do without getting soaked beforehand.'

'Yes, boss.' He saluted, and then stepped forward when two boys got over-exuberant in their attempts to win the prize. 'You two, stop it, now. We don't stand for drowning each other at this nature reserve, whatever you might have heard.'

When Abby made it back inside, Rosa was showing Jonny a pair of high-end binoculars. They had a 20 per cent sale on all their birdwatching equipment, and this was the closest she'd seen Jonny come to actually buying something. Everything was going to plan; she just had the night walk to contend with.

When a packet of felt tips was discovered to be dud, and Abby realized they weren't going to make it through the afternoon with only two orange pens, she took the opportunity to escape the madness and walk to the village shop to pick up some more. She resisted the urge to take the longer route past Swallowtail House. It looked simultaneously regal and slightly spooky at the best of times, but would it seem particularly sinister today? A large, abandoned house was the perfect location for a Halloween investigation, but the padlocks and thick chains would put paid to that, even if there had been anyone brave enough.

Peacock Cottage was quiet as she passed, none of the windows showing signs of life, and she hurried on. On Meadowgreen's main road, she headed towards the shop, the wind whipping her hair against her face. Her pace slowed as she noticed two people standing next to the postbox, chatting.

Abby felt the familiar yet unwanted flicker of emotion as she saw Jack, his hands shoved into the pockets of his expensive jacket. And then she focused on the person he was with, the long blonde hair falling over the shoulders of a smart black coat, and knee-high, tan leather boots over skinny jeans. It took Abby a moment to place her, to realize she had seen her on the television but not in real life.

Flick Hunter was in Meadowgreen. She was even more beautiful in the flesh, the comfortable intimacy between her and Jack clear even from a distance.

Abby hesitated, wondering whether to keep going or turn quickly around. She didn't know why she felt so strange seeing them together, or so reluctant to simply walk past them. Jack leaned closer to Flick, his lips twitching into a smile. Abby scrunched her fingers into fists, hovering uselessly on the side of the road, but then Flick put her hand on Jack's shoulder and steered him to a black Land Rover parked close by.

Abby breathed a sigh of relief, waiting until they were next to the car before she crossed over. But as she reached the shop she noticed a glimmer of movement out of the corner of her eye and turned instinctively towards it. Jack was looking at her, his hand raised in recognition. Her stomach fizzed and she gave him a quick, nervous wave, their eyes meeting briefly, then he climbed in alongside Flick Hunter, the sound of the door closing a heavy clunk that reached her despite the wind.

She decided that she wouldn't tell anyone what she'd seen. She didn't want to fuel a fresh wave of gossip about Flick Hunter and Jack Westcoat, and acknowledging that she had spotted them together made her uneasy, as if she was about to come down with an unpleasant bug. There was no reason for her to feel like that. She hadn't exactly hit it off with Jack, and what business was it of hers if they were good friends or, perhaps, even more than that? Returning to Meadowsweet with felt pens aplenty, Abby went back to the drawing competition. Once it was over, she would have a couple of hours to tidy up the visitor centre before the night walk began.

* * *

They set off as dusk was falling, and Abby could hear the usual excited whispers behind her as they made their way along the meadow trail. She stopped everyone at the end of the path, where a fence looked out across a field. It was part of Penelope's estate, and until a few months ago had been let out to a local farmer for cattle grazing. Abby wasn't sure what had happened to the cows, but now it was empty and, at this time of day when it was in different degrees of shadow, a good spotting place for one of their best nocturnal creatures.

'Now,' she said quietly, 'if we're very lucky, we might just see—'

'There!' someone whispered loudly. 'Oh my God!'

As if on cue, a large, pale bird swooped gracefully over the field, its heart-shaped face clearly visible in the gloom. It was mesmerizing, and almost luminous against the twilight backdrop.

'A barn owl,' Abby said. 'There she is. She roosts over in those trees and is seen frequently by visitors and our reserve wardens. She hunts mainly at dawn and dusk, but she's sometimes out mid-afternoon. The weather can set their hunting patterns off – her feathers aren't very water resistant, so if it's raining she avoids flying.'

'She's magnificent.'

'Stunning.'

'She's like a phantom,' said one, younger-sounding visitor. Abby couldn't disagree.

She immersed herself in the wildlife and her guests' interest in it. This was where she was happiest, and a night walk on a cold October evening was somehow easier than one on a summer's afternoon, because she knew the people who had booked onto it would be a more hardcore breed of nature lover. She wanted to inspire more people, of course, but sometimes it was nice to know that she wouldn't have to work hard at their enthusiasm, that it was already ingrained. The woodland yielded bats, visible coming out of their bat boxes, flying round in wide circles. Abby had brought her monitor, so she could make their weirdly regular clicks audible, and explain how they used echolocation to navigate and find food in the dark.

Everyone was fascinated, the questions kept coming and, as they turned back towards the visitor centre, the darkness almost complete, a Chinese water deer bounded across their path, its large ears and white-rimmed nose so distinctive.

'Thank you, wildlife,' Abby whispered under her breath, as there were low murmurings of delight from those around her.

In the café, Stephan had produced a batch of zombie brownies, with white and pink marshmallow pieces that looked like flesh oozing through the chocolate. He was poised to make hot drinks, and Abby hovered while everyone tucked in, on hand to answer any more queries.

One of the youngest visitors on the walk, a girl of about twelve, came up to her.

'All those things tonight, the owl and the bats and the deer, they're a bit creepy in the dark, aren't they? You can see why people believe in ghosts. If you didn't know what a barn owl was, you might think it was something scarier.'

'That's a very good point,' Abby said. 'I bet our native wildlife could explain away lots of spooky sightings.'

'Is there anything else you see that we missed out on?'

'Not really. We were particularly lucky tonight, though we do occasionally see badgers. It's not that they aren't there, but they're so elusive it's much harder to spot them. I've only seen one once, and I've been here nearly two years.' The girl stared at her, her eyes wide with interest, and so she kept going. 'I was on my way home, and it really made me jump. This huge thing was lumbering through the trees towards me, and suddenly there was this white, striped nose, which *was* a bit ghostly. We looked at each other for a second, then it changed course, going back into the woods. But I can't remember the last time any guests or other staff reported seeing one – we're not usually around in the dead of night.'

'It's been a brilliant walk, though. Thank you!' The girl held out her hand and, surprised and touched, Abby shook it.

'Thanks for staying with me,' Abby said to Stephan as they pulled on their coats. 'Are you cycling home?'

Stephan nodded. 'I'd offer you a lift, except space is quite limited on the saddle.'

Abby laughed. 'I'll be fine. I know the route like the back of my hand, and I've got my torch.'

'Still a bit late for you to be heading home alone. I could walk you back, get on my bike from there?'

'Honestly, Stephan, I'm fine.' She patted his shoulder. 'It'll take more than a few ghoulish masks to scare me.'

They switched off the lights and locked the doors, then wished each other goodnight. Abby listened to the sound of Stephan's bike wheels whirring down the car park, his headlight bright in the darkness.

She started walking, taking her usual shortcut through the trees. She wasn't scared of the dark – she was a night owl herself, only the need to walk Raffle twice a day forcing her out of bed with the sunrise, and she often pottered or watched television until the early hours of the morning. But tonight, after the young girl's comments, and recalling her own encounter with the badger – a moment that had truly scared her – she found that she was on edge.

The wind was rustling through the trees, the woodland was never quiet at night, and she couldn't help picturing Swallowtail House, its dark, hulking shape looming over the village. Her hands shaking slightly, she twisted the back of her torch, checking the beam was on full, pointing it directly ahead, her steps slow and deliberate so she didn't upend herself over a rock or tree root. It was fine, she told herself; she'd done this so often before. But she wished she had Raffle with her, or even Gavin making ridiculous wise-cracks, or Stephan – why hadn't she taken him up on his offer? It would only have been a few minutes out of his way.

Something screeched to her left and she copied it, clamping her hand over her mouth at the ridiculous outburst, knowing the instant she'd screamed that it was one tree branch rubbing against another in the wind.

'Come on, Abby, get a grip.' She surged forwards, seeing the smooth concrete of the road up ahead, and then the glowing, beckoning light of Peacock Cottage. It was just in one downstairs window, but it looked so inviting, so safe, away from the murmuring trees and the darkness creeping in around her. She tried to think of the robins, greenfinches and blackbirds all safe on woody perches, little balls of puffed-up feathers, unconcerned by the wind raging around them. She tried to take strength from her feathered friends, but the pull of the cottage was so strong, her legs automatically turned towards the front door, its bold blue hue hidden in shadow.

And then she thought of Jack's smirk as she'd ranted about his car, the way that, despite complaining to her about ridiculous things, he'd been entirely confident and unashamed in his self-centred opinions. She felt again the disquiet of seeing him and Flick Hunter together. Her anger returning, Abby's train of thought led swiftly and predictably to the fantasy she had conjured up, his strong arms grabbing hold of her, his lips, when they met hers, tender but with clear intent, tasting of lemon-scented Earl Grey tea.

She disliked Jack, what little she knew of him. Her mind had no right to be gallivanting off in these wayward directions. Angry at herself now as well as him, she was distracted, and as she stepped with relief out of the trees and onto the road she missed the biggest, most obvious tree root and got her foot caught, her momentum propelling her forward, the torch clattering to the ground as she put her hands in front of her to stop herself landing on her face.

The light went out. It sounded loud, probably fatal for the torch, and she could feel the sting of her grazed palms, a painful tug in her ankle where her foot had been wrenched out of the root as she fell. She swore and scrabbled in her bag for her phone, switching the light app on and casting around for the bits of torch. She didn't want to risk causing anyone a puncture in the morning.

She worked quickly, finding the black metal casing, the batteries and the spring. She was nearly there, so close to being able to leave the darkness and run home to safety and warmth, when the meagre light from her iPhone was joined by a much bigger, softer, glow. She looked up to find that the front door of Peacock Cottage was open, light spilling across the road, a tall figure silhouetted against it.

'Hello?' Jack said. 'Is anyone there?'

Abby stayed still. Chances were he wouldn't see her – she was just out of the reach of the pooling light – would dismiss it as any one of a number of irritating creatures, and go back inside.

'Hello?' he said again. 'Who's there?' Was his voice wobbling? Abby couldn't tell over the blood pounding in her head.

She spotted the torch bulb and reached inchingly towards it, and then a third, almost blinding light had her in its grasp. Of *course* he had his own, powerful torch. Of course he did. It was probably MI5 issue.

'Abby! Shit, are you OK?' He was at her side in moments, kneeling in the dirt. 'Are you hurt?'

'I'm fine. I tripped, broke my torch. Nothing to worry about.'

'OK, but can I . . . ?' He placed his torch on the ground.

'What?' she asked, but he'd started running his hands down her arms, his touch feather-light, pausing as he turned over her hands and saw the grazes on her palms. She didn't want him to touch her, it reminded her too much of her daydream. She tried to pull away but he'd let go of her hands anyway, was patting his hands gently down her legs, from her knees to her feet. She winced as he got to her right ankle.

'I'm fine, thank you, Jack. I should get home.'

'You have no light – that doesn't count,' he added, when she waggled her phone. 'And you've hurt your ankle.'

'I haven't. It got stuck, that's all.'

'Come inside, let me check you over properly.'

'No, I—' she sighed as he gripped her elbows and pulled her to standing. 'I'm fine to get home.' She put her foot gingerly on the floor, relief spiking as she realized it wasn't that sore, that walking wouldn't be a problem. 'Thank you for looking out for me.' She started putting the bits of broken torch in her bag.

When she'd finished, Jack hadn't moved.

'I'm not letting you walk home on your own with only that ridiculous phone light to guide you.'

'Well, I'm not *letting* you force me into your house so you can do God knows what to me. Are you a qualified doctor as well as a novelist? It seems unlikely! Your pat-down just then was more like you were searching for hidden weapons at an airport than seeing if I was injured.'

He stared, aghast, and for some reason, Abby kept going. 'Perhaps you want to experiment on me, to work out all the gruesome ways the victims in your next book will get murdered. How do I know I can trust you?'

'If I practised my murders before I wrote about them, don't you think the police would have put two and two together before now?' Jack shot back. 'Discovered victims who had reached similarly bizarre ends, and done a bit of digging? I'm not clever enough to commit the perfect murder, and even if I was, right now I'm too cold to even entertain the prospect, and I'm just offering to look at those cuts on your hand for you, check your ankle's OK. I'm sure your parents told you never to talk to strangers, but I'm really not an ogre, whatever our last two encounters may have led you to believe. Come on, I'm not wearing a coat.' He bounced up and down on the spot, and Abby bit back the urge to laugh.

'That's very kind of you,' she said, 'but I have to be at work early in the morning, so I need to get home.'

'At least let me drive you.'

'It's a ten-minute walk! Do you have any idea how much fuel you'll use up in that huge thing doing a completely pointless journey?'

In the light from the door, she saw Jack roll his eyes. 'I

am not going back inside and leaving you out here,' he said. 'Either you come in with me, or you let me drive you home.'

She wondered briefly whether, if she was to take him up on his offer, she'd find Flick Hunter sitting on his sofa. She almost said that he could walk her home if he was that bothered, and then she realized that would involve spending more time with him, and also that she would worry about *him* getting back safely when he was such a city boy and couldn't even cope with a few pheasants.

'Fine,' she said, sighing heavily. 'You can drop me at home. Thank you.'

'Good. Arm?' He held his hand out, and she reluctantly let him take her arm. It was a few short steps to the Range Rover, and her ankle was barely bruised, and yet she found herself leaning into him, feeling the solid weight of his support. He pointed his fob at the car to unlock it, opened the passenger door and waited while she climbed into the seat. It was even more luxurious than it had looked, and she sank into the soft leather, smelt its creaminess, felt sleep tugging at her instantly so she had to pinch her arm to stay awake.

Jack hopped into the driver's seat, started the engine, which was much quieter than she had expected, and reversed expertly out of the driveway. She held her breath, waiting for the telltale crunch that meant there was a stray piece of torch she'd failed to pick up, then relaxed when none came. Jack drove slowly, turning left as she instructed when they reached the junction with the main village road, and then round, past the darkened walls enclosing Swallowtail House, the silent building and whatever ghosts inhabited it beyond, then turned right into Warbler Cottages.

It took no more than three minutes, but Abby spent that

time studying Jack's profile, the straight, proud nose, the high forehead partly obscured by his thick, untidy hair. His fingers on the wheel were long and slender, he wore no jewellery, no rings, but a plain, white-faced wristwatch with a gold surround and tan leather strap. It looked classic, expensive.

'This one?' he asked, cutting the engine.

'Yes, this is it.' Abby looked at her terraced house. It wasn't remotely cottagey, not in the way Peacock Cottage was, but it was snug, it was her home, and she could see Raffle, his nose pressed up to the glass of the downstairs window, waiting for her as if he could sense when she was on her way back to him.

'Is that a *husky*?' Jack asked, peering over her shoulder.

'That's Raffle. He's my rescue husky. Do you want to come in and meet him?' The words were out of her mouth before she could stop them. She looked back at Jack, frozen mid-breath, hoping with equal measure that he would say yes, and also no.

He drummed his fingers on the steering wheel. 'I'd love to, but perhaps not now. It's late, as you say, and I . . . sure you'll be OK?' He gestured towards her hands.

'They're just grazes, fine once I give them a good clean. Thank you for the lift, and for . . . coming to look for me. It was brave.'

Jack frowned and ran a hand over his jaw. 'Brave?'

'Your cottage is in the middle of the woods,' she clarified. 'I'm a fan of nature, as you know, but if I lived somewhere like that, there is no way I'd step outside after dark in response to a noise, not unless I had a weapon with me, not even if it sounded like there was a fairground starting up right outside the front door. I was only there because I had no choice. If we were in opposite places, I wouldn't have come to your rescue, I would have left you to get eaten by bears, or make your own way home, whatever.'

'Which, I seem to recall, is pretty much what you wanted me to do when I found you.'

Abby felt the flush creep up her neck and was glad of the darkness. 'Sorry about that. I was flustered, annoyed with myself for getting scared, and—'

'I was the last person you hoped to see?'

'You were inevitable, considering where I tripped.'

Jack laughed, the sound loud inside the confines of the car. 'I was inevitable?'

'God, that came out wrong! I just meant nobody else would be around, only you.' The words somehow had more weight than she had intended, and she scrabbled to change the subject. 'I saw you venturing out into the village today.'

He nodded, not quite meeting her eye. 'I know Flick Hunter from a charity event we did a couple of years ago,' he said. 'I didn't realize she was here, but it was good to see her. A friendly face amongst, well—' he gestured around him. 'I'm new here, as you know.'

'She's anchoring the television show at the nature reserve on the other side of the marsh,' Abby said quietly.

'She was telling me about it. Has it affected things at Meadowsweet?'

'Not really,' Abby admitted. 'Not that noticeably, anyway. We need to be more proactive about drawing in visitors regardless, so in some ways the push has been good.'

Jack stared out of the windscreen. 'That's often the way, getting forced in a direction you never intended, finding out that it was the right move all along.' He faced her again. 'Let's hope it works out for both of us.'

Abby wanted to ask more, to connect the dots between

his words and what Rosa and Octavia had told her about him, but she didn't want to seem nosy, and now, with Raffle waiting inside and her bed calling to her weary bones, wasn't the time. 'I'll keep my fingers crossed,' she said. 'Thanks again for rescuing me. Your car's comfortable, by the way.'

'Noted.' He nodded, suppressing a smile, his lips lifting at the corners. Abby wondered if she'd conjured them up right in her fantasy, how the lips she was staring at would feel if they were pressed against hers.

'Right then,' she said, her voice paper-thin. 'Night.'

'Goodnight, Abby.' He waited until she'd closed the door, walked up the front path and put her key in the lock. She stepped into her warm, vanilla-scented hallway and turned. He made a gesture that was half wave, half salute, and pulled away from the kerb.

When she fell into a fitful, broken sleep that night, the memory of her fall enhanced by the smarting of her palms, all she could think about was Jack running his hands up her arms, and the concern in his eyes when he'd knelt beside her in the mud.

When she woke the following morning, Abby felt like she hadn't had any sleep at all. She took a longer route to work, walking along the brick wall around Swallowtail House, getting that extra peek of the building that intrigued and calmed her. The wind was still raging, low clouds racing across the sky so the sun had no chance to break through, but it never stopped the wildlife, and Abby paused to watch a pair of goldfinches, their regally coloured feathers flashes of bright in the grey. They bobbed along the high wall then disappeared over it, into a place she longed to explore.

She wasn't the only one who wondered why, if the reserve

was in trouble, and Penelope no longer wanted to live in the grand mansion, she didn't sell it. Did she really hold onto it simply because it was a reminder of her and Al's life together? And if that was the case, then why wasn't she looking after it? The longer it was left, the less likely it was to survive at all. If Penelope wanted to preserve it then handing it over to someone else, and making a profit in the process, would surely be for the best.

But she couldn't suggest it. The older woman would have considered it, would have her own reasons for handling things the way she did, and wouldn't have listened to Abby in any case. Perhaps selling the house had some implications for the reserve, as it was all part of the same estate. She turned away from it and fought her way through the fallen elder to get back onto Meadowsweet's woodland track.

She didn't know why she wanted to avoid the sight of last night's fall, but she felt off kilter, uncomfortable despite the success of the previous day's event. She was gratified that the only disaster had come at her own hands, had harmed nobody but herself, but still she wished that, if there had to have been a witness, it could have been anyone but Jack. And yet, in some ways, she was glad it had happened. She couldn't help but replay their encounter, the softening between them in his car a reconciliation of sorts. There had been no sign of Flick Hunter at Peacock Cottage, and he'd offered up the information about her freely, as if Abby deserved an explanation. She felt as if she was at the edge of a tunnel, knowing she should turn back but desperate to see where it led.

When she arrived at the visitor centre, she had a welcoming committee.

Penelope was standing at the reception desk, her arms

folded accusingly, and Rosa and Stephan were in the shop, pretending to rearrange the display of Halloween chocolates but obviously waiting for whatever dressing-down was about to be handed out. Gavin, never one for subtlety, was leaning against the wall, a piece of grass in his mouth in place of a cigarette. When she caught his eye, he winced sympathetically.

Abby slowed, putting her hands behind her back, suddenly conscious of the grazes on her palms even though, now they were clean, they were hardly visible.

'What's going on?' she asked. 'Is there – did something happen, yesterday?'

'I don't know,' Penelope said. 'Why don't you tell *me*?'

She put the emphasis on the last word, glaring at Stephan, Rosa and then Gavin, reminding them this wasn't a spectacle, but none of them budged and Abby was thankful. She knew that, as embarrassing as it was to be reprimanded in front of her friends, they would also back her up if they could. The only thing was, Abby couldn't think what this could possibly be about. The event had gone smoothly. Unless Gavin had let those boys go too far with the apple bobbing and failed to tell her about it.

'I'm not sure what there is to say,' she said slowly, casting around for anything that might help her understand what had happened.

'Well, would you like to explain this?' Penelope put something down on the desk. It was an envelope. White, pristine and, when Abby looked closely, sealed.

'You haven't opened it?'

'Of course not,' Penelope said. 'It's addressed to you. But I doubt whatever is inside will be particularly complimentary, going by the last one we received.'

Her insides suddenly churning, Abby turned the envelope over. In the slanting, elegant script she now recognized as Jack's, was her name. *Abby Field.* They had come a long way from bee Post-it Notes, at least. A hundred things went through her mind – was he going to complain about the event after all, the swathes of people it had brought to the reserve? Had he meant to do it all along, and only failed to say anything last night because Abby was there alone, and he'd seen her as vulnerable? Or was this because she'd insulted him by saying he was inevitable? She had been encouraged by the thaw between them, but maybe she'd misinterpreted it.

They were all looking at her now, even Stephan and Rosa abandoning their pretence of display reorganization. Penelope's politeness at not opening other people's mail didn't extend to letting them read it in peace, she noticed. She didn't want to open it in front of anyone; she wanted to take the blow in private because, she realized with startling clarity, it *would* be a blow, to see harsh words from Jack aimed at the reserve, aimed at her.

'Come on then,' Gavin said. 'We're all dying of curiosity here. What has Mr Snooty got to say for himself now?'

She took a deep breath and ripped open the envelope, sliding out the folded piece of A4 paper and laying it out flat on the table before she lost her nerve. She skimmed over the words, then read them again more slowly, clamping her jaw together to stop her emotion from showing.

Dear Abby,
How are your hands this morning, and your ankle? I hope they're suitably recovered and not suffering too much from passing up the chance of being tended to by me.

When is your next guided walk? I've been wondering if
I should take you up on the kind offer you spat at me
several weeks ago.
   Yours, JW
   PS. Glad the squashed frog met with your approval.

'What is this?' Penelope asked, her brows furrowing. 'What does this mean? *Squashed frog?* Has he been hurting the wildlife?' She levelled Abby with a piercing, unsympathetic gaze, waiting for full disclosure.

'No no,' Abby said quickly. 'It's a conversation we had, a little while ago. He hasn't harmed anything. But he's not angry, see – he's even considering coming on one of our walks. We've turned things around.'

'What is this business with your hands and ankle? Just what have you been doing with my tenant?'

'Nothing,' Abby said. 'Nothing at all, Penelope. There's really no reason to worry; everything's good.'

She folded the note and put it back in the envelope, then in her handbag, and hurried to the storeroom to take off her coat. She should be mad with Jack – there was no way she wanted Penelope, Gavin or Stephan to know about her ridiculous accident the previous evening, and as much as she would have been happy to tell Rosa, and Rosa, by her keen look, would be more than happy to find out, she didn't want to risk it spreading.

Her feelings for Jack Westcoat, as conflicted as they were, were her business alone, a tempting fantasy to fill her idle moments. They would come to nothing, would fade out as quickly as they had arrived. It was good he was no longer against her or the reserve, and hadn't once mentioned the extra traffic passing by his cottage during the Halloween event, but that was as far as it went. He was a writer, a disgraced one, and obviously as keen on his privacy as she was. She wondered if he would have written the note at all if he'd known that Penelope would force her to open it in front of everyone. They were destined to bump into each other occasionally, but so what? It didn't mean anything.

As she hung her coat up and slipped the note into the inner, zipped compartment of her bag, she found that she was smiling, almost tempted to take it out and reread it, study the slopes and curves that his long fingers, pen held between them, had produced. But that would be taking it too far. She hadn't delved into the background behind the scandalous events Octavia had taken much delight in telling them about, and she didn't want to, even though she knew they would be readily available online. She didn't want to know what had happened, discover something that would damage her view of him, just as, conversely, she didn't want to make him a bigger part of her life than he was.

Jack Westcoat was a mirage in her mind, almost as much a work of fiction as the books he wrote, and that was where he needed to stay. The spark between them couldn't be healthy; she knew that from personal experience, could easily replay the memories of verbal arguments between her mum and dad that had started on the right side of cheeky and ended with slammed doors, thrown crockery, and then, towards the end of their relationship, the abuse her mother had faced at her father's hands. Her own escape, as a child, had been the fields behind her house, the calm and quiet, the colourful flutter of the butterflies and the high, uncon- cerned trill of warblers.

And yet, in her adult life, she had begun to repeat the pattern, drawn towards men whose passion started out as attractive but became dangerous. Jack was obviously next on her list of hopeless decisions, and she needed to stay away from him, even if the pull to see him got stronger.

There was just the small matter of his proximity to the reserve and her journey home, and the fact that now, it seemed, he wanted to come on one of her guided walks, was actively showing an interest in the nature reserve and the wildlife he'd been so against. She couldn't allow that opportunity to pass by, however complicated it made things. Getting people inspired by nature was her job, after all.

She took up her post behind the reception desk and busied herself straightening the already neat maps, spotter books and day passes, ignoring the curious, almost knowing look Rosa was giving her.

Chapter Seven

Barn owls are like ghosts in the dusk. Graceful, honey-and-white birds with heart-shaped faces, they glide through the countryside looking for food. They are not the same type of owl as Hedwig in Harry Potter, which is a snowy owl, but I think they're just as beautiful.
— Note from Abby's notebook

With Halloween and bonfire night out of the way, Christmas seemed to hurtle towards them, and Abby and Rosa agreed to meet early in the visitor centre one mid-November morning to adorn the space with decorations. As Abby left her house and locked the door she found Octavia at her side, wearing a bright-green coat with white fur trim which, on top of her red hair, made her look like a large Christmas elf.

'You're decorating the reserve this morning, aren't you?'

Abby had a brief vision of trying to hang paper chains from the trees. 'The visitor centre,' she said. 'How did you know?'

'Oh, something I overheard. I've been busy.' She thrust

forward bulging carrier bags, and Abby saw they were full of glittering decorations: baubles, strings of tinsel and birds made out of gold, silver, blue and purple wire. They looked homemade.

Abby stopped worrying about where Octavia had overheard her and Rosa discussing their plans, and whether she had started to bug their phones, because she was too distracted by the beautiful decorations.

'These are . . . did you make these? For the reserve?'

'There are some up in the library too, though book themed rather than avian. I thought it would be nice if Meadowgreen had continuity to its festiveness, and was seen as one harmonious village. I'm hoping to convince Ryan to hang up the offerings I've made him in the pub, too.'

'But how much time did it take you to make all these? And what if it's all wasted, and Ryan says no? I'm not going to, of course, and Penelope has got more important things to worry about than Christmas decorations, but . . . won't you be upset if he rejects them?'

'Not a worry, pet,' Octavia said, patting her shoulder. 'I'll bring him round.'

Abby could imagine it, too.

They walked to the reserve, Abby taking her usual shortcut, aware that Octavia also knew it, and if she took the detour she had used for the last couple of weeks the older woman would start asking questions. As they got to Peacock Cottage, Octavia's pace slowed almost comically, and she peered towards the windows. They were dark, the shiny red Range Rover absent from its usual space, and Abby felt a twinge of disappointment as she wondered where Jack had gone, whether he was out shopping or had disappeared back to London for good.

It had been two weeks since he had rescued her from the dark, and then followed it up with his good-humoured note, but since then she hadn't seen or heard from him and had spent far too much time wondering if he was expecting an answer to his question about her guided walks. She had thought it was rhetorical, but should she have let him know the dates? Had she pushed him away? She had been going around in circles, telling herself it was a good thing, and then feeling a sharp sense of loss that she might have done just that.

'No more from Mr Westcoat?' Octavia asked as, her curiosity unrewarded, they trooped through the last patch of woodland before reaching the visitor centre.

'A couple of brief meetings, one more note, but it was much . . . friendlier. I think he's coming to terms with his adopted neighbourhood.'

'That's good to know. I suppose he realizes beggars can't be choosers, and after what he did . . .' She tutted loudly.

Abby prayed that she wouldn't elaborate and was overjoyed to see Rosa waving at them from the doorway.

'This is unexpected, Octavia,' Rosa said. 'Come in, I'll make you both a hot drink.'

'Octavia's brought spectacular handmade decorations,' Abby said. 'It seems right that she should be able to help put them up. Or else just direct us from one of the café pews, whatever you prefer?'

'Oh no, I'll get stuck in, my love. No point keeping these hands idle when I could make the job easier.'

Abby lost herself in it, analyzing angles and viewpoints, working out where the best places would be for Octavia's glittering creations. She hauled the ladder out of the store-room and climbed to the top to hang strings of shimmering, rainbow tinsel from the centre of the domed roof out to the edges, like a maypole.

By the time they had finished, the whole building was dripping in festive, sparkling colour. They had even dared to put a mini Christmas tree on Penelope's desk, and Abby was eager to see what the reaction would be. Would she accept it, smile, even, or ask for it to be removed before she threw it in the bin?

Abby knew so little about her boss, about who she spent time with outside work, whether she had close friends she let her hair down with. She had tried to picture Penelope relaxing, and found she couldn't. She knew, via village hearsay, that Al had been her one true love, that she had abandoned her old life the moment he'd died – everything except the reserve, which she kept alive in his memory. They'd had no children together, and Abby thought she must be horribly lonely. Perhaps, over the years, she had held onto her loneliness, nurturing it, slowly shutting everyone out. It was such a shame.

Beneath the sternness, Abby could sense that there was so much more to Penelope, but perhaps living in a close-knit village, the way gossip whispered through it like wind through the trees, had made her cautious.

'Earth to Abby.' Rosa clicked her fingers in front of her face and Abby started, almost dropping the sparkly purple bird she was holding, unmistakable as a wren with its upright tail, its small, bulbous body and sharp beak. 'Stephan's just arrived, and we're going to get a bacon roll before we open. You in?'

'Five secs,' Abby said. 'Got to pop this little guy somewhere.' She turned in a slow circle, looking for the perfect place for her wren, and chose a shelf in the *Birdseye View* section, between two high-end pairs of binoculars. Secretly, she named the bird Jonny, and went to find her bacon roll. As she approached the table, she realized the others were already deep in a conversation she would have tried to steer them away from, had she been there from the start.

'It's very gloomy and empty looking,' Octavia was saying. 'Has he gone? Had enough of the place? Abby said . . .' She glanced up. 'Oh, hello pet, I was just telling the others that Peacock Cottage seems deserted again. He didn't last long, did he?'

Abby slid in next to Stephan, thanking him for the sandwich. 'He could have gone to the shops.'

'True,' Octavia mused, but Abby knew it didn't fit in with her sense of the dramatic. 'And he's stopped complaining, you were saying.'

'Oh yes,' Rosa said, swiping a glance at Abby. 'The last note he left was almost enthusiastic about the reserve, or certain aspects of it.'

Abby stared at her plate. After Jack's note, the one that had made her smile and thoroughly confused everyone else, Rosa had pressed Abby about what it meant, but Abby had been as vague as she could be, saying they'd almost literally bumped into each other and it was a sort of apology from him. It wasn't the truth, but she thought that if he had something to be sorry for, then his swift change of opinion, from hostile to conciliatory, might make more sense. Rosa hadn't been convinced – she knew when Abby was holding something back – and hadn't entirely let it go.

What Abby was absolutely not prepared to do was give anyone her opinion of Jack Westcoat, for fear that her complicated feelings for him might escape along with it.

'I was saying to Abby,' Octavia carried on, oblivious to the atmosphere between the two friends, 'that if he's really in all that much trouble, and this is – or was – some kind of safe haven, then he isn't in a position to be complaining. But then maybe he's that kind of man, one who does as he pleases, always looks after himself and damn the consequences. Long before this latest incident he'd had a few reckless years, according to newspaper reports. It seems old habits die hard, and I've been debating with myself whether I want to unleash a man like that on the library regulars – but it would do wonders for our profile, having such a famous author under our humble roof. As long as he's not going to fly into a rage, I think it would be worth it.'

'You've not approached him about it yet then, Octavia?' Stephan asked.

She shook her head, her myriad of necklaces jiggling. 'I was giving him a couple of months, but now I see I might have left it too late.'

'Left what too late?'

Abby hadn't heard Penelope approach, and judging by the startled looks of her friends, she wasn't the only one.

'We were wondering if your tenant is still about, Penelope? You know, Jack Westcoat, notorious, bad-tempered author.' Octavia was the only one in the vicinity of Meadowsweet – other than Gavin when he was being bold – who was unfazed by her.

'Mr Westcoat is still in Peacock Cottage,' Penelope said, 'though I'm not sure he would appreciate being a subject at the breakfast table. I do, however, like the way you've made the reserve look festive. I'm sure our visitors will love it, and I believe I have you to thank for the quirky decorations, Octavia?'

'I enjoy a bit of crafting, and what better way of spreading

109

festive cheer than to share that with friends? Glad you approve. That'll be a selling point when I go and see young Ryan later.'

'Indeed. And please, if you have to talk about fellow residents of Meadowgreen, be mindful that what may be shallow gossip to you, is actually very serious for them. He happens to be in a position where his every move is liable to be scrutinized, and I'm sure he'd be grateful if, while he is here, he could at least get some let-up from that. Now, do you have a spare piece of tinsel, Abby? The tree you've left on my desk is looking somewhat forlorn.'

Octavia rustled about in her bag and pulled out a few colourful strands that were the perfect size for the miniature Christmas tree.

'Thank you,' Penelope said.

'Do you want a bacon roll? Come and join us for a bit, maybe?' Stephan glanced up hopefully.

Penelope's thin lips shivered into a smile. 'That's a very kind offer, Stephan, but I have some paperwork to go through. A cappuccino would be welcome, but please—' she held a hand out, stopping him as he began to rise – 'not until you've finished your breakfast. I'm not gasping.' She walked back to her office, twisting the tinsel between her fingers.

'Bloody hell,' Rosa whispered, after they'd heard the door shut. 'What was that about? I was sure she'd be Queen Grinch over Christmas; I remember she was pretty nonplussed last year, but that was while we were all still getting to know each other. Is she softening?'

'Interesting what she said about Jack,' Stephan said. 'Very much as if she knows him personally and is looking out for him.'

'That makes sense,' Rosa said. 'She wouldn't want just anyone staying in one of her houses, she's way too particular for that.'

'How do they know each other, then?' Octavia asked. 'And what does she think of all his antics at the awards ceremony, and the reasons behind it? Did you read up on that?' Rosa and Stephan nodded and Abby joined in, hoping if she pretended to be clued up Octavia wouldn't go over it again. 'I could barely believe it,' she continued. 'I wonder how he's hoping to recover his reputation after pulling a stunt like that? It makes the attack on his friend almost acceptable by comparison.'

'As Penelope says though,' Stephan said cautiously, 'we have to be careful. It's his life, and you never know how much the press have twisted things or blown them out of proportion. He might be a highly decent chap, stuck in a very difficult situation.'

Rosa nodded, her eyes finding Abby's and then sliding away. Abby knew that, as much as her friend wanted to have the full story about the contact she'd had with Jack, she wouldn't put her in an awkward position in front of Octavia.

Octavia, however, had no problem asking the pertinent questions. 'What do you think about all this, Abby love? You've been very quiet, and you've had a couple of encounters with him. Is he author-talk material, or is he as dark as those terrible psychopaths he writes about?'

'I've never read his books,' Abby said, picking up crumbs on the end of her finger. 'He was difficult to begin with, but he was prepared to listen to me. He might even come on one of my organized walks, so he can't be *all* bad.'

Stephan laughed. 'As long as they're a nature lover, they're OK with Abby. He could have punched everyone at the awards ceremony, but if he stopped to look at the bluebells Abby would forgive him.'

'Hey,' Abby protested, forcing a smile.

'Well.' Octavia shook her head, and then her shirt, depositing crumbs on the table. 'Wouldn't that be a turn-up for the books? Jack Westcoat on one of Meadowsweet Nature Reserve's guided walks. That would give Flick Hunter and *Wild Wonders* a run for their money, and no mistake.'

Nobody pointed out to Octavia that, even if Jack came on one of the walks, he was highly unlikely to want the fact advertised to the whole of Suffolk.

The turn-up for the books happened one Saturday morning a few weeks later, when Christmas Day was less than three weeks away, and Abby had started to hum 'Fairytale of New York' on repeat.

She liked Christmas, and loved spending time with Tessa, Neil and the girls. Though their festive period inevitably included a visit from their mum, who would regale them with tales of her burgeoning single life, cruises and wine trips to France, dinner parties and dances in the posh Suffolk village of Lavenham, and a card from their dad, complete with additional scribbled names on the bottom, reminding them of his new, younger family, and how little time he gave to them any more.

Still, Abby knew it was for the best, that new families and scattered lives were bliss compared to that claustrophobic pressure cooker of a house where one wrong word was likely to wreak havoc. While her dad had tried to make amends for what he'd done, she was more comfortable keeping him at a distance. At least everyone seemed more or less happy now.

112

She was trying not to think about what her dad would be doing with his wife Susan and Abby and Tessa's half-brother Shaun (who, despite being fourteen, they had only met on a handful of occasions, and how different their Christmas would be to the ones she had experienced growing up), when she pulled on her extra-thick fleece in the storeroom and went to meet the guests who had booked onto her winter warmer walk.

The first thing she noticed was that Evan was there, with his mum and dad in tow. He had an expensive-looking pair of binoculars around his neck, and a spotter book and pen clasped in his gloved hands. Abby's heart soared, all thoughts of her dad forgotten.

'Evan,' she said, before greeting the rest of her visitors. 'How are you? Still enjoying nature spotting?'

'It's the best,' Evan confirmed. 'We've been all over and I've seen so much stuff, but this is my favourite reserve. Are we going down to the kingfisher hide today? They've seen one there already this morning, I checked the board.'

'Yes, I thought we'd go there. Our kingfishers are pretty consistent, if you stay for long enough you should get a good sighting from the right-hand windows. I'm so glad you're here – you'll have to tell me about all the things you've seen after we get back.' She pointed at his book and Evan grinned, glancing at his mum and dad to check they'd noticed Abby's interest. This, she thought, was why she loved her job so much.

'Right everyone, welcome to Meadowsweet Nature Reserve's winter warmer walk. As you will have noticed, it's a beautiful day, clear and dry, but don't be deceived. Are you all wearing enough layers? Have you got suitable footwear? There's still a deceptive amount of mud out there, hidden beneath that sparkly crackle of frost. I don't want anyone slipping over and being confined to their houses for the Christmas period.'

She made eye contact, nodded to her visitors as they confirmed they were properly attired, and that was when she saw him, standing at the back, partly obscured behind an older man wearing a bobble hat.

Jack stood up tall but his shoulders were raised, his chin buried in the collar of his padded jacket, as if he was trying to remain incognito. She thought with the winter sun he could even have got away with sunglasses, but maybe that would have drawn more attention to him, rather than less. She carried on with her introduction, telling everyone the plan before walking past them – eleven people, not bad when it was so cold – to lead them to the first trail.

She passed close to Jack, and felt his fingers brush the back of her hand. She turned, and he gave her a fleeting smile.

'Hi,' he said. 'You didn't give me the dates of your walks, so I had to look them up for myself.'

'What a hardship for you,' she whispered, but she was smiling. 'Glad it wasn't beyond your efforts to make it down here. I'm guessing you won't be too cold, that your coat is filled with duck down or something?'

He laughed. 'It's warm enough but completely synthetic, so it didn't require the death of any ducks to make it. I'm not entirely heartless.'

'Duck down is a by-product of—' she started, and then realized that he was grinning, and that the other visitors were listening to the exchange. 'Right then,' she said loudly, 'if you'll follow me please. This way.'

The reserve was spectacular, with glistening, sun-kissed

water and frosty, twinkling reeds. Everything shimmered, the air was crisp against her cheeks and lips, and the variety of wading birds, winter visitors, herons and egrets on the lagoon meant that Abby's job was easy; everyone was engaged and she found herself answering constant questions rather than giving a monologue on the different species they encountered. She also left a lot of it up to Evan, whose enthusiasm shone through as much as his knowledge. Abby only stepped in occasionally when he faltered on a bit of detail.

'Bewick's swans come all the way from Siberia,' he said, when someone asked about the smaller variety of swan. 'They'll stay until . . .' He looked at her, and Abby supplied the answer.

'Sometime in March.'

'Then they'll fly back again,' Evan continued. 'As well as the size difference, you can identify them because their beaks are blacker, less yellow than the other swans'.'

Several members of the group made interested noises, and then tried to spot the features Evan had mentioned through binoculars and telescopic lenses.

Jack, she noticed, was standing to one side of the hide, staring across the wintry tableau, not asking to borrow any of the equipment Abby had brought with her or getting involved in the discussions. She thought that he might be observing, soaking everything up ready to note it all down and use some of it in his next book. She longed to ask him about it, had often found herself wondering how he worked, if he had one writing space or preferred variety, where he got his ideas from and why he focused on such dark subjects.

She had almost borrowed one of his books from the library, and then realized that would be a green light to Octavia that her disinterest was a cover, and she couldn't bear the thought of the rumours that would spread as a result. Besides, with his presence common knowledge, she was sure all Jack Westcoat books at the library would have *On Reserve* against them for the foreseeable future.

Online was her next port of call. She could buy any of his books with a single click but, like looking up the details of his indiscretions on the internet, she felt that to read one would be to fall down the rabbit hole. She was still waiting for her confused feelings for him to sort themselves out or, even better, disappear altogether.

'What's that, Abby?' Evan asked, dragging her from her thoughts. As she turned, so did Jack, as if he, too, had been miles away.

Abby stood next to the boy and peered out across the water, in the direction he was pointing.

'Like a heron, only different.'

Abby's pulse increased. She lifted her binoculars to her eyes, trying to pinpoint the spot, finding it easily.

'You little superstar,' she said, unable to keep the excitement from her voice. 'Everyone, Evan's found one of our most thrilling, and hardest-to-see species. If you all grab your binoculars and scopes, look just to the right of that tall, dead tree in the centre, and then down in the reeds in front, close to the water, you'll see a bird that looks like a heron, but is shorter, and browner in colour. It's a wading bird called a bittern, and it *is* part of the heron family. They've got amber status in the UK, and mostly appear in the south of the country, although there are some in Lancashire and Wales and even Scotland. We're establishing a conservation programme here, involving supplementary feeding when the weather's at its coldest to try and help their numbers grow, and a lot of the other reserves in East Anglia are doing the same. Wow, Evan. Well done!'

She couldn't help it; she ruffled his hair. Evan bounced up and down on the spot and then, sensing that he should be professional about his discovery, looked through his binoculars again and began telling the interested walkers all the facts he knew about bitterns.

Abby knew they were in safe hands so she shuffled over to Jack, who was looking in the general direction but seemed at least 85 per cent uncomfortable.

'Want to see?' she asked, holding up her binoculars.

'Oh, I don't think—' he started, then paused. 'Go on, then. What am I looking for?'

She lifted her binoculars over her head and handed them to him, and he crouched slightly, put them to his eyes and let her turn him by the shoulders, in the right direction.

'There,' she said into his ear. 'In the reeds. Standing very still, its head and beak angled upwards. They don't often sit on the edge of such a large area of water, they're much happier nestled in the middle of the reed beds, fishing and surviving away from the other species, out of view.'

'Sensible birds,' he said softly, and Abby grinned. 'Oh, I see it,' he continued, and she felt his shoulders tense as he fixed his gaze on the same spot as everyone else. 'It's very serene. Does it ever move?'

'When it finds a fish it'll dart forward, quick as a flash, and grab it. Blink and you'll miss it.'

'Noted,' Jack said, and Abby was taken back to the plush comfort of his car, the flicker of his smile in the dark. The memory brought a smile to her own lips as she watched him. He was oblivious to her scrutiny, blinkered by the binoculars. His hair curled behind his ears, slightly too long, as if it was the one outward sign of recklessness in his otherwise polished appearance.

She realized she was holding her breath, not wanting to exhale against his cheek, the thought of him feeling it somehow too intimate. She was relieved when Evan, full of exuberance, dragged her away with a question about the bitterns and why they weren't booming right now, as bitterns were known to do, and what it sounded like. She left Jack to his observation, though thoughts of him followed her to Evan's side, and for the rest of the walk.

They arrived back at the centre rosy-cheeked and full of the things they had seen, and Rosa was regaled with the bittern story at least three times, by three separate visitors. The hubbub filled the shop and reception area and drew Penelope out of her office. Evan bounded up to Abby, his spotter book at the ready, and Abby spent several minutes poring over it with him, asking where he'd seen the snow bunting, and the tree creeper, and the hares.

She glanced up to see Penelope and Jack talking. She was struck all over again by how similar they looked, especially seeing them side by side, and the quiet, conspiratorial nature of their discussion made it clear they knew each other.

When Penelope glanced in Abby's direction, nodded briefly and went to speak to Rosa, Jack approached her.

'Good walk,' he said.

'You're glad you came?'

'I am. I can see why you love working on the reserve, seeing these people so inspired by the wildlife.'

'But not you?'

He frowned. 'It made me realize how ignorant I am, and that's not something I'm comfortable with. The bittern was

118

beautiful though, and clearly a coup. I feel privileged to have seen it with you.'

'Oh, right. Well, good. Glad it was . . .' Abby fumbled for words and came up empty.

'I should get back, but have a lovely Christmas. Will you be staying in Meadowgreen?'

Abby nodded. 'I'll spend a few days with my sister in Bury St Edmunds, but otherwise, I'll be around. Wildlife doesn't go on holiday, and the reserve is a lovely place to come for a festive walk, work off some mince pie calories, clear the alcohol fug.'

'Always selling the wildlife,' he said, laughing softly. 'I don't think you have anything to worry about, even in the face of *Wild Wonders*. Meadowsweet, the nature, it's a part of you, isn't it?'

'It's easy to sell,' Abby said, 'because it's so—' she stopped, saw the amusement in his blue eyes, that suppressed grin making his lips twitch, as if it cost him something every time he smiled. 'How about you? What will you be doing for Christmas, do you have family to go and see, or a – a – um, friends?'

'I'll head back to London to see my parents, but I wouldn't have thought I'll be away long. There's only so much of them I can take, and I've got used to my cottage with its night-time visitors, now. I'm sure I'll miss it.'

Abby didn't know whether the night-time visitors he was referring to were the deer barking like dogs, owls calling from the trees, or her, tripping over outside his front door. 'So, you're admitting you're fond of this place? Peacock Cottage, and all that comes with it?'

Jack ran a hand over his jaw. 'More than perhaps I should allow myself to be. Anyway, you have people who want your

119

attention, I'll leave you to it.' He turned to go, and his gaze fell on the mistletoe that Rosa had hung from the ceiling and Abby, a few moments before, had noticed she was standing beneath.

He moved towards her again, ran his fingers softly down the back of her arm and kissed her on the cheek, his lips brushing close to the corner of her mouth. 'I wonder if,' he said, when he'd stepped back, 'after the festive period, you'd like to get together for a coffee? You could come to Peacock Cottage, or – I don't know . . .' He seemed suddenly unsure, his nervousness heightening Abby's tension, and her desire to see him again. 'January's bleak,' he continued, 'and friendly faces help. I think, hope, I can count you as one of those now?'

Abby tried to find her voice, fighting through the warnings sounding like alarm bells in her head. *He hit someone. He's had a troubled past. He's the same as the others.* And then she remembered his tenderness when she'd tripped, his light-as-a-feather touch, and found herself nodding. 'That would be lovely,' she said. 'Friendly faces are important, and I'd like that very much.'

He didn't reply immediately, as if surprised that she'd agreed, and then the smile was back, warmer this time, his eyes alight with it. 'Great. I'll be in touch, then. Happy Christmas, Abby.'

'Happy Christmas, Jack.'

She watched him stride off in the direction of Peacock Cottage and the shortcut through the trees. Her breath was lodged in her throat, her skin tingling where his lips had been. It was a physical effort not to touch the spot, aware that she was standing in the middle of the visitor centre, that her exchange with Jack wouldn't have gone unnoticed by certain people, and she needed it to seem as ordinary as possible. But inside, she felt anything but. Something was happening, something she wasn't ready for, something that – when Penelope had handed her his first letter, written on the bee-adorned Post-it Note, pretentious and full of confidence – she would never have imagined in a million years.

She had seen him only a handful of times, but Jack Westcoat was consuming her thoughts. It was as if he felt entitled to take them over, as well as asking her to remove all traces of wildlife, and humans, from around his rented cottage. How dare he? How dare he take her peaceful, un-dramatic life and turn it on its head? He was haughty, self-righteous, and obviously had an aversion to people. Smiling was not something he did readily.

And yet, when they'd been talking in the café and Octavia had suggested he did as he pleased and damn the consequences, Abby had been on the verge of defending him, so strong was her sense that he wasn't like that. She couldn't be sure – she knew so little about him, had spent less than three hours in his presence, and most of that time with ten other people in tow.

But she was convinced that beneath the hard, handsome exterior, Jack Westcoat was worth getting to know. She had seen glimmers of his kindness and his humour, and she wanted more. She felt it so strongly that it scared her, as did the power of her reaction after the quickest, faintest kiss, and her elation, like a giddy teenager, when he'd asked her out for coffee.

'Abby?' Rosa called. 'Fancy a gingerbread hot chocolate with cream? A customer requested a couple but has changed her mind, and Stephan doesn't want them going to waste.'

'Sure,' she said. 'Over in a second.'

As she waved Evan goodbye, checked the state of the welcome desk and whether Maureen needed any help, Abby tried to push her thoughts of Jack aside. Christmas was on the way, he would return to London and she could busy herself with entertaining Willow and Daisy, firming up the plans for her New Year events. The grim, icy and often unappealing months of January and February would be the toughest to draw visitors in, and she had to be on top of her game if the reserve wasn't going to falter just as she had started to gather momentum.

She wouldn't see Jack again between now and the New Year. Still, she thought, grinning gratefully as Rosa handed over the hot, sweet drink, he had left her with a kiss, his parting gift. Now, she couldn't help but touch the skin his lips had briefly caressed. She would keep her feelings to herself, she thought, turning away from Rosa's curious gaze. Her ridiculous attraction could run its course and burn itself out, and everything would go back to normal. Meeting up for coffee was nothing, a favour to someone who felt out of place in a strange village. Almost two years earlier, she had been in the same position. As irritating as Jack was – and he *was* irritating, wasn't he? – Abby wouldn't wish loneliness on anyone.

She was being a good citizen, that was all. Saving the reserve, sharing her love of wildlife, indulging Raffle, spending time with Tessa and with her friends. This was her life, and it would become her mantra, fuel everything she did. There was no room for a man amongst all those things, and even if there was, it couldn't be someone as dark, as dangerous, and as utterly distracting as Jack Westcoat.

Part 2

The Lovebirds

Chapter Eight

A bittern is a rare, beautiful bird, like a heron, only smaller and with golden-brown plumage. They hide deep among the reeds and are very shy, so when you get the chance to see one, it's a big deal. A male bittern booms when it's looking for a girlfriend, and it sounds really strange – a bit like someone trying to play the bassoon for the first time.

— Note from Abby's notebook

Abby looked out at the courtyard garden, at the row of terracotta pots that had no soil in them and the grey, leaden sky above, and felt her mood darken. She turned away from the unforgiving sight, and back towards the room that, in contrast, was soft and warm, with cream furnishings, walls and carpets, hints of gold from the gilt-framed mirror, the subtle pattern on the cushions and shimmering lampshades.

'You could get some bird feeders,' she said, as her mum walked into the room carrying a tray laden with tea things. 'They would find them.'

'Oh Abby, I can't be doing with all that muck – those birds carry diseases, you know. If you're not careful you can catch something horrible, I hope you wear gloves at that place of yours.'

Caroline Payne, who had reverted to her maiden name after her divorce from Abby's dad, was much like her living room. She was soft around the edges, her straightened hair expensively dyed platinum, her silky top and fitted trousers muted colours of beige and taupe, cream and dusky pink. Her gold earrings were almost a perfect match for the lampshades.

'I'm as careful as I need to be,' Abby said, self-consciously tucking a strand of her own dark-blonde hair behind her ear. 'And you shouldn't believe all you read, either. In terms of the world's most dangerous species, UK birds come low down on the list. And they bring . . . doesn't it make you happy, Mum, when you see a robin, or a great tit, or even a sparrow bouncing about on the bushes outside? Sparrows are in decline.'

'I barely notice them,' Caroline said dismissively. 'Now, tell me what's happening with you. How's that husky of yours, and is he the only male you're spending any significant time with?' She sat back on the sofa, in it for the long haul, and Abby suppressed a sigh.

It was New Year's Day, and Abby was at her mum's modern house in Lavenham. Her sister, Tessa, had meant to come with her, bringing her children, Daisy and Willow, whose presence would have distracted Caroline from asking Abby pertinent questions about the state of her love life. Their absence was down to a sickness bug – not alcohol-induced after a raucous New Year's Eve party, but one that had started with Neil, Tessa's husband, and was making its way steadily through the family.

It had meant that Abby was instructed to stay away and

had spent New Year's Eve at home with Raffle and a night of disaster movies on Film4. Not the best way to spend the last day of the year, perhaps, but certainly not the worst.

'Raffle's fine,' Abby said. 'And yes, he's the only male I'm close to.' She put a hand to her cheek absent-mindedly.

There was no way she was going to tell her mum about Jack Westcoat. But she rubbed her cheek, the spot where, a few weeks earlier, he had kissed her under the mistletoe. She was behaving like a teenager, but she couldn't help it. There was something hidden behind Jack's blue eyes and stern, handsome face that intrigued her, and his suggestion that they meet for coffee once the festivities were out of the way hadn't been far from her thoughts over Christmas.

'Have a cup of Assam,' her mother said, pouring from the china teapot. She was doing that motherly thing of watching Abby while also not spilling any tea. Abby didn't like the look she was giving her.

'So, Tessa said she was feeling a bit better.' Abby sat up on her haunches and added milk from a jug that matched the rest of the crockery. It was unbelievable that her mother should be using a proper tea set. Abby could remember, all too well, a time when not only did the crockery not match, but it quite often ended up being hurled against a wall of their terrace in Bury St Edmunds. Could she really have changed so much?

'Don't alter the subject,' Caroline said. 'Are you telling me the truth, Abigail Elizabeth Field?'

'About what?'

'About the no-man business. I know a faraway look when I see one, and just now you were somewhere else altogether.'

'I was thinking about work, Mum. I need to pull out all the stops. January and February are the hardest months to attract visitors, and if the numbers start to decline now, I don't know whether I'll be able to pull them up again. I need to come up with something big, something that will increase our membership numbers and improve things for good. What would make you come to a nature reserve in the depths of winter, when the ground is crunchy and breathing makes your nose hurt?'

Her mum raised a single eyebrow. 'When you put it like that, absolutely nothing. You need to market it better.'

Abby sighed. 'I'm being realistic. That's what it will be like. But we have some incredible wildlife at this time of year. Marsh harriers, peregrine falcons, deer, a huge flock of starlings that roost in the trees – they can be a spectacular sight before they come in to land.'

'So, talk about those things.' Caroline waved an airy hand. 'You'll be fine.'

Her disinterest was maddening, and Abby clenched her hand into a fist at her side. 'Fine won't be good enough. With *Wild Wonders* sending all the attention to Reston Marsh around the corner, we're becoming the forgotten nature reserve. And I'm sure there's more to it than that, and that Meadowsweet is in more financial difficulty than Penelope's letting on. She's even rented out Peacock Cottage.'

Her mother started. 'That grand mansion that overlooks your village? I thought it was falling down.'

'That's Swallowtail House, Mum. That's still empty. No, this is smaller; it must once have been the groundsman's cottage or something. It's still in perfect condition, at least outside. I'm sure it is inside too, considering who's living in it now.' She chewed her lip.

'Oh? Who's that then?' Caroline sat forward, her hands clasped around her cup.

'He's a writer, from London. He's . . . a bit challenging. He thinks that everything should be done for him, that whatever he wants, he should get. I'm sure he wouldn't stay in the cottage if it wasn't up to scratch, or at the very least he'd ask Penelope to give it a deep clean.'

'And from what you've told me about her, she wouldn't like being given instructions.'

'No,' Abby agreed. 'She wouldn't.'

Silence settled over the room and Abby glanced at Caroline, who was staring at the fireplace, fingers pressed to her lips. For all her confidence, her cushy job as a PA for an executive in Ipswich and her full social calendar, Abby could see the cracks where old wounds hadn't fully healed.

'Are you happy, Mum?' she asked, surprising herself.

'What, darling?'

Abby hugged her knees to her chest. 'You're happy, right? With your life? After . . . Dad?'

Caroline's smile didn't reach her eyes. 'It's been a long time, Abigail – over half your lifetime. And I'm very happy. I have two beautiful, blossoming daughters, two grandchildren I adore – even if there's no sign of more on the way. My weekends are booked up until early March. You don't need to worry about me. It's you I'm concerned about.'

'You just said I was blossoming.'

'And you are, I can see that. Your house, your job, your dog . . .'

Abby rolled her eyes. 'How can you imply that my life is lacking because I don't have a boyfriend, when you're stubbornly single? Pots and kettles.'

'Yes, but Abigail,' her mother slipped down to join her on the carpet, 'I'm not at the beginning of my life. I've been there, done it all – and not very well, as I think we'd both agree.'

129

Abby could only hold her gaze for a moment, before looking at the floor.

'I'm so sorry, my darling. I'm sorry for what I – we – did to you and Tessa. I can't reverse time and stop it all from happening; I wish I could. But I don't want you to miss out on anything because of it. You have to take risks and see where they lead you. Don't wrap yourself in cotton wool now because I failed to when you were young.' She stroked Abby's hair.

Abby swallowed the lump in her throat. 'Mum, I know you did your best, that it was Dad, mainly, and that you were . . . protecting us. And I'm fine. I'm not closed off to anything, I just haven't found the right person yet. I'm only young, there's lots of time.' She wondered if the platitudes would work and looked up to see that her mum's eyes were glistening with unshed tears.

This was not how she had planned to spend New Year's Day. She was surprised by her mum's openness – usually she was the opposite, doing everything she could to gloss over their less-than-idyllic childhood.

'You OK, Mum?'

'Of course I am.' She wiped her fingers under her eyes elaborately, as if she was drawing curls in the air. 'Now, shall we open that bottle of fizz I've been saving?'

'I'm driving,' Abby said.

'One glass won't hurt. And if you stay for dinner, then even better.' She stood and picked up the tea tray, the china clattering as she went into the kitchen. Abby pulled her notebook out of her bag and made a note to buy her mum some bird feeders.

The following morning, her mum's words – her unexpected apology – was playing on Abby's mind. She still found it hard to reconcile the elegant, composed woman with the mum she'd had when she was a child, always on the verge of flying into a rage. She had come to see that her dad had been the catalyst, and that her mum had only been trying to stand up for herself, to protect her and Tessa, picking fight rather than flight. Despite that, Abby couldn't seem to bridge the gap between herself and her mother, still unable to see past those memories, her parents feeding off each other's anger, and the fear and loneliness she had felt as a result. She tried not to think of those last, horrendous arguments, the comparison between them and her mother stroking her hair the day before.

Abby dressed in her winter work outfit of leggings under waterproof trousers, and a Meadowsweet fleece over a black, long-sleeved T-shirt, pulled her hair into a tight ponytail and put on some blusher and mascara. She added a slick of pink lip gloss, and then ran downstairs, wrapping her arms around Raffle as he greeted her and pointedly looked at his food bowl.

'Nice long walk before work?' she asked as she fed him, knowing that of course he wanted that, even though it was January and still dark outside.

The cold hit her like a wall, and she zipped her thick jacket up over her fleece and pulled her woolly hat low over her ears. They strolled through the village, Abby's new torch compensating for the weak glow of the streetlights on the main road. 'Want to walk round Swallowtail House?' she asked, and Raffle looked up at her, his tongue hanging out slightly. 'Of course you do.'

They made their way around the high, redbrick wall, and Abby paused as usual at the gate, shining her torch towards the grand house. She could hear the bark of a deer, the distant call of a tawny owl, the first fluttering of birds as they sensed dawn on the horizon. The bushes behind the house were too dense to walk through, so she took Raffle as far as she could, then turned back, wondering why she had put make-up on when she wasn't even going into work yet.

'What am I doing, Raffle? I haven't seen him for weeks, and I expect he spent his time in London going to posh, glamorous parties and drinking Moët. He probably met a stunning brunette with long legs and a chalet in the south of France, who's created her own line of intuitive make-up – or something equally mind-bending – and who kissed away all his worries, and they're going to be blissfully happy and make the world's most beautiful babies together. I'm sure he's forgotten that he even asked me out for coffee.'

Raffle whined gently.

'I know,' Abby said. 'I don't really care. And if I did, it wouldn't matter. We were standing under mistletoe and he was being a traditionalist. He strikes me as very traditional, doesn't he you?' Raffle panted his agreement. 'Besides, I said he had a squashed-frog car, so really, it was over before it even got started. And anyway, these feelings . . . they're not real, are they?' Raffle barked once, loudly, and Abby gave him a treat. 'You're a good listener, puppy, you know that?' Her husky licked her hand in response.

She dropped Raffle at home, had breakfast and left the house for the second time that morning. By the time she got close to Peacock Cottage, she felt like a child on her first day back at school, unsure what would happen or where she'd fit in. Obviously, it wouldn't be like that in the visitor centre; Rosa would be in the shop, Stephan would be cooking up a storm in the kitchen and Penelope would be in her office, keeping a wary eye on everything.

Abby had firmed up her list of events during her few days off and was hoping to rope Rosa into some technology-testing days, where they could take the equipment to the hides and boost visitor numbers at the same time as sales of binoculars and telescopes. She had also planned several guided walks – some focusing on the birds of prey, others on signs of spring. She wanted to show her guests that even in the depths of winter, nature gave you reasons to be joyful – there would be snowdrops and wintersweet, scented and beautiful, and lots of buds that appeared earlier than people realized.

She also had an idea for a larger event in February, which to so many people was the worst time of year, when the winter seemed never-ending. She knew Penelope was expecting something groundbreaking. This one, she hoped, would attract more attention than most, and at least go some way towards putting Meadowsweet back on the map.

No, the worries about the nature reserve's survival Abby could take in her stride – those, at least, she could do something about. The new-term nerves were all centred around Jack.

She approached Peacock Cottage from the back and walked round the house until its quaint front aspect was visible, the blue front door and the hanging basket, the heather blooms long since gone. The Range Rover was parked outside and Abby's heart jumped. He *had* come back. He hadn't been whisked away to somewhere exotic by a glamorous entrepreneur after all.

She was the first one at the visitor centre, so she pulled out her keys and unlocked everything, switching on the lights in the large, airy space.

The Christmas decorations still hung throughout, shimmering in the weak January sun. Abby believed that once Christmas and New Year were done, any decorations should come down straight away, even more so in a public place. She hauled the stepladder out of the storeroom and set to work, carefully unwinding the tinsel, and plucking Octavia's beautiful handcrafted birds from shelves.

'Abby, Happy New Year!' Stephan took off his coat and cycle helmet. 'Good break?'

'Lovely thanks, you?'

'Not too bad. I spent it with my brother's family, and they're a riot when they get going. I'm exhausted. Can I get you a tea, or do you want a hand with all that?'

'Tea would be lovely, thank you!'

'On it.'

Rosa was the next to arrive, just as Abby had finished de-Christmassing the place.

'Oh, it's all come down,' she said, kissing Abby on the cheek. 'I'll miss the tinsel.'

'New year, new start,' Abby said. 'I hope you don't mind?'

'Not really. Just trying to hold onto that festive feeling as long as I can. This is always the gloomy bit of the year.' Rosa's black curls were loose, fanning out around her like a glossy halo. She looked happy and rested, despite her forlorn thought.

'We'll have to brighten it up then, won't we? Meadowsweet to the rescue!'

Rosa laughed. 'What's got into you?'

'I'm glad to be back, that's all.'

'You didn't have fun?'

Abby wrinkled her nose. 'It was a bit quiet. Tessa and her family got a sickness bug, and I ended up at Mum's yesterday, just me and her, which is fine but not what I'd expected.' She had never enlightened her friends in Meadowgreen about her family history, only told them that she was close to her sister, saw her mum occasionally and her dad barely ever. She wasn't about to start over-sharing now. 'Did you have a lovely time with your folks?'

'Brilliant,' Rosa confirmed. 'I'm sorry about yours, though. No wonder you're glad to be back. And aiming to get a sneaky kiss off someone, I see.'

'Sorry?' Abby's heart skipped a beat.

'Did you think I wouldn't notice?' Rosa pointed at the mistletoe still hanging from the ceiling.

Abby had missed the small piece of foliage that had been so significant that day, after they'd got back from her winter walk. She had held onto Jack's fleeting kiss as long as she could, the memory becoming more distant as the days passed so that now the sensations were dulled, the feel of his lips on her skin something she tried to reach out for but couldn't quite grasp, like a coin dropped to the bottom of a fountain.

'I didn't notice it,' Abby said quickly, wishing she could reach up and yank it down, instead of having to go and get the ladder again.

Stephan brought their hot drinks over, and Abby resisted the urge to hug him.

'How are we all?' came a voice from the doorway. 'Re-energized and ready to roll with the punches?' It was such an un-Penelope-like thing to say that they all froze, speechless, as their boss strode into the room, wearing a long, turquoise coat and carrying a red umbrella. Abby thought she looked like Mary Poppins.

'Yes, Penelope,' Stephan stuttered. 'I—'

'Excellent news. Because this year is not going to be easy

135

on Meadowsweet, but I intend to fight with every fibre of my being, and I need you, my army, to be as galvanized as I am.'

'Wow,' Rosa murmured. 'Rousing speech.'

'I thought I'd start on a positive note,' Penelope said. 'And now, I'm going to go and open the post, and the day will undoubtedly go downhill from there. Stephan?'

'Cappuccino?'

'That would be wonderful, thank you.'

'Amazing,' Rosa said once Penelope was behind the closed office door. 'Do you think her New Year's resolution is to be a bit more human?'

'She's always been human,' Abby said, laughing. 'She loved the Christmas tree, remember? You always forget the times she's been kind and encouraging.'

'That's because they're so outnumbered by sharp looks and reprimands that they pale into insignificance. If she's really turning over a new leaf, then I'm all for it.' Rosa sipped her coffee and drifted towards the shop, a perplexed look on her face.

The visitors were few and far between that morning, but Abby didn't panic. It was only the second of January, people would still be in a post-party stupor, and going for a walk round a nature reserve was unlikely to be at the top of their to-do lists. That was the kind of attitude she needed to change.

'What about hangover walks?' she said, to nobody in particular.

'What are you muttering about over there?' Rosa called, giving her a cheeky grin.

'Why don't we run hangover walks?' Abby repeated,

warming to her brainwave. 'Come and clear the cobwebs away with a brisk walk down to the lagoon and back, ending with a bacon sandwich and a hot drink in the café? I can tailor the information about the wildlife, pick out the fun and grizzly facts. Why are long-tailed tits called bumbarrels? Statistics about adder bites, and the impressive way sparrow-hawks kill and eat their prey. If people realize we're not all earnest, adenoidal obsessives, we could appeal to more of them.'

'It sounds like a grand idea,' Stephan called, her words reaching the café due to the building being so empty. 'And the scopes are bound to interest a few people. You could work that into it, too.'

'I'd planned on doing that separately, but . . .' Abby chewed her pen, then scribbled everything in her notebook.

The quiet lasted close to an hour before Penelope emerged from her office, looking five years older than when she had gone in.

'What is it?' Abby asked. 'Are you OK, Penelope?'

The older woman waved a dismissive hand. 'Nothing you need to worry about. Post rarely brings good news, does it? No, this is your concern. I'm on tenterhooks wondering if it will be another complaint, or if you've won him round alto-gether.'

'Sorry?'

Penelope slid a white envelope onto the desk, Abby's name written in familiar, slanted handwriting.

'Oh.' She didn't touch it immediately and tried to stop the smile that was threatening.

At that moment, two young women walked through the door. Their warm coats and scarves suggested they could be here for an outdoor walk, but their high-heeled boots did not. They were heavily made-up, had perfect, preened hair, and were perhaps a couple of years younger than Abby. Their overall appearance was so out of place with the surroundings that she swallowed the urge to laugh.

She slipped the envelope beneath the counter. 'Hello, welcome to Meadowsweet Nature Reserve – are you here for a day pass?'

'Yeah.' One of the women stepped forward. 'We were wondering about those walks you do – y'know, like the one before Christmas. Are you doing any more?'

'I've got several organized over the next few weeks. They're all up on the website.' She swivelled the computer monitor round to face them and clicked through to the relevant page.

The woman scanned the list. 'Great, ta. And when do I know who's coming on them?'

'I'm sorry?'

'When do I know who else will be on the walks? Do you have a list or something?'

'I lead most of the walks,' Abby said, frowning. 'Sometimes one of the wardens, Gavin or Marek, will give me a hand.'

The woman nodded. 'So, this walk, before Christmas, yeah? I heard that . . . that someone . . .'

'Jack Westcoat,' Penelope finished, stepping forward, her arms folded tightly over her chest. 'You heard that Jack Westcoat had attended one of our nature walks and are here to see if he's likely to come on any more.'

The woman smiled, and Abby tried to hide her anger, wondering why she hadn't worked it out sooner.

'Yeah,' the woman said. 'It's all round the Harrier estate that he was here. I'd love to glimpse him in the flesh. I've read all his books.'

'Young lady.' Penelope hardly gave her time to finish

speaking. 'This is not what Meadowsweet is for. You come to look at the wildlife, not stalk other visitors. He may have visited the reserve, but there's no reason to suspect he will return, and even if he does, that is not information we will be sharing publicly. Do you have no concept of a fellow human's right to privacy?'

The woman took a step back; her friend was almost at the door. 'He's a writer, though. Shouldn't have written books if he didn't want the limelight, and certainly shouldn't have assaulted that bloke and got all over the papers. He's fair game, as far as I'm concerned!'

'Then I suggest you go and work out your frustrations at a hunting party, instead of coming after my— *our* visitors. I hear the Blasingham estate does a good pheasant shoot; you have until the end of the month before the season closes. Goodbye.'

Abby's gaze flicked between the women, standing their ground for a moment before making a swift retreat, and Penelope, who was more riled than Abby had ever seen her. She was actually quivering.

'Are you OK, Penelope? That was amazing.'

'Did they honestly think they could come here to gawk at him, and that we would tell them if and when he had plans to come back? What is the world coming to? I sincerely hope that Jack isn't leaving the cottage as they pass by, otherwise heaven knows what will happen. I'd better warn him.' She hurried to her office and Abby was left alone, shocked by the brazenness of the young women, and wondering how close Penelope was to Jack that she could pick up the phone to him at a moment's notice.

'Seems the Octavia gossip tree's made it all the way to the Harrier then,' Rosa said, handing Abby a fresh cup of tea.

'My neighbours haven't said anything, but then Tim and Bob don't seem like the kind to spread rumours.'

'I don't even think it's Octavia. Remember, Jack *did* come on one of my walks just before Christmas. It was quite well attended and, while nobody said anything at the time, anyone could have recognized him. He was in the visitor centre for a bit afterwards, too. He was never going to stay hidden for long, not if he's as famous as he appears to be.'

'He wasn't that widely known before,' Rosa said, resting her elbows on the counter. 'Though he had more fame than most authors due to his first book getting so much praise, and in his twenties, too. But ever since this punching business, he's achieved a new kind of celebrity status.' She shook her head. 'I wonder how much he regrets that split-second decision? Or maybe he still stands by it, who knows? From what I read, it did seem like the other guy, Eddie Markham, was behaving like a prize idiot, whatever kind of past they have together.'

Abby bit her lip. One question from her and Rosa would explain what Eddie Markham, whoever he was, had done, and then she would be able to form more of an opinion of Jack. And yet, all Rosa would know was what had been in the papers, and that couldn't be relied upon. Abby had something much more valuable.

She waited until the coast was clear; Penelope was back in her office and Rosa and Stephan were otherwise occupied so, doing a visual check of the route from the car park to the front door and seeing no new visitors, she took the white envelope out from under the counter, and opened it.

Chapter Nine

Long-tailed tits are the most beautiful of all the tits. Small and fluffy, with pinky-purple, brown, black and cream feathers and long tails, they're very sociable and fly about in groups, spinning and bouncing like gymnasts in the trees. They're sometimes called bumbarrels, because their nest is shaped like a barrel, with a small hole in the front for them to fly in and out of.

— Note from Abby's notebook

Abby folded the paper out flat as she read.

Dear Abby,

Happy New Year! I hope this finds you well, and that you had a good Christmas. Thank you for the walk, which I know you would have been doing anyway, without me, but even so. I enjoyed it. I was thinking about turning up on another one, or finding something else to complain about, and then I remembered my invitation to you. Are

*you still prepared to give up some of your precious time
to meet me for coffee?*

I look forward to seeing you soon.

Yours, JW

Grinning, Abby put the note back into its envelope and hurried to the storeroom and her handbag. She would take it home and slide it between the thick, illustrated pages of *UK Flora and Fauna* that sat on the bookshelf next to her bed, along with Jack's other note to her. Now she just had to decide when, and how, to respond.

She held out until Friday, when a particularly difficult customer turned a cold but beautiful day into an extreme test of her patience. He arrived at reception with a complaint already on his lips, about how the speed humps on the approach road had dislodged the roof rack of his car, and then moaned about the quality of his lunch when he returned from his walk.

Abby had come to Stephan's rescue and tried to placate the man, but his refusal to back down, not to mention his final comment that *Reston Marsh was much more professional*, left her feeling despondent. By closing time she was in sore need of something to cheer her up and, the irony not lost on her that it was a complaint that had brought her to Jack's door in the first place, it was him she wanted to see.

Though the hour wasn't as late, it was as dark as it had been on her ill-fated Halloween walk home, and she kept her new torch angled towards the ground. Peacock Cottage and its lit window, visible through the swaying branches, felt like a haven. She walked up the path and knocked on the door, listening to the sound of footsteps from inside, trying not to let her nerves get the better of her.

And then the door opened and he was standing in front of her, wearing a thick, sea-blue jumper with a high collar. His hair was wild, as if he'd been tearing at it repeatedly, and he had shadows under his eyes, but he was as beautiful as ever, and Abby was struck by how much she'd missed him. As his gaze met hers he smiled, the gesture lifting his face, though not entirely banishing his obvious tiredness.

'Abby,' he said. 'Happy New Year.'

'You too,' she replied quickly. 'I got your note, and I was wondering about that coffee? Only if you've got time though. I know you must be busy.'

He stepped back. 'Come inside, it's freezing.'

She shook her head. 'Thanks for the offer, but I have to get home to Raffle.'

'Of course. Let me give you my number. We can arrange a date that way.' He held out his hand, and Abby thought for a moment he expected her to take it, but then understanding dawned and she scrabbled in her bag for her phone, unlocked it and handed it to him. He quickly tapped in his number, then Abby heard the shrill sound of a ringtone from somewhere inside the house as he called his phone from hers.

'Good Christmas?' he asked, as he passed her phone back and shoved his hands in his jeans pockets.

'So-so,' Abby said. 'You?'

'Pretty much the same,' he admitted, his smile fleeting. Abby thought that perhaps there had been no glamorous parties after all, that his reality was very different to what she'd been imagining. 'Are you sure you don't want to come in? We could start the coffee trend right now.'

She was sorely tempted, but if she went inside, she would never want to come back out in the cold. And Raffle was waiting for her. 'I can't,' she said, gesturing in the vague direction of her house. 'But I'd love to meet up soon. Whenever you're free.'

He nodded. 'I'll call you. It's good to see you, Abby.'

'You too.' She turned and walked down the path before she could change her mind, and didn't hear his front door close until she was almost out of sight of Peacock Cottage.

'Hangover walks, you say?' Octavia asked, as she whizzed around the library with her trolley, putting returned books back on the shelves. 'You think that will take off?'

'I don't know yet,' Abby said. 'But I'm trying to think a bit more cleverly. If we only appeal to people who already visit us, then our footfall will never grow dramatically. I want to attract brand-new visitors.'

'You can but try, my lovely. I'm hoping to do the same with this place, but at the moment my secret weapon is a little bit *too* secret.'

'What do you mean?' Abby asked, sitting in a faded blue armchair in the reading area.

She loved the old chapel that Octavia had almost single-handedly turned into the village library, with the convenience store in what had once been the vestry. It was a tiny chapel, and yet it seemed cavernous, with several rows of bookshelves, a colourful, bean-bag-filled area next to the children's books and games, and three tables with green reading lamps that passed as the reference library, alongside a tatty set of encyclopaedias. With its high roof, stained-glass windows and that cold stone smell about it despite being carpeted, Abby always felt calmer here. On this particular

Tuesday afternoon, it contained only the two of them, nobody else perusing the shelves.

'The elusive Jack Westcoat,' Octavia said, pushing her red hair over her shoulders and hurrying to the desk to update the online catalogue.

'Oh.' Abby picked at a thread on the chair.

'Not so elusive to you, it would seem. He turned up on one of your walks, I hear. And how was he?'

Gorgeous, Abby thought. *Gorgeous and mysterious and, understandably, a little bit shy. And he kissed me Octavia, just on the cheek but – oh, he kissed me! And we're going for coffee, on Friday.*

'He was nice,' she said, noncommittally. And then, because she had already bad-mouthed him to her own mother to throw her off the scent, added, 'He wasn't remotely rude. He was even slightly interested in what I was saying at one point. And he thanked me afterwards.'

'Well, my love, that gives me hope.'

'You're still thinking of asking him to do a talk here?'

'I am. We cannot waste these opportunities. I picture you all striving at that reserve, doing all you can to combat the threat of *Wild Wonders*, and I know that I have to take my chances too. Hold that thought.' She lifted a finger and disappeared in the direction of the convenience store, which was manned by part-time staff and volunteers, some older people from the village who liked to stay busy and sociable, many of them also covering shifts at the reserve.

'What thought?' Abby called, but Octavia was back in a flash, carrying two cans of Coke.

'Kettle's on the blink,' she said, 'so I hope this will do.'

Abby thanked her and popped the can open.

'So, what do you think our plan of attack should be?'

Octavia asked, sitting opposite her. 'What will Jack warm to – flattery, directness, money? I don't have a lot of that last one, but flattery I could give him until the cows come home.'

'*Our* plan of attack? Octavia, I only came in here to, uhm, look at the books.' Tessa had called Abby to let her know they were all fully recovered from their bug and to remind her that she still wanted the name of the erotic book Abby had conjured up after accidentally blurting out her Jack-inspired fantasy. Abby had thought she had got away with it, but now she was going to have to find a book that fitted her overactive imagination. Octavia, it seemed, had other ideas.

'You know him better than any of us,' she said. 'You have to help me.'

'I don't know anything,' Abby protested. 'I've met him five times in four months. That could hardly be called a friendship.'

'And you're fully up to speed on all that happened, with his altercation?'

Abby made a noncommittal noise.

'You mean you haven't Googled Mr Westcoat?' Octavia gave her an incredulous look.

'I didn't think it was fair, all of us knowing about him when he doesn't have a clue what we're like. He's alone here, and it seemed very one-sided. Besides, you can't trust anything they write in the press.' She didn't want to admit that, over Christmas, she *had* Googled him, but that the first headline – *Is acclaimed author Jack Westcoat heading back to his bad-boy ways?* – made her close down the browser then spend the next three days forcing herself not to open it again.

'But there were eyewitness reports from credible sources,'

Octavia pressed. 'It's quite the thing, Abby. You shouldn't go into this not knowing who you're dealing with.'

'Go into what? I'm not going *into* anything with Jack Westcoat!'

'You need to be aware of the background if you're going to help me.' She bustled over to a large wooden cabinet with at least twenty slender drawers, like a tall map chest. She opened one and pulled out a stack of newspapers wrapped in an elastic band. As she brought them back to the reading area, Abby could see that the pile had a Post-it Note on top that read: *Jack Westcoat*. Abby winced as she imagined him discovering the library had a dossier about him.

'Here we go,' Octavia said, putting her reading glasses on. 'No – first, tell me what you know. I'll fill in the blanks.'

Abby sighed. She was trapped, with no way of protesting or escaping. Octavia wouldn't let her leave until she was fully up to speed. She couldn't even slip her hand inside her handbag and make her ringtone sound, pretending it was someone who needed her urgently, because her neighbour would spot it in a flash.

'I heard that he punched another author at an awards ceremony in the summer, and it's damaged his reputation.'

'Ah,' Octavia said, holding up a hand. 'The punch isn't the worst of it; *that* he could have been forgiven for, it seems. It's what led to the attack that is causing angry ripples in literary circles. Have you heard of Eddie Markham?'

'Only because Rosa mentioned him the other day.'

'Right. Well, it seems that Jack and Eddie were inseparable young sprogs, enduring school friends, something like that. They both went up to Oxford, had some indiscretions as sometimes happens to young men with the world at their feet, and both chose writing as their careers. They ended up publishing their debut novels six months apart. Jack's was a psychological thriller, Eddie's a satire. The satire flopped, but Jack's flung him into the literary stratosphere, and he's been a critically acclaimed, prize-winning author ever since. Until last July.'

She smiled serenely, and Abby thought that if Octavia had been a bird, she would have been ruffling her feathers by now.

'What happened in July?' Abby asked, playing along. She braced herself, ready to hear something she would have to explain away so that Jack didn't fall in her estimation. Or did she want him to? Would finding out about his past banish her growing feelings, and take the unwanted complication out of her life? Maybe she should have done it at Christmas, read all the sordid details and been done with him.

'Eddie sold his story to a national newspaper,' Octavia said, 'and let it be known that, all those years ago, when fame and fortune were beckoning, his first novel, the satire, had been the subject of a plagiarism claim. In the interview, he denies being guilty, explaining that at the time he was prepared to reveal the accusation and protest his innocence, but his good friend Jack Westcoat, on the verge of being an immensely successful author himself, paid for the whole thing to go away.'

Abby rubbed her forehead. 'What? So . . . someone accused Eddie of copying another person's book? And what did Jack do? He wasn't under suspicion too, was he?'

'No, not at all. Jack could have distanced himself from the whole thing, but according to this recent interview with Eddie he swept in like Prince Charming and paid off which-ever journalist had uncovered the scandal and was threatening to go public with it. This was supposedly against Eddie's wishes, mind. It seems that, even before he was successful, Jack's family was fairly well off.'

Abby could believe that. He seemed more old money than new, like he was entirely comfortable with expensive cars and watches and aftershaves. 'But if Eddie wanted to be honest about the whole thing, then why didn't he refuse Jack's offer?'

'Why don't you read the piece, Abby?'

'No, you tell me, Octavia. It sounds kinder coming from you.'

'Fair enough. Eddie claims that Jack was very persuasive and told him it would be much better for both of them if the whole thing disappeared. Eddie even suggests – and this is the worst of it – that Jack did more than just *pay* the female journalist, that there was nothing to stop her publishing her story however much cash he offered, and that he had other ways of sealing the deal.' Octavia raised her eyebrows.

Abby had no idea what to say. Had this Eddie person honestly suggested to a national newspaper that Jack had slept with a journalist to stop a plagiarism claim being brought into the open? Despite Abby knowing very little about Jack, from what she had gleaned from their brief meetings, this seemed beyond far-fetched.

'You've met him,' Octavia said, breaking into her thoughts. 'Is he this handsome in real life?' She held up the newspaper, the double-page spread as much images as it was words.

There was a recent, posed photo of a man about her age, with a round face and short blond hair flattened to his head with gel. His expression was smug and contrite all at once. Obviously, this was Eddie Markham. On the opposing page was a paparazzi snap showing Jack mid-stride, his hand up, ineffectually trying to hide his face. She noticed the telltale darkness of broken skin on his knuckles, and his scowl was deeper than she had ever seen it, but there was also a haunted look in his eyes, like a rabbit caught in the headlights.

She tried to process the revelation. He had covered up the plagiarism claim against this man, supposedly paid a journalist a huge amount of cash, and perhaps gone even further. No wonder his reputation was in tatters. It all felt skewed, dishonourable, despite the loyalty to his friend. She wondered if Eddie Markham had held something over him, something from the troubled past that Octavia had mentioned, that had forced Jack to behave like this. She wasn't sure she believed any of it. But she didn't *know* Jack, she reminded herself, she just didn't want it to be true.

She looked again at the photo of him, how trapped he seemed in that instant. 'He's better looking in real life,' she said quietly.

'Good Lord, is that even possible?' Octavia peered at the photos, the crackle of the newspaper echoing up to the high ceiling.

'So, this all happened a long time ago,' Abby said, 'but Eddie chose last year to suddenly reveal it to the world. Why would he do that? And Jack didn't respond?'

'Except by hitting Eddie at the awards ceremony a week later. After which, he issued an apology through his agent . . .' Octavia searched the pages. '. . . Leo Ravensberg. Short and sweet, but it's done nothing to improve his floundering status, it would seem. Apparently, he was on the verge of being the Page Turner Foundation's new ambassador, all sorts of accolades and responsibilities heading his way, but that's all out of the window now, they say.'

'And what about Eddie?' Abby asked, feeling indignant on Jack's behalf. 'What about *his* reputation?'

'Oh, everyone's cooing over Eddie, the browbeaten, young and impressionable friend, trying to be honest, listening to Jack when he should have stuck to his instincts.'

'He was the same age as Jack, though! How has he got away with it?'

Octavia eyed her over her glasses. 'I'm sensing protective-ness again.'

Abby sat back in her chair. 'I've met Jack, and although I don't know him *that* well, I can't believe . . . what did his apology say? The one through his agent?'

Octavia picked up a different paper and flicked through it, licking her fingers to turn the pages. 'Here we are. *Statement on behalf of Jack Westcoat: "I apologize unreservedly for my behaviour at the Page Turner awards. It was inexcusable, and I will be offering a full, private apology to Eddie Markham, Bob Stevens and the organizers of the event. There have also been recent claims about a plagiarism case in 2010. That matter is in the past, and as such I will not be making a further statement at this time. However, I will say that I believe the decisions I made were the best I could have under the circum-stances, and I stand by them."* How's that for smooth, eh?' Octavia asked. 'But a bit silly of him not to deny it, if it's a load of gibberish.'

'You think this Eddie person's making it up?'

'I think Eddie Markham gave the interview to tie in with the release of his new book, and was on the hunt for publicity. And he looks like a rat, if you ask me. No, on consideration, I would be delighted to have Jack Westcoat at my library. As long as we could get him to sign a disclaimer saying he wasn't going to hit anyone.'

'That might be a bit close to the bone,' Abby said. 'I'm sure we can trust him, unless Eddie Markham turns up.'

'God save us!' Octavia replied, and then glanced around nervously, giving a brief wave to the crucifix that was still nailed to the chapel wall. 'Does that mean you'll help me, love? Get Jack to take me up on my offer, once I've made it?'

Abby thought of the letters lying between the pages of her book, the text messages on her phone arranging their coffee date. Now she knew more about Jack's past she was desperate to delve further, to disprove Eddie's words. She wondered if reading one of his novels would give her insight into his personality, and then realized the easiest thing would simply be to ask him about it on Friday. The thought brought her out in goose bumps.

'Let me see what I can do,' she said. 'But we might have to do it gradually. After all, while everyone in Meadowgreen is aware of *him*, he knows hardly anyone here.'

'Softly, softly, catchee monkey,' Octavia nodded. 'I approve of your approach. Thank you, Abby, you're a doll.'

Chapter Ten

A cuckoo's call is instantly recognizable. It's friendly and familiar, and makes you think of hazy summer mornings and the glittering mere. But cuckoos have a darker side; they lay their eggs in the nests of other birds, then when the cuckoo chicks are born, they push out the other chicks and are brought up by their new, oblivious foster parents.
— Note from Abby's notebook

On Thursday evening, with the rain pounding against the window and Raffle lying contentedly on her feet, Abby undid the Amazon package, the perforated cardboard making a satisfying noise as she pulled it open. After leaving the library she had given in and ordered Jack's latest novel, *The Fractured Path*. The story Octavia had relayed had left her unsettled, and in the absence of having Jack to talk to, she thought one of his books would be the next best thing.

She took out the glossy hardback and spent a long time staring at the dark, brooding cover, and at his name, raised in blue lettering on the front. Then she read the acknow-ledgements, recognizing one name from Octavia's information-dump – his agent, Leo Ravensberg. As far as she could decipher, there was no mention of a significant other, and the tone of his thank-yous spoke of the humour that she'd seen glimmers of first-hand: dry, self-deprecating but undeniably warm.

As she turned to the prologue and read the graphic description of a body being uncovered in a London alleyway after the thawing of days-old snow, she wondered if he used darkness and irritability as a cover: something he could hide behind to stop people getting too close. Only now the barriers were beginning to recede, and Abby found she couldn't wait to see what Jack was keeping behind them.

He picked her and Raffle up on Friday morning in his Range Rover, and drove them to a smart, cream-walled pub called the Queen's Head. It was a few miles away, down twisting, hedge-lined roads, bare winter fields beyond.

The pub was almost deserted mid-morning, but the fire was lit, and Abby picked a table close to it, Raffle barking his appreciation before settling at her feet while Jack went to the bar to order their coffees. He returned with the drinks and a packet of three posh ginger biscuits that he opened on the table between them. He was wearing a black, round-neck jumper, dark jeans and smart tan boots. The fabric of his jumper looked impossibly soft, and Abby had to resist the urge to reach out and stroke it.

'This is where Flick brought me, the day you saw us together in the village,' Jack said.

'Oh, right.' Abby focused on her biscuit.

She could still remember the tightening of her chest when

she had seen the glamorous television presenter talking to Jack on the day of the Halloween event. The woman, it seemed, was determined to muscle in on every aspect of Abby's life.

'Thank you for agreeing to meet me,' he continued, oblivious to her discomfort. 'There's no ulterior motive, just that Meadowgreen is very different from London, and being here is more of an adjustment than I'd anticipated. After Christmas, it feels like a bit of a sanctuary, but there's only so long I can survive with just my laptop for company. I know we got off on the wrong foot, but after your winter walk I feel like we're on firmer ground.'

Abby sipped her coffee, which tasted bitter compared to her usual cup of tea, and nibbled the edge of a biscuit. 'Much firmer ground,' she agreed. 'And I know what it's like to move somewhere new, to leave things behind. I was lucky because I was starting at Meadowsweet at the same time as Rosa, so we were thrown into the deep end together, and I had lots of people to talk to. I can't imagine how hard it's been for you.'

'Even so, my complaints were unnecessary.'

'You can't help how you feel,' Abby said. 'And anyway, they—' she was about to say they led her to him, then realized how that might sound. 'I just have a very long to-do list at the moment. But you've stopped complaining – I can tick you off my list!' She gave him a sunny smile.

'And I suppose without them, we wouldn't be here,' he added, stealing her thoughts. 'So, there's that.'

'Yes.' Abby swallowed. 'There is that.'

'And Meadowsweet?' Jack asked. 'Why have you got so much to do? Is *Wild Wonders* really a threat?'

Abby took a deep breath as she considered her answer.

This was something she could talk about; she was on much safer ground with the nature reserve.

An hour later, Jack probably knew more about Meadowsweet than he had ever expected – or hoped – to. But he seemed interested, interrupting her spiel with questions, laughing as she told him about Stephan's over-enthusiastic singing, commiserating with her about the uncertain future of the reserve, intrigued by the idea of hangover walks and the star species that could be spotted at different times of the year.

She realized, as she finished her second coffee and Jack offered her the last biscuit – Bourbons this time – that he had given up hardly any information about himself. She'd aimed a few questions at him, but he'd deflected them with an ease that probably came with being in the public eye.

He put the empty biscuit packet in his mug and stretched his arms to the ceiling. 'I should think about getting back. I can't avoid the laptop forever.'

'Is your new book going well?'

'I'm working a bit slower than I'd like, but that's often the way at the beginning. And it feels promising, so far.'

The cold hit her as they stepped outside, the previous day's damp pavements drying in a brisk, icy wind. Jack, coatless, hurried to the car, unlocking it as he went.

'There are some days when I don't even have the inclination to be creative,' Abby said as he started the engine. 'When the well is dry I focus on logistics instead. It must be a nightmare when your whole career revolves around your imagination.'

'I have memories and experience to draw from, and I spend a lot of time researching beforehand, so I'm not always working from a blank slate.'

Abby thought of his book, lying a quarter read on her bedside table. It was undeniably dark, but she loved the central character, and she'd had to force herself to stop reading at an ungodly hour the previous night. 'I hope you don't have too much relevant experience,' she said, laughing.

Jack smiled. 'As I said before, I'm not smart enough to get away with murder, but coming up with flawed characters who will do anything to get what they want is part of the fun. And like everyone, I have my fair share of unpleasant memories, situations I should never have got into, things I regret. You just twist those emotions, take them to extremes so that they're truly dark.'

Abby stared at the dashboard. He'd said it in such a conversational tone, as if it was something he tripped out regularly at events, but it brought up images of her own unhappy past, the bits that Abby didn't need to embellish to make darker. She thought of what Octavia had told her; the role Jack had supposedly played in Eddie Markham's plagiarism case, the suggestion of a less-than-perfect past and then the attack, much more recently.

It had been so easy in the pub. She had felt comfortable with him, listened-to and attractive in his presence, her own attraction to him growing. But she had got it so wrong before.

'Abby?' he prompted. 'Are you OK? Did I say something—'

'I'm fine.'

'Are you sure?' She could hear the concern in his voice and resisted the urge to be honest with him in a way she hadn't been with anyone else in Meadowgreen.

'It's nothing,' she rushed. 'I'm interested in knowing more about your writing, and about you. Just – everyone has unhappy memories, don't they?'

As they approached Meadowgreen she felt the car speed

up. He drove through the village, onto Warbler Cottages, and pulled up outside her house.

He undid his seatbelt and turned towards her. 'I find it hard to believe that you, Abby Field, have a past full of dark deeds you wish you could undo.' He spoke softly, as if he was picking his words carefully. He tried a tentative smile, and Abby wanted to roll her eyes and tell him no, of *course* not. But she couldn't.

Instead, she fidgeted in her seat. 'They weren't necessarily *my* dark deeds, but I still wish I could erase them.'

Jack's smile disappeared. 'Abby, I'm sorry.' He ran a hand over his jaw then reached out towards her, his fingers brushing her arm. 'I shouldn't have been flippant. I don't know enough about you. Are you OK? Do you want to talk—'

She shook her head. 'I'm fine, honestly. I should let you get back. But I've had a lovely time. Whenever you need to get away from your book again, just let me know.'

'Are you sure you're all right?'

'I'm good. Really. Thank you for coffee. See you again soon, I hope?'

'I'd like that.' He leaned towards her and kissed her cheek, repeating the mistletoe kiss she'd spent so much time replaying. She tried to capture the feel of his lips on her skin, holding his gaze when he sat back, wishing it could have lasted longer.

Once they'd said goodbye and Abby was inside, filling up Raffle's water bowl, she felt a wave of embarrassment. Why had she opened up to him in a pointless, cryptic way like that, leaving him feeling awkward and confused? 'It should have been all or nothing,' she said to her husky. 'What on earth must he think of me now? What can he possibly be imagining about my past? He'll probably never want to see me again, despite what he said.'

The thought of Jack steering clear of her should have been the answer to all her prayers, but instead it made her feel overwhelmingly sad.

Abby's first hangover walk – advertised on social media and in the local paper – was on a Sunday morning at the end of January. There were seven people on it, and at least three of those looked like they had taken it at face value. Abby had gone to the Skylark with Rosa the night before, but had stopped after two pints, knowing that, while her visitors should be able to identify with her in some respects, it wouldn't help if she was too bleary eyed to notice any of the wildlife.

She introduced herself, told everyone what they could expect from the walk, and then led them down to the heron hide. It was a crisp day, the winter sun casting everything in a whitish hue, bleaching the landscape and making it seem even colder than it was. A pair of marsh harriers kept everyone's interest piqued, and the telescope she had hefted with her proved popular, a couple of the men asking her questions that were technical enough for her to have to refer to the notes Rosa had written out.

'It's great, this,' said one man, whose stubble looked several days old and who, Abby hadn't failed to notice, wasn't wearing any gloves. She had almost said something but didn't want to come across as prissy. 'Can you use it for stargazing? My nephew's dead keen, and we got him one of those cheap jobbies for Christmas, but I'm not sure it spots anything further away than the trees in his garden.'

Abby scanned her notes. 'Yes, it's good for stargazing too.

It's not specifically for that, but it's often used as an entry-level star scope, so – dual purpose.'

'And the tripod comes with it?'

'It's meant to be eighty, but if you buy them together I can do it for fifty-five, which is a pretty sweet offer.' The words sounded alien to her, but the gloveless man was nodding away.

'Come and see this, love,' said the woman he had arrived with. 'All these pretty little ducks, there are hundreds of them.'

'They're teals,' Abby said. 'Beautiful, aren't they? We have a resident population, but gain a lot more in the winter months, when they fly over from colder climates. Like they're all coming somewhere warmer for their winter holidays.'

'Seriously? Couldn't get much colder than this, could you?' someone asked.

'Oh, believe me, it gets colder.' Abby grinned. 'Sometimes, when we're doing surveys, we spend whole days down here. It takes ages for the feeling to come back in your feet, and when it does – God, it's so painful. But worth it,' she added swiftly, not wanting to put anyone off. 'The cold might be extreme, but the views are too.' The hide quietened as everyone looked out over the frostbitten scene, the low sun, the birds, geese and waders going about their business on water that looked like fractured glass.

Abby breathed in deeply, felt the air and the love fill her up as it always did, a kind of euphoria that this sight was a few minutes from her house, that it existed for everyone to see. She wished more people felt as strongly about it as she did, but this morning, reaching out to a new audience, was a start.

Of course, *Wild Wonders* was doing the same thing on a

160

much larger scale, with their fact-filled television programme and their beautiful presenter, but she couldn't think about that; she had to focus on Meadowsweet, and hangover walks were an idea she thought she could develop further.

As she left her visitors in the capable hands of Stephan, the warm café sizzling with the sounds and smells of cooking bacon, Abby went to check the post. It was a Sunday, so there wouldn't be anything from Royal Mail, but she was still waiting for a letter, hand delivered, in response to hers.

It had been over two weeks since their coffee, and she hadn't had even a text message from Jack. She had walked past Peacock Cottage every day, and on most occasions the Range Rover was parked outside, so he was still there, beavering away at his book. Had she scared him off for good? So far, she had resisted the temptation to knock on his door, the awkwardness of their last parting at the forefront of her mind, wondering if what she'd written had somehow made it worse.

Dear Jack,

Thank you so much for coffee the other day, and sorry if things got a bit serious at the end. I'd love to see you again, to talk some more, to distract you from your dark words occasionally.

Hopefully see you soon,

Abby x

PS. I forgot to mention last time that my neighbour, Octavia, is gearing up to ask you a library-related favour. Tell you more when I see you.

She hoped it was this last part that had sent him into hibernation rather than their exchange in the car. She could

161

entirely understand if he didn't want to put himself on display any more than was strictly necessary.

Perhaps he was just so engrossed in writing that he was barely giving himself time to eat or sleep, let alone consider going for more coffee dates with a strange woman that – he had reminded her – he barely knew.

Abby logged her walk visitors into the online system, watching the numbers creep ever so gradually up, and tried to take her mind off Jack. Her next planned event was a new-shoots walk, and she needed to spend a few hours outside, finding the signs of spring that would delight her visitors and plotting a route that encompassed them all. The way her mind was tangled at the moment, time alone in the fresh air would do her good. She checked the volunteer schedule, to see when Maureen or Deborah were working and she could make her escape.

'That sounds like satisfied customers to me,' Penelope said, making Abby jump.

'It does now they're in the warm with bacon sandwiches.'

A frown flittered across the older woman's face. 'They didn't enjoy the walk?'

'Oh, they did, I think. It was very cold today, though. I've asked them to fill in a survey, either online at home or before they leave. I made it clear they were guinea pigs and it was really important I get some feedback – positive or negative – so I hope they'll oblige and I can improve it for next time. I've also given everyone a "bring a friend" voucher, so they can come on another walk for free, as long as they bring someone else who pays.'

'That's excellent, Abby. The guided walks are so important for teaching people that nature spotting can be for everyone. And how is your larger event coming along? Any thoughts about a membership initiative to get numbers soaring?'

'I'm advertising the murmuration event for the end of February,' she said. 'We can take people to the end of the meadow trail, where there's a good view across the fields. And because it's on such a large scale, I thought that we could sell more tickets than usual, about fifty, and get the press to come. That way we could talk about the walks and the spring camping event I'm planning, show off the reserve and give people a taste of the amazing things they can see, so they're more likely to sign up for membership.' She took a breath, aware that she was rambling.

Penelope smoothed down the fabric of her blue dress. Her necklace was made of pink and purple translucent beads, picking out the grey of her eyes. 'Good work, Abby,' she said eventually. 'How many tickets have you sold so far?'

'Eighteen,' Abby said proudly. 'And the local paper have agreed to come, but they haven't confirmed a named reporter yet so I'll chase them tomorrow.'

'Excellent progress. Keep me updated, will you?'

'Of course.' Abby fiddled with her notebook, debating whether to ask her next question, then realizing she might burst if she didn't find out what – if anything – had happened. 'Penelope, have you heard from Jack recently?'

'Why do you ask? Has he been giving you more trouble?'

'No, no,' Abby said hurriedly. 'Not at all. I've not heard from him for a while, and I . . . I wondered . . .' She didn't know what she wondered, except whether he was OK or not.

Penelope's expression softened. 'That poor boy – man – has had a difficult time of things recently. I assume you're aware?'

'I've heard some of it. Mainly from Octavia, and only what's in the press, so I don't know how much to believe.'

Penelope sighed and took a step closer to the desk as a couple walked past, thanking Abby for the walk on their way out. 'The papers are always going to turn to the worst possible scenario,' she said. 'Whatever will have more readers picking copies off the shelves, and you can't blame them for that. But Jack . . .' She shook her head. 'I'm not sure his Christmas was ideal. His father is very exacting.'

He had hinted at a less-than-happy Christmas, but that didn't explain his silence since their coffee. 'Do you know him well, then?' Abby asked.

'I'm beginning to,' Penelope admitted. 'And finding him very agreeable, despite what the world at large is saying about him. But these last few weeks, he hasn't seemed quite himself. Pressures of this new book, the concerns of his editors, the lingering bad publicity. I do think it's beginning to weigh on him, almost like delayed shock after the event. When he first moved here, he was rallying – as you well know, having to deal with his obstinacy. Now though, I'm worried he's too isolated here.'

'I think he's trying to make friends,' Abby said carefully. 'But . . . is there anything else we can do? To help him?'

Penelope scrutinized her. 'His complaints didn't turn you entirely against him, then?'

'No,' Abby said. 'I'm not against him.'

'Good. I have someone I can talk to about it, someone who should be able to help, but thank you. You have a kind heart, and not just for our feathered friends. I'm sure Jack, were he to know about it, would appreciate your concern.' She turned to walk back to her office.

'Penelope,' Abby called. 'Will you let me know how he is? Once you – you've spoken to this other person?'

'I will,' she nodded. 'And if you do see him, and even if

he's railing against one inconsequential thing or another, please bear in mind what he's been through, and find it in you to continue that kindness.'

Abby smiled as she thought of their closeness in the pub, the way he had seemed interested and relaxed in her company. She was desperate to know what had happened to change that. 'Of course,' she said.

Penelope returned to her office, a thoughtful look on her face.

Abby rolled her shoulders, trying to release the tension. She'd had no idea that Penelope would speak so frankly to her about Jack, a subject that had, before Christmas, seemed off limits. But maybe her change of heart was because Penelope was worried about him, and while Abby was pleased her boss had told her, she knew that she would worry even more about him now too.

What had happened since their coffee date? Had there been some setback with his publishers, or was it simply that Abby had got things wrong, had started to open up about her past in a way he had no time or inclination to hear? She had felt something growing between them, the warmth of it expanding her chest, and yet since he'd kissed her on the cheek and driven away, she'd heard nothing. Had she misjudged him after all? Was he a man who had never truly put his chequered past behind him, the punch at the awards ceremony more characteristic of his nature than his kindness when she'd tripped, his generosity and attentiveness in the Queen's Head? Was she making the same choices in men as she'd always done?

She wouldn't knock on the door of Peacock Cottage. As troubling, and frequent, as her thoughts about Jack were, he'd made his decision by failing to respond to her letter. No, it was best to let Penelope handle it, speak to this mysterious person who she thought might be able to help him, and focus on saving the reserve.

She set about editing the page for the murmuration event, trying to inject the blurb with enthusiasm. It had the potential to be spectacular, as long as the starlings showed up and the weather was kind. But when it came to nature, nothing was guaranteed, you just had to do all you could and hope for the best.

Chapter Eleven

Like a lot of water birds, teals come to the UK for a winter holiday. We have some that live here, but thousands more come from Russia and Iceland, because our weather is a lot warmer than theirs. Teals are pretty ducks – the male especially, which has a green eye-patch and a black-and-yellow tail. The male calls to its friends with a high-pitched whistle, and the female quacks.

— Note from Abby's notebook

Getting hold of someone at the local paper proved harder than Abby had expected. She wanted a reporter and a photographer at her starling murmuration event, to help her prove that Meadowsweet could still draw the crowds, even without the help of a perky television presenter.

Finally, on a Friday afternoon, with the winter sun dusting Abby's computer screen with a pale-golden light, she got an email from someone called Brad Kennedy at the *Suffolk Echo*, whose signature declared him to be Lead Event Reporter. His brief email was encouraging, saying he would bring a photographer with him, and asking for various details so they could do a write-up before the event and direct readers towards tickets. Abby fist-punched the air and replied enthusiastically, hoping she looked efficient rather than desperate.

She left the visitor centre at four o'clock, and as she strode through the woodland, the sun almost out of sight, she inhaled, allowing the clear air to fill her lungs, listening to the birds' final songs in the branches above her. Jack's car was outside Peacock Cottage, and she noticed that a downstairs window was open a fraction, as if he wanted the beautiful day inside with him.

It had been almost a week since her unlikely chat with Penelope, and he hadn't been far from her thoughts, but her letter had left the ball in his court, and she had to wait for him to get in touch. Reluctantly, she pushed on past, aware that Raffle was waiting for her.

The following day the good weather returned, and the prospect of a sunny Saturday in early February made Abby's heart lift. She put a Kyla La Grange album on at full volume and gave her house an early spring clean, dust dancing around her as she tried to banish it from the surfaces.

When she was satisfied, she decided to take Raffle for a long walk and pop into the pub for lunch. She set off on a loop right around the village, walking through the fields that backed onto the Harrier estate. The sky was a clear blue, the air pure and full of birdsong. Blackbirds called from the gardens, and Raffle disturbed several green woodpeckers that had been feeding in the long grass.

By the time they stepped back onto the main road, her husky was panting happily, and Abby's jeans were damp with dew above her sturdy walking boots.

She pushed open the door of the pub and was hit by a

wall of warmth and subdued chatter. Raffle raced forward, his extendable lead stretching ahead of her, and Abby followed him inside.

The pub was fuller than she had seen it for a while, with familiar faces from the village enjoying food or a lunchtime drink. Obviously, the sun had inspired more people than just her into coming out of hibernation. But something was different, the atmosphere heightened as if there was a special event on, rather than it being just a normal Saturday lunchtime.

A couple of people caught her eye and pointed in the direction of the snug. Abby nodded bemused thanks – she could find her dog by following his lead – and frowned at the raised eyebrows and smirks that accompanied their help. She stepped through a low archway into the pub's smallest room, and found Raffle, along with the object of everyone's interest.

Jack was sitting on a stool at the bar. He was wearing jeans and a grey woollen jumper, the sleeves rolled up to the elbows. His navy padded jacket was folded on the stool next to him, and he was staring into a glass of what looked to Abby like neat whisky, his shoulders hunched. He didn't look up or acknowledge her when she walked in, and she hovered just inside the doorway, wondering what to do.

All the other seats in the snug, save a couple of stools at the bar, were taken, people clustered onto the benches that lined the wall in a way that couldn't be comfortable. Two older women Abby vaguely recognized from the village, with glossy red nails and carefully styled hair, had their phones out, and she wondered how far the gossip was spreading.

Abby wound Raffle's lead round the leg of the stool next to Jack's, and then slid onto it, resting her elbows on the bar. Still, he didn't look up, just drained his glass and continued to stare at the sticky counter, the crinkled mat advertising a local brand of ale. Abby remained quiet. Even a simple 'hello' seemed too intrusive, somehow.

Then Ryan bustled round from the other side of the bar, raising his eyebrows and nodding in an entirely unsubtle way at Jack. 'Abby,' he said. 'What can I get you?'

'A pint of lager, a portion of fish and chips, and an extra bowl of chips on the side, please. Plus, whatever Jack's having.'

Jack looked up slowly, his eyes widening in surprise when he saw her.

'Hi.' She smiled at him.

'Hello,' he said warily. 'Look, you don't need to—'

'It's fine. Top him up, Ryan.' She turned briefly to the barman.

He obliged, selecting one of the single malts and giving Jack a double measure. He placed their drinks in front of them, and then disappeared to take Abby's food order to the kitchen.

'Cheers.' Abby held up her glass, and Jack clinked his against it.

'Thank you for the drink,' he said. 'Have you come to join my pity party?'

'I didn't know there was one, but it's not how I'd planned on spending my Saturday afternoon. I came for fish and chips – the chips here are hand cut, delicious, you'll find out soon enough.'

Jack shook his head. 'I didn't realize they were for me, I thought they were for Raffle.'

'From my limited experience, getting solidly stuck into a bottle of whisky at lunchtime never ended well for anyone, and chips will help.'

'Abby . . .' He sighed and ran a hand through his thick hair. 'I don't need you here.'

The words stung, but she could see that he wasn't his usual self. 'I don't need you either,' she said. 'We just happen to be in the same place at the same time, and I owe you for two cups of coffee and some great biscuits.' She swivelled on the stool, reached into her pocket and pulled out a treat. Raffle came forward, his tail wagging, and took it, then looked expectantly up at Jack.

Jack eyed the husky for a moment, then, turning fully round, held his hand out. Raffle sniffed it, then licked it, and then jumped up, putting his front paws on Jack's knees. Jack stroked Raffle's ears and the fur beneath his chin, a smile breaking through the scowl.

'He remembers you,' Abby said. 'He knows he can trust you.'

Jack's smile faded. 'He's not a great judge of character, then.' He gently lifted Raffle's paws off his knees and turned back to his whisky.

Abby gave her dog a conspiratorial eyeroll and stroked him until he'd settled on the carpet next to the stools, before swivelling back round. 'What are you doing, propping up the bar on a Saturday lunchtime? It's a free country and everything, but I thought you wanted to keep a low profile in Meadowgreen.'

Jack sipped his drink. 'Don't concern yourself with me, Abby. I'm fine.'

'Bollocks you are,' she said quietly, aware how many eaves-droppers there were in the vicinity. She wouldn't be surprised if Ryan had hidden a microphone somewhere and was beaming everything Jack said to every area of the pub as if it was a Champions League semi-final. 'You're wallowing in self-pity; definitely in self-destruct mode.'

'Have you been reading *Psychology for Dummies?*'

'Only as much as you've been taking lessons in melodrama.' She placed a hand gently on his wrist, her breath faltering at the feel of his skin against hers. 'I thought, after our coffee the other week, we'd gone past bickering. I thought we were starting to be friends.'

'Abby,' he said again, his sigh weary. 'It isn't anything you've done, but I'm not going to be the best company today. Leave me to it and go and have your lunch.'

'What, and let you stumble back to Peacock Cottage through the cold dark woods tonight, pissed as a parrot?'

'This is only my second drink, which *you* bought me, I should add.'

'Even so, I'm sure you're not planning on it being your last.'

Jack rubbed his forehead. 'I was going stir crazy in that cottage. It's not that I don't like it, but it's become a bit of a prison the last few days. I thought a walk, a drink, would help to clear my head. I didn't bargain on . . .' He waved his hand.

'Me?'

'Exactly.'

'But isn't that what I'm here for, to get you away from the cottage when it's driving you mad? We could have gone to the Queen's Head again, instead of here, where the villagers are lapping up your presence so they can go and tell their friends. There are probably dozens of photos of your back online by now, from various different angles. It's a good thing you've got a nice arse.'

Jack's frown deepened and a moment later his glass was empty. 'Just let me be, Abby.'

'Nope,' she said, her pulse ramping up. Was she really being this obstinate? How would she feel if Jack shouted at her, if she severed their already fragile bond? But he had been warm and relaxed the last time they'd been together – nothing like this, and she sensed this was what he needed, that she had to match his stubbornness. 'You're miserable, and alone, and what you need is friendship and chips.'

His laugh was hollow. 'This cannot be solved with chips.'

'But friendship?' She nudged his shoulder and he turned towards her. She felt her chest constrict beneath his gaze, and wondered if she *could* actually be friends with him when every time she had his undivided attention her body went into overdrive.

'I made mistakes,' he said quietly. 'I thought I was doing the right thing, but – I got so much wrong, and now it's coming back to haunt me.'

'And you can't make it right again?'

Jack held her gaze, his hand inches from hers on the bar top. 'Abby, what you told me in the car, about the memories you wanted to erase, what someone else had done—'

'Excuse me, my love,' a voice said, cutting through Jack's words. 'I hope you don't mind me coming over to say hello?' Abby turned to find one of the older, coiffed women hovering behind them.

'Hello,' Abby said warily. Jack twisted his upper body, flicked Abby a questioning look, and then smiled at the woman.

'Hi,' he said.

'I know you're enjoying your afternoon, and I don't mean to interrupt, but I was wondering if I could have my photo taken with you? I love your books, see, and I couldn't believe it when I heard you were staying in the village. Delphi's got the camera ready, it won't take a moment.'

Abby chewed her lip, waiting for Jack's outburst or a cold,

swift dismissal. She could see the muscles working in his jaw, and as he turned fully to face his admirer, she caught a whiff of his expensive, delicious scent.

'I'd rather it didn't appear online,' he said. 'I'm trying to keep a low profile at the moment, as I'm sure you can appreciate.'

'Oh, of course my love. You poor dear. Oh, thank you so much! I really do love your books, and that last one you wrote, *The Fractured Path* – so chilling. My fragile heart when it was getting close to the end!' She shuffled across until she was standing next to Jack, and Abby had to slide sideways on her stool, out of the way. Delphi made a palaver of taking the photo, and then Jack spoke for a few more moments with the woman before she thanked him and returned, beaming, to her friend.

'That was very sweet of you,' Abby said. 'All things considered.'

He shrugged. 'She was perfectly pleasant, and I'm rather over confrontation for the time being.'

Abby thought of her early conversations with him. 'You didn't seem to mind it the first few times we met.'

'That was different.'

'How so?' She tried to hide her smile as she watched him working out what to say.

'I was frustrated, obviously, and then when you turned up with your—'

'My . . . ?'

'You were so forthright, so indignant about my opinions and I didn't have anyone else to talk to. I wanted you to stay.'

'So, you wound me up on purpose, to keep me there? You *enjoyed* it?'

'Couldn't you tell?' He gave her a quick, shamefaced glance, and then laughed at her appalled face. 'Why do you think I asked you for coffee? I like your company. Come on, you enjoyed our sparring matches too. Admit it.'

Abby didn't know what to say. He was right, of course, but she wouldn't dare acknowledge it, because that was a dangerous path she didn't want to head down. Before she could construct an answer, Ryan appeared with their food and Jack ordered another whisky and another pint for Abby. He moved the bowl of chips to the side, and Abby plonked it firmly back in front of him.

'Eat chips,' she ordered.

Jack sighed and picked up a chip, chewing it slowly. Then he ate another, and another. When Ryan gave them their drinks, he asked for some ketchup.

Abby grinned. 'See, friendship and chips. And getting out in the fresh air, I mustn't forget that.'

'Of course not. Your precious nature.' Abby couldn't detect any sarcasm in his tone. 'How did your first hangover walk go?'

'It was freezing but dry, and the visitors seemed to enjoy themselves. Perhaps I should have planned one for tomorrow.'

'I'll be fine,' Jack said dismissively. 'And I'm glad it went well. Tell me more about Penelope's estate. How is Meadowsweet connected to the rest of the village?'

'That is the least subtle subject swerve I've ever heard,' Abby said, laughing.

Jack smiled. 'I'm curious about how it's all linked. Peacock Cottage is fit for purpose, but I could tell it had been empty for a while before I moved in. Some of the appliances are outdated, and there was a slightly musty smell, though expertly covered with plug-in room scent. My agent, Leo, who found me the cottage, said that Penelope inherited the estate from her late husband. I've got to know her a little since I've been here, but she's never been forthcoming about that side of things.'

'She's not forthcoming about anything much,' Abby said. 'The mood you're in, a night out with the two of you would be an absolute *riot*!'

It was Jack's turn to look outraged. 'I've got a fun side.'

'I know,' Abby said more gently. 'I just . . . you were beginning to let me see it, and then this. The whisky, the cold shoulder.'

Jack rubbed his eyes. 'I'm sorry, Abby. I'm an idiot. And instead of fixing it, I seem to have piled more idiotic behaviour on top and made everything ten times worse.'

'That's called digging a hole,' she said, smiling. 'But you haven't offended me, and I'm not leaving you alone, no matter how hard you try and get rid of me. So, I'll tell you. The big country house is called Swallowtail House, and Penelope owns that too. When her husband, Al, died of a heart attack, Penelope moved out immediately. She kept running the reserve, which was Al's passion to begin with, but the house is just this big empty shadow looming over the village.'

'Now who's being melodramatic?' Jack asked lightly. 'Hasn't she got someone to keep it in good condition? Why doesn't she sell it, if she doesn't want to live there any more?'

'I don't know,' Abby said. 'I've been here nearly two years, and I've never even seen the gates open. It's as if she can't bear to go near it but can't face getting rid of it either – despite the problems with Meadowsweet.'

Jack pinched a chip off her plate, his own long gone. His cheeks were slightly flushed, she noticed, his eyes bright. 'You're intrigued,' he said.

'About Swallowtail? Sure I am. It's this huge, grand old

home that's falling apart. I can't imagine anyone *wouldn't* be fascinated by it. I wondered enough about Peacock Cottage before you turned up – who used to live in the house in the woods? It's just nestled there, looking snug and inviting and, while it was empty, mysterious too.'

'And now I'm there it's lost its mystery?'

'As if! You're the most perplexing thing about Peacock Cottage, with your mood swings, your celebrity status and your badass history.'

Jack's brows lowered. '*Badass history?* You mean I lost my temper and hit someone.'

'Despite writing letters of complaint to a nature reserve – which, by the way, is almost akin to drowning a kitten – it doesn't seem your style, somehow. I can imagine you inviting Eddie Markham to a joust or a fencing duel, but not actually, straight up punching him.' She stared at his hand, thought that maybe she could see faint lines on his knuckles, traces of scars where he'd opened his skin connecting with Eddie's jaw. Before she realized what she was doing, she was running her index finger gently along his knuckle line, stroking the ridges, the dips.

'Don't mention Eddie Markham,' Jack said, but it was almost a whisper.

Abby glanced up. He was very still, watching her. She placed her hand over his, then patted it awkwardly as if that's what she'd been meaning to do all along, and tried to stop the pounding in her ears.

'It was stupid of me, I'm sorry.' She felt her skin flush, her confidence draining out of her. She had *stroked* him. Caressed him, almost. 'I should never—'

'It's fine,' Jack said quickly. 'He's my problem, not yours. I just don't want him encroaching on this afternoon. Not when you've turned it around.' He smiled at her, his eyes crinkling at the edges.

'I have?' she croaked.

'You were right,' he said softly. 'I was on my way to the bottom of that bottle, and you've forced me out of it. God knows what I would have done after another three or four of those.' He pointed at his empty glass. 'You've forced me to look on the bright side, to seek out mystery instead of misery.' He slid deftly off the stool and grabbed his coat.

'What mystery? What are you talking about?'

'Come on.' He held out his hand.

Abby scrabbled off her stool, popped her final chip in her mouth and finished her beer. 'Where are we going?' she asked, as she unwound Raffle's lead and took Jack's hand, trying to ignore the thrill that ran up her arm at his solid, warm grasp.

'We're going on an adventure.'

'We cannot go in there.' She glanced around her to check nobody from the pub had followed. She had a disconcerting image of a *Beauty and the Beast*-type procession, everyone with angry faces and flaming lanterns stomping up to the big house to wreak havoc on the intruder in their midst.

Jack rattled the double gates of Swallowtail House. 'Shit, they're locked.'

'Of course they are! It would be overrun with squatters if they weren't.'

He glanced up at the wall, which Abby guessed was at least ten feet tall. Raffle sat and looked at him, waiting for his next move.

'There must be another way in,' he said, turning to her. His face was more open, more alive than she'd ever seen it. His eyes were bluer in the bright sunshine, as if they were charged by sun power, and his jaw seemed less rigid, no longer a fortress that kept any expression outside of a scowl in check.

'There's a smaller gate in the woods,' Abby said, 'but it's as locked as that one.'

'How can it be *as* locked?' he asked. 'Either it is, or it isn't. Come on then, we'll try there.'

'Jack!' Her protest was half-hearted, and she let him take her hand again, let him pull her in the direction she had pointed in, Raffle darting ahead, loving the game. They stepped under the woodland canopy where the sun was muted, where birds chorused and leaves danced gently in the breeze. Abby felt the adrenalin thrill of being with Jack thrumming through her, like a second pulse.

'I don't even know why you want to get in,' she said.

'Because you do.'

'But I'd never *break* in,' Abby protested.

'Nobody will know. And besides, who's to say the house isn't desperate for a little TLC?'

'It's a house. It's not alive.'

'But it is, partly.' He stopped walking and turned to face her. 'Think of all the plants that will have found gaps and worked their way in, the spiders weaving webs in the corners of the rooms. There'll be birds roosting in the roof, bats possibly. It may not have people living in it any more, but I guarantee it won't be empty.'

Abby stared at him, wishing that he wasn't so handsome, or that he'd kept pushing her away in the pub. She wished he hadn't shown this sudden giddiness – whisky-driven or not – and interest in Swallowtail House, that he hadn't given her this image of a place teeming with wildlife, beautiful and unkempt and alive. That was how she'd always seen it, but to know that he felt the same, that he'd thought about it too, wasn't helping her control her feelings.

'Jack . . .' she started.

'Let's go and see, shall we?' He squeezed her hand and started walking.

'It's locked,' she said again, as Jack rattled the secluded gate. 'I told you. Penelope doesn't want anyone getting in.'

Jack rubbed his jaw.

'We should just leave it,' Abby pressed.

'Not yet.' Jack walked in a circle behind her, then crouched and picked up a large rock. He approached the gate, wielding the rock, his face a mask of determination.

'You can't do that,' Abby said, aghast. 'That's breaking and entering.'

'And what if, tomorrow, I replace the padlock with a much more secure one?'

'That you'll have the key to, and Penelope won't.'

'I doubt anyone could get a key into this padlock anyway, it's completely rusted over.' He put the rock on the ground and peered at the padlock.

Raffle barked loudly, and a couple of pigeons flew from their perches, wings flapping madly as they disappeared into the blue. Abby felt a pang of sympathy that their lazy Saturday afternoon had been disturbed.

On a day like today, there would be lots of people on the reserve, just a short walk through the fallen elder and the spreading brambles. What if Gavin or Marek were doing some work close by and stumbled upon them? She tried to remember who was rostered on that afternoon.

'Jack,' she whispered desperately.

'This isn't—' He waggled the padlock, and suddenly there

was a splintering sound and the metal lock was in Jack's hands in two pieces, the chain hanging forlornly. He gave Abby a triumphant look.

'We can't.'

'It was rusted through. I have no idea how old it is, but it wasn't a good-quality lock in the first place.'

'Jack,' she said again.

He held out his hand to her.

'There's no harm in looking, and I'll get a better padlock tomorrow and give Penelope the key, tell her I was walking past and saw that it was broken. We'll be doing her a favour. Come on Abby,' he said, when she didn't move or reply. 'Where's your sense of adventure?'

Abby sighed. She had wanted to get up close to Swallowtail House for two years, and now here was her chance, a chance that also let her get closer to Jack Westcoat.

She took his hand and let him lead her through the gate, Raffle following happily behind.

Chapter Twelve

Just because a bird is common, it doesn't mean it's not precious, and pigeons are unfortunately hated by lots of people. If you look closely at their necks, you'll see their feathers aren't just grey, but shiny green and purple too. Their gentle cooing is one of the most familiar sounds you'll hear in the garden, and is very comforting.

— Note from Abby's notebook

From the moment Abby stepped inside the tall, redbrick wall, the atmosphere changed.

It felt stiller, as if the air was different, as if this was a place that had paused the moment Penelope had left and had been lying in wait for someone new all these years. Raffle padded along in front of them, nose down to the brown, frost-damaged grass. Abby still had her hand in Jack's, and was acutely aware of the pressure of his grasp, his long fingers curving around hers. She didn't know whether to keep hold or to let go, but as they walked past the old stone fountain, long since given up spurting, its curved bowl with a puddle of water and dead, mulching leaves at the bottom, their hands fell apart automatically.

Up close, the house was imposing, the cracks more visible. The yellow paintwork was dulled and the windowsills were peeling, though most of the glass was still intact. Abby crunched over the gravel and peered through the closest window. The room was large and square, faint imprints on the walls where paintings had once hung. There was no furniture, but the plasterwork around the edge of the ceiling and the fireplace was intricate, patterns of flowers, butterflies and birds. The wooden floor was covered in dirt, as if creatures had tracked it through from outside.

All this time she'd been imagining the house's interior as a still life of the day Penelope had left, the furniture in place, a book discarded on the table, a mug that had once held a cup of tea. The reality was very different. The house was empty and yet, as Jack had suggested, also not.

There was birdsong close by, a high, repetitive tune that Abby recognized as a chaffinch. A cluster of starlings sat on the roof, their iridescent feathers shimmering, their chirping, squawking and whistling a cacophony of attention-seeking – *look at me, look at me*. Abby had a sudden, ridiculous urge to tell them about her upcoming event and make sure they'd all be there.

'Abby, come here.' Jack beckoned to her, his gaze fixed on whatever he could see through a window on the opposite side of the house.

Abby walked over and stood next to him, turned to see what he was seeing, and gasped. This room went all the way to the back of the house, French doors leading onto a terrace, and beyond that she could see a hint of the bustling, overgrown gardens.

'What is this?' she asked. 'A ballroom?'

Whereas the other room had pale walls, this grand space was decorated in a dusky blue, which made the white plasterwork stand out even more. Hanging from the ceiling were two intricate chandeliers, their crystal droplets catching the light, some of the jewels clustered together to form rudimentary butterflies.

She tried to imagine the house in its former glory, and Penelope inside it. Had she been welcoming, hosting grand parties alongside her husband? Or had she always been closed off, the two of them stalking through the huge house, barely making use of it?

'I think so,' Jack murmured, but Abby had forgotten what she'd asked him.

'What are you thinking?' she whispered. He seemed transfixed, the pads of his fingers lightly touching the glass, as if he was a small boy enthralled at the window of a sweet shop.

'I'm thinking I definitely need to get Penelope a good padlock tomorrow. And look.' He pointed, and Abby followed the line of his finger, noticing what should have been glaringly obvious, but she had managed to miss. One side of the French doors was open a crack.

She sucked in a breath. 'There might be intruders in there. Squatters, drug dealers – anyone.'

'Or it could have been the wind? An animal?'

'We don't have bears in Suffolk,' she said, more to hide her anxiety than anything else. 'Occasionally there are badgers, but sightings are rare, and they couldn't pry open a door.'

'Let's go and see.' When she didn't move, Jack took a step towards her. 'Nothing will happen, I promise.'

'*How* can you promise that?'

'Because I write this stuff for a living,' he said. 'Empty houses, intruders, suspense. I know all the tricks.' His smile was lopsided, also unsure, Abby thought, but his curiosity was clearly winning out. 'Come with me.'

Those words, from Jack, were like a spell. *Come with me.* She couldn't say no.

As they walked round the side of the house, the grass gave way to a tangle of weeds, a hint of pale-green buds and some apple trees that must once have been coppiced and shaped, but now grew proudly up towards the sky, winter skeletons waiting for the spring. She hurried to keep up with Jack's long, easy strides.

She knew that, were she suddenly afraid, she could take his hand, and that he wouldn't shy away from that simple physical contact. Somehow, that meant a lot. It had been a long time since she had felt this comfortable with a man, and she and Jack barely knew each other.

'Jesus,' he said, as they reached the back of the house.

Abby stopped beside him. 'Wow,' she murmured, because it was truly magnificent, in a creepy sort of way.

The stone veranda ran the full length of the building, with steps down to what must once have been a neat path, weaving through low beds and formal rose gardens, between mani-cured hedges. Now, only the echoes of that formality remained, a rigid past trying to imprint itself on an unruly, chaotic present. Winter weeds crept up between every paving slab, the stones themselves pitching and cracking with the pressure, giving the impression the patio was moving, rippling like the sea. The stairs were mostly hidden by a tangle of ivy, and every rose bush had either grown wildly or died, dark, charcoal-like remains alongside healthy plants, bursting with the promise of new buds in only a few weeks' time.

A small, pale structure towards the back wall of the grounds – a summerhouse – was almost lost amongst the greens and browns.

It was overrun with life: natural, escaped life. Warblers trilled, a blackbird sang from the top of a burgeoning, ever-green hedge, grown out of its topiary shape like a wilful child, and Abby could see movement at the back of the garden, close to where the redbrick wall kept the woodland at bay. A fox or a rabbit, maybe. Possibly a deer. She watched for a moment longer, but the movement stilled as whatever it was disappeared into denser foliage.

'Can you imagine what this will be like in the spring and summer?' The thought overwhelmed her, the wildlife that would run amok in this place that had once been so highly cultivated. 'There will be roses – who knows how many colours and scents – different types of butterfly and moth, the birds making nests, bringing their young up with all this to feed on. It's heaven.'

'It's years of work for someone, somewhere down the line,' Jack said quietly. 'But there is something compelling about it. Shall we?' He turned to the house, and Abby heard the creak of the French doors opening wider. She felt a wave of panic, and then decided that, as they'd come this far, they may as well go the whole way.

She stepped inside after him, their boots – his, Timberland, hers, Merrell – echoing on the wooden floor. Beneath the high ceiling and the chandeliers of the ballroom she felt small, the trails of ivy and cobwebs not diminishing its impact. Jack was already striding through it, towards the hallway. She followed, walking over a mildewed rug that had been forgotten, its pattern indistinct.

The hall was impressive, but without the large windows

seemed gloomy, and the further they got from the French doors, the more cloying and thick the air became. But Jack was exploring the house with a sense of purpose, as if he'd planned this all along, and had used subterfuge and suggestion to make Abby think this was what *she* wanted.

She remembered the accusation she'd flung at him after the Halloween event, that he wanted to use her to test out some gruesome theories for his next book. She pushed the idea away. Jack was grumpy, but he wasn't dangerous. She reminded herself of how he'd behaved with his admirer in the pub, courteous even when he'd been set on drinking himself into a stupor, the way he'd come to her rescue after she'd tripped outside his cottage, refusing to let her go home alone. However miserable he was, she was sure she wasn't about to die in Swallowtail House, falling senseless onto the mouldy rug with a well-placed blow to the back of the head.

'The kitchen's through there,' Jack said, making her jump. 'It's huge, but understandably old-fashioned. If it were up to me, I'd rip all the units out, redo everything in wood and white granite, and put an island in the centre. The windows are large, and there's another set of doors onto the patio so it's got lots of natural light.'

'Do you fancy a bit of interior design, then?' Abby asked.

Jack gave her a quizzical look. 'Aren't you imagining what you'd do with this place if it was yours? Think how incredible it would be if it was restored, in keeping with all the period features, but with modern appliances and technology. What would you do with the ballroom?'

Abby laughed. He was so different; whimsical and relaxed, the hunched shoulders gone. 'I don't know.'

'Let's go upstairs,' he said, not giving her time to protest. Jack tested the stairs gingerly, but they seemed to be solid, no overly loud creaks or splintering of rotten wood beneath his feet.

They toured the bathrooms and bedrooms, all empty of furniture, all at different stages of nature's consumption. One had a bird's-nest on the windowsill; Abby thought from the size and shape it was probably a sparrow's, and too early for it to be this year's. The house was never silent, their footsteps creaking, Raffle snuffling into every corner, the trill of birds reaching them through the thin glass.

Abby warmed to Jack's theme, telling him which bedroom she would use, and which would be reserved for Tessa and Neil, Daisy and Willow. There was a small room, tucked into a corner of the house like an afterthought, but it had windows on two sides, which made it one of the lightest. It had a worryingly impressive spider's web in the corner, with several moths hanging limply in it, but in Abby's fantasy world that would easily be removed.

'How old are they?' Jack asked. 'Your nieces.'

'Eight and four,' she said. 'Daisy's birthday was just before Christmas. My sister, Tessa, is a natural mum. She never gets stressed or wound up, and always manages to look glamorous, though it must be constantly exhausting.'

'Do you see them a lot?'

'Yeah, they only live in Bury, so I try and see them every couple of weeks.'

'It must be nice, being close to your family like that.'

Abby nodded, thinking of her mum and their strange encounter on New Year's Day, and then her dad, who she hadn't spoken to in such a long time. 'I'm very lucky to have Tessa,' she said. 'How about you? Do you have brothers or sisters?'

Jack shook his head. 'No, it's just me. Which is fine, mostly.

I can't exactly miss siblings if I don't know what it's like to have them. I count my friends as pretty much the same thing.'

Abby thought of Eddie Markham, and wondered how close they had been before everything got so angry and complicated. Had his betrayal been like losing a brother? Was that where the punch had come from, the lingering sadness that had seemed to overwhelm him today? She had seen tempers frayed to breaking point, and for much lesser things than revealing a friend's past mistakes in a national newspaper.

'Why is it only *mostly* fine?' Abby asked, taking advantage of Jack's temporary suppleness.

He glanced at her before turning back to the window. 'Because when you're the only one, your parents' expectations are all on you. You have to fulfil all the hopes and dreams that they never achieved and which they've subconsciously – or consciously, in some cases – passed on to you. And you certainly can't screw up, at least not in the way I've managed to.'

Abby winced. 'I'm sorry. It can't have been fun telling them.'

'I didn't have to. It was all over social media before I'd made it out of the venue. I got a call in the car on the way home, which I was lucky to be in, as Eddie could have called the police and had me charged with assault. But as it was, that phone call from my dad was probably as bad.' A ghost of a frown flittered across his face, then it went back to being stony.

Abby wrapped her hand gently around his arm, the thick, soft fabric of his padded jacket, and wondered if he'd even be able to feel her touch. But he glanced down, acknowledged the gesture with a weary smile, and then seemed to snap out of it.

'Which one do you think is the master bedroom?' he asked, walking along the corridor to the front of the house. He stepped into the largest room, which had two windows looking out over the front lawn, and Abby followed.

She could see the gate they had broken in through and the woodland beyond, the trees towering over the brick wall. Over to her left was the spire of the chapel library, and further away, a hint of the yellow paintwork and the tiled roof of the Skylark. The sun was sinking, and she knew they'd have to leave soon or risk being in the abandoned house in total darkness. The thought sent a thrill through her, and not purely out of fear.

'Look at this,' Jack said.

There was something dangling from the otherwise bare curtain rail. Jack unwound the slender chord and pulled the object down. It was an ornament made of coloured glass that, with the north-facing window, would catch the sun throughout the day, as it swept east to west. He handed it to Abby, and she looked at it more closely.

It was in the shape of two birds, facing each other, their wings and tail feathers splayed out behind them. The glass was shot through with all the colours of the rainbow, shimmering like the Murano necklaces Rosa sold in the gift shop, and edged with metal. Purple beads hung on a string below their feet. Even though the design was simplistic, Abby thought she could identify the birds from their shape, the myriad of colours, their position facing each other.

'Lovebirds,' she murmured, running her fingers over the wavy, hand-blown glass. 'Why did Penelope leave this behind? It's beautiful.'

She could imagine her boss and Al lying in a grand bed facing the window, the curtains drawn, knowing that from their impressive vantage point they couldn't be spied on by anyone, the glass of the lovebirds dappling the covers with coloured light.

'Maybe it was too painful,' she said, answering her own question. 'Maybe, after Al died, they were symbolic of what she'd lost.'

'Lovebirds,' Jack repeated quietly, reaching out to touch the glass, their fingers brushing, the briefest touch sending a tingle up Abby's hand, an electric shock that went straight to her heart.

'Lovebirds mate for life,' she said, trying to keep her voice steady. 'And they pine for their companion when they're apart. Just like Penelope and Al,' she added, wondering again at the strength of her boss's grief to abandon the home they had shared, to stay so close to it for all these years, but to never venture inside, or make a decision about its future. 'What if she had things that she'd never told him, things that she regretted? Perhaps that was what was haunting her, but it felt like it was the house, so she had to get away from it.'

Jack didn't respond immediately, and Abby felt the house settle around them, the comforting, distant chatter of the starlings.

'I'm sorry,' he said eventually. 'That I didn't respond to your note, after our coffee.'

'Why didn't you?' she asked quietly, hoping she didn't sound accusatory.

'Because . . . I felt ashamed.'

'Ashamed? Why?'

'What you told me about the memories you wished you could erase, that they weren't your actions, felt too familiar. In the past, I was reckless; I hurt my parents, and my friends. Not physically, but emotionally. And then with Eddie, last year . . . I went too far. All the mistakes I made . . . I can't seem to outrun my history.'

'But you haven't hurt me,' Abby said. 'You aren't responsible for what happened to me. I'm only going on what I've experienced when I'm with you, and surely that's what matters?'

'I've got so much wrong.' His voice had dropped to a whisper. 'Even with you – not responding to your letter, being rude to you in the pub. Those stupid complaints I made.'

'Can't we put the past behind us?' she asked. 'I know that sounds odd when we're standing in an abandoned house, full of the ghosts of other people's lives, but maybe being here is as good a reminder as any. Don't let it drag you down, Jack.'

It felt like she was saying the words to herself as much as to him; the reassurances from Tessa that, despite her tendency to pick the wrong men, she deserved a healthy relationship; the insistence from her mum that her dad's behaviour shouldn't dictate her future. *Was* Jack different, or was she fooling herself into believing he was because she liked him so much?

When he didn't reply, she handed the lovebirds to him and he reached up and tied them back in place, so they fell just below the upper frame of the window, catching the sun's light as it slipped towards the trees.

'We should get back,' he said softly. He seemed subdued, as if he'd given too much of himself away. His jaw was set again, but when he looked at her, he rewarded her with a brief smile. 'It's a beautiful house. It doesn't feel oppressive or sad despite the cobwebs and dark corners.'

'I know what you mean,' Abby said. 'It's still so light, so . . . hopeful.'

'Hopeful of what?'

Abby shrugged. 'Life? Maybe it hopes it'll see human life again one day.'

'Looking to the future instead of the past?' Jack asked. 'I'm sure it will. A place like this can't stand empty forever, however strong Penelope's hold on it is. Maybe she just needs some encouragement to make a decision. Or perhaps, after all this time, she'd like to move back, but is daunted by the size of the task.'

Abby wrinkled her nose. 'This is a big place for just one person, though. That could have been part of the reason she moved out in the first place.' She wondered if Al was still here, gliding through the rooms after dark, looking for his wife. She shuddered and shook the thought away. 'Come on, we don't want to lose the last of the light.'

She led the way down the stairs, back through the ballroom's French doors and down the side of the house. Rabbits had emerged from their burrows and they scattered now, more afraid of Raffle than Jack or Abby, and she watched them bound through the grass; fast, dark shapes with cotton-white tails.

They walked past the fountain, towards the gate and then Jack glanced behind him, stopped and turned fully, touching Abby lightly on the arm. She followed his gaze, her eyes widening.

The windows were full of the lowering, blazing sun, reflecting it back, each one a square of gold as if the whole building was on fire.

'The House of Birds and Butterflies,' Jack said.

'What?'

'That's what this is. Swallowtail House – its name, its occupants.'

'The House of Birds and Butterflies,' Abby murmured. It

was a beautiful, romantic name for this grand old home, standing stoically in its place while nature slowly consumed it.

With the windows on fire and the darkness chasing the sunset, nothing but nature surrounding them, Abby felt like she and Jack were the only human beings left on the planet, and realized she wouldn't mind if that turned out to be true. And then, because that was such an unexpected, over-whelming thought, she left the abandoned, glowing building behind and picked up her pace towards the gate.

Jack wrapped the chain around it to give it the impression of security, while Abby reattached Raffle's lead. When they got to the cut-through that led to Peacock Cottage, she tried to say goodbye, but Jack insisted on walking her home.

The village was almost deserted now, the falling dusk turning the sky turquoise. They reached Warbler Cottages, and Raffle padded eagerly up the front path.

'Do you want to come in for a coffee?' The words were out before she realized she'd spoken them.

'Coffee would be lovely,' Jack said, and Abby's insides went haywire. 'Besides,' he added, 'as if you haven't done enough for me already, there's something I want to ask you.'

'You want me to give you a personal tour of the reserve, so you can work out the best place to hide a body?'

They were sitting in Abby's living room, which in a happy coincidence was gleaming after her spring-clean that morning. Raffle was lying on the rug in front of the fireplace, and Jack was on Abby's rather saggy sofa, which was covered in a purple-and-yellow checked throw. He held a steaming mug of coffee in both hands, his legs slightly open, though not stretched to breaking point in that ridiculous, alpha-male stance that she hated. She could see a bit of grass sticking out of the top of one of his boots, and after the cold of the afternoon, his cheeks were flushed in the warmth of Abby's house.

She was in the armchair opposite, her housewarming present from Tessa and Neil. The fabric was a bold, teal-and-pink flower print, and Abby loved it. She could curl right up in it, between the oversized, chunky arms.

Now, though, she was perched on the edge of the seat, trying to make sense of Jack's request.

'You told me to embrace nature,' he explained. 'And to let it inspire me. After I spent a good three days being thoroughly irritated by your suggestion, I realized there might be something to it. So . . .' He shrugged. 'I rethought the plot of my book, and now one of the victims is discovered on a nature reserve. A cruel, violent death amongst all that life. But I need to know where would work best, and I could spend a morning walking round by myself, but it would be much better if you, with all your knowledge, could spare a couple of hours of your time. I wanted to ask you before today, but I wasn't convinced I should inflict myself on you any more.'

She ignored his last comment. 'You're going to sully the beauty of this place with a death?'

'Not Meadowsweet, Abby. A fictional nature reserve.'

She sipped her tea and stroked her bare foot down Raffle's long, soft back. The dog twitched his ears in appreciation but didn't move from his spot on the rug.

'So, will you?' Jack prompted, his voice so low that it made Abby's tummy flutter unhelpfully. She looked up at him, and found his blue eyes piercing her from beneath his long eyelashes, his hair gorgeously dishevelled. He looked perfectly at home on her squashy, comfortable sofa.

She opened her mouth and found that, despite her cup of tea, it was dry.

'Come with me,' he said. Those words again, casting a spell on her.

Abby got up and sat next to Jack. Raffle's pale eyes fixed on her as if assessing whether his mistress was in any trouble. He must have decided no, because he laid his head back down on his front paws.

Jack shifted round towards her.

'Yes, Jack,' she said. 'I will take you on a body-location tour of the reserve, but you must promise not to breathe a word to Penelope, and you can't mention that we took ourselves round Swallowtail House, and you really can't—' She stopped as he took her hand, his skin hot from where it had been clutching his mug, and gave her a whisper of a smile.

'Abby, I promise. I know I started out as a fly in the ointment, a barrier to your plans to boost the popularity of the reserve, but that wasn't my intention then, and it certainly isn't now. I'm sorry about today, about the way I've behaved, and I know that I'm pushing my luck even asking. I'm already indebted to you.'

Abby thought of Octavia's request for help convincing Jack to do an event at the library, but kept quiet. She didn't want to use up his favour on that; she hated how much she wanted him all to herself.

'OK,' she said. 'OK, I trust you.'

'Thank you, Abby,' he whispered. 'Trust is something a lot of people have lost in me, so to hear you say it, even about a walk, a new padlock, it means a lot.' He frowned, and then banished it with a smile.

He leaned towards her, the sofa squeaking as his weight

shifted, and his lips found the corner of her mouth. She smelt the faintest, lingering trace of bergamot, coffee and the sharp tang of whisky almost drowning it out, felt the brush of his stubble, the press of his hand round her shoulder. Then he moved his head and his lips were against hers, kissing her gently. The tenderness of his touch, the reality after so long imagining it, made her dizzy. She kissed him back, feeling his warmth all around her, resisting the urge to lose herself in it.

He broke away and pressed his forehead against hers, his breathing loud in the silence. She could sense that he wanted more, but that something was holding him back, too.

'I should go,' he murmured. He tucked a strand of hair behind her ear, then stood and pulled on his coat, and gave Raffle a brief stroke goodbye.

Abby followed him, dazed, to the front door. 'I'll check the rota tomorrow,' she said, hearing the wobble in her voice. 'To let you know when would be best to meet you.'

'Thank you,' he said again. 'For that, and for not giving up on me; for the chips.'

She nodded, mock stern. 'Chips have all the power, it's an important fact to remember.'

'Noted,' he said. 'Goodnight, Abby.' Then he was gone, striding towards the main road, pausing to pull out his phone and put on the torch. Abby watched until the light was gone, and his tall figure was out of sight.

She closed the door and slumped onto the sofa, picking up the mug that she'd given him. It was white, with a robin painted on it. Her pulse was racing, her thoughts trying to find their way back to those days in the autumn when Jack had been infuriating her, and she'd dismissed her emotions as anger and dislike – fleeting and insubstantial. They didn't feel insubstantial now.

She had been consumed by his kiss, as gentle and brief as it had been. She wanted to play it on repeat, hold on to the way it made her feel. She already missed his presence in her house, his thick, chocolatey hair and blue eyes, the stubborn jaw and the occasional smiles it let out to tempt her. She wanted to go back to Swallowtail House, to be under its spell with him – the only two people in the world. And she wanted to kiss him again. Despite the shadows of his past behaviour, and his own obvious self-doubt, she needed more.

Already, she couldn't wait to look at the rota, so she could work out when to sneak off with him, down to the heron hide or along the meadow trail, muddy and barren and often deserted at this time of year, and soak him up.

The lesser-spotted Jack Westcoat. He was the species she was most interested in, and surely that couldn't be good for anyone – not him, not her, and definitely not Penelope and the future of Meadowsweet.

Raffle was looking at her, his wide, honest eyes curious, questioning, accusing.

'Oh God, Raffle,' she said, clutching the empty mug to her chest. 'What am I doing?'

Chapter Thirteen

A murmuration of starlings is one of the most impressive sights nature has to offer. Like a black, swirling wave filling the sky, the birds somehow know which direction to turn in so that they all move together. It's like when you and your dance group, Willow, all do the steps at the same time, and it looks like you've been practising for years. Starlings are the dancers of the bird world.

— Note from Abby's notebook

It was only as Abby turned on the computer on the morning of her walk with Jack that she realized the significance of the date. She silently cursed her subconscious and wondered if he had smirked when he got her note, posted through the door of Peacock Cottage in what was becoming a tradition, or if he'd felt a surge of the same complicated feelings she got whenever she thought about him, and about what had happened the last time they had been together.

She had tried to convince herself that she'd been caught up in the madness and magic of the day. She'd had two pints at lunchtime, and then the giddiness of breaking into Swallowtail House had somehow heightened her senses, and her feelings for Jack – because he'd been there with her – had been heightened in the same way. He'd been on the way to being drunk, he was relieved that she was still talking to him after his radio silence, and their brief kiss had been the result of the alcohol and too many swirling emotions with nowhere to go except towards each other.

But there had been no hint of irony or teasing in his returned reply, which she'd managed to read entirely alone, just confirmation that the fourteenth of February would be fine, and another thank you.

The weather was grey. Not even a glimmer of sunshine broke through a solid wall of cloud, the air cold, heavy with promised rain, the smell of earth and damp all-pervading. A cluster of jackdaws pecked mechanically in the ground next to the feeders as Abby stepped outside and zipped her thick waterproof coat up to her neck, their sinister caws punctuating the quiet. She had always had a soft spot for jackdaws; she thought that they looked rather shy and unsure with their black caps, grey heads and beady eyes. She imagined them to be old men, doddering anxiously through life, saying things like, 'Oh do excuse me, I'm terribly sorry,' or else awkward teenagers, bashful and embarrassed about everything.

Maureen was working that morning, and Abby had told Rosa and Penelope that she needed to check the meadow trail and then, if necessary, order some boards that they could place over any particularly muddy areas. She couldn't have anyone sinking or slipping at her grand murmuration event – she just hoped Jack wouldn't mind her multitasking.

He was waiting for her at the top of the woodland trail, his hands shoved deep into the pockets of his jeans. He had his usual navy padded jacket on, and sturdy boots. He gave her a nod as she approached, his blue eyes smiling at her even though his mouth remained impartial.

'Good day for it,' he said, pointing at the sky.

'It does get you in a murderous mood,' Abby agreed, as they started walking. 'I thought we'd go along the meadow trail first, and then make our way around the rest of the reserve. I need to check the path for my event, and we'll pass one of the tributaries, which would be a great place for a body to lie hidden for a couple of days.'

'You've been thinking about this?' Jack sounded amused.

'A little bit,' Abby admitted.

After a few minutes, the track changed beneath their feet, becoming noticeably softer as they emerged from the woods. The view ahead was flat but beautiful, a thin slice of grey-blue water to their right, the dulled green of a winter meadow ahead. Abby stopped when they reached the tributary, which had sharp, steep banks, the river narrow, but, she assured him, quite deep.

'Let me show you.' She scouted around until she found a long stick, left over from some coppicing work Marek had been doing. She knelt on the ground and pushed the stick into the river. Its progress was swift, and she fell forward much more quickly than she had expected, jerking back to try and catch her balance. There was a moment of panic as she realized she wouldn't be able to recover, then strong hands wrapped around her waist and pulled her upright, away from the water, as if Jack had been waiting behind her for that very purpose.

She could feel his breath on her neck as she watched the stick continue down, and then, when it had almost completely disappeared, it stopped.

'Some of that's the mud at the bottom,' Abby said, her voice wavering as Jack released his grip and stood, holding out his hand to pull her up. 'If someone threw a corpse in there, then they might get away with it until the wardens did some maintenance work. The tributaries are too small to have any real current running through them, so it wouldn't get washed up anywhere else, but perhaps there would be a hand or foot sticking up – maybe when it was disturbed by an animal or a swan.' She wrinkled her nose in distaste and tried to dust the dirt off her waterproof trousers. 'Thank you, by the way.'

'I wouldn't want you to go full method actor on me,' Jack said. 'Penelope would never forgive me if I had to explain that you'd accidentally drowned showing me where to lose a body.'

'If you could find her another activity coordinator, I'm not sure she'd be too upset.'

Jack laughed. 'Oh, come on, she's not that bad. Is she?'

They continued walking, Abby stopping occasionally to test the path for slippability and give. A lot of weather could happen in a couple of weeks, and she would probably order some new boards anyway, to be on the safe side, but it was important to check the area for other potential problems.

'Penelope is a wonderful woman,' she said eventually. 'She's passionate about this place – all the things she's doing to try and keep it open – but she . . . lacks a bit of a human touch. I see glimmers of it, but I'm one of the only ones.' She thought back to her frank discussion about the man walking alongside her, Penelope's obvious concern mirroring her own. 'What happened when you replaced the padlock? Did you tell her?'

Jack nodded. 'I invited her to Peacock Cottage for tea and

explained that I'd been walking past and noticed that the padlock was corrupted, so thought it was best to replace it.'

Abby tried to imagine Jack and Penelope having afternoon tea together, all lightness and laughter.

Jack mistook her silence. 'I didn't mention you, if that's what you're worried about.'

'I'm not worried,' Abby said. 'I trust you, remember? Was she grateful?'

'She was. She was very pleasant and asked how I was getting on. I told her things were looking up, that the writing was going well and my ideas were flowing. I didn't tell her who'd given me the much-needed kick up the backside. From what you've said I wasn't sure she'd be pleased to hear you were deviating from your one true purpose in life.'

Abby grinned. 'No, she wouldn't like that. I'm glad if I've helped though, with . . . things.'

'And now you're solving my corpse dilemma too. Where next?'

'The heron hide. There's a lot of knotty undergrowth, and some impressive gorse close to the lagoon. Obviously, the killer would get scratched to bits offloading the body, but that would be worth it to make the location almost undiscoverable.'

'*Almost* being the optimum word. It needs to be found eventually, or my plot rather stalls.'

'Noted,' Abby said, and he shot her a look, which she parried with a sweet smile. 'I'm starting to get into this.'

Jack raised a single eyebrow, managing cynical and sexy all at once, and Abby had to turn away.

The weather remained stubbornly miserable as she led him on a grand tour, sneaking in details about the wildlife and the recent sightings, as well as showing him where she thought a body could be hidden, or where a discovery would be dramatic. Not that, she reasoned, it would ever be undramatic to come across a corpse when you were out for a relaxing stroll.

'And the thing about a nature reserve,' she said, as they left the kingfisher hide, 'is that it can't be locked away. We only man the visitor centre during certain hours, and it's not as if we can fence the whole place off. So, with a powerful torch and balls of steel, you could drive your car into the car park and make your own way down here at three in the morning, hefting a body over your shoulder. Or if you'd cut it into pieces, even better!'

'Just *how* long have you been puzzling this over?' Jack asked.

'Since you asked me, two weeks ago, after the House of Birds and Butterflies.' She couldn't think of it as Swallowtail House any more. His new name for it, somehow so symbolic of the afternoon they had spent together, had pushed the other one aside. 'Are you inspired?'

'Very,' he said. 'It's a shame we don't get vultures in this country. I'd like the body to be found in a particularly grizzly state.' He narrowed his eyes, and Abby wondered if he was teasing her. Surely, he already knew a lot about body decomposition from researching previous books?

'British wildlife will do that almost as well as a vulture, given enough time,' she said. 'Foxes, crows, magpies – obviously I've not seen them eating *human* remains, but they'll go after carrion. Not to mention all the insects that will devour it. Slowly. In different groups, like people waiting their turn for a wedding buffet. Ugh.' She shuddered. 'Shall we go on?'

'Are you sure you want to?' He sounded concerned, but Abby didn't believe it. He was pushing her buttons, as if he wasn't happy without some kind of battle between them.

'We haven't been to the forest hide,' she said briskly. 'And of course I want to continue, I'm not remotely squeamish.'

'If you're sure.' There was definite amusement in his voice.

Feeling her hackles rise, along with a sort of nostalgia at finding Jack infuriating all over again, Abby stomped off towards their final destination.

The forest hide sat on stilts, snuggling into the woodland canopy, and with glimpses of the lagoon through breaks in the trees. They passed a couple of seasoned birdwatchers on the way and exchanged greetings.

'It's a bit quiet up there today,' one of them said cheerfully. 'Still, it's respite from the cold.'

They climbed the ladder, Abby going first, aware of Jack following her and where his eye level might be. The hide was empty, the wooden floor creaking beneath them. She had replaced all the posters at the end of the previous summer and they looked glossy and professional, listing the species regularly found in that particular habitat. Each hide also had a whiteboard and a pen attached with string, so visitors could add what they'd seen. It currently read:

Two siskins
A nuthatch
Bullfinches
Four blue tits
Several long-tailed tits

Abby felt a surge of pride, as she always did, at the variety of wildlife people could see on the reserve. She sat on a bench and opened three of the hatches so that birdsong and the wind, more blustery up in the trees, slipped into the space. She recognized the high-pitched, upward-swooping call of the nuthatch, the peeps of tits as they twirled on branches. Jack was walking around the hide, prowling almost, and it struck her how like a wild animal he was; quiet, dark, a little bit threatening. But also sleek and beautiful, his thick hair so strokable, though she had yet to run her fingers through it. Suddenly, it became her utmost desire.

'Sit down,' she said, and it came out pinched and high, like a schoolmistress. She cleared her throat as Jack gave her an amused glance.

'What are we looking at?' he asked, stretching his long legs over the bench, sitting close enough that she could feel his warmth alongside her.

'This. What do you think?' She indicated the whispering trees and heard a woodpecker's rat-tat-tat in the distance. 'If your character was up here looking for birds, they could easily spot a crumpled shape, or a leg sticking out. Look there, below that huge tree root, or over near those reeds. This viewpoint, it gives you so much more – so much clarity.'

She wasn't really talking about finding bodies any more. This was her favourite spot on the reserve, sitting amongst trees that had grown from a seed or an acorn hundreds of years ago, giving her a sense of perspective. It was like looking at a sky dark with stars, watching meteors shoot, Disney-like, across it. She felt insignificant, knowing that saving these trees, and all the species that lived in them, the plants that grew at their feet or up their trunks, was so much more important than she was.

When she had first got the job and moved to Meadowgreen, she had spent a lot of time in this hide, amazed that this was what she was charged with looking after, with promoting.

It was a hundred times more inspiring than her previous job working as an administrator in Bury St Edmunds, even though it had been for a wildlife charity. She had been helping nature, but she never got to immerse herself in it.

Here, she had found a new, perfect life to slot herself into. It was a small life, but one that she relished. Recently it felt like it had become unwieldy, out of control. The main culprit was sitting next to her, and as she allowed herself to look at him, at the shiver-quick flash of his eyelashes as he blinked, his taught, smooth jaw, and the dark hair reaching the neckline of his jacket, she realized she didn't mind. In fact, the thought of Jack Westcoat not being in her life and making it more complicated made her feel hollow.

He turned towards her. 'What?' he asked softly, and it was as if the view had sent him away too, dragging up thoughts that she would never know.

'What do you think?' she asked again.

'It's beautiful,' he admitted. 'Almost too good to hide a body in.'

'What about the contrast with life and death that you were talking about before?'

'I'm going to have a body discovered here – a fictional here – but that tributary is just what I was after. This place doesn't deserve that.'

'Jack Westcoat,' she said lightly. 'Are you starting to appreciate the wonders of our natural habitat?'

He turned back to the view, a smile chinking the dimple in his cheek. 'Possibly,' he said, then he leaned forward, the shiny material of his jacket rubbing against her arm. 'What the hell is *that*? Is it a robin on steroids?'

Abby followed his sightline. 'It's a male bullfinch. They used to be really common around here, like the blue tits and chaffinches, but their numbers have fallen dramatically. It's always lovely to see one.'

'I guess they're not great at camouflage,' Jack said. 'You're sure it hasn't been dipped in red paint?'

She laughed. 'Listen. Hear that finchy peep – two short blasts? That's him singing.'

'Sounds a bit like my old PE teacher; he was always over-zealous with his whistle.'

Abby tried to hold it in but could only manage a few moments, and then she was laughing so hard she had to turn away from the hatch so she didn't disturb anything. 'That sounds so wrong,' she said. 'I don't even want to know.'

'What?' Jack asked. 'What did I say?' His voice was rough, and then a moment later he was laughing too. 'God. It wasn't like that *at all*.'

'You're sure? Because PE teachers don't have a particularly good reputation, and I would have thought at posh boys' schools it would be even worse.'

'What makes you think I went to a posh boys' school?'

'Oh, come on, Jack. Where else would you have gone?'

He scrutinized her, his laughter gone, and she thought she had offended him, but then he shrugged and rubbed his jaw. 'None of us choose the way we're brought up.'

'I know that,' she said, suddenly feeling awful for judging him, fitting him into a box, and thinking how much she had been shaped by her own upbringing. She wasn't in a position to make jokes about other people's. 'Sorry.'

'There's no need to apologize. Hey, what is it?'

'Nothing.' She couldn't meet his gaze.

'Abby?' He touched her chin with two fingers and tipped it up so she was looking at him. 'What did I say?'

'It wasn't you.'

He frowned, his eyes flaring with frustration. 'I want you to be able to talk to me, to trust me. I've never claimed to be perfect, but if you're prepared to see past what I've done and give me a chance—'

Abby's phone buzzed frantically in her pocket and she pulled it out, seeing Rosa's name on the screen.

'Rosa?'

Her friend's voice was a harsh whisper. 'Abby, where are you? You've been hours! Penelope's on the warpath and some journalist has turned up to see you about the murmuration event. She is going to *literally* spit feathers if you don't appear soon. Have you fallen in a ditch?'

'No, of course not,' Abby said, although that had come close to being her fate. 'I'll be there in ten minutes. Please keep her distracted for me.'

'Keep Penelope distracted? Are you serious?'

'Seven minutes, Rosa.' She was standing before she'd hung up. 'Shit shit shit. We have to go.'

Jack held the door open for her. 'Have I got you in trouble?'

'It isn't your fault,' Abby said, hurrying down the stairs. 'I chose to do this on a work day, I'm the one who's getting carried away.'

'Carried away? With what?'

She stopped at the foot of the stairs. 'Was that OK? Do you have all you need for your book?'

Jack nodded. 'It's been great. When will I—' His voice caught, snagging on his next words. 'When will I see you again?'

Abby swallowed. She couldn't – she'd let him lead her off course enough, at least for the time being. 'The twenty-eighth,' she said. 'Come to my murmuration event. The local paper is going to cover it, but it's at dusk and you could wear

209

a hat . . . I'd like you to see it. If everything goes to plan, it'll be beautiful.'

For a moment she thought he was going to turn her down, and she wouldn't have blamed him. There would be publicity, lots of visitors, and even though their focus would be elsewhere it might still be too much.

'I'll come,' he said. 'But now, shouldn't you be running?'

'Yes. Definitely. Running. Right. Bye Jack, see you soon.' She wondered whether to kiss his cheek, thought better of it and squeezed his hand, her body reacting with thrilled goose bumps. She turned and, leaving the bullfinch, nuthatch and Jack Westcoat behind, raced to the visitor centre, hoping she still had a job to return to.

Abby led the group of seventy-five people carefully down the path as the sun was setting, the icy, cloudless blue gradually being consumed by pink and purple. The weather was colder than it had been in days, so any mud that might have sucked people's shoes in was hidden deep below frozen, solid earth. In the woodland, in patches where the sunshine had failed to reach during the day, the glisten of frost remained, and Abby worried that anyone without a hat or gloves would get instant hypothermia.

At this time of year, the murmuration was a semi-regular occurrence, and Meadowsweet was ideally placed, close to where the starlings made their roosts for the night. She had come down to this spot each evening for the last week, and had watched them perform, so she was hopeful that tonight would be the same. It was freezing, but everything was perfectly set up.

And still, she couldn't forget Penelope's heavy stare when she had bolted back to the visitor centre after her walk with

Jack. She'd barely said a word, which had made it worse, as if Abby's absence was too much for her to talk about. Abby had given her attention to Brad Kennedy, turning on the charm so that he would be drawn in, enthralled by her idea. It must have worked, because the piece was positive and the phone had rung with people wanting to buy tickets for days afterwards.

After that, Abby had made a pact to herself. She wouldn't see, write to, or even think about Jack Westcoat until after the event was over. She had been letting him distract her, and it was starting to impact on her job.

'There was a thick brown envelope in the post this morning,' Rosa had said later that Valentine's day, once the journalist had gone and the two of them had carved out a five-minute break for one of Stephan's hot chocolates. 'It looked official, and Penelope snatched it out of my hands immediately. I don't think it was just you not being there that made her so angry.'

'But she wasn't angry, was she? She was . . . cold,' Abby had said, shuddering. 'I've never seen her so emotionless.'

'I wonder if it was something about the estate.' Rosa had shrugged. 'If there's more behind her need to boost numbers than simply *Wild Wonders* which, after all, doesn't seem to have sucked all the visitors away.'

'I've been thinking that for a while. There's more to this than she's letting on. I wish she'd tell us. How can we help her if we don't know the size of the problem?'

'But if it *is* that dire, and it might affect the future of the reserve along with our jobs, maybe she wants to keep it from us so that we don't worry. It's commendable, but also stupid.'

'We have to work extra hard then,' Abby had said, nodding decisively.

Rosa had looked like she was about to ask something, her full lips parted, but then she'd simply smiled and nodded her agreement.

That conversation, along with Penelope's dark expression, had stayed firmly at the forefront of her mind for the last two weeks. Now, she brought everyone to the edge of the field, turned to face them and took a deep breath.

'Good evening everyone,' she said. 'Thank you for coming to our special event. I'm Abby Field, the activity coordinator at Meadowsweet Nature Reserve. I had hoped, with it being March tomorrow, that the weather would have been kinder, but as it is we've got below-freezing temperatures and clear skies, so I hope you're all layered up and ready for one of this area's most outstanding natural spectacles. It should start any minute now, so keep looking behind me.

'A murmuration of starlings, the sight as beautiful as the name, is when a flock of hundreds, sometimes thousands of the birds get together and perform an incredible aerobatic sky display, changing direction as one, even though they've not practised beforehand. Imagine a synchronized swimming team having those skills!'

She looked over the crowd as they laughed gently. It included Octavia and Jonny, sisters Karen and Joyce, Joyce's white stick bright in the gloom, and many other faces Abby didn't know. Brad Kennedy was there, alongside a photographer, both of them looking distinctly uncomfortable, probably more used to covering indoor events and summer fetes. Rosa, Stephan, Gavin and Marek had all agreed to stay due to the large numbers, and Abby felt well supported as she answered questions and waited for the main attraction.

She couldn't help scanning the faces to see if Jack was there, but if he had decided to come, he'd obviously taken her advice and disguised himself. Anyway, she wasn't allowed to think about him. Even when his note had arrived at reception the day after their walk, thanking her and apologizing for any problems he may have caused, she had given it only a cursory glance and put it in her handbag, ready to tuck inside *UK Flora and Fauna* with the others.

Turning her attention back to her audience, she explained what was known about why the starlings behaved this way, unease churning in her stomach when the skies remained quiet behind her. She glanced at Rosa, then Gavin, their smiles reassuring, but she could see her own uncertainty reflected in their eyes. Was this the one night they wouldn't do it? Had they found somewhere else to roost? Brad Kennedy was looking on expectantly, stamping his feet against the cold, and there were some younger, eager faces at the front of the group.

What if she let them down? She glanced behind her, the sunset beautiful but empty of birds, and nerves began to take over. She scanned the crowd again, and this time she saw him. His tall frame, a thick woollen beanie hat covering his hair, but those blue eyes, the gentle smile he gave her, were unmistakable. She risked a quick smile back, took a deep breath and projected her voice.

'Obviously, as with all natural events, we can make as many educated guesses as we like and examine patterns of behaviour, but we can never predict exactly what will happen. Nature has a way of surprising us, often in the most wonderful way, but sometimes, we do get disappointed. But I hope you'll agree that the sunset is stunning, so if you . . .'

People had begun to murmur, focusing on the view beyond her, no longer listening, and Abby could hear that familiar chatter, peppered with high-pitched screeches and trilling.

213

She turned. The sun was descending, the sky a pink-and-purple canvas, and dancing, centre stage, was a murmuration of starlings, diving and weaving, changing direction at a moment's notice. Abby was mesmerized, and she knew she wasn't the only one. She heard the photographer snapping away, and hoped he could get some good pictures, even in such low light.

She grinned, feeling her knot of tension start to release. The extra boards she had bought hadn't been needed, rain and clouds hadn't ruined the view, nobody had slipped on the icy ground – so far – and the starlings, after giving her a scare, were performing brilliantly. Everyone watched, no commentary needed, until the birds descended as one into the trees at the far side of the field. Their chirping and squawking continued for several more minutes as they settled and then, like a mute button being pressed, all was quiet.

The light was almost gone now, and torches flicked on.

'We'll head back to the visitor centre,' Abby said, 'and my colleagues and I will be happy to answer any more questions while we're warming up with a hot drink and, if I'm not mistaken, some cookies.'

'You're not mistaken, Abby,' Stephan called. 'A selection of homemade cookies await!'

The post-mortem went on a long time, which was a good sign. People were interested, they wanted to know if they could come back and watch without a guide, bring their friends. Abby and Marek fielded the questions while Stephan and Rosa worked in the café. She saw Jonny hovering alone at a table, his gaze trained, for once, on something other than binoculars. Rosa was oblivious, and Abby made a mental note to ask her if she had ever got the impression Jonny had a crush on her. Jack, it seemed, had slipped back to Peacock Cottage.

'That was wonderful,' said Karen, approaching with her sister. 'I was describing it to Joyce as best I could, but it's like nothing else you've ever seen.'

'I heard them though,' Joyce said, smiling. 'That wall of sound, of conversational voices, chattering away like gossip before bedtime, and I could imagine how many birds there were.'

'So, you come for the sounds, the birdsong?' Abby asked.

'And the smells too, the feel of things – bark and leaves. But I am becoming an expert at birdsong,' Joyce added. 'It's the warblers I'm struggling with.'

Abby laughed. 'I honestly don't know what the secret is to telling them apart; they're so similar. When you've discovered it, you'll have to let me know. Have you had a hot drink?'

'Not yet,' Karen said. 'We're on our way there next.'

'Tell Stephan not to skimp on the marshmallows,' Abby called as Karen guided Joyce round the reception desk. She wondered if she had a guide dog at home, and thought of Raffle snuggled up on the rug, or perhaps on her bed, waiting for her return. She felt a pang of longing, aware that he was someone else she needed to give more attention to now this event was done.

She began to tidy up, shuffling leaflets into piles and throwing discarded visitor wristbands in the bin. When Penelope appeared, Abby gave her a wary smile.

'I didn't know you were still here,' she said.

'I'm growing into the chair these days.' The older woman grimaced. 'There's so much paperwork to sort out.'

'Is there anything I can help with?'

Penelope glanced at the busy cafe. 'Keep doing what you're doing, don't lose focus and we might have a chance at saving this place.'

Abby swallowed. 'Is there . . . what are the pressures?'

For a moment Penelope didn't reply, and Abby thought she was about to disappear back into her office, but the older woman surprised her. 'Meadowsweet costs a lot to run, with salaries, maintenance, stock and fees, and we are not doing enough to make a profit. There have been external influences, and I may have to sell some of the assets to keep us afloat, though I will do everything in my power to stop that from happening.'

Abby glanced around her; there was nobody within earshot. 'Assets?'

Penelope met her gaze, and Abby was shocked by the sadness she saw in it. 'Mr Westcoat's new padlock may not be necessary for too much longer.'

'Swallowtail?' Abby gasped. 'No, I—'

'I'd be grateful if you could keep that to yourself for the time being. I am determined that it doesn't come to that, and hopefully it will serve as impetus for you; think what you could achieve if you were 100 per cent focused on the job next time.' She squeezed Abby's arm, a gesture that was so unlike her that Abby dropped her pile of leaflets all over the floor and had to spend the next ten minutes retrieving them from all the places they had slid off to.

It wasn't until much later, once she was tucked up in bed, that Abby realized Penelope had mentioned the new padlock, knowing the comment would make sense to her. Had Penelope discovered that she and Jack had been spending time together, or had she simply guessed and let Abby walk into the trap? She tried to banish the thought that her boss knew all about their visit to her old home, rolled over and waited for sleep.

216

Chapter Fourteen

*The male bullfinch is a chubby, pretty finch with dusky
red plumage, grey wings and a black cap. It is a bit like
a robin on steroids (ask your mum what steroids are).
The female is paler, as if its colour has faded in the wash.
The bullfinch song is high and shrill – two short, squeaky
blasts like a PE teacher's whistle.*

— Note from Abby's notebook

The following morning Abby felt like her eyelids had been
superglued shut. She pulled herself wearily out of bed,
wishing she'd had the common sense not to agree to early
reception duty the day after the murmuration event, and
took Raffle for a walk along paths slick with frost. She stopped
in at the village store and flicked through the local paper,
even though Brad had told her his piece wouldn't appear
until the late edition because he needed time to do the
write-up and sort through the photographs. She would have
to wait.

She greeted Rosa and Stephan at the visitor centre, took

in their equally weary stances, and thanked them both for all their support.

'It's going to be easier from now on,' she said. 'It'll get warmer, being outside will be more fun for visitors, we won't be tensed up against the cold and the wildlife will follow suit. I saw my first daffodils on the walk in today, which is apt considering it's St David's Day.'

'I'm finalizing my spring menu specials,' Stephan added. 'Honey-and-lavender scones should go down a treat.'

'Ooh.' Rosa brightened instantly. 'If you need any tasters let me know.'

The morning was slow. It was still cold, despite the daffodils, and racing, tumultuous clouds were denying them the blue skies of yesterday. No wonder people were staying inside. By eleven o'clock, Jonny was back perusing the binoculars, paying particular attention to a new pair Rosa had ordered in the week before, and Octavia had appeared to talk about the previous evening, and also, Abby soon realized, to give her a telling-off for the lack of progress with the author talk.

'I've been rushed off my feet with this murmuration event,' she protested, which, at least for the previous two weeks, had been the truth. 'I haven't had a chance to ask him.'

'What about that afternoon in the pub? Don't look at me like that, Abigail, the whole village was there. It can't have escaped your notice.'

Abby shook her head, aware that other ears were pricked towards their conversation. 'He wasn't in a fit state to be cajoled into doing a talk that afternoon,' she said, then immediately regretted it.

'What state was he in?' Octavia asked.

'He wasn't very happy, that's all. I was trying to cheer him up.'

'And did you succeed? Is this turning into something we should know about?'

'No, definitely not.' Abby took a sip of too-hot tea and spluttered.

'Not turning into something, or we shouldn't know about it?' Rosa's smile was cheeky.

'Not turning into something,' Abby assured her. 'He's still a bit out on a limb, and I was being a good neighbour, that's all.'

'I saw him last night, I think,' Stephan said, approaching as he dried one of his vintage cake stands with a tea towel. 'He was wearing a beanie hat. I couldn't be sure it was him, but – why would he come to the event?'

'Why shouldn't he?' Octavia asked, her voice high with excitement. 'He's getting into the swing of Meadowgreen life, slowly coming out of his shell. This is excellent news.'

'I don't know about that,' Abby said, 'but he was definitely—'

'Jack asked me to give you this,' Penelope said, striding through the door and handing Abby a white envelope. She nodded greetings to everyone then swept into her office, throwing the visitor centre into momentary silence.

'Come on, Abby,' Octavia urged. 'Don't leave us in suspense.'

'I don't—' she started, and then gave in, realizing the futility of trying to argue. Why didn't he drop them off at her house, rather than at the visitor centre where they were pounced upon like lions on a fresh piece of meat? He knew where she lived now; he could easily have posted it there.

But she opened the envelope, wondering whether she should add some dramatic tension for her keen audience, and unfolded the stiff paper that had been pressed carefully into three. His sloping handwriting was as elegant as ever.

Dear Abby,

Well done for putting on an excellent display last night; did the starlings cost much to hire? I'm sorry I didn't come to see you afterwards. You were the centre of attention, and I didn't want to distract you.

Also, your educational walk has been most helpful, and the (grizzly) words are flowing. I can't thank you enough.

Lastly, I'm sure I saw a badger in the garden of Peacock Cottage two nights ago and am planning on holding a stakeout on Saturday evening to see if it returns. I wonder if you'd like to join me? This isn't a ruse, just an offer of some company, some badgers, possibly a bit of food. Think of it as a thank-you for all you've done for me.

JW

She folded the paper quickly, not daring to look at anyone.

'He wants you to go round and see his badger?' Octavia raised an unsubtle eyebrow.

Abby rolled her eyes. 'I told him how rare badger sightings were around here, so he clearly thinks that I'll be interested – which I am. It would be a wonderful discovery; I could write a blog about it for the website.'

'Leaving out some of the detail, I hope?'

'Octavia,' Abby sighed. 'There is nothing going on between Jack and me. After a rocky start, we seem to have found a bit of common ground. That's all.'

'You should definitely go,' Rosa said. 'I've seen some gorgeous badger merchandise in a catalogue that I'd love to order, and how great would it be if we could tie it in with a genuine sighting? Have Reston Marsh found badgers?'

Stephan shook his head. 'They have a night camera set up, but nothing concrete so far.'

'There you go, then, we could be a step ahead of *Wild Wonders*.'

Abby nodded, pretending to think about it. A couple of months ago, it would have been the thought of seeing a badger so close to the reserve that would have had her pulse racing, and of course it would be wonderful if Jack hadn't been mistaken. But a night in Jack Westcoat's company was the star attraction. The badger, if it reappeared, would be an added bonus.

'I won't be gone too long,' she told Raffle that Saturday evening as she rifled through her wardrobe. She picked a lilac cardigan and a white blouse with tiny blue forget-me-nots, over dark jeans and brown, calf-length boots. She kept her short hair loose, and added eyeliner, mascara and rose-pink lip gloss. She'd bought a bottle of wine and a salted caramel cake at the closest supermarket, and she put them in a tote bag, along with a night-vision scope Rosa had let her borrow on pain of death that she brought it back in perfect condition.

Raffle followed her into the living room, his head low in an Oscar-worthy display of sulking, so that Abby risked dog hair all over her outfit giving him an extra-long cuddle and settling him on the rug in front of the fireplace.

Doing up her jacket, she left the house and made her way quickly along the village road and into the woods, turning on her torch as she left the streetlights behind. At six-thirty it was close to being dark, and Abby couldn't wait for the days to stretch out towards summer, for the heavy warmth of the spring sun on her face. Peacock Cottage looked cosy and inviting, an outside light next to the front door welcoming her; it was the first time Abby had seen it switched on, and the thought that it was for her made her heart skip.

She knocked on the door, heard footsteps padding down the corridor and then Jack was in front of her, wearing a black shirt, open at the neck, jeans with frayed hems, and black socks. He looked completely relaxed, free of the tension in his shoulders and jaw that she had come to expect. He gave her a warm smile and invited her in.

'Hi,' she said, as he took her bag, giving her space to shrug off her jacket.

'Glad you could come.' He hesitated for a moment, then leant down and kissed her cheek, the gesture somehow misplaced, as if he should have done it on the doorstep or not at all.

'Thank you for inviting me,' she said. 'I bought some things.' She pointed to the bag and Jack looked inside, his eyes widening.

'That's very kind. You didn't need to. Is that your scope?'

'No, I borrowed it, but I thought we couldn't take the stakeout very seriously if we didn't have the right equipment. Show me where you saw the badger.'

'Right, of course. This way.' He led her down the corridor.

The walls were painted peacock blue which, while pretty, made it seem dark and narrow, but then it opened up into a bright, compact kitchen. As Jack had mentioned, the appliances looked like they could do with updating, but everything was clean, and a couple of arty postcards on the fridge added a splash of colour. Abby wondered if they were purely for decoration, or if they had been sent to Jack by friends and family in London. On the far wall, a long window over the sink looked out on the back garden, and next to it was the glass-panelled back door.

'I was rinsing a tumbler before bed,' Jack said, leading her to the sink, 'and I hadn't bothered to put the light on, which meant I could see the garden. The long grass over there was shaking, as if something heavy was walking through it, and I'm sure I saw a flash of white, like the stripe on their noses, but it didn't come onto the lawn so I couldn't be sure.'

'It sounds promising,' Abby nodded. Jack didn't need to know that her only encounter with a badger had been terrifying. She hadn't been expecting it before, hadn't been prepared, but now she was – for a badger sighting, at least. She could smell Jack's expensive aftershave, and also something delicious that made her stomach rumble.

'It's just chilli,' he said when she glanced around the kitchen. 'I hope that's OK?'

'It smells amazing.'

'Let me open the wine and get you a drink while it breathes. What would you like? I have gin and tonic, vodka tonic, whisky. No beer I'm afraid – I should have thought of that.'

'No, that's fine. A gin and tonic would be lovely, thank you.'

'Let me show you – here.' He led her back down the corridor, turning right into the room where Abby had so often seen the light glowing from outside.

This room was painted mid blue with white cornicing, but the soft glow of two standard lamps, the pale-blue blanket flung over the back of the grey fabric sofa and the bold peacock print on the wall made it seem snug rather than gloomy. In one corner there was an expensive-looking office chair and a wooden desk. On it sat a closed MacBook and a Moleskine notebook, their edges perfectly aligned. Abby also noticed a sharing-sized bag of peanut M&Ms, and the

223

thought of him crunching his way through them while he wrote made her smile.

'Are you happy to wait here while I sort out the drinks?' he asked.

'Of course.' She sank into a plush sofa cushion that was softer than it looked, while Jack returned to the kitchen. She couldn't detect the musty smell he'd mentioned, and thought that his presence, his life in the house, must have obliterated it. He had helped the cottage breathe again.

Sitting on the back of the sofa was a small, cuddly hippopotamus. It looked old and tatty, but it still had two beady eyes and a pink tongue protruding from its mouth. Abby reached up for it, squeezing its soft fabric. She would never have pictured Jack as a cuddly-toy person – not in a million years.

'Here you go.' He came back with their drinks and Abby hurriedly put the hippo back in its place.

Jack sat next to her, clinking his glass against her own, and she thought he hadn't noticed.

'That's Shalimar,' he said, pointing at the hippo. 'I've had him for most of my life. The one toy that I couldn't bear to get rid of.'

'He's lovely,' Abby said. 'Why Shalimar?'

'My dad named him after the river in Flanders and Swann's "Hippopotamus Song". You know,' he added, when Abby frowned. '*Mud, mud, glorious mud* – you haven't heard of it?'

'It sounds vaguely familiar. It's certainly something I can relate to,' she said. 'You have to love mud to do my job – or not hate it, at least. You'll have to play it for me.'

'I could do that, though Flanders and Swann songs are . . . an acquired taste. Not the kind of music I listen to on a daily basis.'

'And definitely not when you write,' Abby said. 'I remember that. No music.'

'No. I'd forgotten I'd told you that. Oh – except, it was that first meeting, wasn't it?'

'Yup.' Abby grinned at the memory. She was determined not to be awkward or hesitant tonight. They were simply two people getting to know each other, looking for a badger together. It sounded ludicrous, but it was the truth. 'I'm sorry I didn't get to talk to you at the murmuration event,' she added. 'I spotted you, but it was so busy afterwards. I can't even remember what time I got home.'

'I'm not detecting nearly enough smugness,' he said. 'It was a triumph, surely?'

'It went as well as could be expected,' Abby said, but Jack shook his head pityingly.

'You need to blow your own trumpet more. I know you're dogged about that place, that you're probably already thinking about the next event, but give yourself space to take it in, to be proud of what you've achieved.'

'You don't think I'm proud of myself?'

'You don't show it, but of course I have no idea what's going on inside your head.'

Thank God, Abby thought.

'I picked up a copy of the paper,' Jack continued. 'It was a stellar write-up, and the photos were impressive. Has it increased footfall?'

'It's been two days!' Abby said, laughing. 'But I hope it will – lots of the people who came on the walk want to show their friends, and I've seen more cars in the car park at closing time, so some are obviously going to see it for themselves. I've spoken to Penelope about opening later for the next few weeks, so we can answer questions or direct anyone who comes specifically to see it, but she's adamant it would be too expensive. I've told her I don't mind staying later without extra pay – it's only for another few weeks – but she still won't do it.'

'You don't want to wear yourself out,' Jack said. 'But it seems strange that she's so reluctant when it's likely to help your cause.'

'She's properly worried, Jack. She told me—' She stopped, remembering Penelope's request for confidentiality.

'What?' Jack leaned forward, his forearm resting along the back of the sofa, fingertips touching Shalimar.

'She said . . .' Surely when Penelope had told her to keep it quiet, she had meant only from reserve staff – and obviously Octavia. Jack wasn't the kind of person to go gossiping, even if he had people in Meadowgreen he could gossip with. 'She hinted that she was under pressure to sell Swallowtail House, that the reserve is still costing much more than it's making.'

'Really? God. Leo's never mentioned anything about the situation being that bad, and I get the impression he knows Penelope well. He said that my moving up here would be mutually beneficial, that Penelope needed a tenant, and I needed to hide away, write a brilliant book and see if I could drag my career out of the dungeon.' He gave her a wry smile. It was the first time he'd referred to his past with any kind of humour.

'And are you – is it going OK? You said your writing was going well?'

'It's all coming together. And it could be what I need; it could work. I'm aiming to be a bit more daring with this one, step out of my comfort zone. There's still a crime to be solved, but – hopefully – it has more depth than my previous novels. And it's the first one set outside London, which has given it a completely different feel.'

'Central London doesn't have many nature reserves,' Abby said.

'Exactly,' Jack nodded. 'But it's a risk, and if it's a flop then the press will have a field day, saying I've been permanently scarred by what I did, my conscience coming back to bite me. It's a sorry situation and makes me wonder why I got into it in the first place.'

'Because you love writing?' Abby suggested. 'Working on the reserve isn't always comfortable; it can be cold and damp, you can get bitten by mosquitos in the summer or end up waist deep in mud, but I wouldn't do anything else.'

'But none of those things are of your own making,' Jack said. 'They're accepted side effects of working with nature. I was stupid. All of this could have been avoided so easily.' He let out a frustrated sigh. 'Anyway, this isn't round two of the pity party, this is badger watch. Shall we set up after dinner?'

'Sounds good.' Abby sipped her gin and tonic, her fizzing nerves given a respite when Jack went to dish up the food. He returned with wine and glasses, poured two large measures and disappeared again, coming back with steaming bowls of chilli and rice, the soured cream and cheese separate so Abby could add them herself. He placed everything on the glass coffee table.

'I didn't think this through,' he said. 'The dining room is full of things I brought with me and haven't bothered to unpack. I started clearing it this afternoon, but the table is pretty rickety. I thought laps would be safer, if not exactly good host behaviour.'

'Laps are fine,' Abby said. 'You don't have to stand on ceremony with me. Being here is enough.'

It was a couple of seconds before she realized what she'd said. Jack was sprinkling cheese onto his dinner, not meeting her eye. Being here was enough *what*? She cringed inwardly, and ate a mouthful of chilli.

'This is delicious. Do you do much cooking?'

'I ate out a lot in London,' he said, 'so I've had to get back into the habit since I've been here and being on your own makes it awkward sometimes. It's nice, sharing food with someone. It's a long time since I've done that – apart from the chips in the Skylark, of course.'

'Of course,' Abby said. 'You weren't . . . attached, before this, back in London?'

'Not for a while now.' He winced as if that, too, held painful memories.

'Are you lonely?' she asked.

He shrugged. 'I'm a writer, so time alone is productive, but of course I wouldn't choose to live a hermit's existence. When I moved up here it felt like a suitable punishment that I kept alive by being furious about everything – walkers, pheasants, forthright women turning up on my doorstep.' He gave her a quick smile. 'More recently it's been difficult, not being able to call on my friends on a rainy afternoon and go to the pub. What about you? I know you have Raffle, and that you're close to Rosa and the others, but the village isn't that big. Do you ever feel isolated?'

Abby finished her mouthful, taking her time before answering. 'I love it here,' she said, her pulse thrumming even though she was the one who'd brought the subject up. 'And I don't mind being single. In some ways, it's a lot simpler. That sounds awful, doesn't it? Like I'm uncaring, but it's not that. There are things in my past . . . family traits that I don't want to emulate or go looking for.'

Jack left his fork in his bowl, the food momentarily forgotten. 'Like what?'

Abby closed her eyes. She hadn't meant to be this frank with him tonight, to travel down this path. 'My mum and dad had a very turbulent relationship,' she settled on. 'I used to escape into the fields at the back of our house and spend hours there, looking for birds and butterflies, staying out of their way. Mum always told me they were just passionate about each other, but as I grew up, I realized it wasn't healthy, the way they were. My dad, particularly.'

'Your bad memories,' Jack whispered, piecing it together instantly. 'Was it ever physical?'

Abby put her plate on the coffee table. 'Sometimes,' she admitted. 'Especially towards the end. Mum was the main target, but sometimes I got in the middle. They divorced when I was fifteen.' She stared at her knees. 'I'm worried that I might – that things will repeat themselves. I've made some bad decisions with previous relationships.'

Jack didn't speak for so long that she wondered if he was working out how to ask her to leave. Instead, he placed his hand lightly over hers. 'I'm so sorry, Abby.'

'It's not your fault.'

'And yet here you are, telling me something so personal, and difficult, something that has affected your whole life, and all you know about my past is that I'm like him, that I was capable of—'

'No, Jack, I don't think – I mean, I don't know you, really, but . . .'

He looked troubled, weary, suddenly, his forehead crumpled in a frown.

'I don't believe you're like that,' she continued. 'It's hard to explain, but I . . . I've seen first-hand what leads to violence,

229

I've sensed it, balled up inside my dad, so I was always on tenterhooks, ready to rush out of the back door if I needed to get away. I don't feel that with you, not remotely. Not even knowing that you did it that one time.'

She saw his Adam's apple bob. 'It was the biggest mistake of my life,' he said. 'I've regretted it ever since, which I know is no excuse. But you don't trust yourself not to follow your parents' path? You can be sure about me, who you've known for all of five minutes, but you don't think you know *yourself* that well? Abby, you are one of the kindest, most thoughtful people I've ever met. You're prepared to look beyond someone's history, to really see them for who they are, but you're also confident and questioning, you don't suffer fools gladly. I cannot imagine you making a bad decision.'

She felt a lump form at the back of her throat. 'But I have in the past. What if I make the same mistakes again?'

Her words hung in the air, the insinuation that he was one of those mistakes. But Jack *was* different. To Darren, to her father, to anyone she'd met.

'I don't mean . . .' She sighed. 'I'm sure about this. I want to be here, Jack. With you, and the badger.' She smiled, trying to lighten the mood.

'And I can't think of anyone I'd rather spend tonight with, even if I had the choice of all my friends and family in London.'

'That's only because none of them would care about your nocturnal wildlife.'

'Well, of course there's that, but it is also my birthday.'

'What?' she sat up straight. 'Really?'

'Thirty-four today. Happy birthday Jack Westcoat; what a year you've had,' he said dryly, topping up their wine glasses.

'I'm glad I brought cake then, but you should have told me before!'

'There was no reason to, but I am glad you're here. Even if – God, I'm sorry, Abby. If I'd had any idea about your dad, about what you'd been through, I never would have—'

'What? Sent me a note at the reserve, forcing me to come out and see you? Driven me home that night, taken me for coffee, let me go with you to Swallowtail House? I have to have the opportunity to make up my own mind about people. If I let everyone else dictate my life, then I'll never get it right.'

He shook his head. 'You're worried about being in harm's way again, and yet you're trusting your instincts about me, despite what you've read in the press. Why do I get the benefit of the doubt? What makes me different to your previous bad decisions? If it's because you're consciously putting what happened behind you, as you told me to do, then doesn't that prove you're stronger now, that you don't need to worry about the past repeating itself any more?'

She couldn't respond, a wave of emotion threatening to overwhelm her. How could he be so open about it, and call her out on her contradictions without blinking? She inhaled quickly, and it came out as a gasp.

'Abby.' He lifted his hand to her cheek, his thumb grazing her cheekbone. It felt like a lit match against her skin. His expression was tender, but there was something determined about it too. 'You need to know that I would never—'

The doorbell rang.

Jack dropped his hand. 'Who the hell?'

Abby sat back on the sofa, her heart pounding, as he went to answer the door. She could see him open it but not who was beyond, and then there was a loud, familiar voice and Abby closed her eyes. Octavia.

'Oh Jack, we heard about your badger vigil and thought we'd bring supplies! Crisps and popcorn, some of that delicious local cider – you must have tried it by now, but if not, tonight's your lucky night!'

Octavia bustled into the living room and did a visual sweep of their food bowls, the wine glasses, and the dip in the sofa where, until moments before, Jack had been sitting beside her.

'Octavia, what are you doing here?' Abby asked.

'I've come to join the hunt, and I'm not the only one.' Rosa and Jonny stepped into the room, Rosa giving her a bashful wave, Jonny nodding hello. Jack stood in the doorway, his arms folded, and Abby was treated to the scowl she had got to know so well but hadn't seen for a while.

The greetings were stilted, and Jack stood aside, slightly stunned as Octavia took control, rooting through the kitchen cupboards, finding crockery and glassware.

'Hope we're not interrupting anything?' she asked brightly, carrying a tray with five glasses full of amber, sparkling liquid into the living room.

'Oh no,' Jack said. 'Of course not.'

After Octavia had spent half an hour telling Jack about the chapel library and extolling his virtues and the impact he would have on the place – with a few digs thrown in Abby's direction that she should have already suggested the idea to him – Abby convinced them that they needed to move into the kitchen. She took the night-vision scope out of her bag and helped Jonny set it up. He was more embarrassed than any of them, and she wondered how Octavia had convinced him to come in the first place. She turned off the light and then, leaving the three of them peering out at the garden, took Jack's hand and pulled him down the corridor to the living room.

'I'm so sorry,' she said. 'I had no idea they would turn up.'

'How did they even know about it? Did you tell them you were coming?'

'I didn't need to. The problem, when you leave a letter for me at the reserve, is that I barely ever get to open it alone. And considering your first one was a complaint, everyone, including Penelope, is always extra keen to know what you're going to say next.'

Jack's eyes widened. 'So, all my messages to you, they've been read by everyone at the reserve?'

'Most of them,' Abby said. 'I managed to squirrel a couple away before anyone else saw them.'

'God.'

She could see the flicker of a smile threatening to break free. 'What?'

'I was just thinking of some of the things I *almost* wrote.' His voice was low, and Abby's skin prickled. She wanted desperately to ask him what he'd nearly written, but knew that if he told her, even if he was making it up, even if what he said wasn't remotely seductive, she couldn't listen to that deep, amused voice for much longer without taking drastic action.

'Jack Westcoat,' she said, mock-shocked.

'Abby Field?' He took a step towards her, which was more of a shuffle because there was barely space between them as it was. She inhaled his heady scent, and found her fingers reaching out to take hold of his, testing that connection before she dared make another, deeper one. He bent his head towards her and she held her breath, replaying his words in her mind: *Why do I get the benefit of the doubt?* She could spend hours answering that question, but as his lips found hers, and his hand cupped the back of her head to bring her closer, all her thoughts dissolved to nothing. She pressed herself against him, slid her hands up his back as his kiss went deeper.

He pulled away, and then brushed his lips across her cheek, kissing her earlobe, her jaw, her neck. He whispered her name against her skin.

She wrapped her arms around his waist, closed her eyes and—

'Badger! There's a badger!'

Abby jumped, almost bashing Jack's chin with her shoulder, and as he sighed, then stepped back, his fingers trailing along her arm as if reluctant to let her go, she had time to think that if there *had* been a badger, Octavia's screech would have sent it running for the hills.

She followed Jack to the kitchen where the badger, predictably, was gone.

'Dear Lord!' Octavia pressed a hand to her ample bosom. 'I almost got a heart attack! And I swear it looked right at me. On a scale of one to ten, how vicious are they?'

Abby looked to Rosa for confirmation. 'I saw it,' she said.

'And I got a great view through the scope.' Jonny was grinning, his shyness momentarily forgotten. 'I might have to get one of these.'

'But viciousness, people?' Octavia prompted. 'What if I encounter it on the way home?'

'It would run a mile,' Abby said. 'From anyone. They only blunder across people accidentally, and,' she added, thinking of her own encounter, 'they're much more scared of us than we are of them.'

'I'm not sure that's true,' Octavia replied. 'Honestly, my

loves, if I'd realized how dangerous your jobs were, I would have given you more credit.'

Abby laughed, feeling giddy at the absurdity of the situation. 'Badgers aren't dangerous, Octavia. They're beautiful creatures, and I'm glad you got to see one.'

'You missed it, though.' She folded her arms, her eyes boring into Jack.

'We were talking,' he said evenly. 'It's not a large kitchen, and I chose to give priority to my guests.'

'So, if Abby's not a guest, what is she?'

'We were finishing up a conversation from earlier,' Abby said, hoping the lie wasn't obvious. 'I've got more chance than most to see a badger while I'm at work, so I'm not too disappointed.'

'Besides,' Rosa added lightly, 'you can always come back another night.'

'She'd be more than welcome,' Jack replied, and four pairs of eyes looked at him. He ducked his head and ran a hand through his hair.

'Well, that's me done in,' Octavia said. 'Come on, Abigail, I'll walk you home.'

'I can take her,' Jack cut in.

Octavia patted his arm. 'It's no problem. You've had a drink, Jack, and we're neighbours – save you the walk back on your own. And it's getting late isn't it, my love?' she turned to Abby. 'You working tomorrow? I thought so. Come on, we can all go together.'

Abby was on the verge of protesting. She wanted to stay, to be alone with Jack and continue what they had started, but whispers of their earlier conversation returned. She might not see him as violent, but the indisputable fact was that he had attacked someone. How well did she really know him?

235

And, more importantly, could she trust herself to make the right decision? She was convinced that he wasn't another mistake, that he was kind and trustworthy and that this evening hadn't been an act, but hadn't she told herself the same thing in the past? Believed her mum when she'd promised her that Dad had just been angry, that it was a one-off and wouldn't happen again?

And if she did put her fear aside and they started something, what would happen to Meadowsweet, and the looming possibility of Penelope having to sell Swallowtail House to pay for it? She had taken her eye off the ball for a single morning, and her boss had noticed. Could she really allow herself to give in to Jack? Because her feelings for him weren't fleeting or dismissible, they had become all consuming, and that was something Abby didn't know how to deal with, let alone have time for.

'Now, Jack,' Octavia said at the door, picking invisible fluff off his shirt. 'You haven't forgotten what you promised, have you?'

Jack sighed. 'What was that, Octavia?'

'That you will grace my humble library with your presence. I'll be in touch with a selection of dates. So lovely to finally meet you properly. Come on, my love.' She took Abby's hand and pulled her gently down the path.

Abby let go and rushed back to Jack. He was standing on the doorstep, the light of the hallway behind him.

'I'm sorry,' she said, wrapping her arms round his waist, ignoring the shiver that went through her as she felt his solid torso against her. She didn't give him time to reciprocate, instead kissed him on the cheek and stepped back. 'Thank you for dinner.'

His smile was resigned. 'My pleasure. Hopefully we can

try again soon, perhaps without the support party in tow?'

'I'd like that,' she said, despite all the reasoning she'd just done with herself. 'Goodnight Jack – and happy birthday.'

'Goodnight, Abby.'

She turned and ran back to where Octavia, Jonny and Rosa were waiting, sensing, rather than seeing Jack close the door of Peacock Cottage. When she glanced behind her, the outside light was still on. It seemed important somehow, as if it symbolized his hope that she would return.

Abby thought of all the things she had to deal with. There was the reserve, Penelope's new warning and her own conviction, now she'd been inside the House of Birds and Butterflies, that she didn't want it to end up in the hands of some faceless stranger; Jack's growing presence in her life, her attraction getting stronger all the time, and the fact that she was unable to stay away from him, accepting every invite or chance to meet like an eager, hopeful puppy; the knowledge that he felt something for her too, that if it hadn't been for Octavia and the others, the evening would have taken a different turn; their conflicting pasts, the way her parents had shaped hers and the fact that Jack now knew this, and could use it as a way to punish himself all over again; the realization that Octavia would corral her into helping with the library event, making use of her expertise and finding another reason for the two of them to spend time together.

Nothing was simple, or straightforward, or easy.

But spring was coming, the daffodils were creeping up through the hardened soil, and soon the woods would be awash with bluebells. Birdsong would fill the air, the robins and ducks, finches and harriers would start searching for mates, and as long as Abby did her job well, visitors would flock to see it all, to lift their faces up to the sun, smell the spring flowers and let life's troubles drift away.

She had to do her job and forget about Jack; that was the bottom line. A few months ago, Abby wouldn't have let anything get in the way of her event plans, risk assessments and craft activity ideas – there had been nothing more important to her than Meadowsweet's survival. But now, even the simple joys of spring, new shoots and mating birds and fresh, burgeoning life, led her thoughts back to Jack.

As Octavia took her arm and they followed the brightness of the torch's beam through the woods, Abby thought that perhaps it was time for her to step out of the darkness and have her own chance at regrowth. But was Jack Westcoat the right person to do it with? Could a man like that, charming and sexy and warm as he increasingly was, be good for her? Her heart told her yes, but Abby knew from experience that trusting her heart didn't always end well. And her head told her that he was solitary, scowling, so often lost in a fictional world of misery and gruesome deaths, with a troubled past and an uncertain future – one which, she was sure, had Peacock House only as a temporary solution.

No, Jack Westcoat wasn't the easy option. He wasn't simple or straightforward but, Abby wondered, knowing she was betraying her logical side even as she thought it, did any of that matter? Because, when it came down to it, even in the face of a failing nature reserve that threatened the jobs of her friends, the livelihood and estate of her boss, he was all she could think about.

Part 3

Twilight Song

Chapter Fifteen

Badgers are nocturnal creatures, which means they only come out at night. They're very shy, with dark fur, beady eyes and a white stripe down their nose. They're quite large – about the size of a cocker spaniel – and they can't see very well but their sense of smell and hearing is very good, so wear dark clothes and stay very quiet if you are trying to see one. They growl and play fight and make a lot of noise when they're eating, and bushes rustle when they walk through the undergrowth. Coming across one in the dark can be very scary, but remember, the badger will be more scared of you than you are of it. Probably.

— Note from Abby's notebook

Abby's hands were covered in lard, seed and, most unpleasantly of all, dead mealworms. The children standing at the picnic tables in Meadowsweet Nature Reserve's sunny outdoor area seemed entirely happy to bury their fingers – and forearms in some cases – deep in the mixture, their parents less so. There was one small girl of about five whose

241

face was also partially covered, and Gavin, who was ostensibly there to help and who had two girls of his own, was trying desperately not to laugh while her mum picked buggy lard out of her hair.

A robin – was it Bob? – was hovering nearby, hopping between table and floor, aware that there would be rich pickings once the children had finished their craft session.

'How's everyone getting on?' Abby asked, after she had shaped little Benjy's mixture into a ball and wiped her hands on an old towel. 'Does anyone need help?' About ten arms went into the air, and Abby grinned at Gavin before they each went to the raised hand nearest them.

'We did this at the other place, didn't we?' one of the children said to their dad. 'It was *much* better, we had a whole tub to take home, and there were TV cameras and everything.'

Abby caught the man's eye and he smiled apologetically. Abby tried not to take offence at the boy's words, but the knowledge that Reston Marsh was not only threatening the future of Meadowsweet but also running similar activities to them, was a blow she didn't need.

It was a sunny Saturday that was also, as Gavin was at pains to remind everyone, St Patrick's Day. The plan was for the reserve staff to head to the Skylark once they had finished work, but Abby's sister Tessa was coming to visit, and Abby didn't want to share her with her friends on this occasion.

As the session came to an end and the children left, carrying their lard balls carefully in cardboard boxes, Abby's phone beeped. It was Octavia.

T-minus ten days until Jack Westcoat liftoff!! What is there left to do?

Abby huffed in frustration. Octavia was organizing the

author event in the library, and should know exactly what there was left to do. Besides, Abby only had an hour before her afternoon workshop, making nest boxes with older children, was due to start, and she was desperate for a sandwich. She helped Gavin clear up the picnic tables and headed into the visitor centre.

She was surprised to see Penelope poring over the computer on the reception desk and approached quietly, studying the neatness of the woman's grey bun, the rigidity of her thin shoulders and, when she was close enough, what her boss was looking at. It was the events page on the reserve website.

Abby felt her hands go clammy. 'Can I help?' she asked softly.

Penelope turned to her with steely eyes. 'It's looking a bit thin, isn't it? For the next few months, at least. This is the spring, Abby, when blossoms bloom and chrysalises become butterflies and birds sing gloriously, and we should be maximizing on that.'

'Yes, I know,' Abby started, 'but this is only the beginning. I'm a bit behind with the website, but I have a whole series of workshops to add, and there are six schools confirmed for the last two weeks of term.'

'And grand plans?' Penelope asked. 'The incentives and membership boosts that will secure our future, long term? Expanding on the walks is all very well, but you're not thinking big enough, scaling it up in a way that will truly make a difference.'

'A camping event,' she said quickly, because that was a grand plan she'd had, it just wasn't that well-formed yet. 'I thought we could hold it on the field behind the meadow. We can combine nature trails and stargazing, run activities and binocular displays. Stephan and the café could cater, and I can organize local, organic producers to come and sell honey, veg and meat. It would be like a mini festival.'

'Excellent,' Penelope said. 'I'd like to see your proposal for that on my desk by Tuesday, complete with how we're going to end that event with noticeably increased membership numbers.'

Three days away. Shit. 'A – a formal proposal?'

'Desperate times call for desperate measures. *Wild Wonders* is gathering momentum, and we're limping along at a much slower pace, despite the murmuration event and your other, select, successes. It's a few bright stars in a black sky, Abby, when it needs to be a galaxy if we're to have any chance of survival.'

Abby nodded, feeling the weight of Penelope's words. 'And Swallowtail?' she asked quietly.

'I am holding on,' Penelope said, 'my teeth and claws bared, but until I can show the bank that Meadowsweet is firmly in the black, then we're teetering on a precipice. It's not an ideal position to be in.'

'I know,' Abby said quietly. 'I'm sorry.'

'Don't be sorry.' Penelope stood up. She was a good few inches taller than Abby and intimidating in more ways than Abby had fingers to count. 'Just be better. Are any birds nesting in the library, for example?'

'What? No, I don't think so.' She gave a half-hearted laugh.

'That's interesting to know.'

Abby's gaze fell to the floor. Penelope knew that she'd been helping Octavia with the library event. She hoped that Penelope wouldn't also have realized Abby's main motivation for agreeing.

When Penelope spoke again, her voice was softer. 'I've

spent some time with Jack recently, and I'm led to believe that he's doing better than he was. Both by the man himself and someone I'm close to, who knows him well.'

'The person you thought might be able help?' Their previous conversation on this topic was etched into Abby's mind because it was so unlike Penelope to show a caring attitude – and also because Jack Westcoat was her favourite subject, despite all her best intentions.

'Indeed. His agent, Leo Ravensberg. We're acquainted, and both invested in Jack's wellbeing. If he's agreed to Octavia's event, then he's made his bed and will have to lie in it. But it indicates that he's prepared to show his face here, that he's no longer hiding himself away, and that can only be a good thing. There's no need for you to concern yourself with him.' She walked purposefully back to her office, closing the door quietly behind her.

Abby let her arms slide along the desk until she could lean her forehead on them. 'Shit. Shitting shit.'

'What kind of impression are you trying to give?' a familiar voice asked. 'Meadowsweet zombie land?'

Abby stood up, brushing her hair off her face. 'Sorry, I was just—'

'Swearing softly into the desk? What's wrong?' Rosa looked at her with sympathetic dark eyes.

'The usual,' Abby said. 'Penelope doesn't think I'm working hard enough, that I need to up my game. I have to write a formal proposal about my camping idea – by Tuesday!'

Rosa wrinkled her button nose, obscuring some of the freckles. 'But you've been doing a wonderful job.'

'Not wonderful enough, obviously.' She rubbed her eyes. 'And now I have half an hour until workshop number two, and I haven't had any lunch.'

'Go and get a sandwich. I'll book people in. Are you coming to the pub later? It looks like you could do with a chat.'

'Tessa's coming over,' Abby said. 'So I'm going to play it by ear.'

'Bring her too!' Rosa urged. 'It's been ages since I saw your sister, and if you don't come it'll be me and Octavia against the boys.'

'You and Octavia are more than a match for them, but I'll see. Thanks, Rosa.' She hurried off in search of a sandwich, wondering if she could face another evening of Octavia talking about how wonderful Jack Westcoat was and how he was going to singlehandedly save Meadowgreen's library from an early demise. If only she could get him to save Meadowsweet Nature Reserve as well, instead of just putting her off the job of doing it, then maybe she wouldn't be feeling quite so worried.

'You look like a lovesick teenager,' were the first words that Tessa said as she stepped over the threshold into Abby's homely front room.

Abby almost dropped the bottle of wine her sister had handed her, before she took it into the kitchen while Tessa made a fuss of Raffle. Her rescue husky was friends with everyone but had a special place in his heart for Tessa, who brought him organic treats from a pet shop in Bury St Edmunds.

'Uh-oh,' Tessa said, as Abby poured the wine and handed her a glass. 'Have I hit on something? Has the impregnable Abby Field finally let her defences down?'

This was not how Abby had imagined the subject coming up, so she diverted it. 'I'm not lovesick, I'm in trouble. At work. Not trying hard enough with the events, according to

Penelope. As far from a gold star as it's possible to be.' She poured crisps into a bowl and brought them into the living room, where Raffle was waiting eagerly. 'Not for you.' She rubbed his nose as she placed the bowl on the coffee table.

Raffle looked up imploringly and then settled on the rug, his nose on his paws.

'How is that even possible?' Tessa asked, sitting opposite her sister. 'Haven't you spent the whole day doing children's activities? I couldn't cope with that and I've got two of my own. Neil put a brave face on it when I left this evening, but Daisy was having a tantrum because her pink Rapunzel socks were in the washing machine. I thought about staying to help him, but then realized I didn't want to.' She smiled brightly and Abby laughed, always amazed by her sister's relaxed attitude to parenthood. Daisy and Willow didn't often go in for tantrums, and they adored their mum, who looked like she spent her days lounging by a pool with a good book instead of looking after two young children.

'Poor old Neil,' Abby said. 'But I am glad to have you to myself. The others have gone to the Skylark to drink Guinness and listen to Gavin's awful fake Irish accent.'

'We can go if you'd like to?' Tessa said.

Abby shook her head. 'I want you to myself. I wanted to spend time with my sister.'

Tessa sat forward on the sofa, suddenly wary. 'Have you seen Mum recently? Did she say something? What about Dad – has he been in touch?'

'No, nothing like that.' Abby took a long sip of wine, trying to fortify herself. How could she tell her sister how she felt about Jack when she hadn't even mentioned that he existed before? He'd been in Meadowgreen for six months, twisting her mind into knots, and yet she hadn't confided in the person she was closest to in the world. It had been part of her plan to let her feelings for him run their course, but instead the opposite had happened.

'What, then? Come on Abby, you can't hold out on me. This isn't just about work, I can tell.'

Abby glanced at Raffle. He cocked his head, as if he was also waiting.

'Jack Westcoat,' she said, because that seemed like the best place to start.

Tessa frowned, and smoothed her artfully dyed lilac hair from her face. 'Jack Westcoat? That writer who beat his friend up at some award thing last year? What's he got to do with the price of fish?'

'He didn't *beat him up*,' Abby said. 'There was one punch, and things were – are – very complicated between them.'

Tessa folded her arms. 'Why are you defending a famous author? Has Penelope's negativity sent you round the twist?'

'He's here, in Meadowgreen,' Abby said hurriedly, ripping off the metaphorical plaster. 'He's staying in the cottage close to the reserve, and I – I've spent a bit of time with him, gone on a couple of walks.'

'What?' Her sister's voice was low, wary.

'He complained about the reserve, and when I went to challenge him, we – I don't know, Tessa, we've helped each other out. He's been miserable, and I tripped one night, walking back in the dark, and he was—'

'You like him,' Tessa said sharply.

'I don't know.' Abby rubbed her cheeks.

'He hit someone, Abs. He was pissed off about something, and he used his fists to deal with it.'

'He regrets it, more than anything.'

'And isn't that what Dad said every time he got into another row with Mum?'

'That was different,' Abby said. 'So completely different to Jack. Whenever I've been with him, I haven't felt remotely threatened, or that he's even capable of something like that. Not even when he was angry about the reserve.'

'But he is capable though, isn't he? And from what I've read, his past isn't exactly rosy. Didn't he get up to all sorts with that friend when they were at uni together?'

Abby scooted forward, until she was precariously balanced on the edge of her chair. 'All anyone knows is what was reported in the press. How can we judge him when we know nothing about what really happened?'

'But presumably if you're spending time with him, he's spoken to you about it?'

'Not a lot,' Abby admitted. 'But he's been really down, Tessa. He's hiding away to write a new book that he's hoping will fix things, but he doesn't know anyone and he's isolated. He needs a friend.'

'And so kind-hearted Abby Field drops everything as usual to help out someone else, someone who's angry and upset, who's lost control in the past. It doesn't sound like a great balance to me. It sounds like he's using you.' Tessa sighed heavily. 'This is so familiar, Abby. You're walking over old ground, trying to save someone who isn't worth it. Why don't you think about yourself for a change and find someone who'll look after you and won't behave like a prick?' Tessa's eyes were bright, two points of colour on her porcelain cheeks.

'I *am* thinking of myself,' Abby shot back, stunned by her sister's outburst. 'I like him. A lot. And I'm struggling with all the things you've said, and I don't know how he feels about me, not really. But I thought I could trust you. I haven't

249

told another soul and I wanted some reassurance, someone who'd talk it over with me, not – not attack him, or me, in the process!' She felt tears spring to her eyes, as unexpected as her sister's vehemence.

'Shit,' Tessa murmured, and then she was sitting cross-legged on the floor in front of her. 'I'm sorry, but I worry about you. Out here, just you and Raffle. It seems . . . lonely, to me.'

'And yet the moment I find someone I like, you warn me off him. You don't even know him!'

'You're right, I don't. But I do know *of* him, and I can't help but be concerned about that, can I? Doesn't he live in London anyway? Surely he's only here temporarily. You spend so much time saying you can't deal with a new relationship, that you're scared about falling for the wrong guy, and then you find this . . . this—'

'He's not a violent person. It was a one-off.'

'How do you *know* Abby? How do you know he won't turn, and then you'll just put up with it, like you did with Dad?'

Anger blossomed in Abby's chest. 'I didn't put up with it! I couldn't leave, could I? Not like you, disappearing off to university. I had nowhere to go, Tessa! And if they hadn't divorced, it would have gone on, getting worse and worse with me in the middle, without you there so we could look after each other. Don't you dare say I put up with it!'

'Sorry, sorry.' Tessa took both of Abby's hands in hers. 'I know I – I wasn't there. I'm sorry.' Tears filled her eyes too, and Abby bit her lip, trying not to give in to hers.

'Jack isn't like that,' Abby whispered. 'I'm convinced he isn't.' She thought back to his words, to him questioning why she could be so sure of him, and yet unsure of herself.

Tessa sighed. 'So, you're going out with him?'

Abby shook her head. 'No, we're just . . . friends.'

'Then, there *is* something holding you back?' Tessa's voice was soft.

'I was hoping to talk to you, to see what you thought before I took it further. Now I know.'

'I just want to protect you. I couldn't bear it if you got hurt again. Tell me more about him. Tell me what he's like.'

Abby pressed her fingers against her lips. She felt numb that she couldn't, after all, confide in her sister. 'It's OK,' she said. 'Forget I mentioned him. Tell me about Willow and Daisy, how are they getting on? How's the pond? Is Willow still frightened of the frogspawn?'

Tessa stared at her, then wiped elegantly at her cheek and slipped into a familiar, if stilted, monologue about her happy family life.

Abby tried not to let sadness creep in. She'd been expecting Tessa – who was always so adamant Abby needed some romance in her life – to dispel her fears about Jack and encourage her to take a risk. But instead her sister had warned her against pursuing anything with this violent man, and while Abby knew that was a ridiculous summary of Jack, she couldn't help but feel that, at least on some levels, it was true.

Getting involved with Jack Westcoat was a bad idea. Her heart might be clamouring for him, but common sense – and now, as if hammering the nail in the coffin, her big sister – was telling her to stay away.

They settled into a rhythm that wasn't quite normal, and Tessa made her excuses and got up to leave just after ten o'clock, giving Abby a sweet-scented hug on the doorstep, and promising to call her in the next few days, their earlier conversation avoided as if it had never happened.

Abby stood on the doorstep long after she'd driven away. It was cold and misty, the streetlights turned soft-focus by the haze.

'Fancy a quick walk before bed?' she asked Raffle. 'Yeah, me too. Come on then.'

She had something to do that, considering her argument with Tessa, she was even more nervous about than usual.

She'd last seen Jack two weeks ago, on his birthday, when Octavia, Rosa and Jonny had crashed their badger vigil. Since then there had been flurries of texts, interspersed with the notes that were becoming the highlight of Abby's days.

He had continued to deliver them to the reserve, despite her warning that she was never left to read them alone, and now each time they arrived, Abby's anticipation was mingled with trepidation, because the notes were becoming more and more personal.

At first she hadn't believed that he would be happy to lay himself bare in front of an audience, but then she realized he enjoyed it – just as he'd enjoyed their sparring matches all those months ago. She was waiting for one of the *almost* writtens, for him to slip in something too intimate to be easily explained away. It hadn't come yet, but it was a close-run thing.

Dear Abby,

Bullfinches in the garden today. I still think they're like robins on drugs, but they are brightening up the place while the daffodils struggle to break through the frozen earth. I'd like to talk more about their finchy peep soon if possible.

Yours, JW

Dear Abby,

The tributaries have been particularly interesting today – throwing up some unexpected things. Hard to balance when you're peering into their murky depths, I find. What about you?

Yours, JW

Dear Abby,

OP in touch today. Is it normal to be terrified about a library event? I've talked on much bigger stages than this one, but Octavia and her chapel library put the fear of God in me (pun intended). Will you be there to hold my hand?

Yours, JW

Abby had been lucky that Octavia hadn't been present for that one, and Rosa had made sympathetic noises when she'd read it over her shoulder.

It was the latest one, however, which Abby couldn't stop thinking about, and which was probably part of the reason Penelope had given her a thinly veiled talking to today, as she'd been there when it had arrived at the reserve.

Dear Abby,

I've been thinking a lot about our badger vigil, and what we missed out on. Are close calls such as ours normal, or is it usually more satisfying than that? It's been on my mind.

Yours, JW

Abby knew he wasn't talking about the badger, and Penelope wasn't stupid; Abby was sure it was no coincidence that she had allowed Jack to come into the conversation earlier that day.

She knew she was treading on thin ground, unable to resist answering Jack's texts at work, finding herself thinking about him and staring into space when she should have been ordering more membership forms, but she couldn't stop. She picked up the letter she had written before Tessa arrived, and closed her front door quietly behind her. Jack would still be up, she was sure, and as she approached Peacock Cottage she was rewarded with the welcoming glow through the thin curtains of the living-room window.

She tiptoed quietly up the path, slipped the note through the letterbox and hastily retreated, hurrying back towards Warbler Cottages, skirting past the tall, imposing walls of Swallowtail House. Recently, when she'd passed it, she'd had the eerie sense that the house was watching her, as if now she'd been inside she was irrevocably tied to it. In the dark, that sense was increased tenfold. She was relieved that she had Raffle with her, the husky enjoying the jog at her side, his head lifted high to sniff the night-time air.

She silently recited her note to Jack, wondering if he'd found it yet.

Dear Jack,

Close calls such as ours are, indeed, very rare, and – in this case especially – much lamented over. And to answer your earlier question, hand-holding is one of my specialities, but not one I give out freely. In this case, the severity of your situation makes it acceptable to offer my services. OP reminded me that it was T-minus ten days. Hold on to your hats!

Abby

PS. You will ace it, have faith in yourself. x

When she got home she distractedly put more water down for Raffle, gave him a goodnight cuddle and then got ready for bed. She stared at the dark ceiling, trying to put Jack out of her mind so she could get some sleep, but then her phone beeped, and even before she picked it up she knew who it was.

Why didn't you knock?

Abby's fingers hovered over the screen. Even though the truth was far from simple, she didn't want to lie – she found that being honest with Jack was easier than it was with Penelope, Rosa and, after today, Tessa. Somehow their discouragement made her feel closer to him, as if he was the only one she could confide in.

I'm afraid of what might happen, but I do want to see you. Talk after the library event? x

The reply was almost instantaneous.

I feel the same. After the library event can't come soon enough, for all sorts of reasons.

Abby drifted off towards sleep with a smile on her face, Tessa's warnings and her worries about Meadowsweet temporarily forgotten.

Chapter Sixteen

Frogspawn might look strange, like clumps of jelly, but it's an amazing thing to have in your pond, because it means you'll soon have lots of tadpoles, and then frogs, in the garden. You can tell the difference between frogspawn and toad spawn because frogspawn is in little clusters, and toad spawn is in long strings, like a bead necklace.

— Note from Abby's notebook

T-minus ten days for the library event soon became T-minus ten hours, and as Abby arrived at the visitor centre that morning, twenty minutes late and flustered, Octavia was waiting to pounce on her. Her red hair was hanging untidily over her shoulders, and her jumper was unironed.

'Abby!' She grabbed her sleeve and looked at her pleadingly.

'What is it?' Abby asked. 'What's happened? Has the library sprung a leak? Have you lost the key? Has Jack—' Her voice caught at the thought that the star attraction had changed his mind. In some ways she wouldn't blame him, but to leave it to the actual day to cancel was on the callous side.

'Oh no,' Octavia said. 'Jack's fine, the library's fine, I'm . . . I'm . . . Abby . . .' She took a deep breath. 'There are fifty people coming tonight. *Fifty*. The most I've ever had for one of my author talks is eleven, and that's only because it was that man up the road who does whittling, and all his cousins were visiting from America to celebrate his publication day.'

'But that's brilliant,' Abby said. 'How could that be anything other than brilliant?'

'Because I don't have enough chairs,' Octavia whispered. 'Do you think people will mind sitting on beanbags?'

Abby hesitated, wondering how this experienced woman could get to a point where she had sold tickets for an event without assessing her resources beforehand, and then decided not to be too harsh. Octavia had got carried away, and under the circumstances Abby could understand it. 'I'll go and see Ryan at lunchtime,' she said. 'I'm sure he's got a function room somewhere with some stacked chairs. Do you know how many you're short by?'

'Sixteen,' Octavia said, 'and that's if more people don't turn up on speculation.'

'I'll sort it out,' she said, giving Stephan a grateful grin when a cup of hot, milky tea was placed on the reception desk.

'You're a *darling*,' Octavia said. 'And Jack will sparkle. Nobody will care *what* they're sitting on once he starts speaking.'

Abby waved her neighbour goodbye and sipped her tea, watching a pair of greenfinches on the feeders while the computer woke up. A few smatterings of spring rain darkened the concrete, though the sun was trying to break through. She would like nothing more than to spend the day out in the fresh air, answering questions and checking the nest boxes were secured, but she had her camping extravaganza to organize. She had submitted a formal proposal to Penelope, but her boss had been underwhelmed, and Abby had been firming up the details ever since.

She had a list of remaining suppliers to get in touch with during quiet moments and, hopefully, by the end of the day almost everything would be ready to slot into the programme she was pulling together.

She issued day passes to a group of older visitors, all of whom had matching blue baseball caps, one of them explaining that their village pub had set up a social club, and that Meadowsweet had been chosen as their next excursion.

Abby listened as they bickered good-naturedly, and then showed them a map of the reserve, pointing out the different habitats and where the star species had been seen recently. Once they were armed with all the information, they moved away from reception to reveal Jonny, looking fresh and spring-like in a red checked shirt and smart jeans.

'Jonny, how are you?' Abby asked. 'Is there anything I can help you with?'

'Is – uhm, Rosa here?'

Abby hid her smile. 'She's got a day off today. Did you want to see the binoculars? She's ordered in a new, mid-price range that you might be interested in.'

'Oh sure, thanks.'

She led him over to the *Birdseye View* section, which was opposite the till, and next to the storeroom and Penelope's office. The door was ajar, and as she left Jonny perusing what must have been his hundredth pair of binoculars, she went to pull it closed. But the inner door to Penelope's office was also open, and she could hear her voice, a mixture of hushed and exasperated, as she spoke on the phone.

'I'm sorry, Mr Philpott, but I need more time. A few more months.' There was a long pause. 'No, I can't. Not at present. We do – yes, we do.' Another pause. 'No. That can't happen. You're aware of my – yes, indeed. He's been assisting me in those areas. But there is still time, I assure you.'

Abby hovered, the silence now so long she thought the call must have ended without a goodbye on Penelope's part, but then she spoke again.

'There are jobs at stake, not to mention the future of the reserve, the importance of protecting this whole area. This is bigger than you or me, Mr Philpott. No, I do understand, there's no time for sentimentality. If it has to be the house then so be it, but I am confident that it hasn't come to that yet. I can show you when – yes, I look forward to seeing you too. Goodbye.'

If it had been an old-fashioned phone, Abby was sure she would have heard the receiver slam into its cradle, but there was simply the small beep of the call ending, and then a sigh and a rustle of fabric as her boss shifted in her chair.

Her heart in her mouth, Abby walked slowly back to reception. Things were as bad as Penelope had suggested, if not worse, and there she'd been, rolling her eyes at having to do a formal event proposal, sneaking off to the top of the woodland trail so she could reply to Jack's text messages without distractions, daydreaming about him as she refilled the feeders each morning. She felt sick. Her smile when the next visitors arrived was decidedly forced.

* * *

The sense of shame stayed with her all day, and to counteract it she threw a new level of determination into organizing her camping event. She stayed at work until after five, feeling guilty even as she closed down the computer and took her jacket from the storeroom.

'Goodnight, Penelope,' she said softly to the closed door.

It opened. 'It's Jack's event tonight, isn't it?' Penelope looked weary, worry lines creasing her forehead, and Abby wished she could comfort her.

'You should come,' she said instead. 'There's going to be a big turnout apparently, and I'm sure he'd love to see some friendly faces in the audience.'

Penelope nodded. 'Maybe I'll see you there.'

'OK.' Abby smiled. 'That would be great.'

It was still light as she walked home, her pace inevitably slowing as she passed Peacock Cottage. Jack's texts had become more frequent as the day approached; they were self-deprecating and funny, overplaying his nerves in a way that she thought hid genuine anxiety. Suddenly, even thinking about him felt like a betrayal. Abby couldn't let her mind wander any more. She would go to the library event and support Jack, and then she would give 100 per cent to the reserve. She would never forgive herself if it closed down with her knowing she could have done more to save it.

She arrived at the library at half past six, and it was already fuller than she had ever seen it. Ryan had come through, and there were rows of chairs set up theatre-style facing away from the main doors. Not all of them matched, some certainly looked like they had seen better days and, recently, quite a bit of woodworm – Abby hoped they wouldn't collapse under anyone. At the front was a low, unassuming stage, which was where Octavia usually kept her displays of new releases. For tonight, it had been cleared, and there was a table with a jug of water and a glass, and one of the library's most comfortable fabric chairs waiting to be occupied.

Abby glanced at the people already assembled. She recognized a few faces from the village, and Helen Savoury was there, flicking through a copy of one of Jack's books, silver-rimmed glasses on her nose. Abby tried not to let panic consume her at the councillor's presence, and looked around for a friendly face, but instead found the perfectly groomed locks of Flick Hunter. She was two seats away from Helen Savoury, her gaze going frequently to the side of the room, and Abby wondered whether Jack had invited her, or if she had discovered the event in the local press like everyone else. He hadn't mentioned her recently, and Abby had allowed her jealousy at seeing them together to dissipate, so it was a shock to find her in the audience.

Even more now she needed to see someone she knew, and she homed in on Rosa and her corkscrew curls, sitting three rows from the front.

'Rosa, how are you?'

Rosa stood and gave her a hug. 'I'm good! I've spent a lovely day doing almost nothing, and now I get to hear the famed Jack Westcoat speak. I can't get over how weird that night at his house was. I should never have come, but Octavia insisted that she couldn't go alone, and Jonny and I caved in far too easily. Was he properly mad?'

Abby shook her head. 'Not at all. If he had been, he would never have agreed to tonight. He is misunderstood a lot, I think. Especially after what happened at the Page Turner awards.'

'You've got a soft spot for him,' Rosa said gently. 'How soft is it?'

'Getting softer,' she admitted. 'It's complicated, though. There's the reserve, which I *need* to put more effort into, and Jack's life, he's . . . nothing's simple, Rosa.'

'Feelings get complicated when people try to deny them.' She shrugged.

'I wish that was all it was,' Abby said, but the words resonated. If she gave into her feelings, stopped overthinking everything, would all the barriers between them dissolve into insignificance? 'Anyway, tonight should be good. Jack Westcoat in one of his natural habitats. Have you seen him yet?'

'He arrived about ten minutes ago and was immediately herded into the antechamber by Octavia.' Rosa grinned.

'Uh-oh. I'd better go and see what's happening. Speaking of soft spots, Jonny was asking after you. I showed him that new Belkin range, but I'm not sure how taken he was.'

'Oh?' Rosa frowned. 'That's a good make. I wonder why he didn't like them.'

'Because they're not you. Haven't you noticed?'

'What?'

'Jonny is never going to buy anything from your shop because then he'd run out of excuses to see you, and that would break his heart.' She squeezed her friend's arm and then left her, lips parted and eyes wide, as if the wind had changed and she'd got stuck.

When Abby knocked and pushed open the door of the library's small office, Jack was sitting in a chair with a cup of tea, and Octavia was behind the desk, calmly writing notes on a piece of paper. They both looked up when she walked in, Jack's taut expression relaxing into a smile.

'Hey,' Abby said, allowing herself a moment to drink him in. He was wearing a simple grey shirt and a smart, navy blazer, dark jeans that emphasized his long legs, and tan boots. His hair was slightly tamer than usual, and she wondered if he'd had it trimmed for the occasion and, if so, where he had gone to get it done.

'Hi, Abby,' Jack said. 'Glad you could make it.'

'Of course she was going to make it,' Octavia replied. 'She's organized half the thing. Whizzing about on the Facebook page, leaflet-dropping the entire village, and solving my last-minute chair problem. Now Abby, I've written down a couple of questions in case nobody has any.'

Abby stifled a laugh. 'I honestly don't think that's going to be a problem, do you?'

'Be prepared. The scouts had that part right. Jack,' Octavia turned to him, 'obviously in the course of promoting an event like this, we don't know who's picked up on the fact that you're here, but I haven't seen any media types out there – large cameras, trench coats, anything like that.'

'Me neither,' Abby added. 'And I only promoted it on local Facebook pages.'

'Exactly,' Octavia continued. 'But, of course, we can't guarantee that it won't have caught the attention of a wider audience.'

'I understand that Octavia,' Jack said. 'I always knew there was potential for the national press to pick up on it, but I appreciate you considering it too.'

'Good.' Octavia beamed. 'Aren't you a sweetie? The audience are going to eat you up!'

Jack laughed. 'I hope not.'

'Right then. Fifteen minutes to go. I'll do a final round of checks, ensure the mic is working. Abby dear, could you stay here? You can be Jack's fluffer.'

Jack choked on his tea, spraying a mouthful onto his jeans, and Abby stared at Octavia, trying to work out if she'd heard her right. Oblivious, the older woman swept out of the room, leaving an awkward silence behind her.

'So . . .' Abby said, heat rising up her neck.

Jack wiped at his trousers. 'Do you think she knows what that means?'

'On balance, I'd say yes.' Abby sat next to him and gave him a sideways look. 'I'm not doing it, though, if that's what you're wondering.'

'I honestly wasn't. God. Could you imagine?'

'Octavia has a good heart,' Abby said, trying very hard not to imagine it. 'And a very individual way of doing things.'

'She's distracted me from my nerves, at least. And she's been very kind to me, considering I wasn't that hospitable when she came to track down the badger.'

'That's because she barged in unannounced. You were perfectly polite. Do you really get nervous?' She turned to face him, her embarrassment fading.

'I do. Nerves are healthy, and it's been a long time since I did anything like this. The last time I was in a public arena was . . . that night, and so there's more pressure than usual, a heavier weight on my shoulders despite it being off the beaten track.'

'Octavia's sold over fifty tickets. You're a popular man, even in the sticks. What are you going to do? Read something from one of your books, talk about your writing?'

Jack nodded. 'A bit of both. Then the Q&A, which I'm dreading.'

'You'll be fine,' she said quietly.

'I'm glad you're here. Thank you for coming.'

'Of course,' Abby said, but her mind flashed back to the

phone conversation she'd overheard. She should be at home, working on her event schedule, wracking her brains to come up with this game-changing membership initiative that had, so far, failed to materialize. She looked into Jack's blue eyes, at his smooth, stubble-free jawline, and felt hopelessly conflicted.

'Showtime!' Octavia said, appearing in the doorway. 'Ready, Jack?'

'As I'll ever be.'

He followed Octavia out of the room, Abby taking up the rear. When Jack walked into full view of the makeshift auditorium, the cheers and applause were enough to lift the roof. He raised a nonchalant hand, slightly bashful in the wake of so much attention, and took his seat at the table. Abby slipped into a chair against the wall, side on to the stage, as if she was an usher rather than a member of the audience. But she was at the front, her view was good, and she watched as Jack greeted everyone in his deep, smooth voice and then picked up the book that Octavia had placed on the table. It was a copy of his latest novel, *The Fractured Path*, the one Abby had ordered from Amazon and read in only a few days.

He riffled through to a spot marked by a bookmark and started reading.

The crowd was pin-drop quiet as his sonorous voice filled the room, the rhythm of the words gripping and comforting all at once. It was mesmerizing, and Abby found herself getting lost in it, able to remember the passage he'd chosen and its point in the book, wishing he would continue to the end, however long it took. She had to blink herself back into the present when he finished and the audience clapped once more.

Then he launched into a talk about the process of writing,

the research he'd done, a particularly gruesome, no-holds-barred visit to a morgue that made him realize he could never be a murderer himself, because he didn't have the stomach for it. He was funny, humble and disarming. Abby could sense the audience warming to him, wanting to reach out and gather him close. It could have easily been an act, his public persona, except that it was how he was with her – or at least, was starting to be.

Abby could see that Rosa was rapt, Councillor Savoury's expression was a mixture of interest and affection, and Flick was smiling proudly. It was obvious that some people had noticed the television presenter; that she was on the verge of getting as much attention as Jack was. His arms moved constantly while he spoke and he smiled a lot, loosening up as the talk went on. Abby felt a surge of triumph for him that only heightened her desire. When he sat down and took a sip of water, Octavia strode onto the stage, leading the exuberant applause.

'It's safe to say you went down a treat, Jack,' she said, 'and thank you for that fascinating insight into what it takes to write a book such as yours. We have got time for a few questions, so if any of you have a burning desire to ask something, then please raise your hand and I'll bring the microphone to you.'

Dozens of hands went up, and Abby thought she saw fear flash in Jack's eyes. She crossed her fingers in her lap.

'Jack,' said a loud male voice clearly not in need of a microphone. 'What would you say to the rumours that you're hiding out in Meadowgreen because of what happened last summer?'

'I'd say there was some truth to that,' Jack said calmly, 'but that it's also to concentrate on my current book. Sometimes a change of scenery can be beneficial for the writing process, and getting out of London for a few months is never a bad thing.'

'Hi, Jack.' It was a woman this time, her voice fluttering nervously. 'I love all your books, and it's wonderful to see you here in Suffolk.'

'Thank you.' Jack nodded.

'Do you think it's right,' she continued, 'that you didn't face criminal charges after hitting Eddie Markham last year?'

Abby gasped. Jack seemed frozen for a second, and then gathered his composure. 'That isn't something I feel the need to fully discuss here, but I will say that I deeply regret what happened, that I have never before used violence, and will never do so again. I spoke to Eddie after the event and we settled the matter between us.'

'Lovely,' Octavia said hurriedly. 'Who has a question for Jack about his books? Ah you, yes dear, you look kind.'

'Jack,' an older woman said, standing so she was visible above the crowd. 'How can you continue to write, to come here and talk to us so confidently after being involved in a plagiarism scandal? Isn't that like an athlete being found guilty of doping?'

'I really don't think . . .' Octavia started, but Jack held a hand up, stopping her.

'I'll answer, thanks, Octavia.' His voice had lost its richness, the words much more clipped. Abby winced and threw a pained look at Rosa. 'I understand your concern,' Jack said. 'But firstly I'd like to emphasize that I was never accused of plagiarism myself, and the incident you speak of has been fully resolved, to the satisfaction of everyone involved. What the press does with their limited knowledge of it is beyond my control.'

267

'Don't you feel ashamed?' called someone else. 'Doing all that, and then punching a guy?'

'Ladies and gentlemen,' Octavia shouted into the microphone, causing it to shriek with feedback. 'If you could stick to asking Jack about his books and writing, then we won't have to finish the event early! Now, does anyone have a *sensible* question for him?'

Abby could see the tension in Jack's shoulders. He was sitting forward in his chair, his jaw clenched. Why didn't Octavia finish it now, stop the heckling?

'Is there any truth to the rumour you slept with the journalist to get her to drop the story?'

'What does Eddie Markham think of you now? Do you think you'll appear in his next satire?'

'Is it true that you and Eddie did drugs together when you were growing up?'

Jack shot a glance in Abby's direction then looked quickly away, raking a hand through his hair, ignoring the barrage of questions as they kept coming.

'Why have you ended up in Meadowgreen? What is it about this place?'

'Is your career over, Jack? What will you do if nobody wants to buy your books any more?'

People were standing, voices raised, getting out of control. It was more like a political debate than an author event in a sleepy Suffolk village, and Abby didn't think these people really cared, or were genuinely outraged by Jack's behaviour, they just wanted the drama. Unless they were all moles from the national press. There were definitely a lot of people she'd never seen before.

Abby flung another exasperated look at Rosa and she nodded, then stood and took the microphone from Octavia, who barely seemed to notice, her mouth open, aghast as her event disintegrated around her.

'Hi, Jack,' Rosa said loudly, the amplification of the mic drowning out the other voices. Everyone else stopped talking, eager to hear what she was going to ask. They were like a crowd at a hanging, Abby thought angrily.

'Hello,' Jack said, the relief evident in his voice.

'I wanted to ask how being in Meadowgreen is helping to inspire your book? You said it was good to get a new perspective, and I was just wondering what difference it's made so far?'

Abby could have hugged her, and from the look on Jack's face, she thought he felt the same.

'Thank you for that,' he said. 'The truth is, Meadowgreen has been more inspirational than I could have imagined. At first, it was simply a secluded cottage where I could focus on my novel, but it's become so much more than that. I'm close to the Meadowsweet Nature Reserve; these stunning natural habitats, the wildlife that's so carefully looked after from a distance by the reserve staff.

'Even in my worst case of writer's block, walking in the woods helps to bring everything alive. It's also played a pivotal role in the plot, something I can't say much more about now, but will hopefully become clear when the book's published later this year. And finally, perhaps most importantly, I've made some good friends here. As you're all aware,' he said, his voice becoming sharp again, 'the last year hasn't been without its problems, and I won't deny that they're of my own making, but that doesn't make them any easier to deal with. Coming here, on my own, was wise in some respects and not in others. I have been lucky that Meadowgreen, and a few people in particular, have welcomed me, have helped me to see things more clearly and have, in some cases, changed my outlook completely.

'In short – and I know that answer wasn't – coming to Meadowgreen is the best thing I could have done.' He sat back, took a sip of water and gazed around the room. Everyone was silent, a few were shamefaced, and many were gazing at him with what Abby hoped was respect.

'Well done,' Abby mouthed, and gave Rosa her biggest grin. Rosa gave her a subtle thumbs-up in return.

'Well, ladies and gentlemen, wasn't that wonderful?' Octavia said, recovering her voice and taking the mic back from Rosa. 'Thank you all for coming. If you have any books you'd like to get signed, then please form a queue in front of the table, and Jack will be more than happy to oblige.' Octavia bustled up to the front, placed a chair alongside him as he seated himself behind the table, handed him a Sharpie and sat next to him.

Abby felt a flush of gratitude for her neighbour for acting as a bodyguard. While people slowly formed a queue, or pulled on coats and made their way to the exit, Abby raced over to Rosa and flung her arms around her. She smelt of peonies.

'Thank you,' she said. 'Thank you for rescuing him! I was trying to think of something to ask but my mind went blank.'

'That was a harsh crowd,' Rosa huffed. 'I couldn't believe some of the things they asked him.'

'It was like a feeding frenzy. I wonder if Octavia and I should have thought about it more carefully.'

'Jack agreed to do it,' Rosa said. 'He probably wasn't under any illusions as to what might happen – I expect he had a better idea than you. And he did so well, he's still alive and, I think we can safely say, came out on top at the end.'

'Thanks to your brilliant question.'

'Thanks to his wonderful answer,' Rosa corrected. 'I can see why you have a soft spot for him. Do you really think Jonny likes me? I've only ever exchanged a few words with him. Lots of times, obviously, because he's there so often, but . . . pretty much the same dozen words.'

'Of course he likes you,' Abby said. 'I don't know why I didn't see it before. What are you going to do?'

Rosa chewed her lip. 'I don't know. I do like him but – I'd never considered him as more than just a visitor, with his own life and an acute interest in binoculars. I don't know anything about him.'

'That's easily remedied,' Abby said. 'If you want it to be.'

Rosa nodded. 'Anyway, I'd best be off. See you tomorrow?'

'Sure. I'm going to . . .' She pointed in the direction of the stage.

Rosa grinned. 'He could probably do with a hug after all that, and Octavia might be too overpowering.'

'Oh, well then,' Abby said, returning her friend's smile, hoping Flick Hunter hadn't got in there first. 'It must be my turn to rescue him.'

Chapter Seventeen

Sometimes one species of bird will mob another, which means they'll fly at them and sound their alarm call, because they feel threatened by them. Smaller birds in a big group will often attack a single, larger bird – crows often mob birds of prey, such as marsh harriers or buzzards. This can be upsetting to see, but unfortunately not everything in nature is cute and fluffy.

— Note from Abby's notebook

Jack and Abby sat side by side on Octavia's red leather sofa, in a living room that was a clash of colours, bright but slightly chaotic, very like its owner. While her house was next door to Abby's, it was also twice the size. When Abby had first moved to the area, Octavia had told her the long, complicated story about how – over twenty-five years ago, when the price of builders wasn't through the roof – she and her husband had bought two neighbouring houses and turned them into one.

Octavia was in the kitchen fixing them drinks, which

they'd all agreed they could do with – out of relief more than celebration.

'Is she on her own?' Jack asked.

'A lot of the time,' Abby said. 'Her husband works in London, and sometimes stays there during the week, and her two boys are grown up and both live there now too. There's been talk of her and Ian moving down so that they're closer, but I think Octavia needs this – the community, the village. And Ian likes the peace at weekends.'

'Peace?' Jack raised an eyebrow, and Abby laughed.

'Of the countryside. They're very affectionate, whenever I've seen them together.'

'What is it?' Jack asked, after a moment. 'You look wistful.'

Abby shrugged. 'Nothing.' She didn't want to tell him how much she envied Octavia and Ian's long, comfortable relationship. They might spend a lot of time apart, but they made the most of it when they were reunited.

'You've been quiet this evening,' Jack said, refusing to give up.

'Don't worry about me.' She shifted round to face him. 'What about you? You were brilliant, the way you dealt with all those shitty questions.'

'I was very close to snapping,' he said, running a hand through his hair. 'Not – not physically, but . . . I wasn't entirely naive, I was expecting a tough crowd, and it's no less than I deserve. But some of them were . . .' He shook his head.

'Vicious,' Abby finished.

Jack gave her a rueful smile. 'Welcome to the weird world of people knowing all about you, thinking that, in some respects, they own you, and certainly have a right to challenge your behaviour. I didn't get a chance to thank Rosa before she left, will you do that for me?'

'Of course.'

'And thank you, too, for being there. I always feel calmer when I'm with you.'

'Is that because you know you can let off steam if you need to?'

Jack laughed. 'Are we talking about arguing here, or . . . ?'

'For the last time, Jack, I am *not* going to be your fluffer!' She grinned at his shocked expression, and then Octavia bustled into the room with three martinis, complete with olives, on a yellow tray.

'Octavia,' Abby said, 'when you talked about having a drink, I didn't realize you meant this!'

'Nothing beats a good martini and *this*, I promise you, is a good martini. Cheers.' They clinked glasses and sipped their drinks, both Abby and Jack making appreciative noises. It tasted amazing.

'Jack, my love,' Octavia continued. 'Thank you for gracing my humble library with your presence, and please excuse the downright rudeness of some of the crowd. I have a list of names, and I'm going to bar each and every one of them.'

'You can't do that,' Abby said, laughing. 'The whole point of the event was to boost visitors to the library. That would be counterproductive.'

'Please don't take drastic measures on my behalf,' Jack said. 'I knew what to expect.'

Octavia narrowed her eyes. 'Some of the things they said were appalling.'

'Most of them had an element of truth,' he said, picking an olive out of his drink and popping it in his mouth.

'Not the one about drugs though, surely?' Octavia asked. 'I didn't believe that when I read it in Eddie's interview, and

I can't imagine you snorting white powder up your nose in a posh men's club, though I'm not provincial enough not to realize it goes on.'

Jack stared into his drink. 'I've done some things in my past that I'm not proud of,' he said quietly, 'and that was a very long time ago.'

Octavia gasped, and Abby closed her eyes.

The press had made references to his troubled past, and Jack had told her that he'd made mistakes, hurt his friends and family, so the admission didn't shock her as much as it clearly did her neighbour. She just felt sad that, sitting under a public microscope, he wasn't able to put it fully behind him.

'Eddie's interview with the newspaper was, in many respects, as fictional as his books,' Jack continued. 'And he has embellished everything to suit his motives. But I never claimed to be perfect, and there was a time when my behaviour left a lot to be desired.'

Abby squeezed his shoulder, and Jack placed his hand over hers, his grip tight.

'Abby's writing a book you know,' Octavia blustered, her eyes wide with shock. 'A bird guide for children. One day I'll be hosting you at the library, and I'll have to borrow every single chair that Ryan owns.' Her laugh was over-cheery.

'Seriously?' Jack asked, looking up. 'Why haven't you told me before now?'

Abby should have throttled Octavia, but at least the tension in the room was dissolving. 'Because I'm not, it's . . . how did you even know?'

'Because I saw your notebook on the coffee table when I came to borrow some white vinegar that time. Remember?'

Abby didn't have any white vinegar, but she had searched

275

her cupboards on the off-chance and hadn't realized her scribbles had been left out for all – and by all, it only needed to be Octavia – to see. 'I, uhm—'

'Tell me about it,' Jack said eagerly.

'No. It's not a real book, I'm just – I was trying to explain the difference between willow tits and marsh tits to my sister, and Willow wanted to know too, because of having the same name, so I was working out how to explain it in a way that she'd understand, and I—'

'Came up with this ingenious idea,' Octavia finished.

'It's just a few random thoughts. I'm not writing a book. I don't have time, even if I wanted to write one, which I don't.' She laughed nervously.

'It sounds like a brilliant idea,' he said softly. 'Will you show it to me?'

Abby felt her cheeks burn. 'It's not a book,' she repeated.

'I don't care. I'd still love to see your ideas – when you're ready to share them.'

Abby held his gaze, felt the pull of him, and then remembered Penelope's resignation as she'd spoken to Mr Philpott on the phone.

'Maybe one day,' she said noncommittally, and looked away.

They left after eleven, and while Abby wanted nothing more than to invite Jack in, Penelope's overheard conversation was running on a loop through her mind. And she could see that he was exhausted, leaning on her doorframe as she unlocked the door and greeted a delighted Raffle.

'Why are you so quiet, Abby?' Jack crouched and let Raffle nuzzle his cheek. 'I can understand if my admission to you and Octavia has given you second thoughts about spending time with me, but I promise you that's all in the past. It wasn't the reckless addiction Eddie made it out to be, and anyway, you were distant before that. What's wrong?'

'It's not you,' she said hurriedly. 'It's the reserve.' She crouched in front of him, wondering if Octavia was listening, if she'd left her front door slightly ajar. 'It's in even more trouble than I thought.'

Jack frowned. 'How so?'

'I don't have all the details, just some things I overheard but . . . I've not been working hard enough; I've let myself get distracted. I need to put more hours in. I feel like, if I don't, I'll be letting everyone down. What if Penelope has to sell Swallowtail House and the estate, and they turn it into new homes or something? I couldn't live with myself.'

'It won't come to that,' Jack said. 'The reserve's got too much going for it – you're there, for a start.'

'But I'm not doing enough,' Abby protested. 'Penelope's been relying on me, and I've—' She faltered, risking a glance at him.

Jack held her gaze. 'I understand,' he said quietly, and Abby's heart cracked a little bit. 'What can I do to help? If the answer is to stay away, then of course I will.'

She was more torn than she'd ever been. 'I think I do need you to stay away,' she said slowly. 'But I don't want – I mean, I—'

Jack tucked a strand of stray hair behind her ear and looked at her with such tenderness that Abby had to use all her inner strength not to shuffle forwards and let herself be gathered into his arms. 'I know about the pressures of work, remember? And I know how important this place is to you, and Penelope.'

'But you – you won't go anywhere, if I have to do this for the next couple of months?' She sounded pathetic, but she had to be sure. She wondered if Flick Hunter, with her perfect smile, was waiting in the wings, ready to fill the space Abby left.

'I'm not going anywhere.' He gave Raffle a final stroke, then stood and helped Abby to her feet. 'Whatever you need me to do, Abby, I'll do. And if you ever want to see me, you know where I am.' He leant forward and pressed his lips gently against her cheek. Abby closed her eyes, concentrating on his touch, however brief.

She wanted to go back to the night in Peacock Cottage, for there to be no pressure at the reserve, no warnings from her sister about repeating the same destructive patterns, no confirmation from Jack that he had matched that stereotype, however long ago. She wanted the decision to be simple, and it was anything but.

'Thank you for tonight,' Jack said.

'You're welcome.' It came out as a whisper, and she watched him give her a final fleeting smile and then stride down her short front path and turn towards the main road, the walls of Swallowtail House looming up ahead of him in the darkness.

When cars started to roll into the car park on the Saturday morning of the early May bank holiday weekend, and Marek rushed outside in his bright-orange event T-shirt, Abby felt like she was being held together by hope and coffee. She didn't usually drink coffee, but as she'd burned the candle at both ends over the last few weeks she had discovered that a nice, comforting mug of Earl Grey didn't cut it.

The morning passed in a blur of set-ups and questions, and by midday, the field beyond the meadow was filling up with tents, families and groups of friends milling around

278

the stalls and the activity areas, seeing what was on offer.

Gavin was directing the final stall-holders down the track that led from the car park, behind the visitor centre and to the field, and Marek was checking the cordon they'd put in place along the bank of wildflowers, protecting the plants, bees and butterflies from the constant press of feet as visitors used the meadow trail to get to their final destination. There were signs saying the wildlife was to be enjoyed but not touched, and from the flutter of common whites and red admirals, earlier than usual because the weather was so warm, Abby was reassured that they weren't being put off by the extra humans invading their patch.

She shook her head and flapped the neck of her orange T-shirt, wishing she'd paid a little extra for a more breathable fabric. They had averted disaster three times already, and it was only lunchtime on the first day.

When a young couple had realized, following a long drive from Norwich, that they'd left their tent in the hallway at home, Gavin had given them one of the staff tents, high-fiving Abby for ordering spares. Then a caravan had turned up, having ignored the event information and hoping to be admitted, and Abby had explained that it wouldn't be allowed on the field. There had been a few minutes of tension before she had come up with a compromise, allowing the owners to park in the far corner of the car park, enjoy the festivities and return to their caravan to sleep in. Lastly, the mobile bar had discovered that their freezer had broken down en route and their ice was now a large tray of water. Stephan had produced the bags of ice he'd bought on the off-chance, so all was well for the G&Ts and glasses of Kopparberg that would inevitably be drunk throughout the day.

Abby returned to the visitor centre, her head swimming.

Now it was all happening, she was worried it hadn't been a good idea in the first place. Would they have irreparably damaged the field and the meadow trail with all the footfall and tent poles? Should they have allowed alcohol? It wasn't very likely that any visitors would get too raucous, but were the careful cordons they'd set up and all the extra volunteer support enough to stop anyone ending up in the lagoon? Abby had researched events put on by other wildlife-centred venues, and felt hers was in keeping with the spirit of the reserve, but was it too big?

Just as she reached the bird feeders a family approached, a rolled-up tent tucked under the dad's arm. Her smile brightened when she saw who it was.

'Evan, how lovely to see you! You've grown.' She threw caution to the wind and embraced the boy, who was noticeably taller than when she'd first met him back in the autumn. 'You've come to camp?'

'And go to all the talks and events, Abby. I want to see everything I can. Are we allowed to go in the hides at dusk?'

'All except the forest hide,' Abby said. 'Because of the steep stairs. There'll be staff and volunteers on hand to help out, to lead walks and tell you where you can and can't go. I'm so glad you're here! Hi,' she said, greeting Evan's parents as he headed eagerly in the direction of the meadow trail. 'I'm so happy he's still interested, that his enthusiasm hasn't worn off.'

'He's more than interested,' his dad said, laughing. 'I'm convinced he's going to go into wildlife conservation. He's already planning out his options at secondary school, and he's only in year four.'

'I think we've got this place, and you, to thank for that.'

Abby brushed his mum's compliment away. 'The passion

was there before Meadowsweet, we just helped bring it out of him.'

'He's still got that notebook you gave him,' his mum added. 'It sits on his desk, and he writes down everything he sees in the garden.'

'Really?' Abby said, and because her nerves were frazzled and she'd had barely any sleep, she felt the warning prickle of tears. 'That is so lovely to hear, thank you.'

'Thank *you*,' his mum said quietly, and squeezed her wrist as they walked past.

'Abby,' Penelope said, as she stepped inside the calm and cool of the visitor centre. 'You look like you're preparing yourself for a life sentence, not a night in a tent.'

'Are you coming outside?' Abby asked. Her boss was wearing a loose white shirt, khaki cropped trousers, and Birkenstocks showing off purple-painted toenails. Her long grey hair was in a loose ponytail.

'Of course I am. Are you?'

'I just need to . . .' She scrabbled at the papers on the desk, unsure what she was looking for.

'Abby Field,' Penelope said forcefully. 'I know that, despite the event having already started, you've still got doubts. Need I remind you that the reserve will have to close if nobody comes to visit it, and the wildlife may be at peace once that happens, granted, but their habitats will no longer be meticulously looked after, the reed beds will take over, species will be forced out and the bitterns will not get the extra food they need to flourish. And if my efforts fail, and I have to sell Swallowtail House and all its land, then whoever buys it may decide to bring it into the twenty-first century, and everything will be gone, just like that.' She clicked her fingers. 'Replaced with another estate of identical houses, driveways that don't allow the land to breathe, patches of AstroTurf. If I could speak for the inhabitants of the reserve, I would say that a weekend of fun, laughter and noise on the adjoining field was worth holding onto their sanctuary long-term, wouldn't you?'

Abby stared at the desk. 'Yes, Penelope.'

'Oh, dear Lord, I didn't mean to make you cry. You've run yourself into the ground. What on earth is wrong?'

'Nothing.' Abby turned away from her boss and wiped at her eyes. She felt a hand on her shoulder, and then that hand forced her to turn around and she was pulled, awkwardly, against Penelope's slender chest.

'I know you care about this place as much as I do,' Penelope murmured. 'And I'm sorry if I've been harsh on you. I'm under a lot of pressure. But it hasn't escaped my attention how hard you've worked to make today happen. It's your job, but it doesn't mean I'm not grateful for the effort you've put in. Now, run home and give that husky some attention, and I'll see you back here in an hour.'

'Penelope, I don't need to—'

'*Go*, Abby. And when you return, I want to see a smile.' She tightened her hug for a second, patted her twice on the shoulder as if to spur her on, then released her. 'Smile, and you're halfway there,' she added, leaving Abby perplexed, and not a little shocked by her tenderness.

When she got back to the reserve, feeling refreshed after some quality time with Raffle, a ham-and-cheese sandwich and a pot of tea, Abby didn't have time to draw breath before Gavin intercepted her.

'What is it?' she asked warily.

'Two things, neither of which you're going to like.'

Abby closed her eyes. 'Hit me.'

'Number one, Flick Hunter is here, can you bloody believe the cheek of it? Though she does look positively gorgeous.'

Abby swallowed, trying to work out why the *Wild Wonders* presenter would make an appearance at their event. Was she checking out the competition, or had she been to Peacock Cottage and discovered it was happening that way?

'And two?' she asked, trying to push the thought away.

'The storyteller's got gastroenteritis but has only just let us know,' Gavin said. 'So, in half an hour we're going to have an eager circle of children waiting to be brainwashed into adoring nature with a selection of carefully chosen stories, and nobody to deliver them.'

'Can't you do it?' Abby asked. 'You've got young children.'

'I'm hopeless at story time,' Gavin said, holding his hands up in submission. 'Besides, this bloke's supposed to be a proper writer, and if I turn up in my Day-Glo reserve T-shirt and try and pull it off, I'll get lynched.'

'Small children will not lynch you, Gavin.'

'What about their parents? Why not call Mr High-and-mighty-author, see if he can fill in? You're pals now, aren't you?'

Abby bit her lip, barely noticing when Gavin disappeared, refusing to help fix the problem he'd just delivered to her.

Despite Abby's assertion that she needed to focus on the event, and Jack's initial acceptance, their text messages had continued, Abby turning to Jack for reassurance whenever she was feeling besieged by event details. Several times, she had given in and knocked on his door on the way home from work. It was usually late in the evening, Abby staying behind to work once the distractions of visitors and phone calls were gone, but he had always invited her in and made her tea, listened to her problems and then taken her mind off them by talking about his book or his latest garden wildlife sightings, describing the birds he couldn't identify in a way that made Abby laugh.

Sitting on the sofa in Peacock Cottage had felt intimate, and it would have been so easy to kiss him again, to let go of her worries and exhaustion in his arms, but she kept her visits brief and platonic. Jack had respected that, never asking her to stay longer or sitting too close, though the intensity of his gaze showed Abby his feelings hadn't faded either.

Tessa's concerns were never far from her thoughts, but Jack, by assuming the role of the sounding board that Abby needed and honouring her wishes, was proving her sister's reservations were unfounded. And while the logical part of her knew that just because she hadn't committed to Jack physically it didn't mean she wasn't already too far gone, Abby convinced herself she was being sensible; that text messages and cups of tea meant nothing, and she could still walk away if she wanted to.

But the note he had left at reception yesterday, shunning his phone for pen and paper, had made her heart soar more than usual.

Dear Abby

Your event tomorrow will surpass all expectations, of that I have no doubt. When things are less stressful, I'd love you to drop by again. That badger's still waiting for another chance.

Yours, JW x

Thinking about it now brought a smile to her face. She

knew that, once it was over, she would need to take stock of the event, see how much visitor numbers and yearly memberships increased as a result. Then she would have to start thinking about the next one. But there was a glimmer of hope that, during the early stages at least, she could allow herself more time in Jack's company than just a few fleeting tea breaks.

A little girl ran, giggling, past her, reminding her of her predicament. She needed a storyteller and he was her only option, unless Abby wanted to have a go herself, and the thought of doing silly voices to keep the children entertained made her flush with embarrassment. She pulled out her phone and instead of calling, as she knew she should when time was tight, clicked through to her text messages.

Hey, stranger, she typed. Don't suppose I could ask you a huge favour at very short notice? xx

The reply took only moments.

Anything for you. And hey, yourself. x

Abby grinned.

How do you feel about telling stories to a bunch of over-excited children? Keep them entertained, and extol the virtues of nature without mentioning corpses, body fluids or murderers? x

Back came: I wouldn't want to spend my Saturday any other way. Hopefully this crowd will be kinder than the last lot! I'm already here, by the lemonade stand. Penelope said she'd sent you home to decompress. You OK? x

Abby's phone slipped in her sweaty palms. He was here already? And Penelope had told him about her meltdown? Her stomach churned as she typed a reply and walked in the direction of the field.

Are you kidding, they're kids – they'll be horrible! I'm fine. See you in 2 ticks. Xx

She made her way through the crowds of children laughing and playing tag, queues at the food and craft stands, tents being pitched around the edge of the field, some expertly, some not so. She saw two of the volunteers with a small group of people, pointing to the flowers and butterflies beyond the cordon along the meadow trail, and Rosa deep in conversation with Jonny, who looked happier than she had ever seen him.

Stephan, in chef's whites, was strolling through the crowd with a tray of bite-sized bacon-and-cheese scones, and Marek was demonstrating the newest addition to their telescope family to a few interested adults, one of whom was Councillor Savoury, looking summery in a primrose-yellow dress and oversized sunglasses. Abby often wondered if anything had come of her visit to the reserve back in the autumn, but if Penelope had any news about council funding streams for Abby to follow up, she had yet to share it with her.

The lemonade stand was in the far corner of the field, the small cart's green-and-gold livery fitting in with its spring surroundings. Abby peered through the crowd, trying to make Jack out, but was distracted by raised voices to her left.

Penelope was standing in front of the organic carrot juice stand, her arms folded, talking to a short man who, in a dark suit and grey tie, looked entirely out of place.

'Can't you see we're doing all we can? This is out of order, Mr Philpott, and on a Saturday too.'

'Mrs Hardinge,' he said, his voice flat with weary patience. 'These are unusual, pressing circumstances, as I've already explained. Do you wish to discuss it here, or is there some-where else we can go?'

'My office,' Penelope said shortly, her hands clenching at her sides. 'Come with me.'

Abby watched them go, a well of ice settling in the pit of her stomach. Surely, *surely*, he couldn't be here to start the process of taking her assets away in the middle of their event? Didn't they all deserve this chance? She turned away, her progress to the lemonade stand slower.

Then she saw him, and her heart leapt.

Jack was wearing jeans, black Vans, and a navy T-shirt that expertly (and probably expensively) highlighted the definition of his upper body. Her eyes raked over his forearms, his shapely biceps, his hands shoved in his pockets. His hair had grown since the library event, the waves deliciously thick. She sped up again, but then her tunnel vision widened and the ice was suddenly back, chilling her insides.

Flick Hunter could have been the poster girl for spring. Her blonde hair fell in unnatural but glorious curls over her shoulders, her jeans were fashionably ripped, and her tight rose-pink T-shirt brought out her tan. Her delicate features were crinkled in amusement at something Jack was saying and as Abby watched, she squeezed his arm, Jack leaning closer to hear her reply above the chatter around them.

She shouldn't have been surprised. She had told Jack she needed to give all her attention to Meadowsweet and, even when she'd seen him Abby had been the epitome of self-restraint. Why shouldn't he go running to Flick?

And, she had to admit, they were perfectly matched. A wholesome, girl-next-door media professional anchoring a successful nature programme would be just the person to give Jack comfort and rescue his public image at the same time. Abby hadn't stopped at Peacock Cottage for the last couple of weeks, the growing pressure of the event keeping her away. Maybe that was all it had taken for Flick Hunter to charm her way back into his life, or perhaps it had happened before then, and that was the reason Jack hadn't tried to kiss Abby since the night of their badger stakeout.

She took a deep breath, put on her brightest smile and walked up to them. 'Jack,' she said, forcing herself not to stare blatantly at Flick – or completely ignore her – and thus make her jealousy screamingly obvious. 'It's lovely to see you. Thank you so much for saving the day.'

Chapter Eighteen

It is hard to spot the difference between willow tits and marsh tits. They're both tiny birds with brown feathers and black caps, but marsh tits always start their call with a sound like a sneeze, while a willow tit makes a chay, chay, chay sound. Neither are very enthusiastic singers!

— Note from Abby's notebook

'Abby – hi.' Jack turned to her, his smile warm. He glanced briefly at her orange T-shirt, chosen specifically so all the staff would stand out, and then leaned in and kissed her cheek. He smelt of bergamot and sunshine, and the brush of his lips on her skin made Abby feel all at once at home and at sea. Her lips craved the same attention.

'Hello,' she said, nervously. 'Is it – are you—?'

'Of course, lead me to the little terrors. Oh, sorry – have you met before? Abby, this is Flick. Flick, Abby.'

'Hi,' Flick said, breezily. 'Nice to meet you.'

'You too,' Abby replied. 'Are you enjoying it? I know you're

. . . focused on Reston Marsh at the moment. I've been enjoying *Wild Wonders*,' she added, not wanting to seem rude.

'I'm glad,' Flick said, smiling. 'Thank you. We've got a good team there, but this . . .' She gestured to the field. 'It's so lovely. It reminds me of the camping holidays I used to go on when I was young. Is that guy over there teaching those kids to whittle?'

'Oh, yeah,' Abby said. 'That's one of our part-time wardens. It took me a while to come around to the idea of visitors with sharp tools, but it's only the older children, and he did a full risk assessment. So—' She shrugged, wishing she hadn't slipped into health-and-safety mode. That was decidedly *not* sexy, especially when she was standing next to Flick Hunter.

'I think it's wonderful,' Flick said, and Abby was surprised at the sincerity of her tone.

'Thank you. It seems to be going OK so far. Speaking of which . . .' She caught Jack's eye. 'I'm so sorry to interrupt you, but the storytelling is due to start at three so we should get going.'

'I'm at your mercy,' Jack said. 'See you later, Flick.'

'Sure.' She batted her long eyelashes at him, and Jack raised a hand in goodbye and let Abby lead him across the field.

'How are you?' he asked. 'Penelope was telling me how hard you've been working the last couple of weeks. I hope you don't mind me saying, but you look tired.'

'It's been tough,' she said. 'But most things have gone as planned, and it's all been worth it, I think, so—'

'I've missed you.' He grabbed her hand so that she was forced to stop a few metres from where Gavin was standing in the centre of a circle of children and parents, clutching a large book and looking harassed.

She turned to him, inhaling as she did. 'I've missed you

too. I've wanted to come and see you every night on the way home.'

'Why didn't you, then?'

'Because . . . you know why. These last few weeks, there's been so much to do. I couldn't let myself get sidetracked, and you're a distraction, Jack. The biggest possible distraction.'

'I'll take that as a compliment,' he said, his smile half-hearted.

'Are *you* OK?' she asked.

He nodded. 'I wasn't expecting to see Flick here – I bumped into her when I arrived. I came to see the fruits of your labour, and I knew it would be spectacular. Can I talk to you? I know you're too busy now, but . . . after this is over?'

'Sure,' Abby said, swallowing. 'And thank you, for stepping in at the last moment.'

'I'm happy to help. What do you want me to read? I've got some of my own material if you want me to spice things up a bit.' He grinned, but there was something else, a weariness, behind it. He was trying for chipper and falling slightly short. The fact that they had missed each other, even though it had only been a fortnight, made her skin tingle.

'As tempting as that is,' she said, 'I'm not sure they can stomach anything stronger than *The Hungry Caterpillar*. I'll leave you in Gavin's rather frenetic hands, if that's OK?'

She watched as Jack almost lost his arm to Gavin's firm handshake, and then introduced himself to the children and their parents, before sitting on an upturned log. He delivered the opening words of *Where the Wild Things Are* with as much dramatic effect as a production of *Hamlet*, the children squealing in glee before he'd even turned to the second page.

Abby could have stayed there watching and listening to him forever, but Octavia's craft stall had managed to find a rare patch of mud and was slowly sinking, toppling all her crocheted birds towards a sticky death, and two families were getting into a fight about the proximity of their tents, so Abby was called away to a never-ending to-do list. By the time she had a moment to pause, it was close to six o'clock and the storytelling had long since finished.

'Tea, Abby?' Stephan asked, approaching with a steaming takeaway mug. 'You look like you could do with it.'

'You might have just saved my life,' she said, taking it from him. 'I've exhausted my problem-solving capacity, along with everything else. It's been a long time since I slept in a tent, but I can't wait to take the weight off my feet.'

'What's Raffle going to do? I presume he's not allowed.'

'Octavia's looking after him for me. She's not a fan of camping, and I can't say I blame her. It'll be weird sleeping without him, though. God, that makes me sound like a mad old spinster, doesn't it?'

Stephan laughed and shook his head. 'Not at all. Jack told me to say goodbye,' he added softly. 'He saw you were rushed off your feet and asked me to pass on that he'd catch up with you later. His storytelling went down a treat, lasted much longer than it should have done and pacified a lot of children. I think about fifteen mothers wanted to take him home with them.'

'Good old Jack,' she said, trying for nonchalant.

'Don't worry, Abby. He wasn't interested in any of them that I could see, not even Flick Hunter, who was fluttering about him like an impatient hummingbird.'

Abby didn't know what to say to that, so she just smiled and sipped her tea, waving goodbye as Stephan wandered in the direction of the burrito stand.

She attended the stargazing event, conducted expertly by

Rosa and with a very willing, but unexpected assistant in the form of Jonny, and as families sat around the campfire Marek had built and their stories slipped away from the natural world and towards ghosts and witches and other implausible things, her eyelids started to droop.

'Come on you,' Gavin said. 'I'll walk you to your tent before you end up sleeping in the embers.'

'Shit, my tent. I haven't even thought—'

'Don't worry, it's all done. You're between me and the girls, and Stephan.'

'Thank you so much, Gavin,' she said. 'Have your family had a lovely time?'

'My kids, definitely – Jenna not so much, after they'd each had a second ice cream and were bouncing around like Gummy Bears. They're sleeping now, so I'm on pain of death not to wake them. Also, we've set Rosa's tent apart from the rest, in case Jonny makes it back there with her.'

Abby raised an eyebrow, which was about as much as she could manage.

'They make a cute couple,' Gavin said thoughtfully. 'Not as cute as you and Jack, but . . .'

She found the energy to slap him playfully on the arm, and Gavin squeezed her shoulders in response, almost as if he was giving her a massage, which, at that moment, would have been very welcome. They walked in silence to the row of tents, and he handed Abby a torch.

'Your bag's in there already,' he said. 'Sleep tight, event organizer extraordinaire.'

'Thanks, Gavin.'

'You're very welcome, Abigail Field.'

'Oh, and Gavin?'

'Yup.'

'Why did you say that, about me and Jack?'

'Because he's done nothing today except gaze adoringly at you, when he wasn't reading *The Tiger Who Came to Tea* or being talked at by Flick Hunter. She left fairly early, but he stood and watched you for the entire time you were running the birds and butterflies quiz. I think the only reason he didn't join in was because it was easier to ogle you when he thought nobody was watching. But people were watching all right.'

'Gavin, if you're making this up—'

He held his hands up. 'No word of a lie. Ask Stephan or Marek, or Penelope even. He thought he was out of sight next to the bar, but we all saw it. Now, get some shuteye. Breakfasts to organize and a treasure hunt to run in the morning, as I recall?'

'Ugh,' Abby said. 'Don't remind me.'

'At least I've left you something sweet to dream about.' In the torchlight, Abby saw him wink, before he left her and went quietly to his own tent, turned his light off and crawled carefully inside.

Abby didn't care that her sleeping bag smelt musty or that her foam undersheet was thin enough to feel every blade of grass through, because she was exhausted, and because Jack had missed her. She floated away on a cloud of happy exhaustion, Jack's piercing blue eyes and warm smile drifting through her thoughts until sleep took over.

By the time a girl with ash-blonde pigtails called Matilda had won the treasure hunt, and the last tents and food stands had been cleared from the site, it was close to four o'clock on Sunday afternoon. Despite entreaties to go home, Abby stayed to help with the litter pick and to restore the field to its former glory, save for trampled grass and holes where tent poles had been. It didn't look too traumatized, and as she trudged back to the visitor centre with Rosa, she saw a peacock butterfly fluttering happily in the still, sunny air.

'A job well done,' Rosa said, sounding as tired as she felt. 'It's definitely home time.'

'And tomorrow,' Abby asked, 'will you tell me about Jonny?'

Rosa gave her a coy look from beneath her dark lashes. 'Maybe. Can I give you a lift?'

'I'm fine, thanks,' Abby said. 'The walk will do me good.' Even though her feet were throbbing, she had been looking forward to it. Thinking was so much easier when she was outside, pounding the trails or sitting in the forest hide looking out at the view. They exchanged smiles and wished each other goodnight.

Penelope wasn't in her office but as Abby walked past the reception desk on the way out she noticed a white, square envelope with her name on it. Checking that Stephan was happy to lock up, she stepped outside and stopped next to the feeders to open it.

It was a card with a fluffy duckling against a bright-pink background, a green leaf sticking haphazardly out of its mouth, and it made Abby laugh out loud. She opened it up, her throat tightening as she read the brief message.

Abby, wonderful work. I am truly grateful, whatever happens next. Without you, Meadowsweet wouldn't stand a chance. P.

She almost stopped at Peacock Cottage on her way home, but she wanted a long, hot shower and a hug with her husky before she could contemplate seeing him. She needed fortification before she exposed her body, her senses, to Jack Westcoat, so when she found him sitting on her front doorstep, Raffle lying contentedly at his feet, she thought at first that she must be hallucinating.

'Hi.' He raised a hand in greeting.

'How come you're not inside my house, and my dog is outside? How long have you been waiting?'

'When I appeared, approximately an hour ago, Octavia took pity on me and said I could talk to Raffle but that she wouldn't allow me to wait in your house, because it was an invasion of your privacy. I completely agree, by the way. I didn't even ask to be let in.'

'And Octavia didn't offer you a cup of tea?' she asked quietly, bending to stroke a sleepy Raffle, aware that her neighbour could probably hear their conversation.

'She did,' Jack whispered. 'But I declined, because I wasn't sure she'd ever let me go. After I'd been sitting out here for forty minutes, I wondered if I should have accepted.' He grinned up at her.

'Come inside.' She held out her hand and hauled him up, ignoring the burst of heat that she felt at the contact. He followed her into her front room while she dumped her bag on the kitchen counter and flicked the kettle on. He was wearing jeans and another T-shirt, this one black, with a small, indistinct logo on the right sleeve. His arms were tanned, and she wondered how much time he spent in the tiny garden of Peacock Cottage now that the weather was good, reading books or looking over his own words.

'I'm sorry,' she said. 'I promise I'll get you a cup of tea, but if I don't have a shower immediately I might turn into a pile of dirt. I'll be super quick.'

'Of course,' Jack said. 'I shouldn't have turned up unannounced. Can I do anything?'

'Make the tea?' she asked. 'And there are some biscuits in the cupboard. Please help yourself. I don't think you'll find anything terrifying, other than perhaps a Suffolk super spider lurking about somewhere.'

'That sounds daunting, but I'll brave it out. You go.'

She gave him a grateful smile and trudged up the stairs.

Her shower made her feel a hundred times better, even if she was hyper aware of Jack only a few feet below her. She put on a pair of denim shorts and a T-shirt, ran a brush through her damp hair and rubbed some moisturiser into her sun-kissed skin, before going back downstairs.

There were two cups of steaming tea on the coffee table, along with a plate of bourbons. He'd put just the right amount of milk in her cup, and she sank gratefully onto the sofa next to him and picked it up. She rubbed Raffle's flank with her bare foot and turned her attention to her unexpected visitor.

'Thank you,' she said. 'I wasn't sure I'd be capable of speech, let alone anything else.'

Jack raised an eyebrow.

'I meant making tea,' she clarified, smiling. It turned out her pulse still had the energy to race, despite her tiredness.

'That's what I thought you meant,' he said. 'The event was incredible, by the way. I was honoured to be a small part of it.'

'Stephan said you were amazing, and from the little I saw, I agree. Thank you for rescuing us.'

'I was happy to. And they were a much more tolerant audience, whatever you might think. Which is partly why I'm here,' he said, rubbing at a crease in his jeans.

'Oh?'

'I wanted to see you, of course. I mean – that's all it is, really. But it's selfish of me to turn up when you could clearly do with peace and quiet.' He sighed, and his hand slipped from his knee to hers, fiddling with the hem of her shorts in a way that was so unconsciously intimate, Abby's breath caught in her throat.

He met her gaze and froze, snatching his hand away as if it was burnt. 'God, I'm sorry—'

'What is it, Jack?' She pulled his hand back towards her, holding it between both of hers.

'My agent, Leo, thinks it's time for me to step back into the spotlight. My new book is close to being done, page proofs are imminent, and it's due out in August which, well, it's still three months away, but this is when the publicity machine has to start rolling. There's a literary gala, a precursor to the Page Turner awards, organized by the same people and – miracle of miracles – I've been invited. I've been exchanging emails and phone calls with Bob Stevens, the head of the Page Turner Foundation, and I think he's close to forgiving me for what I did. If I still want a chance at being an ambassador, I can't turn this invitation down.'

Abby remembered something from the newspaper article Octavia had showed her, mentioning his promise as an ambassador had been all but lost. She nodded. 'So you have to go?'

'It's a chance to move in familiar circles and see what happens. I won't get my career back on track unless I sell books, and I won't sell books unless I help promote them. Some people may buy it out of grim fascination, but I'd be the first to agree that I want the words to speak for themselves and, conversely, that will only happen if I show my face again, if I champion them. I need to go in with confidence and make the effort to put what happened behind me, even if it's going to be excruciating.'

Abby picked up her tea, put it down again and took a biscuit instead. 'And if you go to this . . . this event, will you come back?'

'Of course I will,' he said quietly.

'When is it?'

'In three weeks.'

'I'm sorry you have to go. Is . . . is *he* going to be there?'

'Eddie?' Jack ran a hand over his jaw. 'In all probability.'

'Shit.'

'The thing is,' Jack squeezed her hand, wiggling it so that she met his gaze, 'when I'm with you I'm calm, in control. It's like I can be myself, and the person I am is . . . well, is OK. Before you, I hadn't felt that way in a while.'

'I feel the same—' she started, and then her tired mind connected the dots. 'Wait, do you—'

'Will you come with me, Abby? It would seem less daunting if you were there. I know it's a lot to ask. Sorry, I—' He raked his hand through his hair. 'It's not fair of me.'

Abby pictured the candid paparazzi photo of Jack from the paper; his dishevelled evening suit, his grazed knuckles. 'It's posh, right? Black tie? I'd have to talk to people, schmooze and socialize?'

'I wouldn't leave your side unless I had to,' he said. 'And Leo will be there. We'd look after you.'

'Doesn't he make you feel OK?' she asked.

Jack laughed. 'Yes, of course he does. But . . .' His voice dropped. 'Not in the same way you do.'

Abby nodded, burying her toes in Raffle's fur. She knew he wouldn't have asked her unless it was important, unless he really felt he needed her. There was no other reason for him to do it – if he'd wanted someone glamorous to hang off his arm she was sure he could have asked Flick Hunter, and he hadn't. He'd asked her.

'Would we have to stay in London? You have a flat there, don't you?'

'I do, but . . . Leo would send a car, drive us down there and straight back, after the event.'

Abby nodded distractedly. 'And I definitely couldn't wear wellies or walking boots?'

'Not on this occasion, no. Sorry.' He gave her an apologetic smile.

She sighed and slumped against the sofa. 'I'll have to go shopping then, I guess.'

Jack's grip on her hand loosened, and then tightened, his eyebrows shooting towards his hairline. 'You'll come with me?'

'I will,' she said quietly. 'But I have to warn you, I've never been to anything remotely like this, and I'll probably trip over the red carpet or say something unforgivable and make everything worse for you instead of better.'

'Abby, God.' Jack pulled her close, hugging her. His chin was on top of her head and she could feel the solid warmth of him, the strength of his arms, her cheek resting against his chest. She slipped her arms around his waist and lost herself in the moment. She wondered if that night would be worth it for this alone.

Then he gently pulled back, so that she was no longer pressed against him, but their faces were close and he was looking down at her.

'Thank you,' he said softly. 'I'm aware how often I've said that to you over the last few months.'

300

He stroked his thumb along her cheekbone, and a shiver ran down Abby's spine. She could see the hesitation in his eyes; they were searching hers, and she wondered if he was thinking the same thing. That if he kissed her now, it would seem like he was only doing it because she'd said yes, because she'd agreed to go with him. And in her exhausted state, if Abby kissed *him*, then she wouldn't be able to stop, and her sister's words still nagged at her: *You're walking over old ground, trying to save someone who isn't worth it. He's using you.*

'More tea?' she said quietly, and Jack nodded, dazed.

She went into the kitchen and put the kettle on, while he sat on her sofa, lost in his thoughts.

Once the adrenalin had left her, tiredness took over, and even though she loved being in Jack's company, telling him about the small calamities that had made the camping event memorable rather than disastrous, her eyelids began to flicker.

She wasn't sure how quickly she'd fallen asleep, but when she woke it was after ten o'clock, the room was in shadow apart from the side lamp, and Abby was lying on the sofa under her purple-and-yellow checked throw. She could smell Jack's aftershave in her hair and wondered if she'd drooled against his T-shirt.

The mugs and biscuit plate were washed up on the draining board, and Raffle's bowl had fresh water in it and the remains of some food that she couldn't remember giving him. Blinking and sitting up, Abby noticed that one of her notepads was open on the coffee table. Jack's handwriting, in her purple biro, was slightly scruffier than usual, as if he hadn't wanted to disturb her by turning on the main light.

Dear sleeping beauty,

Thank you, again, for saying you'll come with me. I understand what a big ask it is, and that you agreed on the spot, so if at any point over the next three weeks you change your mind I will completely understand. Thank you, also, for the tea and the talk. I feel whole again, as if a part of me was missing and you've restored it.

Sweet dreams,

JW x

Abby knew that she could no more turn down Jack's request than she could send Raffle back to the rescue home. That thought, the strength of her conviction, alongside his candid admission about how spending time with her made him feel, scared her more than anything had done in a long time.

Over the next couple of weeks, as the reserve settled back into something like normality, Abby turned her attention to her regular events, membership incentives, online dress shopping, panicking and, incredibly guiltily, Googling Jack Westcoat.

She had only dipped her toe in the water up until now, not wanting to risk reading something that would put her off him for good. Octavia's retelling of the previous summer's events had been as much as she could take at the time, and it was only her panic at the prospect of a high-profile London gala – *with* Jack – that was sending her into overdrive.

Most of the top news stories were about Eddie Markham's original interview, the Page Turner awards and the aftermath. Eddie had done a follow-up with the same newspaper as the first inflammatory article a few days after the awards, complete with a posed photograph that showed in full the damage Jack's fist had done to his face. It looked nasty, but then a photo could be manipulated as much as a story, with lighting, make-up and Photoshop.

Eddie was gracious, saying he didn't blame Jack for lashing out once the truth about that sticky period in their past had been revealed, but he had felt it necessary to unburden himself, had become tired of covering it up when he'd never wanted to in the first place. As Abby read, her panic deepened. Eddie was clearly very clever, portraying himself as the wronged party when he was the one responsible for the alleged plagiarism, and emphasizing the reckless phase of their friendship to ensure Jack came across as conceited, short-tempered and, on some levels, dangerous, whereas he seemed affable – a naive young author who had been led astray by his wayward friend.

She reread a paragraph of his second interview:

I looked up to Jack from the beginning, when we were eleven years old, braving a new school together. He was smart and funny, with a magnetic personality, and I wanted to be like him. So I listened to everything he said, followed in his footsteps to Oxford, to some admittedly dark places, and into the literary world. He thrived on the attention, on being admired. When I tried to be independent, to stand up to him, that's when it went wrong. He'd never made it physical before, but I always had the sense that it was possible. He wants to be in control and when I finally had the courage to reveal what really happened all those years ago, he realized he wasn't any more. This was the only way he could take back that control.

'Oh, sod off,' Abby whispered, but the nerves were creeping back in. *Had* Jack been the influence that had led to Eddie's bad decisions, or was it the other way around? Raffle whined softly, placing his head on her knee, trying to nudge her iPad aside. It was late, and her hot chocolate had long since gone cold.

Once she'd read all she could about the incident – and several of the online news sites had picked up on the suggestion that Jack's persuasiveness to get the journalist to bury the plagiarism story had gone beyond the financial – Abby started to read the older articles, from when Jack's first book was published, when he was a young, talented author who looked like he would go far. There were a couple of fleeting references to his time at Oxford, the indiscretions dismissed as out of character with phrases like *obvious anomaly*, *youthful recklessness* and *blemish on the landscape*.

She found some photos of a younger Jack, his hair shorter and neater, and with a wide-eyed innocence, perhaps apprehension, that she didn't recognize. It wasn't that he'd lost his passion, she knew, but that he was now painfully aware of how brutal being in the public eye could be; how you could go from the golden boy to a villain at the turn of a page.

A couple of the articles mentioned past girlfriends – Hannah during university, and then a book publicist, Natasha, more recently – but there was nothing in-depth.

Abby pored over it all, losing sleep, wishing she'd never started. Her head and her heart seemed to be doing all-out battle. Was Jack like her past boyfriends, destined to hurt her? Her heart wouldn't believe it, the reality of spending time with him was so different to the picture Eddie Markham had painted. All she could think was that it wasn't like him, that some combination of factors must have made him lash out like that, and that his old school friend was full of shit. She wished Jack would tell her the whole story, instead of brushing it aside with comments about trying to do the right thing. Maybe one day he would.

In the meantime, all she could do was focus on the things she *could* control, and one of those was what she was going to wear to this crazy event.

Chapter Nineteen

Once you've seen a kingfisher, you'll never forget it. Flashes of brilliant blue and orange, they sit close to the water on a protruding branch or skim low over its surface. When they catch a fish, they will often take it to a perch and hit it repeatedly, stunning it, before swallowing it head first. Their call is a high, short 'teee' sound.

— Note from Abby's notebook

Abby finished work at lunchtime on the day of the gala. She had booked that afternoon, and Saturday and Sunday, as holiday. Rosa, Gavin and Jonny had told her that she would need at least two whole days to recover from an event like that, but all of them admitted that, in reality, they had no idea what it would be like; whether the bar would be free, or extortionate because they knew everyone could afford it; whether it would draw sedately to a close at ten o'clock or continue into the small hours. Abby's attendance at the event was the new sparkle of interest at Meadowsweet, though it was mostly restricted to the staff because Abby had told Rosa – and then Gavin, Jonny, Stephan and Marek – that they couldn't tell anyone else on pain of a slow and watery death in the least appealing part of marshland on the reserve.

She had only ever intended to tell Rosa, but then Gavin had overheard something, and the inevitable ripples had rippled, and Abby had had to settle with only her immediate friends knowing. Even Octavia, whom she had confided in because she needed someone to look after Raffle for the evening, had promised that she would be discreet – after her initial explosion of excitement on Abby's behalf.

Now, however, it was debatable whether she would even be going to the event, or if Jack would refuse to send the car because she'd spent the last three weeks bombarding him with terrified text messages:

If I buy three-inch heels will you promise to hold onto me all evening? How many stairs are there? Abby x

What if there's someone really famous and I don't recognize them? Abby x

Is there food? Should I eat beforehand? Abby x

How do we refer to each other? Friends, acquaintances? Abby x

What if someone asks me about the punch? Is 'no comment' too much like a criminal suspect? Abby x

Did you know that the collective noun for lovebirds is an orgy? No relation to the gala, but I had to tell you! Abby x

Is this really a good idea? x

Jack's answers were unfailingly patient, and she now knew that it was a ground-floor event, three steps up to the hotel entrance, two steps down to the ladies' WC. (She thought he must have had to ask his agent about that, or phone the venue himself, and she was touched at how much effort he was going to so that she would feel at ease.) There would be posh but tiny nibbles, and they would grab something on the way down or back to fill the inevitable hole. 'No comment' was quite formal but fine if anyone was being irritating. There were hundreds of celebrities he didn't have a clue about, so she shouldn't worry about that. He'd had no idea about a group of lovebirds being called an orgy, but it made sense, and was the kind of fact he should try and get into a book – unless she was going to use it in hers? They were close friends – if she was happy with that description – and yes, Jack would most definitely hold onto her all night, it was the least he could do. In response to her last question, he had been less certain.

I don't know. But if it is a mistake, there's nobody I'd rather be making it with. Thank you, again, eternally. JW x

'All set?' Rosa asked, as Abby picked up her bag and walked towards the glass doors, the bird feeders teeming with blue tits beyond.

'As I'll ever be, which at the moment seems like not at all,' Abby admitted.

'You'll be fine,' Rosa said warmly. 'I have no doubt that Jack will look after you. Punches aside, he strikes me as a gentleman.'

'He is. I just . . . I'm going to stick out like a sore thumb.'

Rosa laughed. 'Not in your dress, you're not. You'll look stunning. Full-length selfie please, the moment you're ready.'

Abby scrunched her nose up, thinking of all the money she had spent on the dress that was hanging from her wardrobe door, and which she'd asked Rosa to come and look at as soon as she'd bought it. Was it the right kind of thing? She had stopped short of sending Jack a photo of it just to check, because she loved his hair and didn't want him to have torn it all out by this evening.

'I need to go,' she said quietly.

'Oh, come here.' Rosa hurried over and wrapped her in a hug. Abby struggled for a moment, then let herself be squeezed. 'Have you spoken to Tessa about all this?'

'She's been so busy,' Abby said, which wasn't a lie, but it also wasn't the whole truth. There was no way she was going to let Tessa unnerve her even further – she would tell her after the event, when it had all gone brilliantly. She didn't need her sister saying that Jack was using her again; the words were on constant repeat in her head anyway.

'I'll have my phone glued to my hand this evening,' Rosa said. 'So if you need *anything* – advice, reassurance, me to Google anyone famous you're confused about, I'm there. And if for any reason Octavia can't take Raffle, let me know and I'll look after him.'

'Thank you, Rosa, you're too good to me.'

'I am nothing of the sort. Now get going before Penelope corrals you to talk about the summer fete.'

'I'm gone.' She hurried out of the door and began the journey home, finding herself taking the longer route back through the reserve, over the fallen tree and to the side gate of Swallowtail House. Her trip there with Jack seemed so long ago, and as she looked at the building, alive with its spring freshness, the green of the grass, the sound of birds calling in the trees, she began to feel calmer. Reluctantly leaving it behind, she picked up her pace, almost jogging the rest of the way. There were three hours before Jack had said he would pick her up. Would it be enough?

There was a light rat-tat-tat on the front door at five past three. Abby had been pacing nervously in the living room for the last half an hour, Raffle lying on the sofa, his large eyes sulkily following her repetitive movements, a sure sign that he knew he was being left out of something. But now he leapt up, beating Abby into the hallway. Taking a deep breath, she held onto Raffle's collar so he didn't charge Jack, and opened the door.

'Wow.' It came out before she'd had a chance to think about it. 'Hello,' she added quickly, but Jack was staring at her and barely seemed to notice she'd spoken.

She glanced down nervously.

'You look stunning,' Jack said. 'The *blue*bell of the ball.'

Abby laughed. 'I, uhm – you don't look too bad yourself.'

He stepped forward, giving Raffle an affectionate stroke, and kissed her on the cheek.

He smelled even more delicious than usual, his scent headier, full of lemon and sea salt and vanilla. Abby closed her eyes. She knew she looked OK, that her satin, strappy dress, in a dusky blue with just a hint of purple – the colour of a bluebell, though she hadn't made the connection until Jack had – a scalloped neckline and a slit up the ankle-length skirt, was stylish. It needed to be at the price she'd paid for it. She'd teamed it with a delicate silver necklace, drop earrings and a sparkly silver clutch, and had a matching grip to hold her straight-dried hair back from her face. She had kept her make-up simple, black mascara and pale, shimmering eyelids with a brush of bold pink lipstick. It wasn't professional, she hadn't been styled by fashion and make-up experts, but she hoped it would do.

And yet Jack looked like a film star.

His dark hair was brushed away from his face, but still had its characteristic messiness, and he was wearing a fitted black dinner jacket and narrow-legged trousers, a white shirt, currently open at the neck, missing its bowtie. A blue silk handkerchief was folded in his breast pocket, which brought out the depth of colour in his eyes. It was a darker blue than her own dress, but the synchronicity still made her smile.

'Are you ready for this?' he asked, running his palms down the sides of his trousers.

'If you are,' she replied.

She whispered goodbye into Raffle's ear, assuring him that Octavia would be round to see him later, and stepped into the warm evening. As she locked her front door, she glanced up to see her neighbour standing, unashamedly, in her window. Abby waved, her cheeks heating, and the older woman blew her a huge, elaborate kiss and then followed it with a wink.

She let Jack take her arm and lead her to a black Mercedes people-carrier that was parked at the end of her path.

'Abby,' he said, once they were sitting in the back. 'This is Gene, our driver.'

'Hi, Abby, great to meet you.' A square-faced man with receding white hair reached back to shake her hand from the driver's seat.

'And this is my agent, Leo.'

Leo turned fully round in the passenger seat, his arm coming out towards Abby around the headrest. He had twinkly grey eyes in a narrow face, beneath dark-brown hair cut neatly short. He looked to be in his mid to late forties, was immediately friendly and, Abby thought, vaguely familiar. And then she remembered the man who'd been calling from the doorway of Peacock Cottage not long after Jack had moved in and realized that it was Leo – good enough friends to help settle him into his new home and also, she reminded herself, a close acquaintance of Penelope's.

'Abby Field, it is wonderful to finally meet you. Honestly, Jack has been—'

'Leo . . .' There was a warning note to Jack's voice, but also humour.

'It's lovely to meet you too,' Abby said, taking his proffered hand.

'Sorry for the awkward greeting. I would have got out of the car, but Jack said you have inquisitive neighbours, and might not appreciate a welcoming party. Though I'm not sure anyone would fail to spot you looking slightly out of the ordinary in that. And when I say out of the ordinary, I mean beautiful. Jack has complimented you, yes?'

Abby glanced at Jack and he rolled his eyes.

'Yes,' Abby said. 'He has. And both of you look very smart.'

'Oh, shush about me,' Leo replied. 'I know you mean our man Jack, and I agree. He's done himself proud, though I fear he could turn up to these things in a pair of white Y-fronts and still outshine all the other chaps there. But tonight requires a little more forethought, which I'm delighted to see he's put in.'

'To see if I'll be allowed back into the inner circle?' Jack asked dryly.

'You pooh-pooh it, but your writing deserves more than meagre book sales, and if you don't have the industry working for you, that's all you'll get. Especially this new one. Has he told you much about it, Abby, or has he kept things close to his chest, as always?'

'Oh, very close to his chest. Though I do believe there might be a tributary in it?'

Leo laughed easily. 'It's a very clever ruse.'

Abby frowned. 'What? The way the body's hidden?'

'The way that whole passage came about,' Leo said, his grey eyes dancing. He was so relaxed and affable, she felt herself warming to him instantly.

'I think we should change the subject.' Jack did up his seatbelt. 'Don't we need to get going?'

'We do indeed.' Leo tapped the dashboard. 'Right-oh, ready Gene?'

'Yup. Everyone belted? Then off we go.'

They headed out of Meadowgreen, past fields hazy with late-spring sunshine, the areas Abby knew so well, and then into unfamiliar territory. Leo was a talker, and after asking Abby a few questions, all of which he promptly said he knew the answer to because Jack had already told him, he turned to the event.

'People pretend they don't care, Abby, but they're all lying. Everyone wants to say the wittiest thing, have conversations with the most noteworthy people – this year, Jack, I'm sure you'll be in the centre of everyone's bingo card. But if we see Eddie Markham, let's not give them an instant bulls-eye – excuse the mixed metaphors – by repeating last year's performance.'

'Leo, how many times?' Jack sighed heavily, as if his agent was a toddler he had to put up with, but Abby had noticed that ever since he had introduced her to Leo, a smile hadn't been far from his lips. They were clearly good friends, even if they wound each other up.

'It never hurts to hammer the point home,' Leo said. 'Especially when it's such an important one.'

The car journey passed more quickly than she had anticipated, and listening to Jack and Leo chat about everything and nothing helped to quiet her clamouring nerves. But when the fields became dotted with buildings, then housing estates, and then the fields were the rarity and the built-up areas the norm, her apprehension grew.

'Are you OK?' Jack asked. 'Even now, there's time to back out.'

'No,' Abby shook her head. 'I want to come with you. I am nervous, though.'

'I'll look after you, I promise.' He slid his hand over hers on the seat between them.

Eventually, the car came to a halt outside an impressive building with three pristine white stairs up to an oversized double door, a man and woman, in a tuxedo and black dress respectively, checking names on a clipboard and greeting people. She watched through the tinted window while, behind her, Jack did up the top buttons of his shirt and tied his bowtie. A myriad of people, young and old, some in obvious pairs, others alone or in small groups, were ushered inside. She rubbed her hands together, and then surreptitiously along the leather seat, though it did little to dry them.

'Good to go?' Leo asked.

Abby turned to Jack, her tummy flipping unhelpfully as the full effect of his outfit hit her, and he nodded. She opened her door, but before she could step down, Jack had come around the back of the car and offered her his hand.

'You, Abby Field, will be the most admired woman there.' He gave her a bright, brilliant smile, leaving her momentarily speechless.

'Only because I'm with you,' she whispered. Fear clouded his eyes for a second, then he helped her down from the car and they walked towards the grand hotel.

From that moment on it was a blur of names and faces, of hellos and small talk, as Jack and Leo worked the room with her between them. Leo took two glasses of champagne off a tray and handed them one each, and Abby closed her eyes in delight at the delicate, fizzy liquid, so much better than her standard Sainsbury's prosecco. Tiny canapés – scallops in their shells, miniature beef and horseradish curls, smoked salmon and dill blinis – were circulated by waiters in black-and-white outfits. Leo stayed with them, Abby kept her hand wrapped round Jack's arm, and he occasionally squeezed it against his side, reminding her that she wasn't forgotten.

The room was huge, the floor black-and-white tiled, its high ceiling disappearing into darkness while the space was beautifully lit with softly glowing lamps and blue fairy lights that twinkled like stars. Jack had assured her that, unlike the awards ceremony, there was no formality to the night, no sit-down meal, only a brief speech from the organizers at some point during the mingling, but even so, intimidating wasn't the word.

And yet, Jack socialized with an energy Abby found exhilarating. He never left her out, always introducing her and steering the conversation to something she could engage with. He mentioned her job at the nature reserve, listening as she talked about it, adding that he'd come to find it a sanctuary when he needed time to think or clear his head. People responded to him, matching his smile like a reflection, laughing with him and reaching out to touch his arm or shoulder. There were unanswered questions in the eyes of some of the men and women they spoke to, but most seemed genuinely happy to see him.

She understood, now, why what had happened last year had affected him so much. If he was this good at the social side of being an author, then losing that role would have had an impact not just on his career, but on him personally.

Perhaps that was why he was so disgruntled when she first met him; not only was there huge pressure on him to write something good, but he had lost a part of his life that it was obvious he enjoyed. He may have been reluctant to come tonight, and there was understandably a nervous anticipation about being back in the spotlight after so long, but the truth was that Jack was a sociable person. He sparkled more brightly than the fairy lights.

'Oh, Jack,' said Cherie, a woman in her fifties with cropped mousy hair and striking purple eye shadow. 'It's so lovely to see you. You must tell me about this new book of yours.'

They had reached the middle of the room, and Abby's feet were starting to ache, desperate for a wall to take some of the pressure off or, even better, a chair. Jack repeated the spiel he'd been giving people all evening, flashing Abby an apologetic smile as he did.

'It sounds positively delicious,' Cherie said, when he'd finished. 'It's been so wonderful to see you again, Jack. And to meet you, dear Abby.'

'Lovely to meet you too,' Abby said.

As they were retreating, Cherie leaned into her and added, 'So good he's found someone who can keep him on the straight and narrow.'

Once they'd moved out of earshot, Jack laughed.

'What?' Abby asked.

'The look on your face. What did she say to you?'

'Nothing.' Abby shook her head vehemently.

'Tell me, I won't be offended.'

'She said,' Abby started, dragging the words out, 'that she was pleased you'd found someone who could keep you on the straight and narrow. How cheeky!'

'She's right, though,' he said, grinning at her. 'Come on, let's see if we can track down Leo and another drink.'

But Leo was already on his way towards them with full champagne glasses. He delivered his news as he handed them out. 'Natasha's coming over, and EM is by the far wall embroiled in a heated discussion with Harvey Poulson.' Abby looked in the direction he was indicating, but couldn't spot anyone who resembled the man she had seen in the newspaper article.

When she turned back, Jack was talking to a slim woman with luxurious dark curls and a shimmering, gold dress. She was gorgeous, radiating the kind of confidence that Abby only felt when she was standing in front of a group of people in her wellies, talking about the migratory patterns of geese.

'That's his ex,' Leo whispered. 'Bit of a messy one, but it ended a while ago.'

'When are endings not messy?' Abby murmured, watching them closely. They were talking amicably, but there was a stiffness to their body language even as she touched his arm. And then, Natasha was gone and before Jack could rejoin them he was accosted by a tall man wearing a claret-coloured velvet jacket.

'Shit,' Leo said. 'That's Bob Stevens. Head of the Page Turner Foundation. Can't break up that little tête-à-tête. Come with me, we'll find a chair.'

They settled on a regal, high-backed sofa in the expansive hallway they had come in through. It was cooler here and Abby felt more able to breathe. She smiled at Leo, grateful that he was looking after her in Jack's absence.

'Jack's a good egg, you know.' He said it in a matter-of-fact way, but Abby sensed that this was important: the good angel sitting on her shoulder, contradicting her sister's cautions.

'I know. I wouldn't be here if I didn't think that.'

'And everything that took place last year, with Eddie Markham, what do *you* make of it?'

Abby clasped her hands together nervously. If anyone knew the whole story of what had happened between Jack and Eddie, it would be Leo. 'I think that,' she started cautiously, 'even if he's not prepared to talk about it, there's a reason he ended up lashing out – that Eddie provoked him. I don't believe he's violent. We had a couple of arguments when we first met, but they were never genuinely angry. I mean, I got worked up, but—'

'But you can never be pissed off with him for long, I know.' Leo smiled ruefully. 'I've been there, more times than you can imagine. The irritating part is that he very rarely loses his cool, can stay placid and reasonable while making your blood boil. But last year, obviously, was different.' He sighed. 'And trying to get him to give *his* side of the story is – well, impossible. It would explain everything, recover his reputation in an instant, but he refuses to do it. It seems I'm destined to be stuck persuading stubborn people to do what I know is good for them, however reluctant they are. In Jack's case, it's like trying to talk to a brick wall.'

'But why won't he explain?' Abby asked. 'That's what I don't understand.'

'Because Jack's stupidly old-fashioned when it comes to things like loyalty, and he won't show Eddie up as the despicable human being that he is, even when Eddie has done everything in his power to ruin Jack's career. Part of me understands it, but as his agent . . .' He exhaled loudly. 'I want to shake sense into him – or leak the story myself.'

'How long have you known him?'

'Nearly ten years now. Since I plucked his novel off the slush pile and made the phone call that changed his life. In many ways he's been a dream client, and then last year it all exploded.'

'Was it just . . . Eddie and what he did, or was there something more to it?' She chewed her lip, wondering if he would tell her.

Leo folded his arms over his chest, his brow furrowed in a frown that was weirdly familiar. 'His dad has always put a lot of pressure on him,' Leo admitted. 'Novelist wasn't ever a solid enough occupation – Charles was an investment banker, before he retired. He never approved of Jack's friendship with Eddie either. They rather went off the rails together, though Jack had the strength of character to bring himself back from the brink, as it were. But when Eddie span that fantasy story to the newspaper, not only was Jack suddenly made out to be controlling and morally ambiguous, but it was more proof that his dad was right, and that compounded the issue.'

'And at the awards ceremony . . .?' Abby glanced behind her, but there was no sign of Jack.

Leo closed his eyes. 'Eddie wound him up. It was bad enough already; the plagiarism story had come out, there was a mountain of speculation and Jack was facing questions and accusations. Then Eddie appeared, smug and perfectly at ease, and brought up Jack's deceased relationship with Natasha, referring to the most flagrantly ridiculous part of his whole kiss-and-tell story—'

'That he'd slept with the journalist he paid off,' Abby filled in.

'Exactly.' Leo pointed at her as if she'd won a prize. 'And Jack lost it. Only once, very briefly, but with enough force that the damage to his reputation was worse than the state of Eddie's nose.'

Abby sighed. 'Poor Jack. I *wish* he'd tell people the truth.'

'And yet you don't know what it is, young Abby.'

'I know what it *isn't*. I've spent enough time with Jack, and I . . . I trust him.'

'Good. I can see why my—' he started, then coughed and rubbed at a nonexistent spot on his shoe. 'I can see why Jack's pleased he moved to Peacock Cottage, for all sorts of reasons.'

'You found it for him, didn't you?'

'I did. I could see that he needed a fresh perspective, and I knew of Meadowsweet, the old estate. I thought it might be a good place for him and I was right. He has more reason now to prove himself than ever before, and not just to his editors and readers. Peacock Cottage has been a real gem.'

Abby sipped her champagne. She liked Leo and felt reassured on Jack's behalf, knowing he had this man firmly on his side, steering him in the right direction.

'Do you think he's OK?' she asked. 'Being left with Bob Stevens?'

'As long as Bob doesn't try and unite him and Eddie like long-lost brothers, all should be fine.'

Just then, the sound of a loud gong reverberated throughout the building.

'Oh goody,' Leo said. 'It's speech time.'

Abby tried to take in everything Bob Stevens was saying, but she found her mind – and her eyes – wandering, looking for Jack, looking for Eddie Markham or any of the people she had been introduced to. And then it was over, there was resounding applause and the talking started up again. Abby's stomach was rumbling – the canapés had stopped circulating a while ago – and her mouth was dry. Her feet were throbbing, and the room was almost unbearably hot.

She smiled at Leo, feeling bad that she was a spare wheel, holding him up from speaking to whomever he needed to.

'I'm just nipping to the ladies' room,' she said.

'I'll be here,' he replied.

Abby took her time in the luxurious cloakroom, washing her hands and dabbing cold water behind her ears and on her wrists. She topped up her lipstick and, giving her reflection a final quick glance, returned to the fray.

At first, she couldn't see Leo. She looked around blindly, and then felt a hand clutch her shoulder, stopping her in her tracks.

'Wait here,' he said quietly, all the warmth gone from his voice. 'I'm going to give this two minutes, and then I'm stepping in.' Abby frowned, then turned to find that the crowd had parted around two people, a buzz of anticipation filling the room.

'Shit,' she whispered, as she recognized the blond, smug-looking man who was aiming a ridiculous grin at Jack, his arms folded over his chest.

'Westcoat,' Eddie Markham said. 'How're things with you? Bit of a tough year, as I understand it?'

Abby swallowed. She could hear Leo's even breathing.

Jack's jaw was set, his shoulders stiff with tension. 'Eddie.' His voice was flat.

'What, not even a pat on the back for your old friend? Don't you think it's time to put our differences aside? One word of apology from you, that's all it'll take.'

Abby saw Jack's shoulders rise in a sigh. 'I've apologized. I've said all I need to, so now, if you'll excuse me.' He turned away, but Eddie slapped a hand against his chest, stopping him. A ripple of concern went through the crowd.

'Come on now, old boy,' Eddie said, laughing gently. 'We can put this behind us, can't we? Doesn't our history mean more to you?'

Jack turned to face him. 'Our history is one of the reasons I should have ended the friendship long before now. So please, let me go.'

Eddie dropped his hand, his face tight with anger as Jack walked away. 'And does your new piece of skirt know everything?' he called, glancing in Abby's direction. Their eyes met for a moment, and she was shocked by how much hatred there was in them. 'I have to say, Westcoat, you've outdone yourself this time. She's gorgeous. Pliable enough for you too, I suppose? You were always the charming one, and it seems no number of fuck-ups can stop you attracting them like flies.'

Jack faltered, closing his eyes. Abby felt Leo shift beside her, ready to step in, and it was as if the entire room was holding its breath. Then Jack whispered something to himself and started walking again, away from Eddie, towards her and Leo, his expression blank. Behind him, Bob Stevens grabbed Eddie by the arm and pulled him away.

Jack stopped in front of Abby and took her hand. 'I am so, so sorry,' he said. 'I'm sorry he said those things, and that you had to hear them.'

She shook her head minutely, aware that the crowd had focused their attention on them now that Eddie was out of sight.

'Cool. As. A. Cucumber,' Leo said. 'If anyone was unsure beforehand about who is the better man in all this, then they're no longer under any illusions. I'm proud of you, and to prove it, I'm going to find us more champagne.'

Jack gave his agent a weary smile, then turned his attention back to Abby. 'Are you OK?'

She squeezed his hand. 'I am. Are you?'

He nodded. 'I hadn't expected to escape the evening without seeing him, but I'm sorry he brought you into it. He had no right,' he added, his voice hard. 'But I should have known he would do this. He has a way of cutting where it hurts the most. Please don't pay any attention to what he said. Don't let him get under your skin.'

'There's no room for anyone else under my skin,' she whispered, and they held each other's gaze until Leo returned with full glasses and insisted on toasting Jack as if his restraint amounted to winning the Booker prize.

'One more circuit of the room?' Leo asked, draining his drink. 'I'm sure everyone's eager to speak to you after that encounter, and then you will have definitely earned your escape.'

Abby watched as Jack physically pulled himself up straight, preparing to put on a performance. 'Sure this is OK?' he asked her. 'We can leave now if you'd rather.'

'I'm happy to stay as long as you need to.'

He lifted his arm and smiled at her, and Abby gratefully slipped her hand through it. Now, more than ever, she wanted to show the world that she was on his side.

Chapter Twenty

The male peafowl, called a peacock, is one of the most stunning birds you can see in this country, but they originally come from India. They're royal blue and display their incredible tails – greeny-gold feathers with gold, green and blue eyespots – when they want to attract a mate. A peahen will pick the male peacock they like the best by looking at the length of their feathers, and the colour and quality of the eyespots on their tails.

— Note from Abby's notebook

Abby sank into the plush leather of the Mercedes and slipped her sandals off, groaning in relief. Jack slid in after her, undoing the top button of his shirt, draping his jacket and bow tie over the seat between them. He gave her a sideways look.

'Painful shoes?'

'It's so good to get them off,' she said, leaning her head against the headrest.

'Here.' He held out his hands.

'What?'

'Your feet.'

'What?' Abby stared at him.

'Swing round and put your feet up here, and I'll massage them.'

'Jack,' she laughed. 'You don't want to touch my feet.'

'I honestly give a great foot massage,' he said. 'Come on, Abby, you wouldn't have sore feet if it wasn't for me, and I can't be responsible for you not making it back to the reserve on time because you can barely walk. Penelope would never forgive me.'

'He's right about that, she wouldn't,' Leo piped up from the passenger seat. 'And I can vouch for his foot massages.'

'Piss off, Leo,' Jack laughed. He waggled his hands, and she swivelled round, lifting her feet onto the seat between them. Jack took hold of them and put them on his lap, and then began slowly pressing his thumbs into the balls of her feet.

'Oh my God,' she murmured. 'That is so good.'

Jack smiled at her then focused on what he was doing, and Abby closed her eyes and let him soothe the aches and pains away.

'I'm not going to keep going on about it,' Leo said, 'but it was entirely serendipitous that Eddie accosted you. You've proved to everyone that last year was a one-off, that you're putting it behind you. You came out of it ten feet tall, Jack. I'm a very proud agent – and friend.'

Jack's hands stilled for a moment, and then he continued pummelling Abby's feet. She opened her eyes and watched him closely, the way the muscles worked in his jaw, his eyes cast downwards. She couldn't help but agree with Leo, even though it was clear the exchange had affected Jack.

'Anyway,' Leo pressed on. 'I think we can say with complete confidence that tonight was a success. Bob Stevens is still keen for you to be an ambassador, you're seen uppermost in people's minds as a professional author rather than an amateur boxer, and with Abby at your side you have positively wowed the crowds. Job well done, Jack.'

'We survived it, at least,' Jack said. 'Thanks, in no small part, to both of you.' He nodded at Leo, gave Abby a brief smile, and then moved onto her arches, his touch firm but tender.

Leo waved away Jack's gratitude. 'Anyone for a McDonald's pit stop? Gene's going to drop me off at home, then take you back to Meadowgreen.'

'Great,' Jack said. 'I could kill for a Big Mac.'

At some point after they had devoured their burgers and licked the salt from the fries off their fingers, Abby fell asleep. Without Leo's endless chatter, and with the repetitive rhythm of wheels over tarmac, she found her eyelids drooping. They hadn't left the hotel until after eleven, and by the time they'd driven out of London and made their food stop, it was close to midnight.

She awoke with a jolt, her eyes struggling to find anything to latch onto in the dark. Then she remembered, and assessed her position. Her head was on Jack's knee, her seatbelt stretched to its limit. His jacket was over her bare shoulders and his hand was resting gently on her hip. She sat up slowly, and Jack's arm slid off her. She looked at him in the moonlight slipping through the window, and the muted lights from the dashboard up front.

He was asleep, his forehead resting against the glass, his eyelashes shadowing his cheeks. He looked peaceful, and

Abby indulged in being able to watch him unseen; the definition of his collarbone through his open shirt, the dimple in his cheek barely visible when he wasn't smiling, the beginnings of stubble along his jawline. She realized she was holding her breath, not wanting to disturb him, wanting to memorize everything about him.

'Abby,' Gene asked quietly, 'do you want me to take you to yours first, then I can drop Jack off?'

'Where are you staying? Are you in the spare room of Peacock Cottage?'

'No, I'm bunking with a mate in Ipswich tonight, so I've not too far to go after this.'

'OK then,' she said, wondering what to do now it was down to her. 'First, we should go to . . .'

'Peacock Cottage,' Jack said gruffly. He gave her a sleepy smile, and Abby's whole body tingled in response. 'The least I can do is offer you a nightcap, toast an evening that wouldn't have been nearly so positive without you there.'

'Then you'll walk me home afterwards?'

He held her gaze. The painful silver sandals, his long fingers massaging her feet were surely not far from his mind, as they weren't from hers.

'Of course,' he said.

'OK,' Abby replied softly. 'Peacock Cottage it is.'

They said goodbye to Gene, then she let Jack help her down from the car, and tiptoed up the front path behind him, her shoes in her hands. Moths buffeted the outside light and the blue paintwork of the door. It was still warm, despite the late hour – the promise that summer was almost upon them. The sky was clear, the moon shining, stars twinkling above the tree canopy like a painted stage backdrop behind a forest silhouette. She waited while Jack unlocked the door, his jacket slung over his shoulder, and then followed him into the hallway.

'Make yourself at home,' he said.

Abby left her shoes in the hall and sank onto the sofa in the living room, hugging Shalimar against her. The cuddly hippo smelt of clean linen and the faintest trace of Jack's aftershave. She closed her eyes, but she no longer felt tired. The way Jack had answered Gene's question, not even consulting her, his voice rough with sleep, made her heart race. She heard his footsteps, the jingle of ice, and he walked into the room, placed two glasses on the table and sat next to her. He slipped off his polished black shoes and stretched his arms up to the ceiling, his shirt pulling out of the waistband of his trousers.

'It's whisky,' he said. 'I hope that's OK?'

He handed her a glass and, when she nodded, clinked his against it.

'Thank you for coming with me tonight. I'm not sure I could have done it without you.'

'Of course you could,' she said, feeling the whisky burn down her throat. 'You didn't let Eddie get to you. You were so calm, Jack. And you had Leo, Gene – you were at home there, confident and charming and . . . desired.' It was the wrong word, but it was too late to change it. And now it was out there, it gave her a rush of her own confidence, of certainty.

'Looks can be deceiving,' he said softly.

'Not to me. Not about you. I know you, Jack.'

'Not everything.'

'I don't need to know everything. But Leo said – why won't you tell anyone what really happened with you and Eddie?'

Jack sipped his whisky, holding the liquid in his mouth before swallowing. 'Eddie begged me to help him cover up the plagiarism,' he said eventually. 'I told him it was best to come clean, but he was desperate to try and save his career – to not ruin it before it had even begun, though I wanted to argue that he'd already done that by stealing someone else's work. But he needed my help, and he was – had been – my closest friend. I gave it to him.' He reached out and ran his hand along Shalimar's soft fur.

Abby nodded. It was the opposite of what Eddie had said in the interview. She believed Jack entirely. Not just because she wanted to, but because it was a truth hard-won, dragged out of him, not like the lies that so easily tripped off Eddie's tongue.

'Thank you,' she said quietly. 'For telling me.'

'That's not all of it.'

'It's enough. For now.'

He was staring towards the window, the thin curtains shutting out the night, his face strained in profile. He had been honest with her and, even though he hadn't asked for anything, she needed to reciprocate.

She swallowed. 'I've been holding back, from you. Worrying that your past, what you did to Eddie last year meant that I was stuck on a loop, choosing the wrong people to care about.' Jack turned towards her, his whole body tensing, but she kept her gaze trained on the hippo. 'The reason I've been hesitant with you is because I told myself that you were no good for me.'

'Abby, I—'

'And what my dad did, towards the end . . . he hurt me as much as he hurt Mum; it wasn't just when I got in the way. Tessa keeps reminding me that I always end up repeating

329

it, finding someone who I can mirror Mum and Dad's relationship with, that I'm drawn towards people who will hurt me.'

Jack inhaled, about to reply, but Abby kept going.

'But I know you're not like that. I knew from the beginning, really, but things – Tessa's warnings, Meadowsweet and Penelope – I couldn't let myself believe it or give in to the way I felt. But it's gone on too long. This time, I know I'm not making the wrong decision.' She took another sip of whisky. 'I can't stay hidden away any more, I have to trust myself. I have to take a chance.'

His fingers were perfectly still, resting on Shalimar's coat.

'On what?' he asked, his voice low.

She put her glass on the coffee table, leaned forward and kissed him. It brought back flashes of their first kiss in this room, the feel of his skin, the thrill it gave her. She knew they wouldn't be interrupted this time, and in seconds she had obliterated that first kiss, had made hers more definite, its purpose clear. And the touch of his lips against hers, unmoving for a second and then responding, kissing her back so that they found their own rhythm, was everything, rewarding her months of wanting and waiting, shattering any last doubts she might have had.

'Jack,' she murmured, breaking off to take his glass and put it down, to move Shalimar behind her, then returning to him with her lips, her arms around his waist. He moved closer, his hands sliding up her back, his fingers pressing lightly, the thin fabric of her dress not dulling the sensation as their kisses became more passionate.

'Abby Field,' he said, in between kisses. 'This was not why I asked you to come with me tonight.'

'Really?' She smiled at him, running her hands – finally

– through his luxurious, dark hair. 'Because it was part of the reason I said yes.'

He looked at her for a moment, then took hold of the silky fabric and pulled the dress over her head, and she undid his shirt buttons, her movements careful and slow, not wanting to rush any of it as she revealed all of Jack Westcoat, bit by beautiful bit, until they were no longer hiding anything from each other.

She woke early, birdsong and sunshine slipping in through the bedroom window, caressing the walls, the duvet cover and the sleeping, still form of Jack. Abby lightly kissed his shoulder. His skin was warm, his head turned away from her. She snuggled up to his back, wrapping her arm around him, and her eyes drifted closed again.

At some point during the night they had made it upstairs, but sleep had come late, and Abby was happily exhausted. A part of her couldn't believe she had been so brazen, had taken the initiative like that, and yet a part of her had known, from the moment he had knocked on her front door in his suit, with the blue handkerchief in his jacket pocket – from long before then if she was entirely honest – that this was what she had wanted. Jack Westcoat, as close as she could possibly get him.

He turned over, so that their faces were inches apart, his eyes blinking slowly open.

'Hello.' He smiled, the dimple half hidden by stubble as he kissed her.

'Morning,' she replied as he pulled her against him, and then his kisses became deeper and words were no longer important.

* * *

When he was sleeping again, she tiptoed downstairs and found paper and a pen. She wrote him a note and left it on the coffee table, placing Shalimar on top to act as sentry and paperweight.

> *Dear sleeping beauty,*
> *I have to go and attend to the other man in my life*
> *– Raffle needs a long walk.*
> *Can I come around later? Text me.*
> *Abby x*

She picked up her dress from the sofa, slipped it on and found a lightweight navy jacket hanging on the hook by the front door. It was far too long for her, the sleeves flapping over her hands, but at least it would distract anyone who saw her from the fact that her outfit was not remotely suitable for a Saturday morning stroll. She added to her note.

> *PS I'll bring your jacket back when I come.*

The morning was warm, and honeybees buzzed lazily around the hanging basket, its heather resplendent once more. Abby took her usual shortcut back to the village, the birdsong loud around her. It always lifted her heart, but at that moment she was convinced she had reached the ceiling; there was nowhere higher for her heart to go.

If anyone saw her walking barefoot, pale-blue dress shimmering below a too-large jacket, hair in disarray, she didn't notice. She was too lost in her own thoughts, the surrealness of the previous evening, the people she had met and the champagne she had drunk, the image of Jack so alive and confident as he charmed his peers, the way he had deflected Eddie's cruel words, showing the strength to walk away, and the constant pinch-me moments that she was at his side, her hand pressed between his arm and his torso. Together.

She tried to think what Tessa might say. Would she suggest that getting Abby into bed had been Jack's intention all along, but he was clever enough to make it look like it had been her choice? He had told Gene to take them back to Peacock Cottage, but that would have been Abby's choice too – she just hadn't wanted to assume that he felt that strongly. No, Jack wasn't using her – he cared about her, she was sure of it.

She unlocked the front door and gathered her husky to her as he greeted her with a wagging tail, his tongue protruding happily. 'Oh Raffle,' she said. 'I have had the best time. I would never abandon you, but you might have to get used to a bit more of Jack, what do you think?' Raffle licked her arm.

She went into the kitchen to top up his water bowl, and found a note on the counter:

Dearest Abby,

Raffle is staying with me tonight, just in case Jack Westcoat does the decent thing and whisks you off your feet, à la Cinderella, and you don't make it back here. ;) I'll drop puppy off in the morning and give him some food.

Love and kisses
Octavia xoxoxo

She was touched by her neighbour's thoughtfulness, even if it made her cheeks burn with embarrassment. Wondering how long Octavia had known about her passion for Jack, she went to take a long shower.

She pulled her damp hair into a ponytail and put on a T-shirt and shorts. Her Converse sneakers felt like soft cushions around her aching feet, and the memory of Jack massaging her toes in the car, and then later, in his bed as he'd started there and worked his way slowly upwards, made her body burn with longing.

'Come on Raffle,' she said, suddenly desperate for fresh air. 'Let's get going.' He didn't need to be told twice.

She walked along the wall of Swallowtail House and peered in through the side gate, Jack's shiny padlock and chain seeming out of place against the rusted metal. It looked the same, though everything was much greener than it had been during their February visit, a new snake of ivy slinking towards one of the ground-floor windows. It wouldn't be long before the whole place was consumed by greenery, and she hoped that when that happened it would still be in Penelope's hands, that its quiet, natural beauty wouldn't be disturbed by a stark future it didn't deserve. She retraced her steps, her phone beeping as she reached the main road.

It was Rosa:

How was last night? I want all the details! xx

Abby grinned, turned in the direction of home and almost bumped into someone. 'Oh, I'm sor—' she started, and then her words lodged in her throat.

Even with his baseball cap and shades, he was easily recognizable, but it took her brain a few seconds to process the fact that he was in Meadowgreen. He didn't belong here. Goose bumps prickled her arm, but before she had a chance to step away, he grabbed her and pulled her against him,

334

angling his head towards hers. She smelt alcohol on his breath and pushed her hands hard against his chest just as Raffle surged forward, barking, jumping up at Eddie Markham with his teeth bared.

Eddie released his grip and backed off, laughing as he removed his cap and sunglasses. Abby tried to blink away her shock, half-heartedly dragging Raffle away, worried only about the implications for her dog if he hurt Eddie.

'What are you doing?' she demanded, cursing her voice for sounding so weak.

Eddie ignored her and turned around, giving someone the thumbs-up. Dazed, Abby followed his sightline, and saw a man standing on the opposite side of the road beside a white van, a camera with a long zoom lens hanging round his neck. He returned Eddie's gesture, then jumped into the driver's seat just as Eddie turned back to face her.

'Abby Field,' he said, eyeing Raffle warily. 'That's your name, isn't it? Didn't anyone tell you not to get involved with bad boys?'

'You can't do this.' She rubbed her arm, the skin tender where he had grabbed her.

'What have I done?' He shrugged elaborately, but then his grin faded, replaced with a hard-set expression. 'Jack owes me for what he did last summer. He busted my nose – I had to pay for reconstructive surgery – not to mention the humiliation he caused me. I would have let it go if he'd been prepared to apologize last night, but he was too busy trying to impress you. I came all this way to sort things out with him, but a few minutes ago he turned me away from that ridiculous fairytale cottage without so much as a hello, even when I took pains to compliment him on his new woman.'

'Why would he want to speak to you after everything you said about him – what you said *to* him last night?'

'Only the truth, darling.'

'You made it all up!' she said, fury building inside her.

'Is that what Jack told you? He really has got you under his spell. Don't feel too bad – we've all been there.'

'Last night showed that people are ready to move on,' Abby said, and Raffle joined in with a low, threatening growl.

Eddie glanced at the husky again. 'Maybe that's true, but when the next chapter in his dirty little story comes out, how he's supposedly cut all ties with Eddie Markham but is happy enough to share his women, it'll come back to haunt him.'

Abby felt winded. 'I did *not* allow you to touch me!'

'Maybe you'd better give someone an exclusive then? Oh wait, they won't care what you have to say, and Jack will think that by staying quiet he can hold onto his integrity, play the loyal, upstanding gentleman. What a fucking joke. Take my advice, Abby. Jack Westcoat is a broken man; it's only going to go downhill from here. Pick someone whose star is ascending.'

'*You're* the joke,' Abby spat back, trying to suppress a wave of panic.

Eddie laughed at her, long and loud, and then sauntered over the road towards the van and his waiting photographer. Abby thought about calling for help, getting someone to stop them, but what would be the point? All they needed was a laptop and an internet signal, and the photographs would be on their way to whichever news desks Eddie had pre-warned.

She took a few steps back and sank onto the grass at the side of the road. It was dotted with buttercups, bees flying eagerly between them without a care in the world except seeking out more pollen.

She was still shaking, her body vibrating with anger. Had Eddie Markham really just tried to assault her, all so it could be caught on film and he could fabricate another story about Jack? Only moments ago she had felt happy and content, full of hope. Last night's gala had been a triumph; she had been sure that it would help Jack move on and the past, however ugly it had been, would be properly behind him.

But in a matter of moments, she could have ruined everything. She had been naive. She should have walked away the moment she realized who he was instead of standing, frozen, like a scarecrow. What would that moment of hesitation cost Jack? And what would it cost her, once he found out what part she had played in it? Would the papers even be interested in this ridiculous non-event? She prayed that they wouldn't be, but she would have to wait to find out. What couldn't wait, was telling Jack.

Raffle nuzzled his head into her lap, whimpering.

'I'm OK boy,' she said, stroking his ears, but she didn't feel it. She pulled her phone out of the pocket of her shorts, and saw that she had three missed calls from Jack, and a text message:

Call me – it's important. Eddie's here.

He must have phoned during her altercation with Eddie – a couple of minutes too late. She was about to call him back when the phone rang in her hand.

'Hello?' Her voice was small.

'Abby, where are you? Are you OK?' Jack sounded breathless.

'I, uhm – he found me.'

337

'*What?* What did he do? Are you all right? Tell me where you are.'

'Five minutes away, on the main road near Swallowtail.'

'Stay there.' He hung up.

Abby wrapped her arms around Raffle and waited. She heard the screech of wheels on tarmac, and the Range Rover came to a halt haphazardly on the side of the road. Jack hurtled out and dropped onto the grass next to her, caressing her cheek, lifting her head up to meet his gaze.

'What did he do?' His blue eyes were sharp with concern.

'Nothing,' Abby said. 'He tried, but Raffle stopped him. But Jack, there was a photographer, I don't know what he got, but—'

'Never mind about that. Come on.' He helped Abby to her feet and led her to the car, letting Raffle hop into the back seat. He did a U-turn and drove back to Peacock Cottage. It took less than a minute.

Once inside, he settled Abby on the sofa, Raffle at her feet, and then disappeared, returning with cups of strong coffee.

'I am so sorry,' he said, running a hand through his hair. 'I should have called you sooner, but – I was so surprised to see him; I opened the door thinking it was you, and then—' His voice hitched. 'Are you sure he didn't hurt you?'

'I'm sure,' Abby said, sipping her coffee. The heat of it was comforting, despite the warm day.

Jack took her hand. Now the anger had dissipated he looked worn out. Their night together had left him with hardly any sleep, but Abby knew it was more than that. The appearance of Eddie Markham in Meadowgreen, when he had believed things had finally begun to turn a corner, was a shock. It had shaken her, too.

'I'm sorry, Jack,' she said. 'I didn't react quickly enough. He made a pass, and waved to this guy with a camera . . . it was a set-up. He told me that you still owed him for breaking his nose, for the humiliation you caused him. He was angry you'd refused to apologize last night. He doesn't want you to get away with it, to get back in everyone's good books.'

Jack hung his head. 'I need to call Leo,' he mumbled.

'He said that you would never give your side of the story out of loyalty. Is that true? Is that the reason you won't talk about what happened? What *did* happen Jack? Will you tell me the whole story? I know last night I stopped you, but . . . can you tell me?'

When he finally met her gaze, his eyes were bright, wary, somehow. Abby couldn't look away. She didn't want him to think for a second that he didn't have her full attention, that she doubted him; that she wasn't there for him.

Because, whatever he told her now, Abby knew what kind of a man Jack was. She had spent too many months tiptoeing around him, believing that because of their early, heated conversations and the whispers about his troubled past, she would be best staying away from him and living her easy, uncomplicated life.

But even while she had been telling herself that her feelings were temporary, heightened by the presence of this new, mysterious man in their village, a part of her had known she was fooling herself. All that time, Jack Westcoat had been working his way under her skin, getting comfortable in her thoughts and her fantasies, setting up home and refusing to leave.

And then, last night, she had finally accepted it. The way she felt about him, the realization that his feelings mirrored hers. They had shed their skins for each other, had stopped

339

holding back. And now, even if what Eddie had said was right, that the damage he had caused – was continuing to cause – meant that Jack's career was over, Abby would stand by him. She didn't give herself up to people easily; she had stayed sheltered in her quiet, comfortable life for so long, and had felt exhilarated and impulsive in Jack's presence, but never, not once, threatened or unsafe. She knew what kind of a man he was, and she wanted him to believe it too.

'Tell me, Jack,' she whispered.

The late May sun streamed through the window, and she could feel the gentle pressure of Raffle's nose on her foot, keeping her close while he dozed. And as a blackbird sang its fluty, soaring song just outside Peacock Cottage, Jack stroked his thumb repeatedly over Abby's hand, looked into her eyes, and nodded.

Part 4

Birds of a Feather

Chapter Twenty-One

The marsh harrier is a large bird of prey with a brown body and a pale head. It feeds on animals that live on or near marshes and drops unsuspectingly onto defenceless creatures from the air. Its courtship call is a kind of mewling wail.

— Note from Abby's notebook

'Eddie Markham was my best friend,' Jack said, and the sound of his voice, low and deep, on the edge of breaking, made Abby's breath catch.

Raffle, lifted his head briefly, and then went back to snoozing at their feet.

'We met at school,' Jack continued, 'and were pretty much inseparable. My background was more privileged than his, and that didn't matter to me, but as we grew older, it was clear that it did to him. I tried my hardest not to ever make a point of it, and I thought we had enough in common that Eddie could see past it, but whenever we got in trouble he'd make quips about my dad bailing me out, how I was untouchable. In fact, Dad came down hard on me without fail, adamant that I had to learn from my mistakes.'

He glanced at Abby then away again, as if it was easier to pretend he was telling someone else. 'As we got close to the end of school, Eddie started to behave outlandishly, splashing money that I didn't think he had to go on expensive holidays, buying designer clothes, burning hundreds of pounds on nights out. And then we went to Oxford together, and things got worse.'

He released Abby's hand and took Shalimar from the coffee table, squeezing the tatty toy between his fingers.

'Worse?' she prompted softly.

'He started taking drugs, disregarding everything except having a good time: wild nights out, turning up drunk or wasted to tutorials, insistent that I should join him, that this was the best time of our lives.'

'And this was what the papers were referring to?' Abby's throat felt as if it was sealed shut.

He nodded. 'I was young, living away from home for the first time, and I suppose I was weak. But it was a few joints, too much alcohol and partying. I never took the harder drugs, never went to the extremes Eddie did, but I'm not proud of the way I behaved. And of course, it began affecting my studies. I told myself I was going along with him to protect him, to stop him self-destructing, that I was still fully in control.'

'But you weren't?'

Jack ran a hand over his jaw, the gesture now so familiar to Abby. 'Not at all. And Eddie laid it at my door, said that I could have anything I wanted, so why shouldn't he be the same? It was warped, but I felt guilty. I wondered if, somehow, I *had* pushed him into it. I couldn't see straight to a way out for him, but when my grades started to suffer, and with Eddie getting more and more reckless, I realized that I had to change. I didn't enjoy being constantly high or hungover, and I didn't want to be part of Eddie's blinkered destructiveness. I told him that I wasn't doing it any more, hoping it would make him see sense too.'

'What did he say?'

'At first, he left me behind, and a part of me was relieved. But then he got his act together, dragging up his grades and knocking on my door, wanting to reconcile. That became the pattern; he'd work hard for a while, and then get lured back into the drugs and start going downhill again.'

'And you stayed friends with him all this time?' Abby asked.

'I realized, after that first time, that I couldn't do anything else,' Jack said. 'I'd grown up with him. How could I live with myself if I left him to fall apart? I continued to go out with him – though it was more as a chaperone. I stayed away from the drugs, stood up for him when his dedication to the course was questioned. And then I had a wake-up call.' He leaned forward and rubbed furiously at his cheeks.

Abby took hold of his wrists and gently pulled his hands away. 'What happened?'

'Eddie spiked my drink with Ecstasy on a night out. He was already wired, I'd refused, as always, and so he took the decision out of my hands.'

'Oh my God.' Abby's stomach twisted. She tried to imagine the panic, the helplessness of something like that happening to her. For Jack, who was always – *almost* always – so in control, it must have been horrifying.

'I'd started seeing a girl, Hannah, and when I got back to our flat I was a mess. I'd worked out what he'd done, but I couldn't think straight. I didn't know how much he'd put in my drink, and Hannah ended up calling an ambulance. She was upset and scared, my parents were called and the college was notified. I was lucky not to lose my place.

'After I'd stopped taking part in Eddie's stupid games and tried to support him, he'd compromised my relationships, my future. I thought, if he can go that far, then what else can he do? I broke off all contact with him and threw myself into my studies. And, over time, I heard he'd improved. He got cleaned up, started studying again, managed to scrape through with a degree of his own.

'A couple of years after I'd graduated, when I'd been writing for a while trying to get a novel finished, our old professor, Ernest Chisolm, contacted me. He said Eddie was writing a book and was desperate to rebuild bridges. I should have said no – to this day I wish I had – but I was curious. I also thought that what he'd done to me had been the catalyst for his own recovery and I felt, somehow, I owed it to him to hear him out.'

'It's understandable,' Abby said, sliding her finger round the rim of her coffee cup.

'Is it? I *knew* that getting back in touch with him was a bad idea, that however much he'd moved on, his self-destructive nature wasn't too far from the surface. But I saw him, and there was a semblance of the old Eddie there. He drew me back in – he's charming, clever, and very good at pulling the wool over people's eyes. We weren't as tightly bound as we'd been before, but our friendship was shakily resurrected. And then, just as we were both getting our careers off the ground, he was accused of plagiarism by Ernest Chisolm. He'd ripped off the work of our tutor, who had stayed in touch with him, helped him, long after graduation.'

346

Abby inhaled. 'Seriously? Your tutor's work?'

Jack nodded. 'Eddie asked me to bail him out. He said he was innocent, that Ernest was making it up, bitter that Eddie's book was being published when his wasn't. He said Ernest was lying but that he could placate him, make it go away. However, there was also a journalist who had uncovered it, and it was someone I knew. I wanted time to compare their work, to see for myself and make a decision, but Eddie told me the story was going to print, that there was no time.

'He was so close to the edge, high on drink and drugs again, worse than I'd ever seen him, and I knew this could tip him over. I agreed to pay off the journalist while he settled whatever he needed to with Ernest, as long as he never mentioned my involvement to anyone, got his life back on track and stayed away from me.'

He looked at Abby, laughing when she was unable to hide her confusion.

'I know,' he said softly. 'I should never have agreed to it. But he was drowning, Abby. And I, all high and mighty with my book deal and good early reviews, thought I could pull him out of the depths. It was about helping an old friend but, looking back, I realize it was about my own arrogance, too. I wanted to show him that I was tired of all his shit, that I was stronger than he presumed, and I could get this journalist to listen to me. Look how that's turned out.'

'Jack.' Abby scooted forwards and took his hands. His T-shirt was faded red, the neckline pulled slightly out of shape. She thought of him putting it hastily on as Eddie had knocked on the door of Peacock Cottage that morning, imagining it would be her, then the shock at seeing him standing there.

'He took my help and disappeared,' Jack continued, clearly

347

needing to get to the end of the story. 'I checked their work, discovered that – of course – he had stolen Ernest's. He'd been lying, I'd helped him to get away with it, and lost the trust and friendship of my old tutor in the process. But I believed that, in doing what I'd done, I'd saved Eddie – perhaps even his life – and that in some respects it was a price worth paying.

'I got on with *my* life, barely heard his name, didn't see any more books after his first, ripped-off novel. Then he started to appear in the red tops, pictured falling drunkenly out of nightclubs, better known for being a troublemaking socialite than a writer. And then, last year, there was news of this new book.

'Eddie's publicity was never going to involve straightforward reviews or a launch event at Waterstones, but I hadn't expected that interview, or the lies in it. The idea that I forced him to brush the plagiarism under the carpet, that he had wanted to come clean, that I bullied him, couldn't be further from the truth. And, if you were wondering . . .' He sighed again, squeezing her hand. 'I did not sleep with the journalist. I knew her, which was the reason Eddie had asked for my help in the first place, so I was more likely to be able to persuade her. Though the substantial sum she asked for was probably the defining factor.'

'I wasn't wondering,' Abby said. 'I didn't believe that for a second. But what did he say to you – at the awards?'

Jack took his hand away and drank his coffee, even though it had long since gone cold. 'He said that I shouldn't be too disheartened that my relationship with Natasha had ended, that there were probably some journalists waiting in the wings to ease my pain, as long as I paid them well enough.'

Abby closed her eyes.

'I know, it's pathetic, but on top of the interview he'd given . . . I'd been called in by my publishers, asked to explain myself, was close to losing my contract. And he'd *begged* me to help him hide the plagiarism claim. At the time, I'd put everything on the line – my career, my reputation, my relationship with my former professor – and then, years later, he revealed it himself anyway, twisting my involvement. And so, when he appeared, seemingly without a care in the world and said that to me – I lost it. It was stupid and reckless. I regret it as much as any other part of this whole, sorry business.' He stood up and walked to the window, pushing it wide open.

Sounds of spring invaded the room, a relief after the darkness of his story. It was horrible, all of it. Their friendship starting out so innocently, Eddie beginning to crumble under the pressure of trying to prove himself, the way he'd held on to Jack and blamed him equally, creating something toxic and destructive between them. And yet, she still didn't understand.

'Why didn't you tell your side of the story? Why didn't you explain to a newspaper, or someone you trusted, what really happened all those years ago?'

Jack turned and leaned against the windowsill. 'Because I didn't want to stoop to his level. I didn't want to bring what would essentially be a playground spat out into the open.'

'A *playground spat*? Jack, he spiked your drink! He stole someone's work, got you to cover for him, then fed all those lies about you to the paper.'

'But I chose to keep our friendship intact,' Jack said. 'I let him back in, and maybe I was partly to blame from the start. Maybe I caused this. His disregard for other people, the drugs, the need to steal Ernest's work to secure his own future.'

'How could you be responsible for what Eddie did, for the way he lived his life? Jack . . .' She pushed herself up and walked over to him. 'From what you've told me, you have given him too many chances. You tried to rescue him when, the truth is, he doesn't *want* to be rescued. The man I met today was cruel. He has caused this pain, and implicated you, deliberately. He's jealous of you, and he can't bear to see you do well. You have to stop protecting him.'

'I will. I have. After what he did to you—'

'He didn't hurt me,' she said quickly.

'But he did,' Jack said. 'Don't brush it away.' He ran his fingers through his hair, blinking rapidly, and Abby suddenly saw how vulnerable he was, as if the boy who had first smiled at Eddie Markham in a classroom all those years ago had returned, only to discover that Eddie had never really been his friend at all.

'Don't worry about me.'

'Of course I do,' he whispered. 'You're everything, Abby.'

He kissed her and she pressed herself against him, the spring breeze caressing her through the window as she tried to believe his words, that he wasn't just reaching out for something positive in the midst of fresh despair.

'I have to call Leo,' he said eventually. 'I have to tell him what's happened.'

'Of course. Do you want me to go?'

He shook his head. 'Stay with me?'

She made more coffee, listening to the cadence of his deep voice through the thin walls of the cottage. The back garden was a riot of spring flowers, of tulips and lupins, a white rose bush, the stems drooping under the weight of its blooms. Bees buzzed, early cabbage whites flittered happily in the still air, and she heard the trill of a warbler in the woodland beyond. Everything outside was peaceful and beautiful, carrying on in a way that made her envious.

When she returned to the living room, Jack was slumped on the sofa, staring at his phone.

'What did Leo say?' Abby asked.

Jack didn't reply immediately. He looked at her apprehensively, and despite the warmth of the day, she felt chilled.

'What?' Abby whispered.

'He's pissed off,' Jack said. 'Understandably.'

'With Eddie?'

'And with me. He thinks I should have seen it coming, that I should have protected you, and he's right. I should have—'

'What? Stopped me from leaving the house? Come on Jack, how could you have predicted this would be his next move? And isn't Leo just firing off because he's panicking? He seemed happy enough last night, unless he was giving you warnings when I wasn't listening.'

Jack shook his head. 'He wasn't. But he thinks I need to face it this time, to stand up to Eddie, and I've told him I'm ready to tell my side of the story. I'm just sorry this has led to you being involved. If I hadn't asked you to come with me last night . . .'

'Stop it, Jack.' She sat next to him and put the steaming mugs on the table. 'What is the point of *if only*? We are where we are, and you need to listen to Leo, do everything he says. Promote your book, show everyone the real you, and prove that Eddie's story is a complete fabrication.'

'You sound so certain.'

'And you sound like you're already defeated. Come on Jack, where's your fighting spirit?'

He gave her a lopsided smile. 'My fighting spirit is here. With you.'

'There you go then,' Abby said. 'Let's see some of it.'

But Jack's smile faded, taking Abby's confidence with it. She suddenly felt weighted down by something, a realization that didn't hit home until Jack confirmed it.

'Leo says I need to go back to London. That I need to be proactive, speak to Bob Stevens about the Page Turner Foundation, get the interviews started. He says I can't do that from here, that I have to throw myself back into the spotlight, bulldoze Eddie's claims with my presence and overwhelm the negative stories with positive ones.'

Abby's mouth was so dry that she could barely speak. 'In London,' she managed.

'In London.'

'When?' It was a whisper.

'He's coming up first thing tomorrow, to help me pack.'

'Tomorrow.'

The room was full of echoes. She couldn't do anything else but repeat his words and try and make sense of the fact that, after tomorrow, Jack wouldn't be here any more.

'Abby, I don't want to leave you, but I don't have a choice.'

She felt the well of emotion, her thoughts whirring, wondering if this return to London was planned all along. If Tessa was right, and he had been using her from the beginning. But then she forced herself to look at him – and couldn't believe it.

'I could come,' she said.

Hope flashed briefly across his face, then disappeared. 'No, you couldn't. Your life is here, in Meadowgreen. With Penelope and Rosa, Octavia, Raffle, Meadowsweet. I could never ask that of you.'

'You don't want me to come?'

'You have no idea how much I want you to come, how painful it is that I know you can't.'

'I could. I—' Her words were swallowed up as Jack pulled her against his chest. She pressed her face into the warm fabric of his T-shirt.

'I should never have let you get dragged into this,' he said. 'I should have left you alone after that first day, when you came to berate me for complaining. You were right, too, but I couldn't help it. Already, I knew I needed to see you again. I invented that rubbish about pheasants damaging my car, I sat at my desk thinking up ways I could get you to come here, or I could come and see you. Even after we'd been for coffee, part of me knew this was just a fantasy, that Peacock Cottage, Meadowgreen – you're too good for me.'

'Don't say that.'

'And now I've proved that I can't hold on to it.'

'Jack, this is not your fault.' She sat up. 'How could it be?'

'I should have stayed away from you. I should have been stronger, and then this – Eddie, going back to London – none of it would have mattered.'

'Of course it would have. How can you say that?'

'Because without you, I . . .' He faltered, shrugging.

After tomorrow he would be back in London, and Peacock Cottage would be empty again. She would be left with nothing but memories and a dull ache in her chest that was already unfurling, blossoming like the roses in the garden.

A single tear leaked out, and she broke eye contact with him. Jack cupped her face and brought his lips to hers, and Abby let him kiss away her sadness. And, as their kisses deepened, ignoring the fact that the curtains were open, or that Raffle was sleeping loyally at their feet, all Abby could think about was standing next to him in front of Swallowtail House as the sun dipped and the windows flamed, and how much everything had changed.

Abby stayed with Jack, returning to his bedroom, glancing at her phone screen but not replying to the persistent messages from Rosa and Octavia, one from Tessa inviting her over tomorrow. Jack, too, focused solely on her, even when Leo's name flashed up on his iPhone.

'I'll listen to his message later,' he murmured, pulling the duvet over them both.

She tried not to think about the photos, and that if Eddie was as intent on hurting Jack as he seemed to be, then the pictures would most likely be online already. She tried not to think about anything but being with Jack.

When the sun began to set, he slipped from the bed, fed Raffle some cold beef, made cheese on toast and cups of tea, and brought them back upstairs.

Abby settled into the crook of his arm as they ate, watching the sky darken.

'London's not that far from Suffolk,' she said into the quiet. 'I could visit you.'

Jack kissed the top of her head. 'The press might follow the story, see if they can get any more on what Eddie's fed them. I don't want to risk you being implicated any more than you already are.'

Abby nodded, trying not to feel it as a rejection.

'And Leo will want me to concentrate on the book, the publicity.' He sighed and put his empty plate on the bedside table. 'I don't want you to stay away Abby, but I need to protect you from some of this. If it gets difficult again, if I—'

'Who will stop you from drowning your sorrows in a bottle of whisky?'

'I promise that if I even think about it, I'll go and get some chips instead, OK?'

Abby laughed, the sound breaking through the quiet. 'OK. You have to keep that promise, though, or I'll worry.'

He slunk down the pillows, pulling her to him. 'I'll be all right.'

'You will?'

He hesitated. 'The thought of you here, striding through the reserve, sitting in the forest hide watching those ridiculous bullfinches, will keep me going.'

She nodded, wondering how she was going to go back to her job, to be bright and bubbly and full of the joys of summer when Jack was living his life without her, back in London.

They slept, they talked, they held each other, and then, long after the birds had woken and the new day had begun, a loud knock on the door dragged them from sleep, and Jack crawled out of bed, pulled on jeans and the scruffy red T-shirt, and went to let Leo in.

Chapter Twenty-Two

The magpie is a large black-and-white bird with a long tail about the same length as its body. They eat almost anything, and often steal eggs and baby birds from nests. They're the subject of a lot of superstition – seeing a single magpie can be a sign of bad fortune, impending death or the devil. A magpie's call is like a harsh cackle.

— Note from Abby's notebook

Abby took her time showering in Peacock Cottage's clean but dated bathroom, hearing the low mumblings of Jack and Leo downstairs. She was pleased that, knowing everything, Jack was ready to give his side of the story, even if she didn't believe her involvement should have been the final straw, that he should have stopped it long before now. His loyalty to Eddie was, in some ways, commendable, but she could also see that he had been trapped by him, stuck between friendship and the guilt of having been brought up in a family with more opportunities.

But in the relatively short time Abby had known Jack, she

hadn't seen him push his wealth in other people's faces, even if that wealth was now due to book sales rather than his upbringing. He wore expensive clothes and aftershave, drove a good car, but he'd always done those things in an unobtrusive way, never showing off. She remembered that at the beginning she'd felt he'd had a sense of entitlement, but she had come to see that as the remains of the confidence he'd had before Eddie's interview thrust him unkindly into the spotlight, and his frustration at the turn his life had taken.

She couldn't imagine any scenario in which Jack was responsible for Eddie's behaviour, but even after a brief encounter with him, she could see how he could get Jack to believe that, could weave his web around his friend in order to bring him down too. Eddie Markham was definitely a storyteller, even if his best ones hadn't made their way between the pages of a book.

When Abby tiptoed into the living room, Jack was standing at the window with his back to the room, and Leo was sitting on the sofa, Raffle lying across his lap. His narrow face was punctuated by worry lines, and his smile, when he acknowledged her, was weary.

'Hi Abby,' he said. 'Your dog's taken a bit of a liking to me.'

'Leo, it's good to see you again. Even when—' She gestured, unsure how to encompass everything. 'Let me get him off, he gets heavy after a while. Raffle, come on dude.' She stroked the fur between her dog's ears and coaxed him off Leo's lap. Raffle gave a single, loud bark and scrambled onto the floor.

Abby sat on the sofa next to Leo and saw the clutch of Sunday papers that he must have brought with him. The first one had a story about a hurricane in America on the front page, the devastation it had caused, but in the bottom right was a small, blurry picture, and Abby felt the shock at seeing herself, her bright-blue T-shirt and denim shorts, her hair looking lighter in the sun.

The photo had been taken at the moment when Eddie had made his move, in the seconds when she'd been too stunned to react, and the headline accompanying it read: *Markham and Westcoat's war turns personal.* Abby closed her eyes, torn between wanting to read what was written, and wanting to bury her head in the sand.

'I'm sorry Abby,' Leo said gently. 'This is the worst one. I would say don't read it, but I think you need to know what they've said.'

He riffled through the pile, pulled out a paper that had nothing about them on the cover, but then he turned to one of the pages inside and Abby saw the headline running across the top in bold font:

THICK AS THIEVES
Eddie and Jack share same woman, hours apart!

Abby forced herself to read the short article.

The rivalry between authors Eddie Markham and Jack Westcoat took a new turn today when, we can exclusively reveal, they were seen snuggling up to the same woman, only hours apart. Eddie Markham, 34, whose second novel, *Stifle,* was published last year, was pictured in an embrace with 31-year-old mystery girl, Abby Field, the morning after the Page Turner literary gala, where she had accompanied Jack Westcoat, bestselling author of *In the Grip of Death* and *The Fractured Path,* among others. Jack and Eddie's once-close friendship blew up last July when Eddie

revealed that Jack had helped him cover up an alleged plagiarism scandal centred around his first book, *The Scoop*. Westcoat, 34, retaliated at the Page Turner awards with a well-aimed punch, and had been in hiding until making a triumphant appearance at the gala on Friday night. With his new book due to be published in less than three months' time, it is yet to be seen what effect this new development will have on his troubled career. It is understood that Ms Field is a resident of the Suffolk village where Jack has been staying, while her involvement with Markham is still a matter for speculation. At the time of going to print, neither of the authors' spokesmen were available for comment.

The rest of the page was taken up with two photographs. A bigger, grainier version of the one she had seen on the cover of the other paper, Eddie's hand around her arm, his face inches from hers, Raffle positioned behind them so that his bared teeth were hidden from view.

The other was a snap from the gala that she hadn't realized was being taken. It showed her and Jack, dressed in their finery, her arm in his as they stepped towards the hotel's grand entrance. Jack's head was angled towards hers, his hair flopping over his forehead, and he was smiling. She was looking down, probably concentrating on the steps, but her pink lips were curved upwards, the sheer fabric of her dress glistening like water under the camera's flash.

If it hadn't been in a national newspaper, used to tell a story that was so far from the truth that it was laughable, she would have wanted to cut it out and keep it as a memento of that night. She realized that she had no photos of Jack, that they had never stopped for a selfie, that she hadn't taken one spontaneously, surprising him when they'd been walking through the woods.

'Eddie hasn't made a statement,' Leo said, breaking into her thoughts. 'Which is a good thing. Maybe he's hoping the pictures will speak for themselves, because he knows that if he tries to claim anything more then it will be quickly denied.'

'By you?' she asked.

Leo nodded, his fingers pressed against his lips.

'We're going to respond to this,' Jack said, turning from the window. 'We're going to say that Eddie staged it, that it was the first time you had spoken to him.'

'We'll keep your name out of it, Abby,' Leo added.

'How? It's already in here.' She pressed her hand over the page, the newsprint dusty beneath her palm.

'But we don't have to confirm it,' Leo explained. 'We'll refer to you as a close friend of Jack's, if that's OK with you.'

'Sure,' she said. 'Look, I – I should leave you two to it, shouldn't I? Packing, and everything.'

Leo stood and gave her a quick, tight hug. 'It's been lovely to get to know you, Abby.' He patted her twice on the shoulder, then stepped back. 'Hopefully we'll see each other again soon. And don't forget to smile, OK? However miserable you feel on the inside, smile, and you're halfway there.'

'I'll try,' she said, forcing a smile, wondering why that phrase sounded so familiar.

Jack walked with her to the front door. She stepped onto the path, into a beautiful day bursting with the heady scents of early summer. She let Raffle's lead out, allowed him to snuffle at the grass, at the tires of Jack's squashed-frog Range Rover that, in a few hours, would be speeding down to London.

'This is too hard,' Jack said, wrapping his arms around

her waist. 'I'm supposed to go back to my flat, stand up to Eddie, talk passionately about my new novel, while you're here.'

'You're going to be fine,' she said. 'Better than fine. You'll tell your side of the story, prove that you don't deserve the accusations, that you've done nothing but try and help him, and your new book will be brilliant. You'll be a huge success.'

'What about you?' he asked, tipping her face up to his. 'Tell me what you'll do.'

'I'll save Meadowsweet,' she said. 'And the House of Birds and Butterflies.'

His smile was strained. 'I don't doubt that for a second. I've seen you at work, seen the way people respond to your enthusiasm, how you're inspiring a new generation of nature lovers, children – fledglings – who will grow up to make a difference. You give people hope, Abby, and I haven't been immune from that. Even in the face of what's happened, I'll go back to London with hope, because of you.'

She exhaled, holding in her tears. 'We'll stay in touch, though, won't we?'

'Of course.' He brushed a strand of hair from her cheek and kissed her. This was the last time, she realized. A parting gift before he left to start a new chapter of his life.

'I need to let you get on,' she said, when they'd pulled apart.

'I'll write to you.'

'You'd better. Goodbye, Jack.'

'Goodbye, Abby Field.'

She walked down the path, Raffle trotting close to her, his fur rubbing against her leg. As she turned away from Peacock Cottage, stepping onto the track that would lead her to the village and home, she glanced behind her. Jack was slumped against the doorframe, a hand covering his eyes, as if he couldn't bear to watch.

When Abby got home, she went straight up to her bedroom, pulled *UK Flora and Fauna* down from the shelf and took out Jack's letters. She removed each one from its envelope in turn, reliving their relationship through his words from that first, haughty complaint to the warmer, tender notes they'd become. Raffle lay alongside her, his nose nudging her elbow, and she wrapped her arms around him and let her tears soak his fur.

The rest of the day passed in a daze. She replied to Rosa's messages as vaguely as she could, apologized to Tessa for not getting back in touch, and texted Octavia to thank her for looking after Raffle, saying the event was fun, but not elaborating. Nobody, she thought with relief, seemed to have seen the papers with her photo in. It hadn't been splashed as widely as she'd feared, but still, appearing on the front of a national newspaper wasn't something she'd ever expected to happen in her life. Her name had been mentioned, the implication that she was having – or had had – relationships with both Eddie and Jack, but somehow the reality of that wasn't able to penetrate the fug in her brain.

Jack was gone, and as much as she tried, she couldn't get Tessa's words out of her head. Her suggestion that Jack was no good for her, that he would use her and then return to London. It had played out as her sister had warned, but Abby couldn't believe that Jack's sadness at leaving her behind was false, that he was going back to his old life willingly and putting on a good show of pretending otherwise.

As the evening slipped towards a cool, perfect night, a nightingale singing while the sunshine whispered at the edge of the horizon, and Abby was sitting listlessly in her cosy armchair, she got a text from Gavin.

You dark horse! Working your way through literary celebs like a kid in a sweet shop. Whatever will Penelope think? ;)

Penelope. Meadowsweet. She had to go back there tomorrow, to carry on with her job and act like everything was normal. With dread settling in her stomach, she cleaned her teeth and crawled into bed, Raffle refusing to leave her side.

Abby woke on Monday morning and for a few blissful seconds had no recollection of the day before. Then it hit her. She stared at the ceiling as sunlight danced patterns across it through the gap in her curtains, then forced herself out of bed to take Raffle for his walk. She got ready for work with a dogged determination, everything on autopilot.

She took the long way in, not wanting to be faced with Peacock Cottage and its emptiness, but walking past the gate of Swallowtail House was as strong a reminder of her time with Jack. The house looked beautiful in the sunshine, its crumbling stonework and cracked sills not visible at this distance, and it seemed to beckon her towards it. She lifted the hefty padlock Jack had bought, and a lump lodged in her throat.

She felt winded, like she'd been hit by a car and her breathing was refusing to settle, everything bruised and tender. She was also angry with herself. Was this normal? Had some of Octavia's air for the dramatic rubbed off on her? She hadn't felt like this when she had broken it off with Darren. She had been sad, of course, but it had been a relief more than anything. Now she felt hollow, as if she would crack open at the lightest touch.

'Get a grip, Abby,' she said out loud, and a robin landed on a branch ahead of her, its delicate beak opening, its song firing something inside her, spurring her on.

The visitor centre was quiet when she arrived, and as she hung up her coat, she heard Stephan whistling 'Dude Looks Like a Lady' loudly and tunelessly. He placed a steaming mug of tea on the reception desk.

'Thanks so much, Stephan.'

'Good couple of days off?' he asked, his eyes finding hers and then flitting away.

Lead settled in her stomach. 'You've seen?'

'Joyce and Karen came to mine for a roast yesterday and, well, Karen's a fan of those online news sites – *Daily Mail* Sidebar of Shame and all that. She reads some of the articles out to Joyce. They were quite excited – they had no idea you were involved with Jack.'

'Shit,' Abby whispered, resting her elbows on the desk. 'It wasn't – I'd never met Eddie before. He tricked me.'

Stephan nodded sympathetically. 'I thought it would be someone playing silly buggers. Your event with Jack, though, how did that go? Always best to focus on the positives.'

'It was lovely,' she said. 'Really lovely. Anyway,' she added, desperate to change the subject, 'did you have a nice weekend? I didn't know you were close to Karen and Joyce.'

Stephan grinned. 'We're getting on, the three of us,' he said. 'Though I've got my sights set on Joyce, as it happens. She's a wonderful, strong woman, Abby. And so funny. I'm quietly confident that she feels something for me, too.'

'Oh Stephan, I'm so happy for you.'

'I haven't asked her yet, planning on officially inviting her on a date tomorrow night, scintillating conversation over a large bowl of paella, and I – uh-oh.' Stephan's eyes widened, and Abby turned in time to see Penelope striding in, followed closely by Rosa, who levelled her with a meaningful stare.

'The three of you,' Penelope said without slowing down, 'in my office in two minutes. No dawdling.'

'Shit,' Abby muttered again, once Penelope's door was closed.

'Abby!' Rosa rushed over to her as she pulled off her coat. 'What on earth is going on? I saw the paper. Are you OK? What happened?'

'It's a long story,' Abby said. 'But the thing with Eddie, it was false. He made it up as another way to get at Jack.'

'Crap,' Rosa whispered. 'And you and Jack?'

'We—'

'*Now*, ladies,' Penelope said.

'I'll tell you later.' Abby followed Rosa towards the inner sanctum.

The sun was streaming through the window, hitting the back of Penelope's head so she looked like she had a halo. Stephan followed Abby and Rosa, carrying a tray of steaming drinks. Abby wasn't sure that would be enough to mollify their boss who, in a high-necked, navy blouse, her hair scraped into its usual tight bun, didn't look like she was in the mood for a natter over tea and cake.

'I was going to keep this discussion between myself and Abby,' Penelope started once they'd all sat down. 'But I have decided it's no use beating around the bush, and that this involves all of you.'

'Penelope, I—'

'I had several important meetings on Friday, one of which was with the bank,' she said, talking over Abby. 'And the situation at Meadowsweet isn't improving. I value all your efforts, and I know you've been working hard to keep this

365

place going. However, it hasn't been enough, and while some publicity is good, some is decidedly not.'

She didn't look at Abby, but her meaning was clear. Abby dropped her head, her neck burning.

'Anyway, that is an aside. My meeting with Mr Philpott was before the Sunday papers, and they had no bearing on his decision. We haven't been making a profit, it's as simple as that, and I cannot hold off the wolves any longer. I was given a number of options; seek an investor in the reserve or sell off some of its assets. While one of those is much more attractive than the other, I fear I no longer have a choice. Running Meadowsweet has never been about making money, it's been about protecting the land, the wildlife, giving people the chance to see it, but without any sort of profit, it can't survive. And now our time has run out.'

'But couldn't we keep looking for an investor?' Rosa asked, her palms pressed together.

'Rosa,' Penelope said, a sigh in her voice, 'I've been trying. A friend of mine has been exploring the options on my behalf, and it's all been in vain. No, the decision is made. I'm going to have to sell Swallowtail House.'

There was a stunned silence, and Abby sank lower in her seat, wondering if things could get any worse.

'Will that impact on the reserve?' Stephan asked eventually.

Penelope pursed her lips, and Abby could imagine how hard it had been to say those words, to admit that the home she had been happy in with Al, that she had fought so hard to hold onto, was now going to be lost. What happened to the reserve was, perhaps, not the point for her.

'It could do,' Penelope said. 'Of course, I own the estate, and am entitled to sell which parts I want, and the house itself is listed. But the grounds directly abut the reserve, and depending on who buys it and what their plans are, it could significantly impact on the harmony, the sanctity of Meadowsweet. Our only option is to move onwards and upwards, and hope that the new owner will be sympathetic to the house's position.'

'I'm so sorry,' Abby said. 'I know what the house means to you.'

'Do you?' Her voice was sharp. 'Do you have any understanding at all, of Swallowtail, of the reserve and their significance – of Al's legacy? Because if you did, I believe you wouldn't have been so casual in your handling of it.'

'Penelope!' Abby gasped.

'I know Jack Westcoat, of course,' she continued. 'I can understand the attraction.' But while you've been allowing him to take up all your time, you have let us down. Planning events half-heartedly, or leaving it so late that you're in such a state by the time they come round, you're unable to deal with problems effectively. That is no way to run a public-facing business at the best of times, let alone when it's in crisis.'

'Now hang on,' Stephan said.

'Not to mention this latest failing.' Penelope kept going, ignoring him. 'While Reston Marsh is bathing in the wholesome publicity of *Wild Wonders*, you have got yourself embroiled in some sort of scandalous love triangle. I don't claim to know the truth and I don't want to know, but this, Abby, is not the kind of press we need. I don't want you to be the only attraction anyone is interested in. First it was Jack, and now he's gone back to London, he's left you in his place. I had hoped, with his departure, the whole debacle would be over.'

'Jack's gone?' Rosa asked, flashing Abby a concerned look.

Abby couldn't move, couldn't blink or breathe or open her mouth to respond to Penelope's accusations.

'I have been considering your position, Abigail, and I'm struggling to see any reason to keep you on here.'

There was a beat of silence, and then Rosa and Stephan started talking at once, leaning forward towards their boss.

'Abby's been brilliant, you can't get rid of her.'

'The whole thing will fall apart without her!'

Penelope held a hand up, stopping them. 'I am still considering it. I'll make my decision by the end of the week. Now, back to work, all of you. And I mean work, not gossip.'

They left her office, Stephan retrieving the tray of untouched drinks. Abby was last, and she half-expected Penelope to call her back, to give her a private dressing-down, or maybe ask what had happened with Jack. Leo had obviously been in touch with her, to let her know he was giving up his lease on Peacock Cottage, which was probably another blow to the finances of the estate.

'She's upset about the house,' Rosa whispered as they walked slowly to the reception desk, where Maureen was talking to a group of visitors. 'She's not going to fire you. It would be a ridiculous, counterproductive move. Either she has no idea how much you really do here, or she's just angry and can't think straight. But what happened with Jack?'

They heard the click of Penelope's door opening, and Rosa hurried back to the shop.

Abby took over from Maureen, and then, when reception was quiet, pulled her phone out of her pocket and tapped a text to Rosa.

It's a mess. Come to the pub with me later? x

Her friend's reply was instant.

Sure. xx

Abby hadn't had a message from Jack since their parting the day before, but maybe he was feeling as shell-shocked as she was. She hadn't sent him one either, and how could she now, when she was on the verge of losing her job, when he'd told her that the thought of her striding through the reserve was keeping him going, and very soon she might not even have that?

Chapter Twenty-Three

Many species of ducks, geese and wading birds are only visitors to the UK, coming here for the food and the warmer weather and returning home in the spring. When you hear the honking call of geese above you and look up, you can often see them flying in a V shape. This is so they can get where they need to go more quickly, the bird at the front breaking up the wall of air, like an arrow. When one bird is injured and can no longer fly, family members stay with it, looking after it until it recovers, and then they all set off again together.

— Note from Abby's notebook

Abby arrived at the pub after collecting Raffle, expecting to find Rosa waiting for her at a table for two. Instead, she was at their usual, large table in the window. And so were Jonny, Stephan, Gavin and Octavia. A pint of lager sat bubbling at the empty place, and Abby, grateful and wary, dropped into the chair, picked up the drink and took a long, fortifying sip.

'Dear Abby,' Octavia said. 'You've had a trying few days. Come, tell us everything, get it off your chest.'

'What happened with Jack?' Rosa asked. 'Why has he gone back to London?'

'Did Penelope really threaten to *fire* you?' Jonny added. 'I can't believe it. Not after all those events.'

'What the fuck were you doing gracing the front page of the *Daily* fucking *Mirror*?' Gavin asked, his pint hovering close to his lips.

Abby leant down to stroke Raffle's head, looking at the expectant faces of her friends, thinking how ironic it was that she'd become the subject of the gossip they loved to share, and wondered if she could bear to go through it with them. But her truth was better than someone else's speculation or lies – she had come to appreciate that much – and these people who cared about her, who had stood up for her, deserved honesty.

She told them everything, stopping short of the intimate details of her time with Jack and the extent of her feelings for him, though she was sure they could see how wretched she felt.

'So, Eddie Markham's a total fucking snake, then,' Gavin said, returning from the bar with fresh drinks. 'Did you report him to the police?'

Abby shook her head. 'He didn't have a chance to do anything other than grab me, thanks to Raffle. And the photo made it look like it was consensual.'

Jonny drummed his fingers on the table. 'The photo-editing software they have nowadays, they can do almost anything.'

'It's sick behaviour,' Octavia said. 'And you've lost your darling Jack because of it.'

'Please don't be sympathetic,' Abby whispered. 'I don't know if I can take it.'

Gavin slung his arm around Abby's shoulders. He smelt of sweat after a day working in the heat of the reserve. 'You'll be all right,' he said. 'Get pissed, chuck things about, usual break-up stuff. And show Penelope how wrong she is – I can't believe she said that you hadn't been working hard enough! What a load of bollocks.'

'Complete and utter bollocks,' Stephan added vehemently.

Abby smiled. 'Thank you – all of you. And I'm sorry if I've been distant, or I've done anything to deserve Penelope's accusations. I got . . . sidetracked. I knew it wasn't a good idea, but I still did it.' She rubbed her forehead. The beer was already having an effect, and she fought the urge to lay her head on the table and have a quick nap.

'Still did what, Abby?' Rosa asked. Abby noticed she was sitting close to Jonny, but that they didn't touch. Rosa had told her nothing had happened at the camping weekend, that they were becoming friends. She wasn't sure that was the full story.

'I let Jack distract me,' she admitted. 'I let him get under my skin, with all his idiotic complaints and his – his bonkers ideas. Going on a walk to find the best place to hide a body, and then that gala – I'm not cut out for things like that, am I?'

'You looked pretty smokin' in that photo of the two of you in the paper,' Gavin interjected.

'I was out of place,' Abby said, warming to her theme. 'And the night with the badger, at Peacock Cottage. Why did I go? And bloody Swallowtail House, I mean, what was he thinking – what was I thinking?' She exhaled, feeling defiant and sick all at once, hating the thought of dismissing the time they'd spent together, but not knowing how else to lessen the ache she'd felt ever since he'd told her he was leaving.

'What about Swallowtail House?' Stephan asked.

'What did you do at Swallowtail?' Rosa echoed.

'We, uhm—'

'Darling,' Octavia said, saving her, 'you cannot guard against falling in love with someone. Nobody would blame you for that. When it hits, it is completely beyond your control. Whatever your current position on relationships, however you profess to detest the man in question, whatever his history, if it's meant to be, then you're at Cupid's mercy.'

'It's nothing like that,' Abby said quickly. 'Jack and I, we were only . . .'

Octavia's eyes were pools of pity and understanding, and Abby turned away from her friends, staring out of the window at a hot-air balloon, a faraway dot of red in the blue of a cloudless sky.

Gavin gave a low whistle. 'It's definitely time for another round.'

'And then we need to come up with a brilliant plan for Abby's next event,' Stephan said. 'If you're going to get back in Penelope's good books, you need to show her exactly what you're capable of. We all know it, and she needs a reminder. Swallowtail House or not, we still have an opportunity to put Meadowsweet back on the map, and it won't happen without you, Abby. Penelope's too smart not to realize that.'

By the time last orders had been called, Abby definitely couldn't say the words *Summer Spectacular* without slurring, let alone get her thoughts in a coherent enough order to work out whether everything they'd discussed would even be possible. She said heartfelt goodbyes to Gavin, Rosa, Stephan and Jonny who, as the only one who hadn't been drinking, was giving the others a lift home, and then Octavia gripped her arm tightly, and they made slow, unsteady progress along the main road, towards home, Raffle walking patiently alongside.

'I *will* rescue the reserve,' Abby said defiantly. 'I can, can't I, Octavia?'

'Of course you can, my love. Nobody else better suited to the job.'

'Even without Jack, I can do it. I don't need him, do I?'

Octavia's response to this wasn't quite as enthusiastic; she simply squeezed Abby's arm, and patted her hand twice.

'I know,' Abby said, rolling her eyes. 'Smile, and you're halfway there, right?'

'What?' Octavia asked, perplexed.

'It's what Penelope says, which is stupid because she never smiles . . .' Her words faltered, because that wasn't the last place she'd heard that phrase. She frowned at Octavia, stumbling slightly as they reached Warbler Cottages.

Octavia walked with her up her front path, rooting in Abby's handbag to find her keys while Abby pressed her forehead against the cool wood of her front door.

'I told him not to drown his despair in a bottle of whisky,' she mumbled, 'and look at me.'

Octavia tutted. 'This is Gavin's doing. And you're not the only one who'll be feeling it in the morning. You weren't drinking alone, Abby.'

She sighed and stood up straight when Octavia gently pushed the door open for her. 'Thanks, Octavia. You're the best neighbour, you know that? And friend.'

'Go and get some sleep, sweet girl. Don't fret.'

Abby nodded, and then waited until Octavia was safely inside her own house before dragging herself up to bed.

Abby's first thought when she woke the following morning was that her head was attacking her from the inside out. The second was, *smile, and you're halfway there,* and the third was that she had definitely sent Jack a text message when she got in last night. She closed her eyes, but it did nothing to lessen the pain or her crawling sense of shame. What had she said to him? She was almost too afraid to look. And she was never, ever drinking beer again.

Raffle whined and nudged his nose into her neck as she reached for her phone on the bedside table. There were lots of notifications on the screen, but she unlocked it quickly, wanting to read everything in order.

Her first message had been sent at 11.54 p.m.

I miss you Jack. Xx

She relaxed slightly. That was entirely true and not at all embarrassing. His reply had arrived four minutes later.

I miss you too. London feels bleak compared to Meadowgreen. I'm sorry for everything. JW x

Her heart ached at his response. She wished she could reach out and hug him, tell him about Penelope, nurse her hangover in his arms instead of at the reserve where, despite all her efforts, she was failing. She moved on to her next message.

Meadowgren is bleak without youo. Come back! Sorry, I now you cant. Peneloppe is going to fire me. xxxxxxxx

Fuck. Abby closed her eyes. She hadn't wanted him to know that, hadn't wanted to send him a drunken message riddled with mistakes. The next few texts were all from him, but there was no response from her – she must have fallen asleep.

Abby, pick up.

Please pick up, are you OK?

The last one was sent at ten past two in the morning, and her nausea deepened as she thought of him in his flat, dragging his hands through his hair, unable to sleep because of her stupid text messages.

Abby I'm worried about you. Why is Penelope going to fire you? Please let me know you're OK. x

When she closed her messages, she saw that she had five missed calls from him. 'Bollocks bollocks bollocks.' She climbed into the shower, trying and failing to cleanse away her hangover, her stupidity and her self-pity.

She needed to stop being such an idiot and get her life back on track. Jack was in London, and there was nothing she could do about that, but he wasn't gone from her life entirely. He cared about her, and whatever the circumstances, she could hold onto that. But she had to focus on the things she could change, the difference she *could* make.

Clad only in a towel, she constructed a message to him, rewriting it umpteen times.

I'm SO sorry about last night – Rosa and the others took me to the pub. I had friendship, but no chips. Penelope doesn't think I've been working hard enough, so I have to prove it to her. She's definitely selling the House of Birds and Butterflies, which must be heartbreaking. ☹ Hope you're OK – sorry if I worried you. PS. What I said about missing you was true. xx

She read it over, wondered whether to add a last bit, and decided she couldn't leave it off.

PPS. How well does Leo know Penelope? xx

She pressed send, flung on her work outfit, forced a piece of toast down her throat, washed down with a large cup of tea, then took Raffle for his walk before heading into work. Hangover or not, she had a Summer Spectacular to plan.

The mood at the visitor centre that morning was understandably subdued, Stephan, Rosa and Abby exchanging weary, guilty smiles as they got their heads down, hoping to look busy while hiding their hangovers from Penelope. The cups of tea arrived at Abby's desk at regular intervals, and she put on her most welcoming expression for the visitors who, encouraged by the sunny weather, flocked to her desk to show their membership cards or ask for day passes.

She wasn't sure whether it was the fact that Jack was no longer only a few hundred yards away, the pact she had made with herself that morning, or the drunken brainstorming session the night before, but her mind was on overdrive, and in between helping with customer queries, she had managed to come up with three pages of ideas for Meadowsweet's most ambitious event yet.

Could they launch a hot-air balloon from the field behind the reserve, the prize in a draw for everyone who signed up for a membership between now and the beginning of August? What about sessions to show families how to encourage wildlife into their gardens, creating their own nature-focused spaces? She could include talks on the butterflies in the meadow, and, she thought – inspired by Jack's words on the doorstep of Peacock Cottage as they had said goodbye – set a challenge for young enthusiasts like Evan, a sort of detective badge with some grand award awaiting them at the end of the weekend.

Depending on Penelope's budget, which she was sure would be limited now the fortunes of the reserve had worsened, she would love to get some large photos of the reserve and its star species printed on canvas, and put them up in the visitor centre to showcase Meadowsweet throughout the seasons. Having hundreds of visitors in for a weekend was all well and good but, as Penelope had been reminding her, the trick was to make sure they came back.

Her new shoots and winter warmer walks, even her hangover walks – about which she felt like an expert today – had been well attended, none cancelled recently due to lack of interest. When she thought of all the effort she had put into the reserve over the last nine months, she felt a surge of anger. She *had* worked hard, in spite of Jack.

'Excuse me,' a voice said, just as she was about to add another bullet point to her list. 'Is this where *Wild Wonders* is being filmed? I was told it was along here somewhere.' It was a man in his late thirties or early forties, dressed entirely in camouflage, with a camera around his neck and thick-rimmed glasses on his nose.

'This is Meadowsweet Reserve,' she said. '*Wild Wonders* is being filmed at Reston Marsh, which is . . .' She hesitated. 'Well, it's near here. But we have just as much wildlife, probably more, because we're a bit quieter.'

'Excellent.' He leaned over the desk as she got out a map and started explaining the different trails to him.

'If you're feeling energetic you can start with the meadow trail, which joins the path along the lagoon here, then wends its way back round to the woodland trail, and the heron hide.' She followed the lines with her biro, enjoying the simple pleasure of showing someone how to navigate the reserve.

'Thanks, that's really helpful.' He took the map, nodding gratefully.

'My pleasure. And don't forget about the café and the shop on your way back. We've got a great selection of cakes and lunches, as well as bird books, gifts and birdwatching equipment, which my colleague Rosa can tell you about.'

'Cheers. I'll keep that in mind.' He waved his map, still hovering at the desk.

'Is there anything else I can help you with?' she asked, her smile faltering.

'Are you Abby?'

'What?'

'You're Abby Field, aren't you? Only—'

'I'd like you to leave now.' Penelope's voice made Abby jump. It was at its most intimidating, clear as a bell, steely, with no room for manoeuvre.

The man raised his camera, and Abby quickly turned her head away. Then Penelope was shepherding him outside and to the car park, as if he was an unruly sheep. When she returned, her cheeks were pink, and Abby resisted the urge to cower behind her computer as she waited for another barrage.

'Would you come into my office, please, Abby?'

'Sure,' she whispered.

Penelope sat behind the desk and indicated for Abby to sit in the chair opposite.

The older woman sighed, her cold expression morphing into a sympathetic frown. 'I need to apologize to you,' she said, her voice unexpectedly soft. 'What I said yesterday was . . . too strong. I was hurting from the realization that, despite all my best intentions, I was going to have to sell Swallowtail House. I came down on you unfairly. You have worked hard for this reserve, your passion is evident, and I was being crueller than necessary to try and inspire you into upping your game. I also appreciate that you didn't bring the publicity on yourself. Jack Westcoat has a lot to answer for.'

'No, Penelope, it isn't—' She was stopped by a raised hand.

'And when I see him again, I will ask him, politely, not to fall in love with any more of my employees.'

Abby blinked, replaying the words in her head.

Penelope's eyes glinted with amusement. 'One is enough, don't you think? And,' she added quietly, 'he's in good hands.'

'Leo,' Abby managed. 'You know him well, don't you? You asked if he had anyone who could move into Peacock Cottage. He didn't just find it listed on a website somewhere, did he?'

For what must have been the first time, Abby thought Penelope looked distinctly uncomfortable, colour rising fully to her cheeks.

Abby's tired, aching brain tried to fit it all together: the connection between Penelope and Leo, their use of the same, unusual phrase, and Penelope's words, only moments earlier. Did she know Jack that well, or was she just surmising how close Abby had got to him? She didn't like the word *love* being bandied about by Octavia and her boss, or the way it sent a shiver over her skin, her mind firing memories at her, of Jack's touch, his blue eyes, his hands in her hair and his breath on her face.

'Leo is an acquaintance,' Penelope said haughtily. 'I told him about Peacock Cottage and my desire to rent it out, yes. I thought he might have someone suitable.'

'How long have you known him?'

Penelope opened her mouth to reply, but the door barged open and Gavin came into the room, followed closely by Rosa and Stephan.

'What on earth is this?' Penelope asked, her voice rising.

'Sorry, boss,' Gavin said. 'But I didn't think this could wait. Fuck me, Abby, you look worse than I do! Penelope, we had a session in the Skylark last night. The creative juices were flowing after pint number four, weren't they Abs? Whatever she pitches to you next, remember it's a collaboration. We all came up with the slice of genius she's putting on this summer.'

'All our events are a collaboration,' Abby said quickly, flushing as Penelope raised an eyebrow at her.

'What is so important that you had to come screaming in here?' Penelope asked, indicating the newspaper Gavin was holding.

Abby froze. She had been too embarrassed by him laying bare their drunken night to notice it.

'Jack Westcoat,' he said. 'I wouldn't have known about it, except Jenna's a fan of a broadsheet. She found this.' He put the paper on the desk and turned to the page he'd been marking with his finger. Rosa and Stephan looked over his shoulder, and even Penelope was peering closely at the newsprint.

'Come on,' she said impatiently. 'Read it out to us. Chop chop.'

Gavin looked shocked for a second then, grinning, leaned over the desk.

'Righty-ho. This is what it says: *The critically acclaimed author, Jack Westcoat, today released a statement in answer to stories published by the* Daily Mirror *and* Daily Star *newspapers, regarding fellow author Eddie Markham, who last year very publicly accused him of helping to conceal an alleged plagiarism claim.*

'"*The recent allegations, supposedly validated by photographic evidence, that Eddie Markham and I are both engaged in a relationship with the same woman is entirely false. I attended the Page Turner Foundation Gala with a close friend, and Mr Markham, for reasons known only to him, staged the photograph that appeared in several newspapers two days later. Before that moment, the two of them had never spoken. Firstly, I would like to offer my sincerest apologies to my friend, who I do not wish to name, for her unwitting involvement in this, and secondly, I can confirm that I will be addressing all of Mr Markham's claims about me, both current and past, over the coming weeks."* The article goes on to say,' Gavin continued, *'Jack's new thriller,* The Hidden Field, *will be published at the beginning of August, and this public spat aside, it is undoubtedly one of the most hotly anticipated releases of the summer.'*

He closed the paper triumphantly.

'Wow,' Rosa said. 'That's super-gallant.'

'It's very bold,' Stephan agreed. 'And he's going to address the other accusations too? Golly. I thought he was the strong, silent type.'

'I would suggest that this latest move of Eddie Markham's is a step too far,' Penelope said, turning her gaze on Abby. 'Some things, evidently, are not to be messed with, and Jack's come to his senses at last.'

'Guys, did you not hear?' Gavin asked. 'His new book is called The *fucking* Hidden Field.'

'The *fucking* Hidden Field, Gavin?' Rosa said, giving him a cheeky grin. 'That's a pretty perplexing title.'

Gavin huffed. 'The Hidden Field. The. Hidden. Field. Don't you get it? He's writing about Abby.'

Abby's heart leapt, even though what Gavin was suggesting was ridiculous. 'If I'm in it,' she said, 'I'll probably end up as a dead body rotting slowly away in a tributary.'

'Nah.' Gavin shook his head. 'He couldn't kill you off, not even in fiction. He's too besotted with you for that.'

'Perhaps he allowed Meadowsweet to inspire him after all,' Penelope suggested, 'after his first, inauspicious comments about his surroundings. Maybe the title is a nod to that? Now everyone, that seems to me to be enough excitement for one day. Shall we all get back to work? I find three spoonfuls of sugar in my tea works wonders for a hangover. Stephan, if you'd like to oblige? News from Jack, defending the honour of our star event coordinator, is a good omen. So, chin up, everyone!'

'Smile, and you're halfway there, right, Penelope?' Abby said as she stood. She couldn't help it – she was on the verge of discovering something momentous.

Penelope nodded once, her brows knitted into a frown as she waited for them all to leave.

Gavin gave Abby his copy of the newspaper and she read Jack's piece again, unable to hide the elation that, for a few moments, made her headache disappear.

'Do you love him?' Rosa asked, when it was just the two of them.

Abby shrugged, her palms suddenly hot. 'I don't know,' she whispered, and hoped Rosa would accept the lie.

The clock dragged its way round to five o'clock, and Abby stepped out into the balmy evening. She looked at her phone and saw that she had three missed calls and a message from Tessa that read: ????, which meant she had seen a newspaper or the photo online. She also had two messages from Jack, which had been sent that morning, not long after she'd stowed her bag in the storeroom.

She set off for home, and soon found herself sitting against the wall of Swallowtail House, next to the side gate and Jack's padlock. She hadn't yet accepted that Penelope had made the decision to sell it, that it would soon no longer be the abandoned, mysterious building that she had come to love, that held precious memories of her day with Jack. And if it was this hard for her, then how hard must it be for Penelope, who had spent years of her life there with Al?

She pulled her phone back out of her bag as a bumblebee flew lazily by, his buzz a mini-chainsaw against the forest background. A blue tit chirruped from a tree above her, and the ground felt dry and dusty beneath her jeans.

She read Jack's first message:

I'm so glad you're OK! You don't need to apologize, but next time don't forget the chips. How's your head? Sorry about the house of birds & butterflies, but if Penelope's being forced to let it go, maybe it can have a new lease of life? Also, she won't fire you. However angry she is, she believes in you, like I do. Have faith in yourself. Don't know re. Leo and Penelope, though he'd mentioned her and Meadowsweet to me long before he suggested Peacock Cottage, so they must go back a fair way. Why? I'm missing you more with every passing day. JW xx

His second message read:

I put something in The Times today. It doesn't make up for what happened, but hopefully goes some way towards it. You were right about Eddie, and I should have accepted it long before now. JW xx

She lifted her face up to the sun, soaked up the calm and quiet of the woods, and took time over her reply, luxuriating in this contact with Jack, even though he was no longer around the corner. She could call him, could FaceTime or Skype him, but she knew that he was dealing with a lot, busy with the final stages of his book, upcoming interviews, and sorting out what he was going to say about Eddie. That last one, she knew, he would find particularly tough. Jack was obviously a loyal person, and all that Eddie had done couldn't completely wipe out the memories of their childhood friendship.

And she couldn't be distracted from her task. Penelope might be losing Swallowtail House, but Abby would not allow the reserve to follow. Her plans – along with the ideas of Rosa, Jonny, Gavin, Stephan and Octavia – were ambitious, but they needed to be. They needed to reach towards the stars if they had any chance of getting things back on track. And, she realized, as she pressed send on her reply to Jack and took out her notebook, it was as much about Meadowsweet saving her, as it was about her rescuing Meadowsweet.

Chapter Twenty-Four

Goldfinches are an unlikely success story, their numbers growing despite all the threats they face. They're unmistakable gold-and-black birds with red faces – though they have nothing to be embarrassed about. They have a liquid, twittering song, and the sight or sound of them can brighten up even the greyest day.

— Note from Abby's notebook

Over the next two months, Abby lived and breathed Meadowsweet Nature Reserve and the Summer Spectacular. She woke with the sun, walked Raffle over dewy fields, listening to the warblers, wrens and goldcrests chorusing in the trees, and was often at the visitor centre long before opening, sending emails, revising her map, rejigging her programme of activities, talks and walks. She was planning on using the field behind the meadow again, as it had worked so well for the camping event and would leave the reserve itself free for exploring in smaller groups, making the most of the wildlife without disturbing it.

One of Meadowsweet's best features in the summer months was the meadow trail, with its wild flowers and butterflies: peacocks and red admirals, orange-tips and meadow browns. She wondered if, with the warm weather continuing, they would spot a swallowtail – either a visitor from the continent, or an interloper from the Norfolk broads – taking the reserve's all-time sightings up to three.

She sometimes wished she could control the wildlife, and had felt almost powerful when, on the evening of her murmuration event, the starlings had flocked and dived just as she'd hoped they would. But that was part of the joy of nature – the anticipation, and then delight, of seeing something rare or remarkable, and not provided to order. Zoos held a certain appeal, but for Abby, they couldn't come close to the wild beauty of the reserve.

Wild Wonders was due to finish its year-long run at Reston Marsh at the end of August, and Abby wondered if that would make a difference, if her grand plans for growing their membership at this event, combined with the end of the live broadcasts, would turn fortune in Meadowsweet's favour. Even if it did, she knew it wouldn't be enough to save Swallowtail House.

While she had been investigating hot air balloons and planning challenges for young nature buffs, Penelope had been shut in her office, accepting visits from Mr Philpott from the bank, and a suave-looking gentleman who announced himself as Travis from the upmarket estate agency Home and Country. He seemed as sharky as any traditional estate agent, and Abby was fearful on behalf of the house about whose hands it might end up in.

She was also no closer to establishing the connection between Penelope and Leo, though she was utterly convinced there was one. She'd tried to have a roundabout conversation with Octavia about it, two weeks after the night at the pub where, in her drunken state, she'd had a lightbulb moment, but the woman had jumped on her comments like a sparrowhawk on a young sparrow.

'Octavia,' she'd said, when they were sitting in the older woman's manicured back garden, glasses of white wine cooling after the heat of the day, 'Penelope and Al *definitely* didn't have any children, did they?'

'No, dear, that's a well-known village fact. Why do you ask?'

Abby rubbed her finger along the armrest of her picnic chair. 'Leo, Jack's agent . . .'

'Ah, lovely Jack. What I wouldn't give to have him in my library again.'

Abby didn't voice where she wanted to have him, and she was trying her best not to think about Jack, or imagine what he was doing at that very moment, what he was wearing or where Shalimar was sitting in his London flat.

'What about Leo?' Octavia asked, when Abby didn't join in with the Jack admiration.

'There was something so *familiar* about him. Some of his mannerisms, some of the things he said.'

'Like Penelope?' Octavia stilled, the crocheted butterfly she was in the middle of making temporarily forgotten.

Abby nodded.

'How old is he? What makes you think that . . . that Leo is Penelope's *son*?'

'He's late forties, I guess, which would make Penelope twenty, a bit younger maybe, when she had him.'

'*If*, Abigail. This seems like two and two making sixty-five to me. As far as anyone knows, Penelope and Al were

388

dedicated to each other, and the decision not to have children was mutual.'

Abby's shoulders sagged. 'You're right. I'm being ridiculous, looking for things when they're not there. But Penelope knows Leo, knew him long before Jack rented Peacock Cottage, and there have been a couple of occasions . . .' She tapped her fingers against her lips.

Octavia's expression was sympathetic. 'Don't you have enough to think about without adding some fruitless mystery to your worries? How is this summer fair coming along?'

'It's all going to plan. No major disasters yet, and it's bigger than anything we've done before.'

'I knew you could do it,' Octavia said. 'And your lovely sister, Tessa?'

Abby frowned. Tessa had not been pleased when, finally, Abby had confessed everything to her; what had happened with Jack, and how her picture had ended up in the paper. She didn't tell her sister the extent of her feelings for him, but she didn't need to – Tessa knew her better than anyone. They had spoken since then, and Abby had been round to spend time with her nieces, but things still felt strained between them.

'She's fine,' she settled on. 'Busy with Willow and Daisy, but they're happy now the summer's here. They'll basically live in the garden for the next few months. I'm going to see them this weekend.'

'Sounds like things are looking up for you.'

'Yeah,' Abby said. 'Though I may as well marry my job.' She kicked the event plan lying on the grass at her feet. It accompanied her everywhere, like a shadow. While Abby was excited about the scale of their ideas, and the possibility for new members if they pulled it all off, it couldn't entirely banish her sadness at Jack's absence, the hole inside her shifting and changing shape each day, sometimes so small she could barely feel it, sometimes gaping and aching so much that she was worried it would swallow her up.

'Heard a lot from him?' Octavia asked softly.

'A bit. Text messages, mainly. He's on publication countdown now, so it's all pretty hectic.'

'*The Hidden Field*,' Octavia said. 'I saw an early review of it in the *Guardian*. They gave it five stars and said it's his best yet – *A shocking triumph*, apparently. I think lots of the credit for that needs to go to Meadowgreen and, probably, to you.'

Abby laughed. 'I don't think so. We distracted each other.'

'Distracted, or saved?'

'Octavia.' She rolled her eyes.

'We all know he was in a bad place when he arrived and look what's come out of it; this incredible, career-resurrecting book. And you – these last few months, you've been more alive, more determined than I've ever seen you. All Penelope's words about you not putting enough effort into the reserve are claptrap. You and Jack, you gave each other new breath.'

'Even if that's true,' Abby said, Octavia's turn of phrase feeling entirely accurate, 'I can't think about Jack now. I have to concentrate on the Summer Spectacular.'

But Abby couldn't stop thinking about Jack. Their text messages continued and, three weeks after Jack had left Meadowgreen for London, she received the first letter. It was waiting on her doormat when she arrived home late, after working all evening on the event budget. The envelope was damp, because while she had long ago persuaded a fat-pawed young husky that tearing up the mail was unacceptable, he still couldn't resist the odd, gentle chew.

She picked it up, leaning against the wall as she recognized the handwriting. It was so familiar to the letters he'd left her at the reserve, except this time it was her whole address instead of just her name. She tore the envelope open, her breath faltering as she unfolded the paper.

Dear Abby,

I thought of you today as a small brown bird landed on my windowsill in the sunshine. I have no idea what it was – I knew you would have told me in an instant. How is Meadowsweet? I'm imagining the woods full of bullfinches, like out-of-season Christmas trees with red, tweeting baubles, and you walking beneath them, your head full of new ideas for the reserve's next, brilliant event.

All is heading in the right direction here, and I'm meeting with Bob Stevens tomorrow. It seems my hopes of being an ambassador aren't entirely lost, but I still need to make a good impression.

The first reviews of the book are coming in, and I wish you were with me, to soothe my nerves, make me laugh, remind me that I can still do this.

JW x

She sat in her armchair, reading it over and over, and then found a fresh, smart notebook, so she could write a reply and send it to the address in Shoreditch that he'd printed neatly at the top of the letter.

Dear Jack,

I got your note, and nobody else read it over my shoulder – it was all mine! ☺ Your bird was probably a sparrow, but if it appears again try and take a photo.

The reserve is beautiful at this time of year, all soft greens, sunshine and colourful butterflies, the lagoon sparkling like sequins. I saw a pair of bullfinches yesterday and immediately thought of you. The summer event is coming on in leaps and bounds, but if I think too much about all the things that could go wrong I get a bit panicky, so I've stopped doing that now! ☺

You must have had your meeting with Bob Stevens by now – how did it go?

You can most definitely do this! You can do anything you want to, but I wish I was with you too. Every single day.

Abby xx

She could have written pages and pages, but somehow it didn't seem right to make it any longer. Their notes should be in keeping with the previous ones, despite the distance being greater, their meetings now non-existent instead of infrequent.

As the weeks passed and the event got closer, Abby scoured the newspapers and the internet for news of Jack; for reviews of his book, and for the article that he had promised, setting the record straight about him and Eddie.

It appeared on a Saturday morning early in July, in one of the weekend magazines. She saved it until after work and then, sitting cross-legged on her living-room floor, a plate of chips cooling next to her, she opened the thin, slippery paper to find a black-and-white portrait of Jack accompanying the interview.

He was looking straight at the camera, his hands clasped in front of him, a flop of thick hair half-obscuring one eye. She could see the line of his strong shoulders through a tailored shirt, the hardness of his jaw, softened slightly by the hint of a smile that gave her such a flash of familiarity it was almost as if he was in the room with her.

She tore her eyes away from his image and turned her attention to the words, and the cringing, overwritten introduction from the journalist:

I meet Jack Westcoat on a sunny June morning in an obscure, noisy café in East London, close to his flat. He's smartly dressed, his hair the dishevelled mane of a man who wants to give the impression that looks are unimportant, but not even he would deny that he's attractive, almost disarmingly so. A film star of an author, and perhaps that's partly at the root of his recent, public troubles. He greets me warmly, but there's an unmistakable wariness in his piercing blue eyes, as if he already knows the unflinching questions I'm going to ask him.

'Ugh.' Abby rolled her eyes and read on. The interview focused on the furore with Eddie Markham as much as it did his new book, and Abby read through a less candid version of the story Jack had told her that morning in Peacock Cottage. He left out the admission that Eddie had spiked his drink but was open about the plagiarism and his role in it, and set the record straight about Eddie's claims about the journalist, assuring readers it was purely monetary.

'Nothing else happened, though that alone is surely bad enough. I did what I felt was right at the time; maybe disloyal to the literary world, but at that stage, I could think about nothing except helping my friend. I know now that it was wrong, that I was fighting a losing battle, but hindsight is a wonderful thing.'

The article moved on to *The Hidden Field*. The interviewer asked him about his self-imposed seclusion.

'It saved me, really, that time in Suffolk. And not just because I had the space to think and to write, but also because it helped me put things in perspective. I discovered something that is more important than all of this, than Eddie Markham, than writing – certainly more important than my pride or reputation.' I ask him what that was, and he smiles – the first genuine smile he's given since I arrived. 'That would be telling,' he says simply and, asking if I want another coffee, deftly changes the subject.

Jack's two-page spread hadn't escaped the attention of Abby's friends, and when she arrived at the reserve the following morning, she found that someone had carefully torn out his interview and photo and pinned it on the wall behind the reception desk. There was a heart-shaped Post-it Note stuck next to his head, with the word *Dreamboat* written on it. The cheeky sentiment was surely Gavin's, but she was certain the handwriting was Rosa's.

As her event drew ever closer, Abby's to-do list got longer rather than shorter, and when the printers sent her the first batch of membership sign-up forms with the pages printed in the wrong order, she almost had a meltdown in the middle of the shop. She had to be soothed by Karen and Joyce, who had come to sample Stephan's new meringue cakes.

Added to that, sharky estate agent Travis was spending more and more time with Penelope, often walking out of her office rubbing his hands together and winking at Rosa and Abby in a way that, they agreed, made their skin crawl. And Jack's pre-book publicity was ramping up, his name appearing in a new online article almost daily, usually a rehash of the Saturday paper interview tacked onto the standard spiel about *The Hidden Field*. It was being published on Thursday the 2nd of August, the day before the Summer Spectacular started and, Waterstones' website told her, would be celebrated with a launch event that evening in one of their flagship London stores.

On Wednesday evening, publication-eve, she sent him a text, though she'd already posted a card to his flat – a photo of a bullfinch – along with a box of the luxury Fairtrade chocolate truffles they sold in the shop.

Her message read: Good luck for tomorrow. I hope your publication day is full of bubbles, and the launch goes well. I want to see photos! xx

He replied half an hour later.

Thank you! I wish you could come, but I know it's T-minus two days to your summer fair. All set? x

Yup, though drinking champagne and hearing your speech sounds much more fun. But Meadowsweet will survive, even if the House of Birds and Butterflies is out of our hands. I miss you. xx

Ditto, Abby Field. x

* * *

After a run of glorious weather, on Thursday morning Abby was woken by rain pattering against the open window, the scent of hot, damp gardens reaching her on the breeze that drifted through it. Raffle lifted his sleepy head, gave a long, grunting whine and shifted position, lying his nose on Abby's ankles.

'I know,' she said. 'But we have to go out, rain or shine, remember? Besides, it's a big day for me. And Jack too, obviously.'

She shrugged on a thin mac over her shorts and T-shirt, put on her walking boots and took Raffle for his walk. She could sense the greenery unfurling in the rain, and a bedraggled coal tit sat cleaning itself in a tree close to Peacock Cottage as they walked past. The sight of the pretty cottage, now devoid of lights or that ridiculous car outside, never failed to dampen her spirits, ironic today as the rest of her was already soggy, and she considered whether she would have been more open with Jack if she'd known how limited their time was.

By the time she'd taken Raffle home and set out for the reserve, the sun was peering through the trees. It was the day before the event, and some of the craft and food stands were arriving that morning, along with the hot-air balloon, which was being carted in on a huge lorry.

'All right, Abs, how are you today?' Gavin asked, as she stepped through the doors of the visitor centre. 'Prepared as fuck?'

'I am as fucking prepared as I'll ever be,' she replied, and Gavin laughed. 'Has the balloon arrived?'

'It has indeed. Want to come and take a look? Then we can start getting this fair off the ground. Literally.'

Abby was pulled in a hundred different directions, setting

aside half an hour to respond to telephone queries, then greeting the owners of the hog-roast van, the mobile bar and the Mediterranean delicatessen stand, the smell of fresh olive oil making her stomach rumble. The rain shower hadn't been long enough to muddy the parched ground, and with the forecast set to be sunny for the whole weekend, she wasn't too worried that her fair would turn into a mire more suited to hippos than humans. She thought of Shalimar, of Jack hugging him as he told her about his history with Eddie. She blinked the thought away.

Once she'd spent fifteen minutes on the phone giving directions to a man who was delivering a talk on wild living – which seemed ridiculous when his address was in Brent Cross – and eaten a very late lunch, she settled down to answer the emails that needed to be responded to. She relished the idea of a quiet half hour, leaving Gavin and Marek to deal with the Jenga-type puzzle of stand holders the field was becoming.

She'd just hit reply to a message when Octavia bundled through the door, clutching a parcel to her chest.

'Oh Abby, I'm so glad you're here!'

'What's wrong?' Abby asked. 'The marquee for your book-shop and craft stall has arrived on time, and it's not meant to rain for the whole weekend.'

'Oh, it's not that. This is much more important. Where's Penelope?'

'She went out about an hour ago,' Rosa said, joining them. 'Why?'

'Because . . . I have news.' Stephan peered in their direction and Octavia beckoned him over. 'Gather round, children.'

Abby laughed. 'Did you actually just say that?'

'Shush. So, here it is.'

They all waited while Octavia dragged out the silence, as if she was Tess Daly announcing the winner of *Strictly Come Dancing*.

'Get on with it.' Gavin had crept up behind Abby, and smelt distinctly of fudge, leading her to wonder who else had arrived to set up while she'd been busy elsewhere.

'Swallowtail House has been sold,' Octavia said, giving a little whoop of triumph.

'It has?' Stephan asked.

'How do you know?' murmured Abby.

'Prove it,' Rosa and Gavin said at once.

Octavia grinned. 'While you've been working hard here to get your event set up, those grand, double gates have been unlocked, and a van has driven inside.'

'But it – it's uninhabitable,' Abby said. 'Nobody could live in it in its current state.'

'We don't know what it's like inside,' Rosa replied, and Abby's cheeks flushed.

'It wasn't a removal lorry,' Octavia said. 'It was from a high-end surveying outfit. Not the kind you get as part of a mortgage, but an independent, exclusive company, come in to assess the state of the building, what structural work needs to be done on it.'

'How do you know that?' Stephan asked.

'I wrote down the name on the van and looked them up on the internet,' Octavia said, entirely unembarrassed.

'But surely that's someone who's just *interested* in the house,' Rosa protested. 'You wouldn't spend a whole heap of money on somewhere like that unless you knew it wasn't falling down, so I don't see how they can have bought it yet.'

'The For Sale sign has disappeared from outside,' Octavia said.

Abby gasped. How had she failed to notice that? She walked past it, pinned to the wall next to the gates, on her way to and from work. 'Shit,' she murmured. 'So it's really happened, then? Poor Penelope.'

'Maybe she's glad,' Rosa said. 'Maybe if it means the reserve is no longer in trouble, she's happy she's done it.'

'But there has to be a reason she hasn't sold it up to now,' Abby said.

'She probably didn't want it falling into the wrong hands.' Stephan shrugged. 'People sniff at sentimentality, but I know what it's like to lose the person you love most, your whole world, and the urge to hang onto inanimate objects that remind you of them is overwhelming, even though it will never bring them back, and your memories don't need the place, the thing, to survive.'

Octavia nodded, silence hanging over them for a moment.

'Hopefully that means she's convinced the buyer will do it justice, then?' Rosa said quietly. 'After all, she'll still be here, working close by, so it's not like she can avoid it.'

'Fingers crossed.' Abby thought of the tangle of foliage in the gardens, and tried to imagine it with topiary hedges and nail-scissor grass.

'And what's this?' Gavin asked, pointing at the parcel Octavia was clutching. 'Have you been intercepting their post as well? I know you're curious, but that's going a bit far, isn't it?'

'Oh this?' Octavia waggled it. 'No, this came for Abby. The postie knocked on my door because it wouldn't fit through the letterbox.' She thrust it forward, and Abby felt a strange sense of *déjà vu* as everyone peered in to see what it was. She wanted to shout that it was her personal post, for God's sake, and had *nothing* to do with the reserve. But then she saw the handwriting, and all thoughts of protest left her.

'Is it from Jack?' Rosa asked.

Abby nodded. She turned it over, peeled open the jiffy bag and slid out a large, hardback book. It was silky to the touch, and she took in the detail of a cover she'd seen tiny images of online, alongside the reviews. It was black, with the raised title, *The Hidden Field,* written in yellow along the top. Below it was an image of a windblown, desolate field beneath grey, thunderous clouds, emerging out of the black background as if the cover was night and the landscape was being lit with a powerful torch. At the bottom, in raised, silver foil, was his name: *Jack Westcoat.* Abby shivered, surprised at the strength of her emotion at seeing and holding his finished book.

'That,' Rosa said dreamily, 'is a *gorgeous* hardback. Wow, feel the finish on the jacket.' Hands pawed at it, her friends' attention not fading now the book had been revealed.

'Open it then,' Gavin said. 'Has he signed it?'

'Of course he will have,' Stephan tutted.

On the title page was Jack's neat handwriting, a slight smudge to the ink suggesting he had used a fountain pen:

Dear Abby,
    Was it really worth all the fuss? I'm sending you a copy regardless.
    All my love,
    Jack Westcoat
    Xx

His signature was smart and flamboyant, and Abby felt her throat tighten as she reread his note. Then she flipped quickly away from the title page and found herself reading the dedication instead.

To Abby
For friendship and chips
&
The House of Birds and Butterflies

Tears burned in the corners of her eyes. He had dedicated his book to her. Not just this one with its personalized inscription, but every single copy. He had acknowledged her as a part of his life, wanted everyone who read it to see, to know, she meant something to him.

A hand landed on her shoulder, and she was surprised to find it was Gavin's. 'That's a pretty impressive gesture, Abby,' he said quietly.

She managed a smile in return. 'I need to go and see how Marek's getting on with the set-up.' She picked up Jack's book and, hugging it to her, fled from the attention and sympathy of her friends. She would allow herself ten minutes to think about Jack, and then she would put him to the back of her mind, at least until the Summer Spectacular had drawn to a, hopefully triumphant, close.

Chapter Twenty-Five

Wrens are my favourite. A tiny, dumpy brown bird with a sticky-up tail and a pale stripe above its eye like it's wearing make-up, it stays close to the ground, searching for bugs. It's very loud for such a small bird – sound familiar, Daisy? It has a beautiful, trilling song and a rattling alarm call when it's worried about something.

— Note from Abby's notebook

The cursor blinked, waiting for her to add to the message, but she didn't know what else to say, other than:

I hope last night was a success. Thank you for my present.

He had dedicated his book to her. Did he love her, the way she had come to realize she loved him? Surely he must, to want to put her there, indelibly, on the page like that. But what was the point of love when it was separate like this? Abby almost longed for the simple, straightforward relationship Tessa had been urging her to find when Jack had come into her life, without drama, perhaps without passion – comfort, warmth, someone to confide in. Jack had been all those things, but he'd brought drama and passion too.

But she couldn't express her love through text messages and the occasional, handwritten letter. She felt like a lovebird pining for her mate, unable to consider the prospect of living at a distance from him. She wanted to feed him chips, the way lovebirds fed each other. She wanted to be close to him, and the fact that she couldn't made her chest ache.

She added a couple of kisses to the end of the message, pressed send, and forced herself out of bed. The birds were only just up, but Abby had work to do.

By midday, Meadowsweet Nature Reserve was busier than Abby had ever seen it. Volunteers were leading walks to the different hides, each one twenty-people strong, all with bingo cards of bird and butterfly species to tick off whenever they were spotted. Those who got a full house would get a 50 per cent saving on a year's membership, others with a row or a line would get discounts in the shop or the café, or a pair of day passes every month for a year.

The key, Abby had decided, was to give a little, but encourage more. If she promoted the memberships to the hilt, hopefully even those who didn't win would be interested in signing up. Everyone who joined over the three days would get a free birdwatcher's pack containing the latest Collins bird guide, a spotter's notebook and a thermos for those cold, winter mornings when the lure of the café was almost – but not quite – greater than the wildlife.

'Thank you for coming,' she said to two adults who had arrived with an army of children, from gangly teenagers to toddlers. 'If you make your way down there,' she pointed, 'and follow the signs to the field, that's where the action is.

Here's a programme of everything that's happening over the weekend, and if you have any questions just look for one of us, we'll all be wearing these fetching orange T-shirts.' She gave a silly grin, and a couple of the children laughed.

'What's this about Meadowsweet Fledglings?' the woman asked. 'I heard something about it at school.'

'Ah, excellent,' Abby said. 'It's our new membership scheme for young people. We want to encourage as many children and teenagers as possible to get involved in nature, to find out how fascinating it is and what they can do to look after it. So if their parents or guardians join at a discounted fee, payable monthly or yearly, the children can have free access to Meadowsweet and work their way towards getting their Fledgling medal. There's a checklist of things they have to spot, and activities they have to fulfil away from the reserve – making a nest box, setting up a community wildlife area somewhere local to them, that sort of thing – and if they come back with everything completed within the year, they get a prize, and another year of discounts for their family.'

'Wow!' The woman's eyebrows rose. 'It sounds wonderful. Do you have any more information?'

'Here's our leaflet and membership form, which you can also fill in on our website. We ask for a diary as evidence, which they complete as they go, either online or in a physical notebook – with accounts of their trips to the reserve, their activities, and any photos. At the end of the year, that acts as proof of their achievements.'

Abby, Rosa and Gavin had spent a sober day in the pub coming up with all the details of the Fledglings scheme. Abby admitted it had come to her because of Jack's words on the doorstop of Peacock Cottage, the morning he had returned to London. It seemed fitting, somehow, that he had left her with a nugget of inspiration, something that could change the fortunes of Meadowsweet. She only wished he'd said the words, or she'd come up with the idea, sooner, and that Swallowtail House could have been saved as well.

First, Abby, Rosa and Gavin had worked out whether their small reserve had enough capacity to do the associated administration. They had decided that, yes, they did, and anyway, Rosa knew someone who could help them with the online side of things, setting up the diary software and the Fledgling membership form to go alongside the standard, adult version.

'So Jonny's got his uses after all,' Gavin had said, whistling. 'And has he actually bought a pair of binoculars?'

'No.' Rosa had smiled coyly. 'But I don't mind that.'

'Made up for it in other ways, has he?' Gavin's eyebrows had gone skywards.

Rosa had picked that moment to go and replenish their lemonades.

Now, it seemed that all their hard work had paid off. People were interested, the pile of membership forms was rapidly decreasing, and it was only the first day of the event.

The sun continued to shine, and after Friday's success there was a warning on the local radio on Saturday morning about *increased traffic to the Meadowsweet Nature Reserve's Summer Spectacular – please allow extra time for your journey, as queues are expected!* They'd never been the subject of a traffic warning before, and it made Abby's heart swell with pride.

If only, she thought, Jack could be here to see it. He could have run more storytelling sessions, for adults as well as children, reading creepy excerpts from his book as the sun went down. He hadn't replied to her message, and she realized that hers had been too brief, too cursory, considering his heartfelt dedication to her.

She vowed that she would call him when this was over, perhaps even plan a trip to London to see him. There was nothing stopping her, and the pace of both their lives would become less frantic after this weekend, with his book published and her biggest event over. Maybe they could see if long distance was a possibility.

Sunday was the last day of the fair, and Abby had a celebratory ending planned, after which she would go home, rest her weary feet and hug her husky. Raffle was restless at being left alone for such long hours, but there was no way he could go with her to the reserve. The carefully cultivated habitats of Meadowsweet couldn't be disturbed by four-legged friends, and so the closest she had ever taken him was the fallen elder at the perimeter of Swallowtail House.

She took him for an extra-long walk, unable to hide her curiosity following Octavia's gossip about the grand old mansion. She stopped at the side gate, and at first glance it looked the same as it always had. But then she peered more closely and saw that, creeping up the back corner of the house was a tower of scaffolding. It was only visible from the side, but it was definitely there. Someone was fixing it, or at least starting to, which meant it *had* to have been sold. Surveys were one thing; scaffolding was another matter altogether.

By the time she got to the visitor centre, buzzing with the new information, Rosa was already there. Her dark eyes were creased at the edges, but her friend smiled warmly as she ripped open a cardboard box and pulled out a pile of Fledgling membership forms.

'Last box,' she said, triumphantly.

'What?' Abby squealed. 'But I had three thousand printed! Has someone dumped a whole load in the lagoon?'

'Nope. They're *flying*. OK, they're not all going to get filled in, but just think, if we get even a quarter back, even an eighth, Abby, that's three hundred and seventy-five new Fledglings, with their parents paying for discounted memberships. Can you imagine? You're a genius!'

'*We're* geniuses,' Abby said. 'All of us. Shit, this could save the reserve, couldn't it? With the sale of Swallowtail House, and a new influx of members, Mr Philpott will be off Penelope's back for ages.'

'Alleged sale,' Rosa corrected, but Abby shook her head.

'It's got scaffolding up,' she said breathlessly. 'Swallowtail House. Someone has committed to doing work on it, which they wouldn't do unless they'd bought it. Octavia only saw the surveying van on Thursday, but the sale must have been agreed a while ago if the scaffolding's gone up already.'

'Oh my God! Why hasn't Penelope told us?'

'She's probably waiting until the end of all this.' Abby flung her arms wide. 'It's not like we need a distraction, is it?'

'True dat,' Rosa said, and Stephan came over with steaming cups of tea that, Abby thought, she might now solely run on.

Abby helped carry the leaflets to the field, where the atmosphere reminded her of the outdoor fairgrounds she had visited as a child. Stalls were opening up, the smells of coffee and sugar assailed her, and the sun was rising blissfully over the trees, making the dew-covered grass sparkle. It might well be a long day, but really, was there anywhere better to spend it?

She was hijacked at lunchtime by Marek, trying and failing to keep up with an over-exuberant Evan. His mid-brown hair was longer and curlier than the last time she'd seen him, his eyes bright with their usual enthusiasm.

'Evan!' she said, delighted. 'How's it going?'

'I saw a swallowtail butterfly,' he panted. 'That's super-rare, right?'

Abby's eyes widened. 'They're almost unheard of here. Yours is only the third sighting at the reserve since Penelope and Al started keeping records.'

'Yes!' He jumped up and down, fist-bumping the air. 'It was awesome, wasn't it, Marek?'

'Yup,' Marek agreed. 'It was incredible. Abby, they're fu— frigging *huge*! And so beautiful.'

Abby grinned. 'You, Evan, are officially a Meadowsweet Fledgling, did you know that? We're launching the scheme this weekend, but you were part of the inspiration behind it, so you are officially our first. You'll get in free, and your parents' membership will be discounted for the next year.' She had checked his mum and dad were already members, rather than simply frequent visitors, before deciding to announce Evan as the inaugural Fledgling. 'I'd love you to complete a diary of all your sightings, your involvement in nature, between now and next summer, and I'd like to give you something at the end of the day, if you're still around?' She pulled one of the leaflets out of her back pocket and handed it to him.

He stared at it, and then her. 'Seriously?'

'Seriously.'

'Wow, cool! I have to tell Mum and Dad – about this, and the swallowtail!'

'We'll be presenting everything at four, if that's OK?'

'I told them we had to stay to the end!' Evan called over his shoulder, racing off to find his parents.

'A swallowtail, huh?' Abby said.

Marek nodded slowly. 'I know. Pretty spectacular.'

'Maybe it's a sign?'

'Of what, Abby?'

Abby thought about Swallowtail House and its scaffolding, all the Fledgling leaflets they'd shifted, the glimmers of good humour, and something close to friendliness, she'd seen from Penelope recently, as if she was trying to make up for threatening to fire her. 'Of better things to come?'

She watched as the fair continued around them, pondering whether a rare butterfly sighting really could be symbolic, or if her exhaustion was getting to her. And then, through the crowd, she saw a familiar face, and all thoughts of butterflies went out of her head.

'Mum!' she exclaimed, as Caroline embraced her, her floral scent overwhelming. 'What are you doing here?'

'I came with this lot.' She stood aside to allow Tessa and Neil, and then Daisy and Willow, to hug Abby. 'We couldn't miss your event – not this one. I have to say, Abby, it really is wonderful. Are there still walks left for us to go on?'

'A couple,' Abby replied, in a daze. She glanced at her mum's feet, and saw that she had trainers on, her usual kitten heels left sensibly at home.

'Hey, sis,' Tessa said. 'How are things?'

Abby grinned. 'They're good! Busy, obviously, but – all OK.'

'Fab. We should . . . catch up. Soon? Come for a roast and a bottle of wine. Also, Daisy and Willow are dying to read your bird guide.'

Abby laughed. 'It's only a few scribbles in a scruffy notebook.'

'Don't care,' Tessa said. 'We want a grand unveiling. You can read the whole thing aloud, maybe down by the pond?'

'I'd love to come to that,' their mum said, and Abby tried to hide her disbelief.

'That would be great, Mum.'

'Anyway,' Tessa added, looking at the floor, 'it can't be far off being published, not with the company you've been keeping. Some of his talent must have rubbed off on you.'

'What's this?' Caroline asked. 'Who are you talking about?'

'Oh God, Mum—' Tessa's hands went to her mouth. 'You don't know anything about it? The photo, the – Abby, you didn't *tell* her?'

Abby felt her cheeks flush and saw the apology in her sister's eyes. 'It's been a busy time,' she said, unconvincingly. 'But I promise I'll fill you in on everything. At this notebook reading, or whatever it is.'

'Next Saturday,' Tessa said quickly. 'OK? You can both stay over; we've got room.'

Caroline nodded, but her attention was fixed on Abby. 'That sounds wonderful.'

'Abby? You're in, right?' Tessa prompted.

Abby chewed her lip, trying not to imagine what her mum would say when she told her the truth about Jack. 'Yes,' she said. 'I'm in. Now, do Daisy and Willow want their faces painted? Destiny is world class – well, the best in Suffolk, at least. Come on, I'll take you to see her.'

Penelope was handing out the prizes and bringing the Spectacular to a close at four o'clock.

Abby had organized a microphone, and Gavin had created a makeshift stage from a few pallets in an attempt to raise her above the crowd. That, along with her height, meant she could look imperiously over everyone, something that Abby knew from experience she excelled at.

Abby handed her the relevant envelopes, and Penelope announced the winners of the prize draw, and gave Evan his gift – a high-end birdwatching kit that Rosa had sourced from one of her suppliers – as recognition of his dedication to nature, and as a means of highlighting the Fledgling scheme. The remaining crowd was exuberant, and the claps and cheers were slow to die down.

Penelope thanked everyone for coming, and Abby was about to bring the event to a close when Councillor Savoury, resplendent in a grass-green dress and wide-brimmed hat, stepped onto the pallet-stage. She was followed, a few moments later, by Flick Hunter.

Abby stared, mouth agape, and the audience started murmuring excitedly. Flick was wearing a short dress the colour of strawberries, her blonde hair tied away from her face in a thick, luxurious plait. She gave Abby a warm smile.

Snapping out of her daze, Abby handed Helen the microphone and stood aside.

'Thank you, Abby,' Helen said. 'I know this is a little unorthodox, but Flick and I wanted to congratulate the staff of Meadowsweet for hosting such a wonderful few days at their impressive and, dare I say, important reserve.

'It is no secret that I have been fully behind this place since I was elected last year, and I know that resources are hard to come by, and that other, external factors have also had a bearing on its future. Events like this are vital, both in showcasing what is within arm's reach of the public, and also in boosting profits so that all who work here, with passion and dedication, are able to continue their good work.'

Helen took a breath and smiled at the crowd. Abby was

treated to a spectacular eye-roll from Gavin and tried not to laugh. While it was kind of the councillor to show her support, Abby wasn't sure what she had contributed to the reserve other than turning up to walks and events, and thought she was probably making her presence known, being seen to support the community, to boost her next election campaign. She was more interested in what Flick was doing alongside her.

'Now,' Councillor Savoury continued, 'I am aware that Mrs Hardinge and her son Leo have spent the last year seeking investment for the reserve, to ensure it has a healthy future in what are troubling times.'

Abby gasped, her heart skipping a beat. She looked at Penelope, who was studiously avoiding her gaze, and then at Rosa, whose dark eyes were wide with shock. The suspicions that had been bubbling away since she had been introduced to Leo on the night of the gala had suddenly been confirmed, seemingly as an aside, by someone she barely knew.

Unaware of the significance of her words, Helen kept going. 'I have long wanted to contribute something to Meadowsweet, and it was by happy accident that I ran into Flick Hunter at an author event in Meadowgreen library, earlier this year. It turned out we were singing from very similar song sheets.'

Helen handed the microphone to Flick and she stepped forward, eliciting a few cheers from the crowd.

'Hello, everyone,' Flick said in her bright, confident voice. 'I've had the most wonderful year in Suffolk, presenting *Wild Wonders* from Reston Marsh, and have fallen in love with the beautiful countryside here. I always knew Meadowsweet was on the other side of the marsh, but I didn't have a chance to visit until the spring. I can see how dedicated the staff are, how much they care about protecting the wildlife, and we're delighted to announce that the reserve has been awarded a conservation grant from the local council. This isn't really my news to share, but I've also arranged with the production company of *Wild Wonders* to do a special, one-off show about Meadowsweet, to highlight the work of the team, and the changes the grant will make.' She grinned and stepped back, and the audience threw themselves into a hearty round of applause.

Abby forced herself to clap. She felt dizzy, as if this was a surreal fantasy brought on by working too many long, hot days in a row.

Helen took up the mantle again. 'There were a number of sites under consideration for the grant, but I championed the reserve and, with Flick's support, was successful with my application.' She turned graciously towards Penelope and handed her an envelope. 'This is for Meadowsweet, to help it thrive.'

Penelope stuttered a thank you, and as she opened the envelope and announced that it was a grant for £30,000, Abby replayed Helen's words in her head.

Mrs Hardinge and her son Leo.

She hadn't misheard.

Councillor Savoury, Flick Hunter and the cash injection received the loudest cheer of the afternoon, and then, realizing that was the end of the excitement, the crowd started to disperse. Abby watched as people drifted towards the car park, happy and sun-kissed, children ready for baths and bed, and tried to comprehend what had just happened.

The council had given them £30,000. Flick Hunter was going to host an edition of *Wild Wonders* at Meadowsweet.

Leo Ravensberg was Penelope's son. None of these facts seemed ready to sink in.

She went to check on Marek and the volunteers who were staying to help with the initial clear-up. Many of the stall-holders weren't leaving until the next day, and Abby had agreed to be there for that, along with Rosa and Gavin. She had just given Marek a hug when Penelope took hold of her arm.

'Come to the visitor centre,' she said. 'Rosa, Stephan and Gavin are on their way.'

'Is this about what Councillor Savoury said?'

'Tush, girl. Can't you wait a few more minutes? I don't want to have to repeat myself.' Penelope had a glint in her eye, her long fingers wrapped around Abby's arm as they walked.

The visitor centre was quiet save for a couple who were collecting membership forms from a tired but jubilant-looking Rosa. 'Thank you,' she was saying. 'We hope to see you again very soon.'

Once the couple had left, Penelope checked the place was empty, then shut and locked the door. 'To the café, everyone.'

Abby widened her eyes at Rosa, and then noticed the sightings blackboard next to reception. It had the usual birds and butterflies on it: robin, heron, bearded tit, marsh harrier, peacock butterfly, dark-green fritillary, and then at the bottom, someone had written: *The Lesser-spotted Jack Westcoat.*

She gritted her teeth. For most of the day she had almost, *almost* forgotten about him, apart from when her mum and sister had accosted her, and also when a children's author was telling a group of small, enraptured children about the hungry caterpillar, and then when she'd seen a faded toy hippo on the local air ambulance's bric-a-brac stall. OK, so she hadn't managed to put him at the back of her mind, but this was taking it too far.

'Abigail Field, stop gawping and go to the café. I'll join you in a moment.'

Penelope shooed her through to the open space, bright with the early evening sun, the shimmering perfection of a cobweb glistening on the outside of the glass.

'Thirty grand, huh?' Gavin rubbed his hands together. 'That'll help pay for a few hide repairs. Not that I care about the reserve as much as I do that Flick bloody Hunter's going to grace us with her delectable presence again! All my Christmases have come at once.'

'It's incredibly decent of her,' Stephan said, sitting at one of the largest tables and pulling chairs out for the others. '*Incredibly*.'

'That's not the most shocking news, though, is it?' Rosa said. 'Leo Ravensberg is Penelope's son!'

'He's that agent bloke, isn't he? Friends with your dreamboat Jack.' Gavin turned to Abby and she nodded, still stunned by the revelation, even though she had suspected it for a while.

'I wonder why she's kept it secret,' Stephan said. 'Why she felt the need to pretend that she was alone, without family.'

'Maybe councillor Savoury got the wrong end of the stick,' Gavin suggested.

'No, it's definitely true,' Abby said. 'I know it is.'

'How come?' Gavin swivelled his chair round and sat on it backwards, fiddling with the cigarette shoved behind his ear.

'Let's wait and see what Penelope has to say, then I'll tell you how I worked it out.' She grinned when Rosa and Gavin groaned in unison.

Abby decided that bright orange had been a good choice for their T-shirts, except perhaps for Gavin, who hadn't so much tanned over the weekend as boiled, his nose dangerously pink.

'You're all great, you know that?' she said, surprising herself as the words popped out. When three puzzled faces looked at her, she knew she needed to explain. 'Whatever Penelope is about to tell us, whatever impact this grant has on the reserve, I want you to know that I think you've all been wonderful, that this year has been tough, and that Penelope was right to say I dropped the ball occasionally. But it never rolled too far, because you were all there to pick it up. I'm so grateful, and I hope we get to keep doing what we're doing, here at Meadowsweet, for a long time to come.'

Rosa's eyes had become decidedly watery, and Stephan was examining something non-existent on the table top.

It was Gavin, unsurprisingly, who broke the silence. 'Well, I think you're a fucking legend Abby Field, and don't let anyone tell you otherwise.'

'Cheers, Gavin.'

'Rousing pep talk,' Penelope said, gliding in, sitting next to Gavin and placing a bottle of champagne, its sides slick with condensation, on the table. 'I almost couldn't have said it better myself.'

'Penelope, jeez.' Gavin turned the bottle round to read the label.

'Five glasses please, Stephan,' she said.

Stephan got up and hurried towards the kitchen, bumping into a chair on the way.

Abby felt dangerously on the edge of hysteria. *Champagne?*

'Have you finally lost it, Penelope?' Gavin asked. 'This is good stuff.'

'No, Gavin, I have not *lost it*, as you so eloquently put it. But I felt we deserved a little something after all the hard work of the last three days – and the months leading up to it. I have to say, however, that wasn't quite the ending I was expecting. Helen Savoury knows how to steal the limelight. Gavin, if you'd do the honours,' she said, once Stephan had returned with the glasses.

He did, and soon their straight-sided juice glasses were brimming with bubbling, golden liquid.

'I am sorry,' Penelope continued, and those words alone were enough to send anxious glances shooting around the table, 'if I haven't been the easiest person to work for over the last year. As you know, it's been a trying time, and I've had to face up to a few home truths. The nature reserve is Al's legacy, and so to see it on the verge of closure has been almost unbearable. Despite all your best efforts – and I do mean *best*, Abby, despite what I might have said before – there was no chance of us turning Meadowsweet into a profit-making business without some significant changes that I was unable to afford. Selling Swallowtail House was the inevitable choice, but I tried to hold off for so long, believing that our efforts could somehow make enough of a difference. It was mine and Al's home, and that was equally precious to me, even though the thought of living in those rooms without him was too difficult to contemplate.'

She stared at her glass and Abby shifted in her seat, knowing the others would be equally disquieted at the honesty which was in part, she was sure, forced by Helen Savoury's revelation. Stephan, who was best qualified to speak, filled the silence.

'It's an impossible choice,' he said. 'Do you stay where you used to be happy, but which now also has heartbreaking memories, or do you let go and allow yourself a completely fresh start? I chose to stay where Mary and I spent our best years, but I still wonder if I made the right decision.'

'It was a much more sensible one than mine,' Penelope said. 'I didn't stay in the house, but I couldn't let it go either, and it has stopped me from being prudent where the reserve is concerned. Even without *Wild Wonders* on our doorstep, this would always have happened. Swallowtail House, as I'm sure you know by now, has been sold, and I'm confident the new owner will restore it to its former glory, as well as bringing it into the twenty-first century, something it is in sore need of.'

'Can you tell us who's bought it?' Rosa asked. 'Although, maybe that's not fair – we should give them a few days before the Meadowgreen gossip starts doing the rounds.'

Penelope smiled and shook her head. 'All in good time,' she said. 'There's a lot of work to be done before the house is fit to live in, but they have a suitable alternative while the necessary repairs are carried out. But I've let the house go, I have more money to put into the reserve, and along with Councillor Savoury's very generous grant – which I didn't know about – and Flick Hunter and *Wild Wonders* set to bring some much-needed publicity to Meadowsweet – something I *was* aware of – I'm planning on making some improvements over the next few years. Of course, I'll need your input and imagination to make my thoughts a reality.

'And in the meantime,' she continued, 'we've had over a hundred Fledgling applications, and that's only those that have registered online since Friday, so there are more to come. Abby, we'll need a way for members – new and old – and visitors to have their say on the changes we're making, so that they truly feel the reserve is theirs.'

'Of course.' Abby pulled out her trusty notebook, but Penelope put a hand on her arm.

'You won't forget that, I'm sure. This isn't a brainstorming session, it's a thank you, to all of you, for keeping this place afloat when, in all honesty, the solution was there the whole time. I was simply too stubborn to accept it. And so it's also an apology, that I have kept you in the dark, had you labouring under somewhat false pretences – though in many ways this year has been wonderful, and has shown me what's possible.'

'What made you change your mind about Swallowtail?' Stephan asked.

'A number of things,' Penelope said. 'We had run out of road, and Mr Philpott was forcing me to make a decision about the future of, essentially, the whole estate. But I was also given a pep talk by someone who has my best interests at heart, who coaxed me out of my blind determination to hold onto the past, and made me realize that it's the future that's important. For far too long I've held onto a secret, something I spent years believing was a mistake, but which was one of the most wonderful things I'd ever accomplished. Now, I no longer have the option of keeping quiet. He forced me to face the fact that my stubbornness was making me wretched, not to mention harming Meadowsweet. He convinced me that it was time to let go of Swallowtail House.'

She gave them a rueful smile that made her seem entirely approachable and, Abby realized, so like Leo it was scary.

'Your son,' Abby said, keeping her gaze on Penelope.

'So Councillor Savoury hadn't got the wrong end of the stick?' Gavin asked. 'I thought she was being a fruit loop.'

'No, Gavin,' Penelope said. 'She was not being a fruit loop. Over the course of the last year I have spent a lot of time with Helen, and she has had the pleasure of meeting Leo, though her idea of discretion leaves a lot to be desired.'

'Is it – is he Al's?' Rosa asked tentatively.

'No,' Penelope admitted. 'I had him when I was eighteen. A flirtation that went too far with a boy who lived near us in London. Ironically, I met Al here, in Suffolk, not long after Leo was born. My parents decided that I should have my child away from London, that a few months convalescing in the countryside would be the most practical solution. I doubt they expected me to find my future husband, and once I'd met Al, they made me promise not to tell him the truth, for fear that it would end any potential match. By the time Al and I realized we were serious about each other, it seemed impossible to backtrack, to change the foundations of our whole relationship.'

'What happened to Leo?' Rosa asked.

'He was given up for adoption.'

'Jesus,' Gavin muttered. 'And Al never found out?'

'No. There were physical signs, of course, but even though I met him soon after the birth, it was a long time before things . . . progressed, and I was able to keep from him what I needed to. If he ever suspected anything he never raised it with me.

'I lived with that lie our whole marriage. After he'd died and I'd moved out of Swallowtail House, once the shock and grief had started to fade, I searched for my son. And I found him. We've had a relationship ever since, exchanging emails and phone calls, and I visit him whenever I'm in London. He has accepted me, though of course I didn't raise him. But tracking him down felt like a betrayal to Al, and while I reasoned with myself that it was justified, somehow getting rid of Swallowtail House was not.

'I told myself I could have Leo in my life if I held onto Al's family home. I couldn't live in it, and yet I couldn't fail him by letting it go.

'But then I had to choose between the reserve and the house.' Penelope's gaze was firmly on the table, as if she was talking to herself rather than her stunned employees. 'And while I initially tried to keep both, in the end, there was no contest. The reserve gives pleasure and purpose to so many, not just you and the other staff and volunteers, but the visitors and locals, not to mention the wildlife that lives here. The house can start again with someone else, but the reserve is too important to me; to all of us.'

'Hear, hear,' Gavin said quietly.

'And it was Leo who gave you the final push?' Abby asked.

She nodded. 'On the day of your gala, in fact. He came to see me before you all drove down to London, and left me with some uncomfortable truths to wrestle with over the weekend. That is why, Abby, I was particularly hard on you when you returned to work that Monday. Not only was it unfair of me to take it out on you, but by the time I saw you Leo had been in touch again to tell me that Jack had left Meadowgreen, so my anger was doubly cruel when you were already suffering. You didn't deserve that, and I'm truly sorry.'

Abby brushed the apology away, the mention of Jack's departure threatening to overwhelm her after the revelations, the emotion, of the afternoon. 'It doesn't matter.'

'But it does,' Penelope said. 'You have done so much for Meadowsweet. You're kind, generous with your time, and you're smarter than I sometimes think is good for you.' She gave her a gentle smile. 'I knew you'd worked it out, about Leo. I've had cause to be in touch with him a lot recently, since I asked him to look for an investor for me – a fruitless task, as it turned out. He had much more success helping me find a tenant for Peacock Cottage. I was hoping to raise some extra money for the reserve and ended up getting decidedly more than I bargained for. I didn't anticipate your and Jack's burgeoning relationship, and that you'd end up spending time with Leo yourself, and so spot our similarities.'

'Does Jack know?' Rosa asked.

'Leo's and my relationship has always been . . . private. The complications were as much on his side as mine, because he has a very close adoptive family, but also because Meadowgreen isn't the most discreet place, and many of the villagers grew up knowing Al. It seemed pointless stirring up village gossip when Leo was here so infrequently – it wasn't anyone's business but ours.

'When Leo suggested Jack could be the perfect tenant for Peacock Cottage, we both agreed that there was no reason to tell him about our connection. But Jack has been a good friend of Leo's for almost ten years, and while he was staying in Suffolk we spent time together. He may well have come to the same conclusion as Abby, though he has had other things on his mind, and I certainly wasn't his main focus while he was here.'

Abby's triumph faded. Suddenly the thought of going home to a ready meal and a glass of wine felt like an anticlimax, even though she knew Raffle would be waiting for her.

'Anyway,' Penelope said, 'I have kept you here long enough with my tales of heartbreak and indecision. I felt it was useful for you to know my reasoning, but I really brought you here to say thank you. For keeping Meadowsweet going, for being dedicated to the cause, even as I was dithering. Without you, this champagne wouldn't be required. So, to my wonderful team, and to a blossoming future for Meadowsweet.'

'To the team, and to Meadowsweet!' Everyone echoed the words, clinking glasses.

Abby took a long sip of champagne. She was tired and aching, in need of a shower and some food. She was pleased that Penelope had Leo, though she was still stunned that it was true and that her boss had hidden the truth for such a long time after Al's death, but she hoped it meant that she would see more of him in Suffolk. She tried not to think about how tantalizingly close that would make Jack, or knowledge of him, at least. She would focus on her job, and all the new possibilities it held. She would work harder, live up to Penelope's expectations, especially as, she thought sadly, she no longer had any distractions.

'And to you, Penelope,' Gavin said. 'The scariest, most secretive but, above all, most lovable boss anyone could ask for.'

'To Penelope!' They touched glasses again.

'Right, then,' Penelope said, smiling. 'Off you go. Get a good night's rest.'

Drinks were downed and chairs were scraped back, and as Abby went to leave, Penelope put a hand on her arm. 'I do have one final thing for you, Abby,' she said quietly, and Rosa, Stephan and Gavin stopped in their tracks.

Penelope glanced at them, sighed as if their interest was inevitable, and took something out from under the table, where it must have been sitting in her lap. It was a crisp white envelope.

She handed it to Abby, her smile reaching her grey eyes, and as Abby looked down at where her name was written on the front of the envelope in neat, slanted writing, with no address or stamp or postage mark, she tried to remember how to breathe.

Chapter Twenty-Six

The swallowtail is the UK's largest butterfly, and also one of the rarest. Its larvae live on milk parsley, and in England, it can usually only be seen in the Norfolk broads. Very occasionally, Suffolk will have a visiting swallowtail from over the sea in Europe, but it's a once-in-a-lifetime sighting. Its swallow-like tail mimics antennae, and it has red spots on its wings that look like eyes, so it can confuse other creatures into thinking it has two heads.

— Note from Abby's notebook

'What does it say? Oh my God, Abby, what does it say? We're all about to die of suspense here.' Rosa's voice was high-pitched, but Abby barely heard it.

Dear Abby,
Meet me at the House of Birds and Butterflies whenever you're free. I'll be waiting.
JW xx

She blinked, passed the note to her friend, and stared at Penelope.

'Go on, then,' Penelope said.

'What the fuck is the House of Birds and Butterflies?' Abby heard Gavin say, but she was already grabbing her bag from the storeroom and running out of the door, past the bird feeders, where a squirrel was hanging upside down, helping himself to sunflower seeds, and down to the start of the woodland trail, the signpost pointing towards the meadow trail, the heron hide, the kingfisher hide. She followed the path towards the forest hide and then cut off to her right, down the barely visible track which wasn't signposted to anywhere but led to her destination.

The sun was beginning to slip towards the horizon, and she could tell, even though she was beneath the canopy of trees, that the glare of the day was fading, leaving behind a warm evening. She found the fallen elder, navigated carefully through the brambles, but still managed to scratch her legs, bare below her denim shorts. She thought of what she must look like: scraped legs, fluorescent-orange T-shirt, hair pulled back in what would now be a dishevelled ponytail, and realized she didn't care.

Jack was here, and he was waiting for her, perhaps allowed this one, final dalliance on Penelope's property before she no longer had any claim over it.

She could hear the short, high-pitched song of a tree creeper and, somewhere in the distance, what sounded like a nightingale singing for all it was worth, the notes rising high into the clear sky.

A few more steps, and the brick wall that held Swallowtail House and its grounds came into view, and then the side gate, where all those months ago Jack had broken apart the padlock and invited her to trespass with him. Now, Jack's shiny new chain was wrapped around the gate, but it was loose, the padlock missing.

Abby's breathing quickened as she pulled open the gate and peered towards the house. It was resplendent in the evening sun, its windows shining, the scaffolding at the back of the building gleaming like silver.

She hurried through the long grass and saw two figures on the wide front steps. One was laid out flat, head on his paws, large ears twitching, and the other was sitting still, his elbows resting on his knees. He stood up as she approached, and ran a hand through longish, thick dark hair.

Abby's heart soared like the nightingale's song, and she found she was jogging, running, white rabbit tails scattering as she disturbed them. As she got closer, Jack walked towards her. He was wearing pale jeans and a white, casual shirt, open at the neck. She soaked up the sight of him, his smile – once they were close – warm, though there was apprehension in his eyes.

They stopped a few feet apart, and Abby tried to catch her breath.

'I got your note,' she said.

'And you came straight here,' he replied, the low sweep of his voice jolting through her, firing her senses as much as the sight of him.

'I felt it warranted an immediate response.'

'That's what I thought, too.' He took a step towards her, and Abby did the same, deciding that she'd been controlled for long enough, that now his intoxicating bergamot smell had reached her she couldn't hold back for another second. He was here, within touching distance, and it filled her with happiness.

His hands slid down her arms and he laced his fingers through hers. His eyes, so vividly blue in the sunlight, held hers for a moment, and then he kissed her, and all Abby's sadness shattered, dispersing like a cloud of butterflies. He wrapped his arms around her, pulling her against him, closing any last gap, not even the whispering wind given room to come between them. She clutched at the thin fabric of his shirt, pressed her fingers against his back, his shoulder blades, feeling him, solid and warm and here.

He leaned back to look at her and stroked her hair away from her forehead. 'Abby, God,' he said, 'I have missed you.' He kissed her again.

'Ditto,' she murmured, returning his kisses, keeping her words short, not wanting them to get in the way.

Eventually, they broke apart, and he took her hand and led her to the steps of Swallowtail House. They sat close together, their bodies angled towards each other.

Raffle raised his head, and Abby stroked her husky's nose.

'What are you doing with my dog?' she asked, fixing on the least pressing of all her questions.

Jack smiled the half-smile that she had missed so much, though his eyes were dancing, no hint of a frown furrowing his brows, all apprehension gone. 'Octavia let me take him, once she'd stopped screeching at me.'

Abby laughed. 'I can imagine that seeing you again was a bit of a shock for her. I know how she feels.'

He squeezed her hand. 'I'm sorry I didn't tell you about this before.' He gestured around him.

'About what? Coming to visit?' She wondered, through her elation, how long she would be able to spend with him, whether she could cope with another goodbye.

He stared at her. '*Visit?*'

'You came back to see me, and I – Jack, being with you is perfect, I'm so happy, but when you go again, I—'

'Hang on, Penelope didn't tell you?'

'Tell me what?' Abby felt like everything was slowing down, that the sun had stopped sinking, the birds had given up preening, the rabbits were all frozen, their heads raised, waiting in the long grass. She held her breath.

'I've bought Swallowtail House,' he said. 'I'm moving here, permanently. Penelope has said I can stay in Peacock Cottage until the foundations have been stabilized and at least a couple of the rooms are finished, but I'm taking a few months off writing to focus on getting it done. I . . .' He faltered. 'Abby, you really didn't know?'

Abby swallowed desperately, trying to find words – any words – and failing.

So instead Jack kissed her again, his thumb grazing her cheek where the tears had started to fall.

'I cannot live without you, Abby Field,' he whispered. 'The last couple of months have been unbearable. I thought you would have realized that by now?' He looked suddenly bashful, as if admitting this much was too exposing.

'You bought Swallowtail House so you could be near me?'

He glanced behind him. 'I did. And also because that kitchen is crying out for some white granite worktops, and I can't remember feeling as at home, as content, as I did looking out of those windows over the trees towards the reserve and the village. I have space to write here. I can be myself. I can walk along the trails and think through storylines and character motives and dialogue. And most of all, I can spend time with you, if you'll have me?'

Abby didn't bother to wipe her tears away. 'But it's so big,' she said, because that was the easiest of all her thoughts to say out loud.

Jack laughed and took her hands again. 'It is, but I was thinking that, in time, I might have someone who would want to share it with me, and bring their large, affectionate dog with them. Someone who will help me redesign the garden – though I'm planning to leave some of it at nature's mercy – and who might ask their sister and her family to stay sometimes, her nieces to take charge of that small bedroom with windows on two sides. And we'd need to make use of the ballroom, so I could host Page Turner Foundation evenings here – publishing's far too London-centric anyway, though Bob Stevens will need a bit more persuading before he agrees with me on that – and maybe Octavia would like to run a book group for the village, or invite other authors to give talks, as long as the audiences promise not to heckle, of course.'

'You want me to – to live with you?'

He narrowed his eyes. 'At some point, further down the line, I'm hoping that might be a possibility. I know we've barely started, that there's so much to find out about each other, but going on our recent experience, and considering how I feel about you, I'm hoping that in a few months we'll still like each other enough to want to spend more time together. As long as I promise not to complain about the wildlife.'

'If you're not keen on wildlife, then you've bought the wrong property, Mr Westcoat.'

'I know that,' he murmured.

'And I could, possibly, see that in the future I might still like you enough to want to spend some time here. Would I get any say in the decoration?'

'Of course,' he said. 'That's going to take months, by the way. There's a lot that needs bringing up to scratch.'

'So you'll be at Peacock Cottage for a while?'

'I will.'

'When are you moving back?'

'I've done it. Shalimar and the squashed-frog Range Rover are already waiting for us.'

'They are?' Abby's soul lifted further, threatening to sweep her off the ground, untethered like the hot-air balloon.

'I've bought a bottle of champagne and a packet of oven chips, and I wondered, Abby Field, if you would be happy to spend the evening with me, to see if we can finally nail down that badger in the garden.'

She grinned. 'That sounds perfect, if I can have a shower first? Maybe nip home and change this T-shirt for something a bit more comfortable?'

'What's wrong with Day-Glo orange?' Jack asked. 'You look gorgeous, sun-kissed.'

'Like I've been Tangoed,' Abby said.

Jack hesitated, his head on one side. 'Possibly a bit. I will allow you to go home and change, as long as you're back at mine within half an hour, otherwise I can't guarantee that the chips won't be burnt. I'll take Raffle with me as insurance.'

'Deal,' she said, laughing, knowing it would be the quickest shower of her life. She let Jack pull her to her feet, and they stood looking up at the house, the sun sinking, burning amber, classier than her T-shirt but no less blinding as it lit the glass with its fire.

Swallowtail House, the House of Birds and Butterflies, Jack's House and, perhaps in time, a home for her and Raffle too. Abby breathed deeply, trying to take it all in, knowing that she was sure, *so sure*, of one thing, and that was the man whose hand she was holding, who was standing along-side her, as awed by the simple beauty of nature as she was.

They turned away and walked slowly towards the side gate that would lead them to Meadowgreen and Peacock Cottage.

'Speaking of my nieces,' Abby said, 'Tessa has invited me to hers next weekend, as a sort of unveiling of the ridiculous bird guide that I've been writing.'

'It's not ridiculous, Abby.'

'It started as a joke. Something to help Willow and Daisy identify the birds and want to find out more about them.'

'Which is brilliant, and important, especially when you're trying to encourage more people – young people, notably – to show an interest.'

'Meadowsweet will be doing a lot of that with its Fledgling programme, something I have you to thank for.' Jack frowned, but Abby kept going, wanting to get her question out before she lost her nerve. 'I'll tell you about it later. But Tessa, all of them, want me to read this thing out loud, next Saturday, at their house. And Mum's going to be there.'

Jack glanced at her. 'How do you feel about that?'

'Nervous. OK mostly, but a bit nervous. I was wondering, would you – if I checked with Tessa that it was all right – would you come with me?'

Jack grinned. 'I'd love to. I'm intrigued about this bird book, and I'd love to meet your family.'

Abby nodded, exhaled. 'If it's too much too soon, then—'

'It's not,' Jack said. 'Not for me, anyway.'

'Good.' They smiled at each other, looked away. 'And if you could resist passing judgement on my reading,' Abby continued, 'that would be great, because I'll get enough of that from Willow and Daisy, and I'll need at least one person on my side.'

'I'll be the perfect publicist,' he said. 'And I'll quash any heckling the moment it starts. Unless – how scary are your nieces?'

'Daisy, especially, is terrifying.'

'I'll bear that in mind. At least you're starting with a difficult crowd. In some ways that's best, getting the toughest events out of the way first.'

'Like sleepy little Meadowgreen library?'

'Exactly,' Jack said. 'That was hard work.'

'Octavia still feels terrible about it.'

'She doesn't need to. I deserved most of what was said.'

'You didn't,' Abby replied forcefully. 'And you proved it with that interview in the Saturday paper.'

'You read that?'

'Of course I did! I read everything. I inhaled all I could find about you online, in the papers, while I couldn't inhale the real you, your smell and your touch, and your laugh.'

'Abby—' he started.

'*He's smartly dressed, his hair the dishevelled mane of a man who wants to give the impression looks are unimportant, but not even he would deny that he's attractive, almost disarmingly so,*' she quoted in an over-serious voice.

'Oh God,' Jack clamped a hand over his eyes. 'Please don't. I've had enough teasing from Leo about all that.'

'The interviewer was pretty terrible,' Abby said, laughing, wondering whether to raise the subject of Leo and Penelope, then deciding she didn't want to right at that moment, when she'd just got Jack back. They had all the time in the world to talk about it. But there was one thing that couldn't wait. 'I'm glad you told the truth about Eddie, though,' she said. 'You deserve more than what he did to you.'

Jack nodded and squeezed her hand, and Abby knew that was all that needed to be said, for now at least.

They had almost reached the gate, Raffle walking patiently alongside them, his acceptance of Jack so absolute that, if nothing else had convinced her, Abby would have known that he was a good man, one who could be trusted. But she had so much more besides her dog's acceptance, not least her own instincts, which she had finally allowed herself to listen to, telling her that she had found someone she could be truly, exquisitely happy with.

'I've been wondering,' Jack said, breaking into her thoughts, 'about your motto, friendship and chips.'

'Oh yes?' she asked, wincing as she remembered the night she had failed to listen to her own advice, and the embarrassing text messages that had ensued.

'I wonder if we could amend it slightly?' He stopped and faced her, the reflected sun turning the right side of his face golden, his eyes like the shimmering surface of the lagoon.

'What to?' Abby asked, having to force the words out because she was struck by his beauty all over again, and by the new, wonderful truth that this man was hers, that he had given up his life in London for her, wanted her as much as she wanted him.

'The chips part is fine,' he said. 'But friendship is a bit too . . . it doesn't convey my feelings well enough. It seems a little half-hearted.'

'So, you want to change it to . . . ?'

'To true love,' he said. 'I love you, Abby, and it's the most real, genuine thing I've ever experienced. I'm not ashamed to admit it, and if you feel even a fraction for me what I feel for you, then I will be happier than I ever thought possible.' His expression was intent, his lips parted slightly, waiting.

Abby didn't want to torment him for a second longer. Her

smile threatened to split her face apart. 'I do,' she said. 'I love you too. I have been bursting with it, miserable without you, trying to conjure up a world where I would be OK with us apart, and failing. I love you, Jack Westcoat. I accept your amendment to the motto, to change it to true love and chips. It's perfect, perhaps even good enough to be the title of your next book.'

'Not a chance.' He leaned down to kiss her, taking the breath from her body with one expert, electrifying touch. 'It's far too happy,' he said, trailing his lips down her neck. 'It wouldn't be an accurate representation of the death, destruction and bleakness within.' He planted feathery kisses along her collarbone, as light as a butterfly's touch, and as powerful as the wind that whipped across the water on icy March mornings. 'Besides,' he added with a smile, when Abby was leaning into him, her breathing ragged with desire, 'there are some things that aren't for public consumption, and now that I've got you back, I want you all to myself.'

The sun continued its slow, steady progress towards the horizon, and the House of Birds and Butterflies stood stoically in its grounds, its flaming windows looking over the village of Meadowgreen and the Meadowsweet Nature Reserve, as Jack and Abby sank into the long, dewy grass, the chips waiting for them at Peacock Cottage forgotten, at least for the moment.

Above them, a robin trilled a last, cheerful song into the still summer air, and a swallowtail butterfly passed close by, unseen by anyone except Raffle, who lifted his nose as it fluttered out through the gate, following a determined, dancing path towards the meadow trail and the milk parsley growing in the hedgerows.

Chapter Twenty-Seven

Lovebirds are small, rainbow-coloured parrots that come from Africa. They mate for life, and pine for their partner when they're not together. They also feed each other (though not chips). The collective name for a group of lovebirds is, appropriately, an orgy.

— Note from Abby's notebook

Penelope opened her mouth to speak, and a nearby blackbird started singing. She glanced in its direction and raised a solitary eyebrow, and everyone laughed.

The candles on the birthday cake, thirty-two of them, shifted and danced, adding to the heat mirage of the sweltering late-August day, but there was hardly any wind in the reserve's picnic area, and no risk of them being blown out.

'As I was about to say before one of our residents so rudely interrupted me,' Penelope said, 'thank you all for coming today to this momentous event. The birthday of someone who, I think we can all agree, is at the heart of Meadowsweet

Nature Reserve. Abby,' she continued, turning to her, 'you are an invaluable member of this team – our newly promoted events manager, in fact – a good friend and, if rumours are to be believed a soon-to-be author of a bird book for children, something which will tie in neatly with Meadowsweet Fledglings.'

Abby's skin flushed, and she covered her eyes as there was more laughter. 'That's never going to happen,' she said. Jack squeezed her waist and she leaned into him, feeling the heat of his skin through his thin cotton T-shirt. She peeled her hands away and risked looking up.

'No,' Penelope said, her eyes dancing with amusement. 'But I understand it was an entertaining afternoon.'

'Oh, it was,' Tessa grinned. 'Abby must have been pissed off with someone when she wrote about how kingfishers bash fish's heads in before eating them whole, and she definitely doesn't like magpies. Daisy saw one in the garden the other day and ran inside, screaming.'

'I am *so* sorry,' Abby said.

Her sister carried on, unperturbed. 'But the highlight was when she told us about the lovebirds, and Willow asked what the word "orgy" meant.'

'Fucking hell,' Gavin said, chuckling. 'Why did you have anything about lovebirds in there anyway? They're not native to the UK.'

Abby shrugged, wondering why she had allowed Penelope to persuade her to have a gathering for her birthday, when it was clear that the embarrassment she'd expected was nothing compared to the reality. 'It was . . . important to have them in there,' she explained, glancing up at Jack.

'I thought it was a triumph,' he said, kissing her forehead. 'Kingfisher brutality and lovebird orgies aside.'

'Not that you're at all biased.' Tessa flashed him a smile, and Abby felt another rush of happiness that, upon meeting Jack, all of her sister's fears had been dispelled. By the end of the bird-book unveiling day, the two of them were regaling Abby, Neil and Caroline with ropey renditions of Flanders and Swann songs after too much red wine. 'The Hippopotamus Song', was, understandably, the highlight.

'Guys,' Stephan said, 'the candles are dripping wax all over the icing, so . . .'

'Of course, Stephan, thank you. Everyone?' Penelope lifted her arms and counted them in to a rousing chorus of 'Happy Birthday'.

Abby giggled, wondering what the birds must think of such a haphazard cacophony, and then when it was over, she bent forward and blew out the candles on the huge chocolate fudgecake Stephan had made. Everyone clapped, and she started to cut it into slices.

'No speech, Abby?' Leo asked.

Abby shook her head. 'Speeches really aren't my thing.'

'You could have fooled us,' Gavin said. 'What about that day in the café after the summer event?' He pressed his hand to his chest, his voice wobbling dramatically. '*I want you to know that you've all been wonderful.* It was like a bloody Oscars acceptance.'

'Shut up, Gav.' Rosa slapped him on the shoulder. 'We were all knackered, and we'd just heard Helen Savoury announce that she was giving the reserve £30,000, and also let slip that Penelope had been keeping something rather monumental from everyone.' She looked pointedly at Leo, and he laughed.

'I like the idea of being monumental. Usually my job is to thrust other people into the limelight.'

'I still can't believe you didn't tell me,' Jack said. 'What did you think I would have done with the information?'

Abby had told Jack about Penelope's revelations the evening he'd returned to Meadowgreen. He'd been shocked and had admitted that he hadn't picked up on the similarities between the two of them, a fact which, Abby knew, had annoyed him. He'd told her that he knew Leo was adopted, and that he was in touch with his birth mother, but that his agent had never been more forthcoming about that aspect of his life, despite their years of friendship. Abby had re-assured Jack that it was only the coincidence of them both telling her to '*smile, and you're halfway there,*' that had made it twig for her.

'Jack,' Leo said, sighing, 'you expect me to believe that if I had revealed your landlady was actually my mother, you wouldn't have told Abby? Almost from the moment you moved here, our communications were sprinkled with titbits about this woman you'd had a run-in with. "*She's so infuriating Leo, how am I expected to write? Oh Leo, did I tell you she wants me to go on one of her walks so that I can learn to embrace nature? Did you know she has a husky, Leo? She has the loveliest eyes, Leo, I can feel myself falling into them!*"'

'I did not say that!' Jack shot back, laughing.

'It was bloody close enough, though. You changed the entire plot of your novel just so you could find a reason to spend hours walking around the reserve with her. The most significant tributary in history.'

'Yes, all right,' Jack said, his cheeks colouring. 'Everyone knows I'm besotted with Abby, there's no need to humiliate me.'

'Well, I think it's adorable,' Octavia said, cutting off a delicate piece of cake with her fork. 'I could tell you were softer than you looked, like a tiger cub playing at being a stealthy killer.'

'Or a baby hippo,' Abby said, feeling Jack's eyes on her as she joined in. 'Hippos are very dangerous, but I'm not sure a young one would be that threatening. What's a baby hippo called, does anyone know?'

'A calf,' Gavin supplied. 'It could still break every bone in your foot if it trod on you. Not sure I'd peg Jack as a hippo. More a hyena, something like that.'

'Jesus,' Jack muttered. 'Do we really have to debate what my spirit animal is? Shouldn't Abby be the centre of attention here?'

'No, no,' she said, laughing. 'I've done my bit blowing out the candles. But I will just say—'

'Oh, here we go,' Gavin said. 'I knew you couldn't resist it.'

'I just want to say thank you,' Abby continued, ignoring him. 'For this – for the cake and the presents, and for all coming today to celebrate with me. I couldn't think of a better way of spending my birthday than with the people I care about the most, and you're all here – well, apart from those who have decided that Flick Hunter and *Wild Wonders* setting up a kingfisher hide is even more appealing than birthday cake, which I have to say makes me a very proud auntie, even if I'm a little worried that you're coming down with something, Gavin?'

'You're more important than Flick,' he said, shrugging. 'Besides, Jenna told me that if I flirted with her I'd be sleeping in the spare room and the mattress in there's crap.'

Everyone laughed.

'That figures,' Abby said. 'Though I'm not sure a crush on Flick Hunter can explain Mum's foray into the depths of

Meadowsweet – has she had a brain transplant in the last couple of months, Tessa?'

'She was showing off her new wellies earlier, but then they are gold. And she's bought a birdbath for her garden, to go with the feeders you got her. You've got another convert.'

'It took long enough,' Abby said. 'But I'm happy, even if she is angling for her own television appearance.' She exchanged a smile with her sister and felt Jack's grip on her tighten. 'Anyway, that's all I wanted to say. Thank you for coming, now eat cake and be merry!'

The day at Tessa's, with her mum and Jack, and the grand unveiling of what amounted to a series of scribbles in various notebooks, had been better than she could have imagined. Other than her sister and her boyfriend hitting it off, Caroline had been relaxed and non-judgemental and, Abby could tell, making an effort. They couldn't bridge years of pain and discomfort in a single afternoon, but they could take small steps towards a proper, emotional reconciliation, and Abby felt that now she had the tools – the confidence and self-belief – to start down that path. Not to mention someone she could talk it over with, who would support her and, whenever she needed, simply be there for her.

As everyone tucked into the cake, Willow, Daisy and Evan came rushing through the café, their legs splashed with dirt, Neil, Caroline, Karen and Joyce, and Evan's parents following behind. Jonny brought up the rear, a pair of shiny new binoculars round his neck. Abby watched as he gave Rosa a kiss, her nose crinkling as she laughed in response to something he'd said. Abby waved at Evan, who was cutting slices of cake for the latecomers.

'How are the production team getting on?' she asked.

'Amazing,' Evan said reverently. 'Flick's going to let me do a piece to camera, about how Meadowsweet inspired my love of nature and the incredible Fledgling Programme that's going to safeguard the future of the reserve for years to come.'

Abby struggled to hold in her laughter, wondering at Evan's capacity to memorize the words that had, obviously, come from someone else. It seemed that Flick Hunter's appeal wasn't limited to men over twenty-five.

'That's wonderful, Evan. You're the perfect spokesman for the Fledglings. You'll have to let me know when it's going to happen so I can watch.'

'You're doing it with me,' Evan said, a forkful of cake hovering inches from his lips. 'Flick said it had to be you, that you were the *best*.'

Abby raised her eyebrows. 'She said that, did she?'

Evan nodded, the cake now firmly in his mouth.

'She thinks you're ace, Abby, like I do,' he mumbled, crumbs spraying everywhere.

Abby felt her neck redden and could only smile in return. Satisfied that everyone was content, she took Jack's hand and pulled him aside, until they were standing at the edge of the picnic area, the lagoon shimmering ahead of them, the sky a perfect, cloudless blue.

Jack had been back in Meadowgreen for three weeks. Three glorious, sun-filled weeks in which they had talked and laughed, walked through the reserve and spent every night in the same bed – sometimes at Peacock Cottage, sometimes at No. 1 Warbler Cottages. They'd had long, lazy evenings sitting at the picnic tables outside the Skylark with Abby's friends – who were quickly becoming Jack's friends too – or on Peacock Cottage's tiny patio, the butterflies dancing around them.

When Abby finished at the reserve she would head to

Swallowtail House, to find Jack discussing schedules or partition walls with the builders, his jeans and T-shirt covered in dust, specks of plaster in his thick hair. Or he'd be perusing catalogues full of furnishings and fittings, or sometimes, just leaning on the railing along the veranda at the back of the house, looking out over the wilderness that was now his.

Once, she had found him sitting against the back wall of the house, the sprawling gardens ahead of him, his attention fixed on a notepad balanced on his knees. He had a cold cup of tea at his side, and several screwed-up bits of paper littered around him.

'What's this?' she'd asked lightly. 'Someone else you've found to pen notes to?'

He'd told her he was writing to Eddie, saying all the things he hadn't had a chance to. Abby had sat alongside him, closing her eyes as the sun beat down, staying quiet while he tried to get everything out, reading it through when he asked her to. His words, as always, were eloquent and heartfelt, and her throat grew thick as she was reminded of all that had happened between them.

And yet, while Jack's letter was unflinchingly honest about how Eddie's actions had affected him, it wasn't devoid of compassion, and Abby had been struck again by the differences between the two men, and how good Jack's heart was.

Finally, he'd folded the paper up, slipped it inside an envelope and laid it on the stone railing, ready for posting, then replaced the cold tea with two bottles of beer from the mini fridge humming quietly in the kitchen. They had sat on the baked patio slabs and wordlessly clinked bottles, and it was only Raffle, returning from a foray into the bushes with a wild rose between his teeth like some kind of Romeo, that had shattered the sombreness of the moment.

Raffle and Jack were almost inseparable now, her husky delighted that he had someone to spend time with when she was at work, no longer left to his own devices at home or with Octavia on the few occasions she was free to walk him.

It still felt like a dream. But the best dream, one that Abby was slowly beginning to accept was actually real. Her happy, content life in Meadowgreen was still just that, but it was slowly expanding, growing to encompass all her hopes and ambitions, even though some of those, she hadn't realized she'd been harbouring.

The reserve had a new lease of life too, and with her promotion to events manager – which Penelope had offered her the week after the Summer Spectacular, rather than in the café on the last day of the fair when enough bombshells had already fallen – she had more responsibility, more challenges, than ever before. Work on a new wildlife pond was already underway, Marek and Gavin digging it out, returning to the visitor centre muddy and red-faced, Penelope assuring them that manual labour at the hottest time of the year was character building.

Abby had an engagement campaign to plan, to let all the members – old, new and Fledgling – know about their proposals to update the reserve and involve them in the decisions. They had the opportunity to make Meadowsweet outstanding, for visitors – of course – but most importantly for the wildlife that lived there, that sang and fished, fluttered, bred and slept within its parameters, and Abby was champing at the bit to get started.

'It's looking particularly beautiful today,' Jack said, turning to face her. 'It probably knows it's your birthday.'

Abby nodded. 'I went around the reserve a couple of days

ago shouting about it, so everyone knew they needed to pull out all the stops.'

'That sounds like something you'd do.'

'It does?'

'Definitely. I heard you telling Raffle all about your plans for Swallowtail's grounds when you came back from your walk yesterday.' He raised an eyebrow, and Abby flushed. 'I had the window open, and you were out there for a while, chatting away.'

'There was a red admiral. I was watching it, and I hadn't realized . . .' She tailed off, remembering that she'd been chuntering to her husky about how she had got a taste for alfresco lovemaking after her and Jack's reunion at Swallowtail House, when they had taken longer than expected to make it back to champagne and chips at Peacock Cottage, and how she hoped those rambling, secluded gardens would provide more opportunities while the weather was good. 'Oh.'

His lips were twitching and it wasn't long before his face broke out into a full, unhindered smile, something that, she had noticed, he did a lot more easily now. 'I think it's an excellent idea,' he said softly, dropping his head so that his words reverberated in her ear. 'I think Swallowtail House as a whole has a lot of potential. Though of course, it's crawling with builders at the moment, so we'll have to time it carefully.'

Abby shivered happily, suddenly reminded of the evening in Peacock Cottage when Octavia, Rosa and Jonny were looking for the badger, and Jack had found out that his notes to Abby were often read by more than just her. She remembered the hope and the tension, the rush of feelings as he'd kissed her, and her uncertainties that night. She wondered, with Jack here beside her, his fingers laced through hers, how

444

she had ever had a second of hesitation about him, let alone months.

'I'm glad you think expanding our horizons is a good idea,' she said, and felt him stiffen slightly. 'What is it?'

'When you say expanding our horizons . . .' He gave her a quick smile. 'Leo's been approached by a crime-writing festival in Madrid. *The Hidden Field* has been published in Spain, and they'd like me to be one of the panellists. It's in a couple of weeks' time, but I was wondering if Penelope might let you have a few days off so you could come with me? It would only be a long weekend, but I know how much work you have to do here.'

Abby's heart leapt at the thought of a long weekend with him, of being able to explore a new city together. 'I do have annual leave written into my contract,' she said. 'And the last time I took any was for the Page Turner gala.'

He nodded, neither of them needing to remind the other of the significance of that night. 'So . . . you might be able to come?'

'I would love to come. But are you sure you want me there?'

'There'll be a one-hour talk, some networking with the organizers and other writers, but other than that we'll have the time to ourselves. Suddenly, all these promotional events are looking more appealing.' He kissed her, his lips tasting of chocolate.

Abby laughed. 'You love them really.'

'I do. But I'll enjoy them even more if you're there.'

'We'll have to ask Octavia to look after Raffle, but I doubt she'll mind. She'll do anything you ever ask, now that you're supporting the library.'

'Libraries are an invaluable resource, and Octavia's one of

the most dedicated people I've met. I have to be involved now that I'm a resident of Meadowgreen.'

'Resident of Meadowgreen, eh?' Abby said. 'I like the sound of that. I still can't quite believe it. That you're here, with me, permanently.'

Jack's eyes searched hers. 'Believe it, Abby. I'm here to stay. You're well and truly stuck with me. I've got your present at Peacock Cottage – I wanted to save it until this evening. But there's something I'd like to show you at Swallowtail, as soon as this is over.'

Abby looked over at her friends and family. Stephan was pouring out glasses of his homemade lemonade, Evan was showing Willow and Daisy a meadow brown butterfly that had landed on one of the picnic tables, and Jonny and Leo were laughing about something as they each took a second slice of cake. She wondered how she had got so lucky, what she had done to deserve such a brilliant group of people in her life, and then realized she didn't need to search for an explanation. They were here, and that was all that mattered.

'Soon,' she said, squeezing Jack's hand, and they went back to join the party.

Epilogue

Swallowtail House no longer smelled musty, but of paint and plaster, the fumes of renovation that got inside Abby's nose and made her sneeze. And it wasn't quiet, either, with repetitive banging noises coming from the kitchen, which Jack had chosen as the first room to update. They had talked about how it would be the main focus of the house, with its space and the light from the large windows, Jack's eyes bright with excitement at all the possibilities.

It was no longer the mysterious, dilapidated place that Abby had gazed at from a distance, wondering at Penelope's reasons for holding onto it for all those years. Now the secrets were uncovered, and the house was getting its own chance at a fresh life.

Jack led her up the stairs. They had collected Raffle on the way and he followed placidly behind, happy to be inside out of the heat.

Jack stopped on the landing and put his hands on her shoulders. 'Close your eyes,' he said, and then, when she did, he kissed her forehead, took her hands and led her forwards.

They walked a few steps, his pace slow and careful, guiding her gently over the floorboards. 'Now. Open them.'

She did, and her gaze immediately landed on the startling new object in the otherwise empty room. They were in the master bedroom, the one that, on their visit all those months ago, they had stood in, looking out towards the reserve and the village. Now, instead of the lovebirds Jack had discovered, hanging down from the window, catching the light of the bold, summer sun, there was a swallowtail butterfly. It was glass, the detail of its black patterning – so like stained glass anyway – picked out in lead, the red dots of colour at the base of its yellow wings glowing like rubies.

'It's from the same craftsman as Penelope's lovebirds,' he said. 'When I gave them back to her, she told me where they came from, and I was curious. I wanted to see if this woman, Phyllis Drum, was still around, still making things all these years later, so I looked her up, and that's when I found the swallowtail. I'll have to take you one day, her workshop is a treasure trove.'

'You gave the lovebirds back to Penelope?' Abby felt a swell of tenderness for Jack, for his sensitivity towards her boss who, even though she was warming to them all, her revelations breaking down barriers between them that could never be rebuilt, was still not the most emotionally open person. 'What did she say?'

'I knew that you were right, that they must have meant a lot to her, and that, despite the pain of losing Al, despite leaving them behind, she would never have wanted us to get rid of them. She was shocked, I think, when I handed them to her, and I didn't want to push the issue. Leo was there, so I left her in his capable hands, but she did tell me where

448

she'd got them. She bought them as a present for Al who, after all, had inspired her love of nature.'

Abby turned back to the butterfly hanging in the window, casting patterns of yellow and red light over the bare, dusty boards. 'It's beautiful, Jack. I don't know what to say.'

'I just thought that, when this room is finished, when *we're* in here – I don't know.' He ran a hand over his jaw. 'I wanted to show you how much you've inspired *me*, how much you've changed my life. I wouldn't be here, surrounded by all this, with a future I can truly look forward to, if it wasn't for you. God,' he said, 'for someone who spends their life wrestling words into place, I'm finding this very difficult.'

'Finding what difficult?'

'Telling you how much I love you, conveying the strength of my feelings.'

'You could write it down,' she said, knowing that he didn't need to do a thing, because she could see it in his face.

'I could,' he agreed. 'We seem to be rather good at letters. And if I did that, if I wrote everything down on a piece of paper, for you to read at your own leisure—'

'Then I'd reply, of course. Though I'm not sure it would be a very long reply.' She tilted her head up, pressing herself against him as she found his lips with hers, kissing him slowly, luxuriously.

'Why wouldn't it be very long?' he murmured. 'Because you don't feel the same?'

'No, not that,' she said. 'I think you know by now that I do. My letter would be short because it would only need one word to let you know that, after all your hours of heartfelt thinking, tearing your hair out and trying to conjure up exactly what you wanted to say to me, I felt the same. I'd let you do all the hard work – you are the wordsmith, after all.'

She smiled at him, inhaling as his gaze trailed from her eyes, to her lips, to her throat, as if identifying all the places he needed to kiss her next.

'So, what would it say then, this letter?' His words were whispers on her cheeks, tickling her hot skin.

'It would say *ditto*,' Abby said quietly, and she kissed him again, beneath the glare of the sun, the yellow and ruby-red glow of the glass swallowtail, and the watchful, patient eyes of Raffle. She was in the house that, from the moment she had moved to Meadowgreen, she had gazed upon with intrigue and longing, and she was in the arms of the man that she loved, a man that she would learn and grow and laugh with, who brought drama and passion into her life, and a sense of belonging like nothing she had ever felt before.

Abby Field was off the reserve again – and this time, she knew exactly how it had happened.

Acknowledgements

This book wouldn't have been written without the help, advice and general cheerleading of some amazing people.

Kate Bradley, as always, who is an unfailingly encouraging and brilliant editor and friend, and who makes the job of being an author fun, exciting and easier than I'm sure it should be.

The wonderful HarperCollins team who do so much to turn my words into the finished thing, and then make sure it finds readers. Big thanks especially to Eloisa Clegg, Charlotte Brabbin, Katy Blott and Kim Young. To Kati Nicholl and Dushi Horti, for fixing my mistakes and making those final, invaluable changes.

Lindsey Spinks and Holly Macdonald, for creating the most beautiful, unique covers that I still can't quite believe are for me. They are so perfect for my book, and I can't stop looking at them.

My wonderful agent Hannah Ferguson, who keeps me on

course and never runs out of patience or ideas. I am so lucky that I get to work with you!

Amazing author pals who squash my worries and who are so wise when I'm feeling like a rabbit in the headlights, not to mention the best people to hang out with. Kirsty Greenwood, Cesca Major, Alex Brown, Katy Marsh, Isabelle Broom, Miranda Dickinson and Helen Fields – you are all beyond ace, and I am so lucky to call you my friends.

To Kelly for frequent bubbles, Anne TT for cocktails and gossip, Kate and Tim for introducing me to Bury St Edmunds and somewhere to base Tessa's house on, though I know your front door would never be pink! To Kate G for entertaining me with incredible, gruesome stories that I couldn't/ shouldn't/wouldn't ever use in my books. To Rachel, fellow waster and wonderful friend. To Nicola and Darren, who run the best deli and coffee shop in SE London – my bank balance is grateful I don't still live there – and who always make me laugh.

To Katy C for fun Sundays, cute wildlife Instagram posts and introducing me to the delights of Thor, though I still think he's much better with short hair.

Mum and Dad, who never get bored of me rambling on about the weird, wonderful world of being an author, and who have given – and continue to give me – whole mountains of support, advice and encouragement.

LC, who is braver than I could ever be, and who so patiently explains the cryptic crossword clues to me. Maybe I'll understand how it works one day . . . a very long way in the future.

David, who is quite simply amazing. Who gives me time to write, brings me coffee, makes me laugh and makes me feel better about everything. All those walks at Minsmere and Strumpshaw wouldn't have been the same without you.

Every day is better because you're in it. And you have the best hat.

To all the bloggers and readers of my books, who write reviews on Amazon or get in touch on my Facebook page, you make being an author the brilliant, pinch-me job that it is. I treasure every message and comment, because they let me know that my pages are being turned, that my characters and stories have meant something to you and that all the hours of writing, editing and hair-tearing have been worth it. Thank you, and I hope you like this one too!

And finally, thank you to the nature reserves. To Minsmere and the adder I nearly trod on, the nightingale that David found by accident, the otter that had me bouncing up and down like a small child and the amazing sausage sandwiches. To Strumpshaw Fen, for the unforgettable dawn walk and the bittern hiding in the frosty reeds. To Titchwell Marsh, where the robins will occasionally take food from your hands, and where I saw my first bullfinch – just at the right time for him to get an important cameo. To Sevenoaks Wildlife Reserve and the kingfisher I spotted all those years ago. Without those places, and all the staff and volunteers, the other birdwatchers who are patient when we are ignorant, this book wouldn't exist. I hope that any mistakes I've made describing the wildlife aren't too glaring, and that Meadowsweet is a worthy representation of how special and beautiful those places are.